GONE MISSING

CARLY SEYFERTH

This is a work of fiction. All names, characters, places, and incidents are products of the author's imagination or are used fictitiously and are not construed as real.
Any resemblance to anything listed above
is entirely coincidental

Copyright © 2018 by Carly Seyferth
Published via Kindle Direct Publishing

All rights reserved. No part of this book may be used or reproduced in any manner whatsoever without written permission, except in the case of brief quotations embodied in critical articles and review. For more information please address Carly Seyferth at hear.me.shout.art@gmail.com

Cover by Hampton Lamoureux: ts95studios@gmail.com
Formatting: https://serendipityformats.wixsite.com/formats

Printed in the USA
ISBN-13: 978-1986218788
ISBN-10: 1986218783

Visit us on Facebook @CarlySeyferth for additional info

To Heidi Smit
For sticking with me till the very end

CHAPTER 1

PA'S six bushy fox tails flicked back and forth in irritation. Frustration twisted his angular face. He wore a form fitting tunic with a high collared battle jerkin. Two long slits extended from the tunics hem to his waist, revealing a tan tunic beneath which draped over his billowing pant legs. A brown obi sash tightly cinched everything together.

Shadows lurked within the corners, as if waiting to pounce. The firelight had chased away most of the darkness but had failed to ease the tension within the clan head's lodge. We, the Myobu, the servants of Inari, were at war and lives were being lost to a Nogitsune clan. Pa clutched the pommel of his sword which hung from his belt. His black boots scuffed along the dirt floor. His tall shadow stretched swayed against the flickering firelight as he unveiled his foreboding report. The two scribes beneath him hunched over their parchment. Eagerly they scribbled down each word.

"A group of Nogitsune called the Shadow Clan have been relentless. They have barricaded the passageways in to the Kyoto Mountain, leaving us at a disadvantage. We're blocked in. We have no way of keeping the villagers safe. Each night the terror among our people increases. Our homeland, Mount Kyoto, is brimming with chaos. We must keep the Shadow Clan contained. If not then their chaos could spread throughout all of Gaia and cause civil unrest."

Two scribes scratched away at their parchment. Their feathers flapped and whipped frantically with each word. They were preparing two letters. One letter was to go east and the other west. Pa insisted that we alert the other Myobu clans and keep them informed on what was going on in Mount Kyoto. The Myobu are servants of Inari, a goddess of prosperity. They do her bidding. She had put our clan in charge of watching over the people of Mount Kyoto. Myobu are not limited to one region. There are multiple Myobu clans that exist within Gaia, the realm of the supernatural. We happen to belong to one of the Celestial clans and we reside within Mount Kyoto's forests.

Our job is to protect the villagers that live on or at the base of the mountain. Any Kitsune who practices selfless acts and protects one of Inari's precious humans on a selfless basis is considered a member of the Myobu. The Nogitsune are Kitsune too, however they do not answer to Inari. They do as they please. Their actions are what define them. Pa has told me that not all Nogitsune are bad. However, the members of the Shadow Clan are. They would devour anything in their path if left undeterred and their thirst for power is endless.

Silently, I fingered the embroidered trim on the hem of my sleeve. Uneasiness uncoiled inside my stomach like a cobra waking from its sleep. I didn't like the fact that the Shadow Clan was attacking my city, my people and my family, but I didn't know what to do about it. The scribes paused. Pa raked a large hand through his shaggy hair. His temple throbbed and he then ground his jaw before continuing,

"We need to get access to the lower grounds in order to feed ourselves. If we can't get down from the mountain we will eventually drain our land dry."

My fists tightened around the fabric of my skirt. If we end up barricaded in here with no escape then we'd have to resort to feeding off Gaia's elemental energy. Kitsune are elemental spirits. We can obtain our sustenance by feeding off the spirit of another being or off of the spirit of Gaia herself. If left unchecked we can drain both living creatures and Gaia dry.

Our feeding habits can cause living creatures to go into a great depression. Emptiness, exhaustion and even death would fill the land. When dipping into Gaia's life force we draw from different elements like water, fire, earth, air and spirit. However, this can lead to blights, stale air, dead water and death if we are not careful. We can feed off fruits, vegetables or meat but regardless, our main nutrients needs to come in spirit form.

My stomach knotted at the thought of draining my homeland dry. Pa paused and sucked in a controlled breath. His lips puckered and he turned to me. His almond eyes narrowed into little slits. They burned into me. Waiting for my input, for me to take control of my leadership and to participate in the development of the letter. I was the daughter of the clan head after all. I licked my lips. *What did he want me to say? Did he expect me to rally our troops? Maybe come up with a poetic statement about how perseverance brings victory? What influence could I possibly have over a situation such as this?* After a minute had passed I finally gave in.

"We will have to make do with battle." I mumbled begrudgingly.

"We will force them to let us through the passageways."

Pa scoffed. "Force them?"

I continued to grab at straws.

"We cannot afford to drain our land of its elemental energy."

His forehead wrinkled with concern.

"What else would you have us do, Pa?"

The firelight cast multiple planes of shadow across his angular face, making him look haunted. His disapproval pricked my heart but my face remained still as stone. *So much for being helpful.* I thought bitterly to myself. I prepared myself for a lecture and stared into the flames, losing myself in their mesmerizing dance.

"We cannot force them my child. We have been trying to keep them at bay for weeks. They dwell in those passageways. To attack them within their home base would be mass suicide. They know those tunnels like the back of their hands."

Irritation bubbled within my chest. I rubbed the space between my eyes. I didn't have time for this. Ethan was waiting for me out back near the forest. Pa was the head of the clan right now, not me. I had no idea why he wanted to discuss these options with me. His behavior had already made it clear that I have no experience with battle strategy.

What help could I possibly be? Pa's long fingers stroked thoughtfully at his neatly trimmed goatee. He paced to and fro, rattling off various strategies we could pursue.

His deep baritone rose and fell like the ocean waves crashing against the sandy shore. In the meantime, the scribes eagerly awaited his decision with their pens poised. I tuned him out and stared into the flickering flames as they licked eagerly at the crackling logs. The heat of the fire caressed my cheeks. Fingers of smoke curled and twisted as they stretched languidly towards the ceiling of the lodge. I itched with anticipation. Any moment now I would go hunting with Ethan and leave all of this behind.

"Well there is one option left."

Pa paused and thoughtfully rubbed at the stubble on his chin as he pondered aloud.

"Kayne, the leader of the Shadowclan, has offered a peace proposal in exchange for your hand in marriage to his eldest son."

My world fell apart, and so did the log that I had been watching. The wood crackled beneath the flames before crumbling into the glowing embers with a violent hiss.

I shot up, dropping the blanket at my feet.

"You want me to marry *him*?" I hissed incredulously.

I made sure to emphasize the word 'him'. Maybe if he heard the disapproval in my tone he might change his mind. *You can't blame a girl for trying, right?* Pa's hand tightened around the pommel of his sword while the other worried at his brow.

"My dear girl, we don't have much of a choice. The war has left us with no other options. The Shadow Clan has our backs up against the wall. Kayne is offering a peace proposal in exchange for your hand in marriage. He insists you marry his son or the warfare against our people will resume. You of all people should know we aren't equipped to handle a war against the Shadow Clan."

I released a weary groan and rubbed at the corners of my eyes with my fingertips.

"But, Pa! It is Noah. Of all people you are asking me to marry Noah."

Pa flashed me a scornful scowl.

"Now honey, don't be ridiculous. He can't be that bad."

My stomach writhed and twisted into knots.

He couldn't be seriously taking this into consideration could he?

I narrowed my eyes.

"Pa. He snuck spiders into my bed last summer and hexed me with night terrors. He may be a prince but he isn't prince charming, that's for sure."

Pa grimaced and shifted his weight as he raked a hand through his hair.

"I am sure it was all just for fun. He is a Nogitsune after all. They are known for their trickster ways."

He flashed me a reassuring smile.

Regardless, worry clouded his visage.

The hairs on the back of my neck prickled with unease. My blood chilled as I came to a single revelation. He was trying to reason with me. Cold shock boiled into fury, pushing me past the ability to reason.

"You're going to sell me in exchange for peace?"

It was more of an accusation than a question.

His brown eyes lowered. They were clouded with pain.

"Honey, you know that's not what I meant." He began.

"What about what I want? What if I don't want to marry the bastard?"

Bitterness welled up within me.

Pa's face hardened with resolution. "Now don't start. The two of you were designated as a potential match before this war even started."

"*Father, please see reason*!" My voice had cracked with desperation.

"It's time. you do what's best for your own people, Alexandria."

"But Father!" I sputtered in disbelief.

He remained stone faced.

The silence was confirmation. He had finally made up his mind. His expression emphasized the crinkles around his eye and forehead. He had aged since the war had started. Leaders tend to age quicker when their people were victims of guerilla warfare and fear. Especially when they know there's nothing they can do about it. Dread shivered down my spine like little spider legs.

Desperate, I tried again.

"You do realize he's only interested in obtaining our lands, in whatever way he sees fit. The chaos isn't going to stop here. It will keep on going."

It was all about the land I thought bitterly to myself. Kitsune are territorial and when not kept in check we get greedy. We thrive off the energy of the land and life force of the people who surround us. However, if we don't keep ourselves in check we can end up taking in too much. When this happens we exhaust the environment and those who are around us. If we lose control we leave destruction and death in our wake.

That was what happened to the Shadow Clan. They inherited a leader who was too greedy for his own good. Kayne had his own territory, just like the rest of us. He had used up all the resources within his land for his own gain and now he was battling other clans like ours so he could have more. He specifically picked our clan because we specialized in healing. We were plump for the picking. We had everything he wanted, land, wealth and power at virtually no cost. The Celestial Clan wasn't equipped to deal with his guerilla warfare, terror and dark magic. He knew that and took advantage of our good nature.

"Once we are wed we will be required to participate in the first hunt. That ritual will bind our clans together. Our land will become one with theirs. We will be sharing both territories."

The scribes watched this whole ordeal with great apprehension.

Pa shifted uncomfortably and his lips puckered with distaste.

"Do not lecture me on our marriage rituals."

I gushed forth, not giving him a chance to rant.

"Both you and I know that the Shadow Clan has exhausted their resources and their land is destitute because of it. Once the first hunt is done Noah's father will see to it that our wealth, territory and people will be used to his advantage. They will drain us dry and cast us aside the first chance they get. As the head of our clan you should find another way."

Pa's cheeks reddened. Any sympathy had vanished. His face flashed with anger.

"What do you know about leadership? You are but a girl who avoids her studies and fails to take care of her responsibilities." Each word dripped with scorn. The fire snapped and crackled like a whip. Pa shivered with restraint. He kept a white knuckled grasp on the pommel of his sword. I opened and closed my fists. My own fury boiled within me. The scribes exchanged looks of concern.

I snorted and barked out a bitter laugh.

"My responsibilities? Father, I am only two hundred years old and you want me to throw my future away. *All for an unstable peace treaty!?* Do you even comprehend what that will do to me?"

The scribes grimaced, it wasn't proper to argue with the head of the clan.

Meanwhile, Pa's face darkened.

The eyes of his fox shown through his gaze, glowing as they reflected the firelight.

"This isn't about you." He growled, revealing his upper canines.

A shiver rippled down my spine.

"It's about our people. You are the next in line as clan head. You have a duty to your people. You owe them a sense of safety. It is our responsibility to maintain the wellbeing of our people. In this instance some sacrifices must be made to ensure that our people survive."

I threw my hands up into the air.

"Well what if I don't want to be next in line for the clan head?"

How could he expect me to make such a large sacrifice? Didn't he understand that being the clan head's daughter was not something I ever wanted? His mouth tightened. A muscle in his jaw popped on reflex. His eyes were cold and flat like stones in a riverbed.

"That is not for you to decide."

The pent up fury inside me exploded.

"I never asked to be born into this position!"

I abhorred the idea of sitting in on meetings and taking responsibility over matters that weren't mine. Leadership wasn't really something I had wanted but Pa insisted that it was my destiny. I can't really blame him since I was the only heir ma had gave him before she died. The idea of having to be shoved into such a situation infuriated me. Marriage should never be about politics.

Nor should I have to sacrifice my life for someone else's gain. I had just turned two hundred years old. Yes, as a matter of fact we Kitsune happen to live for a long time. Two hundred is quite young for my species. You could say I am practically in my teens. Sure we married but at two hundred? That was a bit young and to imagine my destiny would be linked to an insufferable creature like Noah? That thought in itself made me recoil with disgust.

What would ma say? Surely she'd say no. The thought of her nearly broke my heart. I never had the chance to meet her. She died while giving birth to me. Bitter bile built itself up within the back of my throat. My heart ached.

"What would ma say in a situation like this?" I mused aloud. My voice came out haunted. The fire crackled and spat out a puff of ash. The room went still. The scribes exchanged looks of concern. They had tried to become one with the wall. My mother was a touchy topic among my people. She was well loved, but her life was short. The very topic of her brought pain. However, since I was her daughter I thought I had a right to know what she would say in a situation like this.

"Alexandria.." Pa rumbled dangerously.

"What? I am her daughter after all. It is my given right to know what she would say."

Tentative shadows crept within the corners of the cabin. The air thickened. Smoke swirled. Pa's face twisted with pain. His back straightened and his body tensed.

"Leave us.." He hissed.

The two scribes scuttled out of the hut .

"Don't pull her into this Alexandria."

The anger within me burned brighter.

"You know she'd say no. She'd say find another way."

Pa spoke, his voice came out frosty and flat.

"Your mother isn't here and if we don't act now our people will die."

My stomach twisted into a ball of knots. He wasn't going to give.

I was doomed for an eternity of unhappiness and there was nothing I could do.

Pa straightened to his full height.

"Alexandria. I have made up my mind. You will marry Noah. Nothing you say or do will change my decision. You are a daughter of a clan chief. You do not have the luxury to marry whomever you choose. It is time that you take responsibility and do what is best for your people. Our clan's survival depends on this marriage. My decision is final."

I flinched as each word punched through me. Marrying Noah wasn't an option, it was an order. My throat constricted. I charged for the door. Salty tears threatened to spill down my cheeks. The golden gaze of Pa's fox burned bright within his eyes like the embers of a dying flame.

"Alexandria! Pull yourself together!"

He grabbed for me. I ducked out from his grasp and burst into the hot midday sun at a full sprint. He had no chance of catching me now. My father may be strong but I outranked him in speed. Crisp mountain air filled my lungs. Salty tears spilled from the corners of my eyes. The pads of my feet pattered against the rocky earth. I whizzed past cylindrical wooden huts with conical straw roofing made of thatch. Villagers bustled around me, tending to their daily tasks. Meanwhile, Father's voice called out to me, demanding my return.

Like hell. I had thought to myself. If I was going anywhere it was hunting. I skirted past two men wearing loose fitting kimono tops, billowing pants and sandals. I nearly collided into two women who wore flowing strapless dresses with high waistbands. Their slim torsos were sheathed in form fitting kimonos that were tightly wrapped in place with a thick obi sash. The laundry baskets they balanced on their heads wobbled precariously. Maybe they wouldn't be able to witness the tears streaming down my cheeks if I didn't meet their gaze. I mumbled a haphazard apology. Their disapproving scowls burned into my back as I headed towards the forest.

The spaces between the houses grew and the mountain grass lengthened. Their blades bit into the exposed skin above my heels. Ethan waited off in the distance. His figure leaned against the base of a gnarly oak tree. Knowing him he had probably took a nap. A cool breeze rustled through his rusty red hair. He chewed on a blade of grass. His face broke into a lopsided grin. He had balled up his obi sash and threw it off to the side.

He sat there, relaxed. His kimono top hung open, exposing his bare chest. Ethan doesn't wear much clothing or at least his clothes don't stay on for very long. Being a werewolf can do that. Their clothes get torn to shreds if they wear them during an unexpected shift. This time we'd be transitioning. So naturally he'd take them off to avoid any damage.

"Took you long enough."

I skidded to a stop and did my best to catch my breath.

He shrugged off his top.

I gasped for air in between each word.

"Sorry. Got held up by Pa. You won't believe what I had to endure before getting here."

He arched his brow and flashed me a mischievous smile.

Rusty waves of hair fell into his emerald eyes. "Oh yeah?"

I pushed my hair back and stood.

"Pa wants, no *demands*, that I marry Noah."

Ethan froze. "Is that so?"

His shirt hung limp at his elbows.

"Yeah, he babbled on about some bull shit responsibilities."

Ethan spat out the blade of grass as if it were venom.

"But you hate Noah."

I released a weary sigh and slid my spine down the side of a tree trunk. "Yep."

"Why would he insist you do something you're not comfortable with?"

"All for the good of the people I suppose."

A moment of silence hung between the two of us. Birds chirped. Two squirrels bounded from one tree to the next, chattering manically. A cool breeze tickled my cheek. A flicker of disappointment danced across his emerald gaze only to disappear as quickly as it had come.

"Well that settles it." Ethan said crisply and then began to pull his top back on.

I perked a brow.

"Settles what?" I demanded as he grabbed for his obi sash.

He moved like a wooden doll.

"Hunting. I take it you aren't in the mood to go. Not after hearing that news. You probably want to be alone." Ethan didn't meet my gaze. His expression remained guarded but I knew he was disappointed. My heart stopped. This was my chance to get a release, to be away from all the crap waiting for me at home. My hot sweat turned cold with panic. I couldn't let him take that opportunity from me, not today. I snatched his belt up before he could reach it.

"Are you kidding me? I need to blow off some steam."

His jaw tightened and he looked away with a sullen expression. His molars chewed on the inside of his cheek. Curiosity kindled inside me. *What the hell was his problem anyway?* A few seconds passed then something in me clicked. A smile curled at the corner of my lips.

"You're jealous aren't you?" I teased, half bewildered and half amused.

His green eyes narrowed into little slits. The freckles on his nose bunched up. It was then that he tried grabbing for his belt but I stepped out of reach.

"Not at all. I just don't think it'd be a good idea for you and Noah to get hitched."

I poked at him and flashed him a mischievous grin.

"Is it because you want me all for yourself?"

Ethan bristled. His pupils shrank, becoming more wolf like.

"Oh shut up." He glowered. His lip curled, revealing a sharp fang.

I danced around, waving his belt in the air as I sang.

"You want to love me. You want to hug me. Don't you?"

He grabbed for it. I twirled out of the way.

"Can you just give me back my belt?" He snarled.

"I can't just walk back into town half undressed."

I flashed him a playful grin. "You want it? Then come and get it."

I took in a deep breath. I released my elusive barriers and plunged into my true form, the shape of a fox. I sprinted away with Ethan's belt within my maw. Cold dirt squished between my black toes as I dashed into the forest. Broken beams of sunlight broke through the canopy. Crisp mountain air filled my nose with the earthy scents of pine, cedar and wet leaves.

Squirrels chattered. Birds chirped. A rabbit stirred the underbrush as it zig zagged off into the distance. I weaved in and out of the massive tree trunks. Ethan's black wolf came crashing in from behind. Twigs snapped beneath his paws.

A soft humming sound thrummed through the forest. My ears swiveled towards the source of sound. I veered towards the noise. Forest undergrowth cracked beneath the pressure of my weight. The humming increased as I ran towards the grove. Static electricity crackled along my fur. I sped around a towering cedar and almost collided into a swirling mass of purple light. Gasping, I dug my toes into the grass and skidded to a halt. My legs tangled beneath me. I tripped, tumbled and rolled.

Plumes of dust billowed into the air as I landed face first into the earth. *So much for grace.* I had thought sourly to myself. Note to self: work on your landing skills. If I was going to be the head of the Celestial clan I'd need to learn how to run without falling face first. I needn't bring my clan to total humiliation by tripping during the first hunt like some clod hopping drunken maid .When two leaders from two different clans marry they participate in what is known as their first hunt. We foxes are a bit territorial so each clan has its own land to hunt upon. However, if two different clan heads marry then their land, property and people become one. The first hunt symbolizes this union because both husband and wife hunt on their newly shared grounds and make their first kill together.

Ethan's wolf nearly collided into me as he rounded the corner. I hopped to the side and he skidded clumsily to a halt beside me. Clouds of dirt flew up into the air. The portal swirled in front of us like an enchanting pinwheel. The twirling mass thrummed with power, making the earth vibrate beneath our paws. Panting, we both stared at the swirling mass of light in front of us. Ethan and I exchanged looks of concern. Why would a portal pop up in a place like this? Sure the war had marred the land with magical energy but I haven't heard of a portal being around these parts for a thousand years.

Ethan's emerald eyes stared back at me. His pink tongue lolled about the side of his massive jaws. He sat back on his haunches and let out a high pitched whine before itching the bottom of his chin with his back paw. *How typical.* Ethan is a werewolf and I am a fox spirit. Despite being shapeshifters we cannot converse when we are in our animal forms. For some reason foxes and wolves speak different languages. It might be because we are two different species. However, if two werewolves were together they could mentally converse amongst each other. They call it a pack mentality. So it made sense that he couldn't hear my thoughts.

With a swift pop I transformed into my human form, clothes and all. That's the gift of being a master of illusion. I can create any set of clothes with the flick of a thought. Ethan's transformation slowly followed suit. Despite being a werewolf Ethan still had the ability to choose when to shift, the only time he didn't was when it was a full moon. Being born with the gene allowed him more room for control than his bitten counterparts. Being a Kitsune has its own advantages too. Unlike werewolves, we can transform quickly because some of our magic is based solely on illusion. We also tend to keep all our garments on once we transform back into our human identities because they are not clothes at all. They are illusions woven by our own magic.

Ethan and his kind tend to run around stark naked each time they turn because the change in mass usually ruins the clothings' fibers. I watched as every muscle in his body contorted, shortened and lengthened. His long black snout shrunk down into a human jaw. Large paws flattened out into human hands as the nails shortened into a man's stubby fingernails. His human shaped green eyes looked up at me, black pupils still the size of a wolf's.

"What is it?" He had asked, his voice losing its rough growl.

I shook my head and ran a hand through my auburn tresses.

"No clue." I mumbled as I stared at the swirling portal.

I reached out towards the spinning mass. Curiosity has always been one of my weak points. My fingers felt like they were moving through cobwebs. The air around me tingled and crackled with power. Ethan snatched my hand away from the mesmerizing pull of the portal's energy. The center pulsed with power. A wave of static crackled through the air. The colors of the forest mixed into its purple core like a spinning paint palette. The portal itself had the proportions of a door, maybe more.

"The only thing I can think of is that it is a rift or a portal to another realm. I remember Pa saying sometimes rifts occur in the barrier when there is magical unrest but I swear he mentioned they didn't exist anymore. The mages of the old world had sealed them away once they learned how to use the elements to create stability. These things haven't made an appearance since the great flood and the very birth of Gaia."

Ethan inched a bit closer. Despite his wolf ancestry Ethan had the curiosity of a cat. His freckled nose wrinkled a tad as if sniffing would provide some sort of answer.

I rolled my eyes.

"Oh mighty great wise one. What does your all powerful nose say?" I teased.

Maybe if I laughed he wouldn't hear the tremor in my voice.

Ethan peered at me from the corner of his eyes.

The corner of his thin mouth tilted into a wolfish grin.

"It says." He paused for dramatic effect.

"That the mighty Princess Alexandria did not do her studies this morning'."

My mouth dropped into a large O.

Well I'll be damned, someone was keeping tabs on me this morning.

Keeping up on studies has never been my forte. I was wondering when my geezer of a teacher would realize I hadn't been studying at all. I brought my hand to my chest and feigned complete innocence. "Why my dear good sir. I know not what you are speaking of. Why would you accuse me of such a treason?"

Ethan held his hand up. "Wait."

He furrowed his brows and took in another large whiff. I tensed at his change in character. Moments passed before his face broke into a brilliant smile.

"It also smells bull shit from a mile away."

I snorted and gave him a playful shove.

"And you will do best to not tell my father." I warned and turned towards the portal again. I tilted my head to get a better look at the swirling colors.

"No but really, where do you think it goes?"

I cautiously explored the space with an extended finger. The humming became more concentrated. Vibrations buzzed through my bones.

Ethan shrugged his shoulders in an empathetic gesture.

"No clue maybe- Lex?!"

He was cut off by my scream.

The portal had swelled with light and then began to suck me in.

I tried to squirm away, but to no avail. It kept pulling me closer to its center. Ethan wrapped his arms around my waist. It was a game of tug of war and I was in the middle. A ripple of fear ran down my spine. *Was this thing going to eat me alive?* The portal gurgled hungrily in an attempt to engulf my body. Together our feet dug a trail into the mossy ground. As soon as the light touched Ethan's skin the portal buzzed more fervently. The gravitational pull began sucking Ethan in too.

Together we fell forward. The ground beneath us sunk in and gave way to a black abyss. It was like the forest floor had transformed into quicksand. The ground gave way to darkness and then we were falling. Our bodies twisted and turned. Icy wind whipped through our hair. I opened my mouth to say something but we made impact with something solid, so hard that the breath was knocked right out of me. My vision blurred and my head buzzed. Before I knew it I was out cold.

CHAPTER 2

SWEET INARI, I awoke with an earth shattering headache. Spinning doubles haunted my vision. My eyes watered but eventually everything began to clear. Slowly, the doubles merged into one face. A pair of amber eyes studied me through long lashes. They belonged to a young woman that was easy on the eyes with fair skin. She was in her late teens, maybe early twenties. Her black winged spectacles cast my own reflection back at me.

Sweet mother of Gaia here was a goddess of beauty and I looked like the local swamp monster dredged from her sleep. Strings of my auburn tresses fell in my face. The tumble had left my hair in a tangled mess. Dirt smudged my face and twigs stuck out of the top of my head. The portal must have spat us out above a tree and we had to of toppled through its branches. I held my breath, half expecting her to scream. Any normal person would if a girl and a naked man fell from the sky and landed at their feet. She on the other hand, found the whole aspect of it quite amusing.

Casually, she removed her glasses, cleaned them off on her dress and pushed them back upon the bridge of her nose. She had freckles just like Ethan. She flashed me a winning smile and extended her hand. When she spoke her voice came out as a breathless purr.

"Hello there. My name is Astrid."

My uneasiness faltered. My entire thought process went down the drain.

She was a goddess of beauty with mulberry lips. *Oh what I could do with those mulberry lips.* A shiver of pleasure rippled down my spine. Her soothing aura caressed me with its rosy kiss. Shaken, I shook my head. Something wasn't right about this one. She wasn't human, that's for sure. Maybe that's why she didn't scream? No human aura has ever managed to send my hormones roaring out of control.

I cast an apprehensive glance towards an unconscious Ethan who happened to be drooling. The fall must have knocked him hard on the head. My eyes shifted back to Astrid. The breeze rustled her silken black hair. She smelled of peaches and honey. Her euphoric aura dulled my apprehension. Something about her was different. She had an appealing aura but everything about her screamed sex. She wore a black dress that clung to her hourglass figure and flared out at her hips. Her plunging neckline emphasized the curve of her breasts. I said a silent prayer and steeled myself for the inevitable. *Whatever happens Lexi, do not focus on her boobs.*

"Um, hello Astrid." I began.

I tried not to get lost in her cleavage but the sisters were just hanging there in front of my face. The tops of them looked so soft and silky smooth like downy pillows.

I wonder what would happen if I were to touch one?

Just one touch couldn't hurt. Right?

Focus Lexi! Now is not the time to let your mind wander.

An awkward silence hung in the air as Astrid stood there with her hand still extended.

Ugh, it was like I was some god damned animal.

I cleared my throat and returned the greeting. Who knows what sort of trouble this one may bring. On the other hand maybe we could have some fun? I resisted the urge to reach out and adjust her dress and zoned in on her heart shaped face instead.

"I'm Alexis" I said stiffly.

I cleared my throat. "I mean, Lexi."

An lazy smile curled at the corner of her lips.

A blanket of fire spread itself across my cheeks.

What else could I tell her? It is not like I can say, Hi my name is Alexandria Marie Adams and I am a kitsune and Ethan is a werewolf. We just happened to come from another world called Gaia just to stop by for the scenery. So sorry for the intrusion, we should get going now because my people are at the brink of war with the Shadow clan. Who was I kidding? I couldn't even tell her my full name. Names had power. Once someone knew a spirit's true name that was it, they would have full control over you. She pulled me up as I turned towards the crumpled mess beside me.

"And this is Ethan." I added as an afterthought.

"Oh?" Astrid said as she took him in.

"Er, pleasure to meet you?" I began.

Ethan laid there curled up in the ball. In the nude. These things tend to happen to werewolves when they turn back into their human form. Astrid simply adjusted her glasses as her eyes roamed from the toes of Ethan slowly up to the top of his head.

The corner of her lips turned up in a satisfied smile.

"No really, the pleasure is all mine."

"Yeah um about that, do you know what just happened?

Astrid casually and flicked a hefty set of black curls over her shoulder.

"Oh you just happened to fall from the sky, went through a bunch of trees and landed smack dab in the middle of a public park. I was on the way home when it happened."

I gaped at her, completely shell shocked by her reaction.

"And is that normal?"

A sly grin curled at her mulberry lips.

"No, not quite. Most people would run in the other direction screaming."

I brushed at my lap. "Where are we anyway?"

She lifted her hand and indicated to a spot on the flesh of her palm.

"You're in Grand Rapids, Michigan."

"Is that some sort of greeting from where you come?" I asked with a suspicious frown.

"Is that the sort of attire you wear on a daily basis?" She quipped back with raised brows

"Or did you just happen to hop into a kimono and skydive from a cosplay convention."

I tensed. *Now I had done it.*

I had forgot all about my high waist dress and overcoat that was tightly held in place by my thick obi sash. My clothes were going to blow my cover for sure. I fingered my flowing skirt, trying to bide time.

"Yeah, um about that. It's actually a ruqun with an overcoat. Not a kimono."

Why did people always assume that we only wear kimonos?

A muffled groan erupted from the ground and up popped Ethan.

"And you must not be like most girls." Ethan grumbled.

We both turned to look at a naked Ethan.

Quickly, I shielded my gaze with a modest hand.

"Hm?" Astrid inquired, completely unabashed.

"Unlike most girls, you didn't go running."

Astrid did the unthinkable. She broke out into a grin.

Ethan eyed her, as if daring her to stare upon his nudity.

Instead, she got down on one knee and brushed one slender finger across his swollen lip. His body stiffened from the gesture. Her rosy aura pulsed at his response. He must have felt the same thing I did, sexual tension. She leaned in, letting him get a good look at the tops of her breasts. Ethan's aura flickered like a flame in the wind. Her mulberry mouth hovered near, petal lips almost touching his ear. She whispered with a voice as soft as silk.

"It depends on what you deem as normal for a girl."

Traces of gold swirled within her amber gaze. Ethan took a short breath and held it. His pupils dilated. A little bit of his spirit had left him just then. She flashed him a playful smile as she traced the outside of his mouth with a red nail. A tiny bit of his life force swirled around the tip of her finger.

"I'll let you be the judge of that."

The glimmer of gold inside Astrid's amber eyes flickered. Just like that, the connection between them was severed. As I had already concluded, she definitely wasn't human. Astrid rose with a satisfied smirk, leaving a dumbfounded Ethan in her midst.

She rummaged through her picnic basket and tossed him a blanket.

"Now cover yourself before you poke some innocent child in the eye with that thing between your legs." Her tone was brusque and clipped.

His cheeks flushed as he wrapped the blanket around his waist.

Astrid perked a brow as her eyes slid down Ethan's chiseled abs.

Ethan's lip curled. "Like what you see?"

I rolled my eyes and let out a weary groan.

"For the love of Inari, Ethan put your tongue in your mouth you wolfish fiend."

Astrid flashed a stunning smile, the sexual tension increased.

Did he even know what he was getting himself into?

"Perhaps." She said

She flipped her hair and sauntered away before calling out over her shoulder.

"I suggest you two keep up. Ethan I advise you to keep your goodies covered. It would be a bummer if you got arrested before I had time to play."

I looked at Ethan then at Astrid.

"Where are we going?"

She spun a set of keys around her index finger. Her heels clicked against the stone.

"Isn't it obvious? I am taking you home with me."

Ethan glanced at me and then I at him. I have come to a simple conclusion. We were officially screwed. I gave him a feeble shrug before chasing after her. Who knows, maybe Astrid would know how to get us back to Mount Kyoto. It was a worth a try, right? On the way home we passed another park.

Speaking of parks, for some reason the natives of this world have this peculiar tendency to try to control nature. They have this pure obsession with mowing grass and keeping manicured pathways. However, they have no problem leaving their trash. We happened to stumble upon a few papers as they tumbled after us along the sidewalk like tumbleweed. One of them was a missing person's poster.

GONE MISSING

A picture of a woman in her early thirties with caramel skin stared back at me with hazel eyes and curly black hair. The poster read, Anna Johnson missing person since June 30th 2016, please contact authorities if seen. Her mousey expression sent a foreboding shiver down my spine. Hastily, I crumpled up the paper and threw it into a trash bin.

We passed a few buildings that shot up towards the sky. They reminded me of the castles back at home. According to Astrid the humans call these things skyscrapers. What surprised me even more were the smooth black rivers on which the humans rode their metal dragons. *Who knew humans could control metal dragons in the shape of boxes on wheels?* Astrid calls them cars. I called them abominations. Something that size shouldn't move at that speed. Astrid clicked some sort of remote and the car unlocked.

Dread bubbled within me as I slid into the front seat. Tight spaces have never been a forte of mine. Ethan scooted into the back seat. There was a jangle of keys, a few odd beeping noises and a click. Within seconds, the engine rumbled to life and the earth moved beneath our feet.

"Sweet mother of Gaia." I crowed as the ground began to move

"It's like a horse." Ethan breathed as he put his head between his legs.

"*What in the world is happening?*" We inquired in unison.

Astrid bubbled with laughter. "We are driving you fools. Sit back and relax."

I tried focusing on the passing scenery but the view was too quick for my eye to catch. The process of it all was extremely overwhelming, so I tried focusing on conversation instead.

"So, what are you anyway?" I asked, desperate to distract myself from the landscape that whizzed past my window.

"I am a succubus." She turned the vehicle.

My stomach churned and both Ethan and I gripped the handrails with all of our might.

"A succubus?" Ethan asked.

Astrid nodded, but her expression remained grim.

"So you do a bunch of weird sex stuff?" I asked.

Astrid's cheeks flushed. She looked away and pushed her winged spectacles up further upon her nose. Realization bubbled through me. I gasped involuntarily.

"That's why your eyes were glowing! You were working your sexy vibe on Ethan at the park!"

Her flush deepened.

"It is NOT a sex vibe."

She paused, desperately searching for a logical explanation.

"It's, it's more like absorbing someone's life force."

Ethan gaped at her in horror. "You were trying' to *eat* me?"

I snickered. "Ethan, girls don't eat boys silly. It's the other way around."

Astrid shook her head and took another turn.

"You have such a dirty mind Lexi." She purred, her eyes twinkling. "I like it."

"Easy tigress." I teased as I brushed my fingers across her bare arm. She tensed. A flame of pride stirred within me. She stole a glance my way. Flecks of gold danced within her amber irises. Her rosy aura twisted hungrily around her. I couldn't really blame her for absorbing someone's life force through seduction. I myself use seduction at times to obtain sustenance.

"You should keep your eyes on the road. I'd hate for us to crash."

Normally I'd play with Astrid, get her all hot and bothered. We fox demons don't tend to be too picky when it comes to gender and we sure do like to play. Unfortunately, the whole falling from the sky thing still had me a bit rattled. Nor did I know how strong Astrid's abilities were. Last thing I needed was to get my ass kicked by a succubus.

Astrid cleared her throat.

"Anyhow. Ethan would have been able to handle it."

Ethan scowled. *"Oh is that so?"*

I didn't think he cherished the idea of being someone's snack because his green eyes were blazing. His temper could also be easily attributed to his werewolf heritage.

"And what makes you think that?" I asked.

Astrid giggled. Her laughter sounded like tinkling bells.

"Because he's a werewolf silly."

His face twisted with confusion. "How did you.."

"For one you smell like a wet dog. For two you were butt naked in the middle of a park. For some reason werewolves think that they can run around in parks and not be caught. Maybe it is because the humans sometimes mistake the wolf for an abnormally large dog. However, that is not always the case."

Ethan's forehead wrinkled with concern.

"Wait a minute. You guys have werewolves?"

Astrid scoffed, purely amused.

"Of course we do. We have loads of them."

She wiggled her eyebrows at him. "Maybe you'll get a chance to meet the pack."

Ethan went silent.

We didn't have many werewolves at Mount Kyoto. In fact, Ethan was the last surviving member of his pack. Various thoughts and emotions flickered across his face. She jutted her chin towards the books peeking out of the top of her picnic basket.

"I also do a lot of research on supernatural beings. Those are only *some* of the books from the library that I have been reading. That was where I was coming from when I saw you guys fall from the sky."

Her voice got husky when she said the word library.

I snorted and rolled my eyes.

"Seriously? You are a succubus and you are getting a hard on over books?"

"What?" She frowned and pursed her lips. "There's nothing wrong with reading books and having the desire to expand your intelligence. Besides Lexi, hard-ons are for boys. Girls are more likely to get wet."

Her hand trailed over towards my lap and slowly slid down the side of my inner thigh.

Tingles of electricity shivered down my spine.

"Do you want me to show you what it means to get wet Lexi?"

"Alrighty! No thanks. I am sure Alexis is good." Ethan said with a tone of finality.

Astrid let out a petulant sigh. "Oh fine. You're such a spoilsport, Ethan."

Moments later she rolled down the windows and turned on some tunes.

Meanwhile, Ethan and I had a blast when we stuck our heads out of the window like a pair of domesticated dogs.

I enjoyed the rush of air as it ripped through my long hair. Thankfully we ran into Astrid or we probably would have been hit by an oncoming car. The thought of the cool wind whipping through my hair made my stomach flip. The rush reminded me of how the wind would ripple through my fur as I ran through the forest in my true form. A dull ache pulled at my gut. I missed home.

I closed my eyes and imagined myself sprinting through the forest on all fours. Pine, ash and the crisp scent of cedar filled my nose. The music vibrated through my veins. The tempo of the drums reminded me of the ceremonial festivals we had back at home. I opened my eyes and expected to see my people dancing around a fire. Unfortunately, the smoke that I had smelled was just a pile of burning leaves in someone's yard. The car slowed down as we passed a series of huts with fancy windows and finely manicured bushes. Astrid called them houses. There was still so much to learn in this new world.

CHAPTER 3

WE PULLED up to a Victorian house with white bay windows that looked out upon a perfectly manicured lawn. A patch of blooming stargazer lilies guarded the front of the porch without a weed in sight. Their fresh blossoms bobbed and swayed delicately in the summer breeze. Together we got out of the car and followed Astrid up to the porch. White gravel crunched beneath our feet.

We climbed the stairs onto the freshly swept veranda. Ethan and I left a crumbling trail of grass and dried mud within our wake. *So much for their efforts,* I had thought to myself. Astrid rapped on the French door. Two suspicious blue eyes peeked through the blinds. Moments later the lock unhitched only to reveal a suspicious woman with a thin face, silky blonde hair and porcelain skin. She wore a checkered apron. Beneath the apron were freshly pressed dress. She wore her blonde hair in a tight French twist. Not a silken tress was out of place nor a wrinkle in sight.

"Oh good morning Astrid." She said in a sing song voice.

"Yes, it is, isn't it?" Astrid replied with a polite smile.

"Senator Benson, I am here to introduce to you Alexis Adams, and her friend Ethan."

The woman stiffened once she took in our muddy appearance. Her eyes followed the trail we had left upon her porch. Perfect lacquered nails dug into the door frame with restrained irritation. Benson struggled with to say something.

"They looked like they've just came off the street." She said.

"Is that the best you have?" I asked.

Benson's spine straightened but Astrid blundered on.

"That they have." Astrid agreed with an incline of her head. "Now, can I keep them?"

Benson's scowl deepened when her sapphire eyes locked onto Ethan's exposed abs. Her lips puckered with distaste. Astrid offered her a cajoling smile. I couldn't really blame the Senator, Ethan had the body of Adonis. So who wouldn't be disgusted?

Ethan's tongue clucked with disapproval.

"Now, now It's not polite to stare."

The woman flashed him a scathing glare.

Astrid gave him a good jab in the ribs.

"Careful, Ethan." Astrid grumbled out of the corner of her mouth. "She happens to be the most influential supernatural creature within the entire city."

All pleasantries melted away from Benson's face.

"Oh I am so sorry, I was distracted by your lack of clothes."

She paused and her sapphires widened in disbelief.

"Nudity- Oh mother of God! Astrid you didn't have a threesome did you?"

Ethan gaped at her like an open mouthed fish.

"Not today." Astrid replied with a petulant sigh.

I took this as my cue to step forward and extend a dusty hand.

"My name is Alexis Adams, please call me Lexi."

She took a step back and eyed my hand as if it were a snake.

I hooked a thumb in Ethan's general direction.

"This is Ethan Matthews." His full name was really Nathaniel Jay Matthews but I wasn't going to go into the specifics. Like I said, names have power. "The view on the porch here is quite nice. However, do you plan on letting us in any time soon? It's a tad bit drafty for some if you know what I mean."

I waggled my eyebrows at her, hoping she would get my point. There was a long pause. Briefly, Benson stared at my hand and sniffed.

"The hose is out back. Astrid, you know what to do."

She then shut the door, leaving me standing there with my hand still extended.

Together we stood there in stunned silence.

The hose?" I asked with raised brows.

The word itself felt foreign to me.

"Yes, the hose." Astrid confirmed grimly.

Ethan's emerald eyes shifted from Astrid then to me.

"What does she mean by the hose?" He asked with a hint of trepidation.

Astrid flipped some hair over her shoulder.

"You'll see, come now, follow me."

Astrid led us to the back of the house. Ivy foliage sprawled and clung against the ten foot brick wall that surrounded the backyard. The gate swung open to reveal a large court yard with a stone paved patio. A three tiered fountain with Greek basins carved out of granite sat in the corner, gushing with water.

In the other corner there was a pool of water built into the ground with liquid as clear as crystal. Benson stood a few feet away in a black swimsuit. In her manicured hand she held a green snake that actively spat out water. Three crisp white towels sat on the stone table top.

"What magic is this?" I inquired.

"Before you enter my humble abode. I kindly ask that you rinse yourselves off."

She offered the hose to Ethan but he didn't take it.

Her lips thinned into a straight line.

"Mr. Matthews." Blue eyes narrowed into little slits. "I would appreciate it if you would be so kind to look at my face and not at the top of my breasts. Thank you."

Apprehension hung in the air. A hot flush crept across Ethan's cheeks. In his defense I couldn't quite blame him. Those perky puppies were sitting up high on that swimsuit top. I myself had a bit of trouble averting my gaze. The people of this world were quite revealing.

"Now strip." Her flat tone rang with authority.

Something told me that Benson was a woman of power and she didn't take kindly to the word no. A cool breeze rippled across the water in the fountain's basin.

"Excuse me?" He squeaked.

A storm brewed behind those ocean blue eyes. Her expression became grim.

"Did I stutter Mr. Matthews? I said strip." She enunciated each word clearly.

Ethan shifted his weight for show and batted his lashes at her.

"But, Miss Senator I feel a bit rushed. Aren't I supposed to take you out to dinner or something first?"

A snicker bubbled up inside me.

"You people sure do have strange customs."

She scowled, clearly not amused. Her aura crackled and thrummed with power. Her life force swirled about her in blue rivulets. The water in the fountain began to bubble and gather. I tensed. Astrid and I exchanged looks of concern. I opened my mouth but Astrid pressed a finger to her lips and slowly shook her head.

Who was this woman? Was she a witch? An elemental spirit? What gave her the power to possess the gift of water casting? An uneasy Astrid shifted her weight. Electrical energy began to gather at my fingertips. The static made the hairs on the back of my neck stand on end. Benson rubbed the space between her eyes in a gesture of frustration. Astrid stayed my hand and slowly shook her head. I lowered my crackling fingertips.

"Look we can do it the easy way or we can do it the hard way. Your choice. Regardless, I am not letting you into my house until we rinse that filth off you."

She spat out the word filth as if it were venom. I had to admit we both were a mess. We had twigs and leaves sticking out of our hair. Mud, dirt and dust caked our bodies. We looked like a pair of swamp monsters that just hobbled out of the forest. Something told me that she didn't find swamp monsters appealing.

"What? You don't like dirty boys?" Ethan teased.

Benson's mouth thinned into a small line.

Astrid cleared her throat.

Ethan didn't pay attention. Nor did he stop to ask Astrid what was wrong. A globe of water hovered out of the rippling fountain and began floating towards him. My muscles tensed. I held my breath. *Wasn't Astrid going to do something? Why did she stop me from launching my previous attack?* My fingers tingled with electrical energy, ready to launch at any given moment. The wet orb rippled and danced, collecting the sunlight within its liquid belly.

"Not one bit." She said before releasing the tension that held the water in place.

The mass of liquid exploded, releasing huge sheets of water upon Ethan's head. The pressure pushed him down to his knees and into the earth. He flailed about, arms flapping and waving like a fish out of water. He sputtered and gasped.

"It looks like you have chosen the hard way. Pity, really."

A few koi flapped about on the pavement.

Benson flicked a towel at a sputtering Ethan.

"If you think you are entering my house in the condition you were in then you can think again. I spent hours cleaning today. No way in hell will I let a hooligan like yourself mess up all my hard work."

She towered over him. Her legs were long and lean.

A muscle popped along Ethan's jaw line. A moment passed as he glared up at Benson through his dripping red bangs. Emerald eyes boiled with rage. I broke the building silence with a chuckle. The electrical energy running up and down my arm fizzled away.

"You look like a drowned cat!" I crowed.

Together, Astrid and I bubbled with laughter.

Ethan opened his mouth to retort but nothing came out. A moment passed before his lips curved and his shoulders relaxed. The tension slipped away. He sat there dripping as all of us laughed at him. A tiny koi flapped about on top of his head. The corner of Benson's mouth quirked for a brief moment. After a few more minutes of arguing Benson begrudgingly gave Ethan the hose so he could rinse the rest of himself off while maintaining his dignity as a man.

"Alright Lexi. It's now your turn."

"Aw, Senator why must you take away all the fun?"

"Are we going to do this the hard way or the easy way?"

"It depends on what you consider hard, *Senator?*" I teased.

Astrid watched the whole moment with mild amusement. In the meantime, my stomach rumbled with hunger. The journey here had taken a lot out of me. That brief attempt to gather lightning had drained me dry of what little energy I had. Maybe, just maybe I could seduce some life force out of her for my own gain.

"You see I sort of like things rough if you get what I mean"

I gave her a playful wink.

Benson's brow wrinkled with disapproval.

"Shall I just rip your clothes off for you?" She suggested coolly with a will power as strong as steel.

"Perhaps." I flashed her a charming smile and twirled a strand of hair between my fingers. "I may play hard to get though."

Benson was not impressed.

"Look child, I live with a succubus. Do you really think you can seduce me?"

Damn, she didn't take the bait. What made this woman so uptight anyway?

"I like it when they play hard to get." Astrid chimed in.

"Thank the Gods. At least someone has a sense of humor."

Senator Benson on the other hand was not amused.

"Get to it child, we do not have much time."

I had almost forgotten Astrid was there . Yet, there she was leaning against the house. Her eyes flickered gold eyes through the shade. Meanwhile, a sullen Ethan was wiping himself down.

"I do happen to have a pair of handcuffs upstairs. Though, it'd be a pity to be late to the party tonight, but I am always open to making an exception if it is for play."

Benson flashed her female counterpart a motherly scowl.

"You will do no such thing. First of all we are meeting with Carmen Garcia and secondly it is an official meeting, not a party. The whole coven will be there. The very last thing you will be doing is arriving late. Must I remind you? This is a business matter Astrid *not* a fraternity house.

Astrid's luscious lips turned upside down into a classic pout.

"Look, even you yourself said the whole coven will be there.

Besides the meeting doesn't even take place until late this eve. How will she keep everyone distracted beforehand if there isn't any entertainment? I am telling you it is going to be a party."

I stiffened, all games were set aside.

"A party? Oh no we can't be late for something like that."

Benson's ice blue eyes narrowed into little slits. She became dangerously serious. "You will not be late for that. Being tardy is not an option. Punctuality is imperative!"

Astrid let out a petulant puff of air.

"Now Lily, don't get your panties in a knot."

Benson's small hands tightened into little fists.

"Astrid I am serious. This meeting is critically important. You need to take this seriously. I have a whole community to look after and I need your help in convincing the local coven to help with this investigation."

Immediately I began to tug at my obi sash.

"You see where I come from being late to a party would be an insult."

I tossed the sash off to the side and began wiggling out of my over coat.

"And where exactly do you come from?" Benson asked imperiously as she eyed the kimono overcoat and obi sash with great suspicion.

I kicked off my slippers. "From a land far, far away."

No way was I going to tell this crazy lady where Ethan and I came from. Knowing my luck Benson probably had the ability to transport between realms. I could only imagine how horrified she would have looked when she learned about our dirt floors back at home.

Astrid sensed my apprehension.

"You do realize Lily isn't a threat, right? She is a selkie. She can't teleport and has no interest in harming your people. In fact, she is the one who took me in when I had nowhere else to go."

Her and I had a conversation during the ride here. Thankfully, with Ethan as the only one present. Ethan's forehead wrinkled in confusion. "What's a selkie?"

Benson sighed as she picked the twigs out of my hair.

"A selkie is a Norse version of a mermaid. Our homes are underwater but unlike mermaids we don't turn into fish. Instead of becoming part fish we take on the shape of a seal. When we come of age we can shed our seal skin and come onto land. We have to hide our seal skins because we cannot fully transform into our true form nor can we go back home without them." Benson took great care in the act of rinsing my skin as she briefly explained what she was.

Enthralled with her story, I asked, "Why aren't you living at home then?"

"I was young. Despite my father's warning I fell in love. The man took my seal skin and ran. I've been stuck here ever since." Her voice held a tinge of regret.

Astrid broke the awkward silence and tilted her head towards the door.

"Come on Ethan. The past isn't something Lily likes to talk about. Let's go and I will show you how to use the shower. We'll get you cleaned up and ready for the party." He nodded and followed her inside.

Benson winced when she saw a dripping Ethan head towards the house.

"Please make sure he doesn't drip all over the wood floors."

Astrid frowned. Mischief danced in her amber eyes.

"Now why would a let him do a thing like that? Honestly Lily. I thought you'd have more faith in me." She said with feigned innocence.

Benson plucked a leaf out of my hair and flicked it off to the side before letting out a defeated sigh. "Alright. I suppose that's going to be the best that we can do until we get you in the shower."

"A shower?" My nose scrunched.

"Yes, a shower." She threw me a towel and I began to dry myself off.

"I take it you don't use showers back at home?"

I thought about telling Benson how we usually transform into a fox and jump into the stream as a form of bathing. I thought better of it after looking over her flawless French twist and finely manicured hands.

"Nah, we normally do baths." She turned the hose off. "Well I'll show you how to work the shower. You won't be able to show up on time for the gathering if you do a bath. Being late is not something Miss Garcia looks kindly upon. It's really easy. I promise."

"I am always down for easy." I said as I followed her into the house.

It was then that an icy draft of air blasted me in the face as I entered the doorway. Benson frowned at my unexpected gasp.

"Sweet mother of the Gods, I swear old winter must have caressed me himself!"

"Yes, I do apologize about that. I tend to be a huge fanatic of air conditioning."

She blamed the cold on my bad circulation. I blamed it on her lack of need for heat due to her frozen heart. A bitter cloud of what I had learned later to be bleach hung heavily in the air, making my eyes water and my nose burn. Despite being in human form I still maintained my fox like senses. The smell itself was overwhelming. Then again, I had to give it to her, she had great organizational skills. Everything had a place here and some things even had labels. If Mr. Clean had a wife it'd be Benson. Not a speck of dust was in sight. Maybe she massacred all the baby dust bunnies during the detailed clean. I arched a brow at the leather furniture, which she had encased in some sort of clear wrap. Benson called it plastic.

My eyebrows shot up in surprise.

"Really?" I poked at the plastic with my index finger. "Is this really necessary?"

"What?" She demanded defensively. "It keeps the furniture from staining."

I snorted. "A bit much don't you agree?"

"Well you never know what Astrid will bring home. You think this is the first time there has been a naked man in my house? She is a succubus after all. Enough now, come this way. The bathroom is just down the hall."

She led me into a cozy little room with gray walls and marbled flooring. On one side an oval mirror with a silver rim hung above a black vanity with polished knobs. There was a stainless steel lamp on each side of the mirror with ivory shades.

I let out a low whistle.

"So this is what you call a bathroom. A bit fancy don't you think?"

Senator Benson flicked a finger across the light switch.

"Yes I suppose but beggars can't be choosers. Now can they?"

The two stainless steel lamps flickered to life, filling the room with a soft white light. On top of the vanity sat an ebony wash basin with black handles that reflected off the sleek white marbled countertop. Across from the vanity was a black tub with a white interior and frosted glass doors. She called it a bathroom, I called it a wash room. It was all the same to me. It too reeked of cleaning products. Benson gave me a quick tour of the bathroom and a brief rundown on how to work the showerhead. She prefers to put the massage dial on full blast but level one worked fine for me. I wrenched the window open as soon as she shut the door. She hadn't take long to explain how to work the shower.

Regardless, the toxic fumes had given me a pounding headache. Gingerly, I stepped into the shower and allowed the hot curtain of water envelope me in its wet embrace. Steam clung to the air, making it thick and muggy. The heat reminded me of the hot springs at home. The thought of home made my chest twinge.

I thought of Pa and my so called "responsibilities". I remembered the hint of disappointment in Pa's eyes just before I had left. Regret and sorrow clawed at my throat. *Maybe I shouldn't have left in such a hurry. Maybe I shouldn't have said the things I had said.* Something inside me twisted. *Why was I upset? Didn't I have a right to be angry?* He wanted me to give up my life, something I wasn't ready to do yet. I scrubbed furiously at my skin with the soapy washcloth as I grumbled sourly to myself.

"What are you going to do now Lexi? Kyoto is at the brink of war. The Celestial clan and the Shadow clan are pitted against each other." I snorted with disgust. "Figures. It was only a matter of time till something like this would happen. Why am I not surprised? Our people have been at odds since the beginning of Gaia, we're like oil and water. Of course with that being said the Shadow clan just had to start a war, didn't they?"

Disgusted, I flicked a leaf off of my shoulder and tossed a tiny twig onto the floor. Benson had done a decent job cleaning out the debris but she could only have done so much. I growled. I couldn't contain my boiling frustration any longer. I unsnapped the cap to the shampoo and squeezed a generous dollop onto the top of my head before slamming the container back onto the rack. Fuming, I resumed my scrubbing and scolding.

"Of all people Pa just had to arrange you to be the ticket for peace didn't he? Instead of doing what you were told you just had to run off, didn't you! Now look where that got you. Now you are stuck in some place called Michigan where they use their hand to tell you where they live."

I clawed at my face, trying to get the stinging soap out of my eyes. Maybe if I had listened I wouldn't be in this mess. Pa himself believed that my marriage with Noah would have created stability between our clans. Why didn't I listen? What was he going to tell the Shadow clan's leader? Oh I'm sorry Kayne I lost your son's bride? I'm sure that would not have gone well. Who was going to keep the shadows at bay? They are malevolent in nature and are creatures of darkness.

CHAPTER 4

ASTRID HAD MANAGED to push her way into the bathroom with an armful of dresses. She insisted that I try each one. A few moments later, after some much needed persuasion and some succubi influence I found myself trying to wiggle my way into multiple outfits.

Never did I know that dressing without magic would be such an acrobatic endeavor. I managed to get my arm stuck in the first dress, the second one I couldn't fit over my hips, the third I tripped over and dove face first into the vanity, the fourth had so many layers I got lost and the fifth one's zipper got stuck in my hair. Finally, I managed to wiggle my way into an outfit and forced the zipper close before inching out into the hallway.

Astrid's face puckered with disapproval.

"Oh no, no, we can't do that. That one makes you look fat."

I bristled with irritation.

"Why thank you Astrid, for making me feel like a whale. Your honesty is *greatly* appreciated."

She grimaced and gave me an empathetic shrug.

"Well you know what they say. First impressions are the ones that count the most. You are going to be meeting very important people today. Don't you want to look your best?"

I snorted and glanced over at Ethan who sat back on the leather sofa, thumbing through what I had later learned was a newspaper. Thankfully he was wearing clothes now. I hadn't realized Benson had any men's clothes. According to Astrid they belonged to some guy named Frank. Apparently Frank wouldn't mind Ethan borrowing them either.

"Ethan, what do you think?"

He peered over the newsprint and signaled for me to turn.

I twirled on command. The fabric stretched against my skin, threatening to split.

His eyebrows rose in surprise.

"You really want to know what I think?" He asked as he folded the newspaper neatly onto his lap. He wore a relaxed pair of creamy khakis and a black polo shirt.

"Yes, as a matter of fact, I do want to know what you think."

He tilted his head, inspecting the fabric that clung tightly to my skin. He rubbed his chin. Red rusty curls fell into his emerald eyes.

"I think it's too tight Lex."

I stuck out my bottom lip.

"Give it time and the dress will rip right down the middle of your crack."

Astrid threw another dress at me.

"Try this one on for size."

I let out an irritable sigh.

"Look Astrid. This isn't working. I appreciate you trying to find something for me but I think I can manage on my own."

I was beginning to realize how hard it was going to be to hide what I was. Nothing was fitting me and using my magic would be so much easier than trying on dress after dress. Time was running out and we were going to be late if we didn't hurry up. Being late would be unforgivable. It was either I go and be on time or not go at all. Not going wasn't an option. From where I come from a party is a huge social event where we celebrate important things or meet important people. To arrive late would be an insult to the one holding the gathering. Besides Benson mentioned that we would be meeting a group of very important people. Who knows, maybe they were powerful enough to open a portal that would lead back to Gaia? I refused to miss out on such an opportunity.

Astrid scoffed. "You think you can manage?"

She arched a brow at me and placed a slender hand on one of her curvy hips.

"Trust me Lexi, you are beautiful but I highly doubt that you will be allowed into the party in just your birthday suit."

I opened my mouth to protest. Ethan eyed me warily. Astrid already knew who he was but she had no idea what I was. I wasn't planning on telling her my deepest darkest secrets anytime soon. Besides, illusion was right up my alley. I could easily create a suitable dress using my own energy but was it really worth exposing who I was to someone I barely knew? I struggled for words. My fingers tingled as I began to gather energy.

The door busted open before I could begin my transformation.

Senator Benson stepped in with an armful of clothes.

"I'm back!" She rang out in her sing song voice.

"I went to the store when I heard you were in need of an outfit. I managed to come back with a large selection!"

I gaped at her in complete bewilderment.

"How did you afford all of this?"

Astrid giggled, somehow she found my exasperation amusing.

"Lily is quite resourceful and she is filthy rich. She is a successful senator after all." Astrid said as she rushed over to Benson and began plucking the multiple dresses from her arms. "How do you think she would be able to afford this house and all the other places that house the supernatural?"

Ethan peered over his newspaper.

"She has other houses?"

"Loads of them." Astrid replied.

I rubbed at my forehead with my forefingers.

"I don't understand.." I murmured more to myself than anyone in the room.

"Oh never mind that my child. Please do try some of these things on. We are almost out of time and I don't want you to be late for the gathering. Everything will be explained to you, all in good time." Benson said with a warm smile.

I eyed her with great suspicion as she shooed the rest of the goons out of the room. *Who knew shopping could warm that woman's heart?* I looked over my selections.

Benson had conservative taste. Many of the dresses did not go above the knee. All of them reminded me of the business lady Astrid had pointed out to us earlier this morning. None of them revealed much. It wasn't like I was expecting to walk out looking like a hooker but how in the hell was I supposed to compete with Astrid in this crap?

I took in a deep breath and closed my eyes. I released the breath through my nose. Silently, I began to gather energy into my fingertips. Thankfully, no one was present. Warmth tingled across my fingertips and slowly trickled through my veins. A soft breeze rustled through my hair. A stream of fox fire trickled up out of the ground and swirled around me like a storm of leaves caught up in the autumn breeze, engulfing me with its light.

New fabric began to materialize beneath the flames and wrap itself around my body. In moments the flames faded away, leaving behind a black halter dress that hugged my torso and flared out at my hips. I turned in front of the full length mirror and cursed. Two fluffy fox tails swished playfully from side to side, white tips whipping through the air. Sometimes when I use magic my kitsune form reveals a part of itself. Someone knocked on the door. My heart stuttered.

"Just a minute!" I replied hastily as the knob began to turn.

Quickly, I twisted my hands above the tails. Cold fire swirled around the tails and any evidence of them disappeared in a puff of smoke. I adjusted my breasts making sure those puppies could compete.

Astrid's head peeked in. "You about ready, sister?"

"Just about." Quickly, I applied some kohl around my round fox like eyes and faintly dusted some blush upon my cheeks. I've never been the type to overcompensate so I left the room without applying Astrid's scarlet lipstick. I stepped out of the bathroom, praying that the illusion I had just created would look similar if not exactly like the halter dress Astrid had shoved at me earlier. I stepped out of the bathroom and into the hallway.

Benson peered warily at me over the rim of her tea cup, her eyes calculating.

Ethan stole a peek at me before setting the newspaper down.

"Well well, look at you." He cooed teasingly.

"You found something after all!" Astrid crowed with a brilliant smile.

I sauntered over to them and twirled for show.

He caught me and gave me a twirl before letting go.

"Not too bad. It fits you just right."

Benson watched from where she sat, her expression remained cryptic. Something had soured her cheery mood. She sipped her tea daintily with her legs crossed. Her lips were set in a straight line. Before I could ask what was wrong Astrid strode into the room. Her heels clicked against the wooden floor with purpose. Benson stiffened at the sound.

Astrid tossed me a piece of clothing.

"Here, this should keep you warm once it cools off tonight."

Benson schooled her face into a polite but tight smile.

"Astrid, my dear. How many times have I told you not to walk on my wood floors with heels?" Benson inquired, with strained patience.

"Oh, sorry Lily it sort of just slipped my mind." She shrugged with an apologetic smile.

"I see. Well next time it slips your mind I might slip some money out of your next allotted allowance for the repairs." She replied coolly.

I grimaced. *So much for the shopping high lasting for a while.* I had almost asked how she'd react to the dirt floors we had at home. I glanced at the plastic wrap around the couch and reconsidered. Ethan wrinkled his nose.

"An allowance?" He asked as him and I exchanged looks of confusion.

A flicker of gold briefly danced across Astrid's eyes but she held her tongue.

"Come on you guys. We are going to be late."

Benson's jaw tightened, at the very prospect

"Punctuality is critical Astrid. You know this."

I could practically hear Benson grinding her teeth all the way from the front door.

Astrid slammed the door behind her.

"Yes, an allowance." Astrid hissed as she shoved me unceremoniously towards the car. "Benson may be a nut about her house but regardless she is quite generous. She happens to be an extremely successful senator and has learned how to integrate herself into this world without anyone noticing she is a selkie. There's no sense in arguing with her when she was the one who took me under her wing when I had nowhere to go. We have a mutual relationship. I help her out and she pays me. She calls it an allowance, I call it a paycheck."

Ethan's face went white.

"You mean, you don't.." He struggled for the right words.

The tips of his ears turned crimson. "You aren't..."

Astrid flashed him a tight smile as she drove the car through the neighborhood.

"Her escort?" She purred.

He nodded.

Was this seriously was coming from a guy who ran around half naked all the time? Astrid's amber eyes narrowed into little slits.

"No, you prat. I am her web designer." She replied stiffly.

"Come again?" I arched a brow.

"I am her web designer."

Ethan chimed in. "You're a what and a who?"

He peered over my shoulder from the back seat.

"I use computers to design websites. When Lily first met me I was a hacker. She caught me hacking into her company's server. Once she realized I was doing things like that to survive she then offered me a job as her website designer and software technician."

"So let me get this straight. You're not only a succubus but you're also a spider woman, who controls a site with her webs using soft wares? And Senator Benson met you after you brutally hacked into her server. Why in the world would she hire someone who murdered her server?"

41

Astrid bubbled with laughter, her amber eyes sparkled with amusement.

"No silly, that's not how it works."

Astrid briefly explained what a computer was and clarified what she meant by a website. Apparently Gaia was a bit behind the times. Astrid accused us of living under a rock. Which I couldn't necessarily blame her. We didn't technically live under a rock but we did come from another world. She tossed me her cell phone and briefly explained how to use it. Ethan ignored his seatbelt and leaned over my shoulder to watch. I could practically feel his wet breath on my neck.

"It's like magic." He whispered, eyes wide as saucers.

"All these lights and information just appear at the swipe of your fingertips." I mused aloud, totally mystified by the whole ordeal.

We had never seen a cellphone before. The humans sure do create some nifty gadgets. I guess they do have their uses after all.

"You think that's cool? Watch this."

She tapped a few numbers into the touch screen and swiped her thumb over a green button. The phone let out a shrill ring. Ethan and I both tensed.

"Hello?" Loud music echoed in the background.

Together our mouths dropped in surprise.

"Hi Frank. It's Astrid we're turning on your road as we speak."

"Alright. Sounds cool, see you soon." The voice disappeared with a click.

We both stared at her.

Ethan was the first to break the silence. "What is this type of sorcery?"

Astrid chuckled.

I scowled and eyed the phone warily.

"What do you NOT do?" I asked, strongly emphasizing the word not.

Her lips curved into a sly smile.

"What can I say? I am a jack of all trades. Look. Honestly, I am not a witch. It's called technology, not magic. Besides, anyone can do it. You'll see. Benson and I will get you guys set up in no time."

We pulled into a gravel driveway that crunched beneath the weight of Astrid's silver Prius. We pushed through the shadows of pines to reveal a house on a hill. The dark silhouette of a ranch house stood in stark contrast against the bleeding sunset. All of the windows twinkled with light. The sound of music increased as we neared. A strong bass vibrated through the house. Off in the distance people stood in the front yard with cups in their hands. Some were nursing their drinks while others tended to the crackling bonfire. Their skin reflected the fire's glow and their eyes soaked in the burning sunset. We approached the house at a decent speed, climbing up the gravel driveway.

Until a cackling woman stumbled drunkenly into the driveway only a few yards off. She stopped mid stride, mesmerized by Astrid's bright headlights. She swayed like a snake caught up in a snake charmer's tune. Bleary eyed she stared into the light of Astrid's oncoming car. Brown eyes widened into large saucers. The light of the car's headlights reflected off of the whites of her eyes. Ethan sucked in a breath. She stepped back, too drunk to think clearly as Astrid stomped on the brakes.

Adrenaline rushed through me like wildfire. We lurched forward, so did my heart. *We were going to hit her, weren't we?* I tried to call out to her but nothing came out. *Why wouldn't she move?* Ethan smacked into the back of my seat with a disgruntled grunt. Astrid's tires struggled to stop against the loose gravel.

"Whoa, Bessie." She hissed as she wrenched on the steering wheel.

Despite Astrid's efforts the car slipped and slid towards her. Fright danced across the woman's eyes before her body crumpled to the floor. Something black darted across the terrain. My nails dug into the black upholstery. Ethan groaned.

"I think I'm gunna be sick."

A violent retching sound followed promptly afterward. Clouds of dust and dirt rose into the night sky. Bile tainted the air within the car's cabin. Something blurred across my visage but I couldn't tell what between the dust and the debris. We skidded to a stop. The engine ticked and popped. A wide eyed Astrid gripped the steering wheel with white knuckles, her posture remained rigid and her jaw was clamped shut. Music still reverberated off in the distance.

A shadowy form on the side of the road rose from its kneeling position, silent, swift and graceful. I couldn't distinguish who he or she was. Dust billowed everywhere. The smell of crisp pine, smoke, sweat, and alcohol mingled in the air. A strange mixture of ancient earth and dried blood haunted my nostrils as the shadowy figure began to approach us with predatory grace. Something wasn't right. An unnatural sense of dread tickled the hairs on the back of my neck, like the legs of a thousand scuttling spiders. Ethan and I exchanged glances. Whatever it was, the smell wasn't human.

CHAPTER 5

ASTRID UNBUCKLED her seatbelt with a trembling hand. Ethan finished heaving in the back seat. My throat constricted as the sour scent of his vomit flooded my nose. Astrid coughed as waved at the air in a futile effort to disperse the scent of bile. The dust settled only to reveal a lanky man in his early twenties. He wore a white button down shirt and black dress pants. He paused. His piercing gray eyes peered towards us, uncertain if he should proceed. A rich voice called out into the night, it was peppered with what I later learned were soft Italian undertones.

"Astrid is that you?"

"Frank?" She called out as she stepped out of the car.

His thin lips spread into wide smile, crinkling the corners of his steely gray eyes. He had a square shaped face with a long nose, a thin mouth and an angular chin.

"Astrid! I am so glad you can make it."

He took a few long strides with his spindly legs and swept up Astrid in a spinning hug. The breeze rustled through the top of his tapered haircut, tickling my nose with his scent. He looked human, but didn't smell like it. He had an earthy smell, like pine trees, dirt and fresh rain on a spring day but the scent of old blood and smoke clung to his clothes like a disease.

I stiffened. In fact, the whole premises stank of old blood and alcohol. Ethan glanced my way, his muscles tense and his jaw tight. He too could smell the blood. Shivers rippled down my spine like little spider legs.

"Is she okay?" Astrid asked as she peered around his shoulder, searching for any evidence of a woman that may have been hit by a car.

Frank flashed her a congenial smile. "Hmm?"

He chuckled once he realized who Astrid was searching for.

"Oh. Brenda? She is right as rain. Had a tad too much to drink if you ask me. No worries, I snatched her up before you made any impact. You gave her quite a scare though." He hooked his thumb over his shoulder to indicate Brenda's current location. "She's sleeping it off over there in the ditch."

Relief melted her fear away.

He peered over her shoulder. His expression turned quizzical.

"I see you have brought friends"

"Well aren't you Captain obvious." She teased.

His smoky eyes analyzed us with speculation.

"I told you I was bringing them." Astrid whispered as she ran a playful finger down his cheek. He batted the hand away absentmindedly, his steel gaze honed in on us. Her hazel eyes glittered with gold. His life force remained intact, despite the golden flicker in her gaze. She gave him a gentle push our way. "Frank, this is Lexi and Ethan. They are *my* friends. Upon Benson's request I was asked to bring them to the coven's gathering."

Frank's spine straightened at the mention of Benson's name.

Her full lips pressed into a thin line.

"If there are any issues with this arrangement they need to be brought to Lily herself."

She spat the word *issues* as if it were venom.

Surely we wouldn't be too much of a hassle, now would we? I mean how much trouble could two shape shifters cause anyway? On second thought, I didn't bother with listing the different possibilities. Frank gave me a tight but cordial smile before extending his hand in greeting.

"Hello. My name is Francesco but you may call me Frank."

I flashed him one of my winning smiles and shook his hand.

Ethan eyed him warily as he wiped spittle off of his mouth with the back of his hand before offering it to Frank. "Name's Ethan, Ethan Matthews."

Frank grimaced and wrinkled his nose. A hint of contempt flashed across his gray eyes. He eyed Ethan's hand as if it were the plague. Astrid stared at him expectantly. Begrudgingly, he shook Ethan's hand with very little enthusiasm.

"Pleasure." He said stiffly.

He held his breath for a moment and then rubbed Ethan's spittle onto his pant leg. "Right then." He stood there with a polite smile frozen upon his lips. Silence impregnated the air. Chirping crickets pierced through the awkward silence with their nightly song. Off in the distance music thrummed and people chattered.

"Now that is settled. Astrid dear, might we have a word?"

Without hesitation he grabbed Astrid by the elbow and steered her away off into the distance to what he presumed was out of our hearing range. The hairs on the back of my neck prickled.

"Care to explain why you would bring two shapeshifters to the coven's gathering? Most importantly a werewolf?" He whispered urgently.

She gave him a disapproving glare.

"Now don't be rude, Frank."

He stole an apprehensive glance our way before continuing.

"What in the world were you thinking?" He hissed.

Astrid slapped his hand away. "I told you it was at Benson's request!"

His eyes darted over towards the party before gushing on.

"Do you realize how much trouble this might cause for tonight's gathering? Did you take into consideration on how my people might react?"

Astrid's amber eyes narrowed with contempt.

Great. We were the uninvited guests to some stuffy old party. *So much for first impressions.* I had thought bitterly to myself. *How on earth were we going to get these people to open a portal to Gaia if they don't even* want us here? Was it even a possibility that they could help us in the first place?

Astrid gave him a flinty glare, the specks of gold in her eyes glowing.

Frank lifted his palms in an acquiescent gesture.

"Look, I know Garcia has been trying to extend the olive branch per Lily's request. Regardless, you and I both know they won't appreciate having two weres as unexpected guests. This type of request could cause an uproar. We're still trying to mend broken pride and old wounds from the last war. You must realize this, don't you?"

Ethan and I exchanged knowing looks.

"Well, this sure isn't awkward." I said.

"No, not at all." Ethan replied flatly.

Regardless, the two of them continued to argue as if we didn't exist. Astrid bristled. Her pink aura flared red with irritation. Gold flickered through her amber eyes. When she spoke it was with strained patience.

"I am well aware of this, Frank, and we do appreciate your people's attempt to adapt to the modern ways of society. However, peace amongst the community has not been concretely established. Instead, it is teetering on thin ice. In order for peace to occur both the local coven and the local wolf pack need to work together." Her voice came out flat and acidic.

"Easy chica. I am just looking out for you."

Apprehension tainted his tone.

He cast a worried glance our way and then back at the party.

Astrid kept plowing through as if he hadn't spoken a word.

"Keep in mind Senator Benson's goal is to create a peaceful environment that is inclusive of *all* species. Don't forget, Frank, people are going missing. We need to work together. Benson has connections. Think of Anna. Lily can use her connections to your people's advantage or disadvantage if need be. Would you rather it be the latter?"

The silence between the two of them was tense.

"On a different note." She continued primly, quickly changing the subject.

"I am sure your *guests* don't appreciate being talked about as if they weren't there." She flashed the two of us an apologetic smile.

I knew there was a reason why I liked this girl.

"Couldn't have said it better myself." Ethan said with a smug smile.

"Yeah, funny you should mention that because I was thinking the same thing." I said.

"It's not like we couldn't hear you or anything." Ethan added, his green eyes glittered with mischief. "What really peaks my interest is how you knew we were shapeshifters?"

Frank cursed beneath his breath.

"More importantly why does this place reek of blood?" I added.

Frank rubbed the space between his eyes and muttered something about half-wits and dogs.

"I beg your pardon?" Ethan crowed.

Frank ignored him. It was his turn to speak with strained patience.

"Look, you happened to have stumbled upon a vampire gathering. Oddly enough, our diet happens to consist mainly of blood. So I would assume it is only natural you would be able to smell it at the party. Lucky for you, I just so happen to be vegetarian." Frank replied with an arch smile.

"However, I will be more than willing to bite you if you get out of line."

He had added this last comment with a hint of disgust.

I snorted. *"A vegetarian vampire?* Come now, you can't be serious."

We had vampires back at home. Gaia happens to be filled with various supernatural creatures. Vampires were only one out of the many supernatural species. However they weren't prevalent in my home town. The fang heads had a tendency to appreciate larger cities more so than small villages. More humans meant more prey.

Not many people lived around Mount Kyoto, due to the mountainous terrain. The people there were simple rice farmers. Once in a great while we'd stumble upon a vampire roaming our lands. If they ever became a threat we would quickly dispose of them. Back at home we were the servants of Inari, the goddess of agriculture and the villagers were her people. We were trained to attack anything that would cause them harm. The villagers were our food supply. Their emotions and life force were what fed us. In exchange, we protected their crops and helped them flourish. If we allowed vampires to suck them dry then there would be nothing left for us but empty carcasses.

Astrid fiddled with a strand of her hair.

"Contrary to popular belief there are vegetarian vampires. Frank here drinks animal blood instead of human blood. That is why vampires consider him a vegetarian." She paused for a moment, searching for the appropriate wording. "Human blood tends to make him go batty, if you get what I mean."

Her amber eyes glittered with amusement.

"No pun intended." Astrid added with a stifled giggle.

She couldn't be serious, could she?

Ethan and I exchanged looks of uncertainty.

It was Ethan's turn to proceed with caution.

"You do realize vampires don't have the capacity to turn into bats, right?"

"Come now, cant you take a joke?" Astrid scoffed.

"How is that possible?" I sputtered in disbelief.

Frank let out a flustered sigh and raked a hand through his black hair.

"It's simple really, animals and humans contain life force in their blood."

Ethan and I stared at him as if he were some sort of unnatural phenomenon. We waited for a more detailed explanation but Frank simply cleared his throat and averted his gaze.

"Look let's just say I have issues with self-control when I feed. Regardless, my feeding patterns are not important right now. Onto your first question. How do I know you are weres? Well Ethan, you smell like a wet dog. Which happens to be a common trait among werewolves."

The muscles along Ethan's jawline twitched. "Ruthless, much?"

I couldn't help but chuckle.

Ethan elbowed me in the ribs.

One of these days my mouth was going to get me in trouble.

Frank continued. "And Lexi you happen to smell like a mix between a fox or skunk."

My jaw dropped in complete horror.

Ethan's mouth, however, curved with smug satisfaction.

What the hell was this guy's problem? Weren't vampires supposed to be polite and charming? Astrid simply smiled and shook her head in silent amusement.

"A skunk? Is that the best you can come up with?" I scoffed in disbelief.

Ethan tried to stifle a chuckle.

I flashed my werewolf counterpart a dirty glare and bared my teeth.

"Well at least a wet dog sounds more enticing than a skunk." He mumbled quietly to himself as he rubbed at his neck.

I shot him another deadly glare.

"What?" He shook with laughter.

"Alright chuckles. That is enough."

Frank grumbled and massaged his temples.

"Regardless, none of you smell like human. Anyhow, Astrid has a point. What is more important is Lily requested that you come to the gathering. Do I like it? No. I don't like it one bit, but if we don't adhere to Lily's requests then the coven loses its connections with the local police force. I am sure Garcia would have my head if I were the cause of that happening. Astrid, will you do me the honors?"

Astrid tossed him the keys to her silver Prius.

He caught him in midair with cat like grace.

Lily this, Lily that. Why did the topic always veer back to Lily anyhow?

I rolled my eyes and let out a puff of air through my nose.

"I don't see why everyone's so hyped out about this Benson lady. I mean she seems a bit up tight if you ask me." I grumbled more so to myself than to anyone in particular.

Frank froze mid stride and turned to me. The keys dangled limply in his right hand.

"Wait. You met Lily?" Frank asked with a hint of surprise.

"Yeah, what's the big deal anyway?" I asked, my mouth tightened into a thin line.

My fox tails twitched beneath my human illusion. I didn't like how she was dangling her power over the coven's heads. It just didn't seem fair.

Ethan cringed at my sharp tone. "Lexi." He warned.

Frank gawked at me, in complete bewilderment. He closed his mouth and schooled his expression. I continued on, as if Ethan hadn't spoken.

"What?!" I replied defensively.

"I wanna know why everyone is so googly eyed over her anyhow?"

Frank stared at me like I was stupid.

Astrid let out a controlled breath and massaged her temples with her forefingers.

"Lexi here is new to the community Frank, so please excuse her ignorant behavior." My pelt bristled with irritation.

"*Please excuse me?*" I scoffed.

"Oh boy, here we go.." Ethan grumbled beneath his breath.

"Excuse me for what? I have every right to know what is going on just as you do. Besides, who are you calling ignorant anyway? Let's remember, I'm not the one who thought vampires could turn into bats."

"That was simply a joke, you babbling baboon."

For a brief moment the crickets were the only ones responding to my question.

Astrid watched me with her cat like gaze.

The boys stood there in stunned silence.

"Is anyone going to answer me?"

It was then that Frank cleared his throat.

When he spoke it was slow, he made a valiant effort to enunciate each word.

"Well, she just so happens to be a powerful senator. She also plays a huge role in this city's governmental politics. She has tremendous power and maintains a strong connection with the police force. She also happens to work closely with the supernatural community and has been able to maintain our community's secrecy for decades. Senator Benson has had a significant impact on modernizing the supernatural society. She has been helping both werewolves and vampires move past their differences and has also played a large role in each side's rights. She has strongly pushed for the humane treatment of both vampire and wolf. Without her we would probably have been exposed by now.

She has used her resources and wealth to support halfway houses for the orphaned supernatural. Without her Astrid wouldn't be here and you guys would probably have been torn to pieces by the media." He paused and looked at me quizzically with his stormy grey eyes. "To belittle her or act as if she has no significance would truly mean you are not from around here. Or at least I am hoping you are not because if you are then that would make you a complete idiot."

My stomach tensed.

I opened my mouth to retort but he held his hand up.

"That'll be enough for now." He replied curtly.

"Let's be going now" Astrid's voice came out clipped.

Together they swiveled on the ball of his foot and walked away.

Something told me that he didn't like Benson much.

Ethan and I glanced at each other, perplexed.

"Where are you going?" I asked.

Frank's eyes narrowed with irritation.

"Isn't it obvious? I am taking you to the party. It's now or never, so let's go."

Together we hopped into the vomit ridden Prius. Thanks to Ethan the car stank of bile. Thankfully, Ethan was gentleman enough to sit in front of his own mess and the ride itself didn't take long at all. We broke through the forest and stepped out of the car and into the night. The earthly smell of vampire clung heavily to the air, mingling with the smell of smoke, lust and human sweat. Flickering firelight kept the darkness at bay. Laughter and conversation grew louder as we approached. Music boomed while shadows danced across the side of the house. A handful of people stood around the crackling fire.

The swaying flames cast playful shadows across each person's face. Some people danced, while others nursed their drinks. A couple stood off in the distance, locked into an intimate embrace. The hackles on the back of my neck prickled. Something wasn't right. I couldn't put my finger on it just yet. She had her face buried into the crook of his neck. The aura around him flickered dimly like the flame of a dying candle. His blood tainted the air. His life force spooled out of him and trickled into her. She was feeding on him. My stomach flipped.

She was taking too much. My heart stuttered. I held my breath. A few more moments passed. *Why wasn't anyone stopping her? How could people just stand around and chit chat while this man wilted in this black widow's arms?* Anger boiled through my veins. Energy crackled at my fingertips and fear shredded at my nerves. By no means should his aura be flickering so faintly. Anytime aura flickered like this it meant the person was at the brink of death. I stepped forward to assist but Ethan snatched my arm and pulled me back.

"Stop, you don't know what you are going up against." He whispered urgently.

"What the hell are you doing?" Frank hissed.

"Do you have any idea who that is!?" Astrid whispered.

Before Ethan or Frank could steer me away I released a ball of electricity towards the vampire in front of me. The crackling ball of energy slammed into her spine. She dropped her prey with a hiss. His body crumpled to the floor. She spun on her heel, snarling and spitting like a wild cougar, baring her sharp fangs. Ethan tensed, ready to pounce. Astrid brought her hands to her mouth. A handful of people gave her a wide berth and backed away.

Frank released an anguished moan and dragged his hands down the sides of his face. "Do you realize who you just attacked?! That is Carmen Garcia, the head of the local vampire coven. Are you *fucking* insane?!"

A shadow whipped across the courtyard at lightning speed. The shape of a man manifested in front of me. *Could this be the black widow's bodyguard?* I stared into his empty black eyes, mesmerized by the reflection of the dancing firelight. He wore a pair of dress slacks and a button down shirt. His square face was cleanly shaven and he wore his brown hair slicked back. His icy skin reeked of spice and earthy aftershave. He hissed, revealing his own set of blood-stained canines. I grimaced as some of his spittle sprayed my face. *Don't these people know that spitting is not polite?* Within seconds, he lifted me off the ground like a rag doll, my throat crushing beneath his vice like grip.

"So much for the pleasantries, eh?" I choked out each word.

My fingers clawed at his hand.

"Give me one reason why I should not snap your pretty little head right off your skinny little neck?" He asked, his accent crisp, clean and sophisticated.

His breath however, was not.

I flashed him a lopsided smile. "I have mints?"

His grip tightened. I rasped with laughter.

"Well someone does not appreciate my humor."

Ethan tried lunging forward but Frank pulled him back by the scruff of his neck. He tried arguing but Frank simply shook his head. Ethan shifted his weight and stared at me, his face frozen from shock. A thousand thoughts flickered behind his eyes. A horrified Astrid clamped one hand over her open mouth.

"A little help here Frank" I sputtered, struggling to breathe.

Frank mumbled something foul.

"Now you've done it. We are all screwed. Screwed, you hear me?" He hissed.

I kicked my legs back and forth and tried to wiggle free.

The man with the crisp accent held me firmly in place.

"Not helping Frank!" I managed to gag.

Laughter and conversation dwindled to a soft hush.

"Put her down!" Ethan snarled, baring his own set of canines.

His pupils dilated and the eyes of his wolf had shown through his furious gaze.

The music went silent. The dancers stumbled to a halt. A handful of spectators looked our way, their expressions tense and their voices hushed. A few humans glanced around with a dazed expression, as if waking up from a drunken stupor. Laughter and conversation came to an awkward halt. A soft murmur fell over the crowd. The vampires mumbled quietly to one another, their lips tainted with scarlet. The air stank of copper and blood. The fire crackled and popped. Crickets chirped. Tense silence held everyone in place. The hairs on the back of my neck prickled in anticipation.

Someone's musical laughter splintered the silence, followed by a slow singular applause. The crowd parted for a woman of Mediterranean descent. Everything about her screamed elegance, from her glossy black hair to her olive skin all the way down to her leather boots. She wore a black pencil skirt and a dressy white blouse. She approached us with the grace of a predatory cat. Her clicking heels pierced through the tense silence. She stopped a few feet away and rested her hand on one hip. Humor quirked at the corner of her scarlet lips.

"My, my Dante. What do we have here?"

CHAPTER 6

SO THIS WAS the legendary Carmen Garcia. She stank of scorched skin and burnt hair. Her brown eyes glittered with calculation. The queen of the night watched me with a keen interest. I had hit her square in the back. Burnt skin crackled and peeled as new skin began to surface beneath her damaged flesh. *Damn vampires and their damn healing abilities. Why couldn't they just die like normal critters?*

The fire popped. Ash fluttered to the ground. A handful of humans shifted their weight. They exchanged glances looks of silent uncertainty. The vampires stood like statues in the night.

"Mm, what do we have here?" Garcia inquired with a lazy smile. Seconds later, she closed her chocolate eyes and breathed in, scenting her surroundings like a panther ready to fight. Frank remained frozen, his vice like grip still held a tense Ethan in place. Garcia let out a breathy chuckle.

"It looks like we have a wolf."" She paused and held up her hand.

The crowd stared at her with an intense impatience.

She sniffed again. Disgust twisted her perfect features. "And a skunk."

The crowd murmured in agreement.

She just had to compare me to a skunk, didn't she? Couldn't she use some other word to describe me? Like a mongoose? Or a weasel? They too had similar scent glands to a fox. Or maybe she could simply describe me as what I am, a fox.

"Surely, you mean fox. Not skunk." I rasped as I dangled from Dante's grip.

She let out a puff of air and gave me a leisurely shrug.

"I care not what you smell like, or what you are. You are a nuisance to me, nothing more than a pest. I am more interested in learning how you managed to strike me at my own gathering. On what grounds do you have to attack me? Have you no manners child?" She had a thick velvet voice, rich with Italian undertones.

She circled me like a hungry cat.

I watched her out of the corner of my eye.

Ethan leaned forward, ready to pounce.

Frank pressed him back with the weight of his arm.

I wiggled beneath Dante's grasp.

"You were attacking an innocent person." I croaked with accusation.

Garcia scoffed. "I don't know where you come from but you smell foreign. You have no authority here, little skunk. Here we have rules. He was an active participant. As a blood servant he knew what he was getting into. I as well am bound to a duty. It is my responsibility to keep him safe."

"Does that include draining him dry like a juice pack?" Ethan countered.

This conversation proved to be going nowhere. Thanks to pretty boy here I couldn't use any incantations to summon magic. *So much for trying to get the fire pit's flames to do my bidding.* I may have been able to control the flames with my mind alone, if I was a few hundred years older. However that was not the case.

Time for plan B.

I dipped into my own body heat, an elemental source that was already accessible to me and simply maximized it. That is what kitsune do. We twist the natural elements and use them to our advantage. I was famished. I hadn't ate in a long time and I had already used a bit of my magic earlier today for my outfit. Would I even be able to pull this off? Possibly, maybe if I focused my energy on a specific area. My body heat increased in temperature until the area of skin beneath Dante's hands glowed like an ember. Dante released me with a hiss and clutched his burnt palm. I crumpled to the ground like a discarded doll.

"The bitch burned me!" Dante snarled.

"Hmm, it seems like the little skunk has many tricks up her sleeve." Garcia mused aloud.

Dante reached back to slap me but then Ethan lunged.

Thankfully, Frank scooped him up into a bear hug before he got too far. He snarled and struggled against Frank's hold. His fingers had extended into sharp claws. Ethan may be a big bad wolf, but even he couldn't handle a pack of vampires. I sent up a silent prayer of thanks, I don't know what I would do if anything had happened to him on my account.

"I swear if you lay hand on her I will make you pay." He growled, baring his teeth. Firelight reflected in his wolf-like eyes. The vampires around him tensed. Sharp fangs clicked into place. The sickly scent of fear and smoky smell of rage polluted the air. The skin around their cheekbones tightened. Blue veins tickled out from the corners of their eyes. Black pitch pooled into the whites of their sclera. Shadows danced across their faces making them look like the risen dead.

A nervous titter threatened to escape my throat. My heart thundered inside my chest. Some of the human blood bags shifted their weight. The vampires inched forward with the grace of a predatory cat. I pushed my fear down, forcing my heartbeat to slow. Vampires can smell fear. It excites them. Tension strained at the crowd's fragile state, threatening to burst with violent chaos.

Garcia's voice cut through the impending chaos.

"That is enough!" She thrummed with power.

Her vampire counterparts froze, muscles coiled like springs.

"I do offer my humblest apologies and must express my appreciation for your participation. However, due to an unexpected series of events we are moving the gathering to a new date."

A soft murmur of disappointment rippled through the crowd.

When Garcia spoke again, her voice came out frosty and flat.

"I said we are moving the gathering to a new date. You are all dismissed."

A handful of fang heads flashed us a pointed glare before they dispersed.

Meanwhile, a scrawny woman with darting eyes shuffled up to Garcia.

"Mistress, do you think it wise to leave yourself unattended with these formidable creatures?" She stammered as she wrung her hands.

Garcia's cool demeanor slid away. Darkness bled out from her irises, filling the whites of her eyes. She took the woman by the throat and lifted her into the air. Blue veins trickled out from the corner of her hooded eyes. Her face became more angular. The woman gasped and cowered beneath Garcia's flinty glare. When Garcia spoke, her tone was as flat as an icy river bed stone.

"Maybe I did not make myself clear, *human*. You are a guest here only because I allow you that luxury. By no means are you given permission to stomp upon my hospitality and undermine my authority. Now I suggest you leave before I lose my temper." Garcia chucked her aside. Her bottom skipped across the ground like a stone over water. She tripped over herself in a feeble attempt to scramble away.

Papery laughter tickled at my raw throat.

Garcia herself cast me a murderous glare.

In the meantime, Dante cradled his burnt hand. The melted flesh was slowly repairing itself. He eyed me warily. His eyes were as sharp as knives. I struggled to stand. Frank held back a fuming Ethan, while Astrid was nowhere to be seen. *So much for reliability*. I thought bitterly to myself. Later Astrid and I would have to have a talk about dependability.

"My, my, we have a temper don't we?" I croaked, my voice paper thin.

A cool mask foreshadowed Garcia's demonic expression.

"So the rat has a sense of humor. I do have to say I am quite impressed that you were able to touch Dante with your magic." Garcia replied.

She cleared the amount of space between us within seconds.

Honeysuckle and old earth filled my nose.

Inky black eyes looked me over thoroughly.

I swiveled on the ball of my feet and watched her warily as she circled me like a predatory cat.

"What are you anyway?" She asked.

It was then that Ethan lost it. He tried bursting through Frank's hold but Frank grabbed him by the collar and pulled him back.

"If you so much as touch her I'll rip out your spleen and eat it for dinner!" He seethed.

Garcia's face puckered with disapproval.

Frank grimaced and murmured a half hearted apology.

"Tut, tut, temper, temper" She clucked patronizingly. "Please do refrain yourself, before I rip out your tongue and shove it down your petty little throat."

She offered Dante a petulant sigh.

"I swear the young these days lack in manners. Dante will you do the honors?"

Dante's muscles coiled. He open and closed his hand as he lowered into a crouch.

"Tell your little pet dog to stand down." He growled.

Ethan bared his teeth, green eyes glowing.

"And if I don't?" I couldn't resist testing the waters.

"Then I will simply kill him."

I paused and sized Garcia up. *Could I take her on?* I already knew I couldn't take on Dante but if I took on Garcia would I even have a chance? She did heal quickly. During our conversation her back managed to knit itself back together. She also managed to toss a grown woman across the yard like a rag doll. If my calculations were correct then any vampire could do that. However, she did dismiss a whole gaggle of vampires with the wave of her hand. Judging by her character she was Dante's equal if not more. One vampire was a possibility, but two? My shoulders slumped in defeat. I had to pick and choose my battles, this one not being one of them.

"Stand down Ethan." I said with a reluctant sigh.

Ethan flashed me a bewildered frown. "Excuse me?"

Frank's grip on Ethan's shoulder loosened in relief.

"I said stand down." I growled through gritted teeth. I never really liked losing to an argument but keeping Ethan from killing himself was more important now. Reluctantly, his shoulders slackened beneath Frank's grasp. Wolf eyes slowly transformed back into that of a human.

A satisfied smile curled along the corner of Garcia's scarlet lips. "Ah, it is a pleasure to see that we are ready to have a civilized conversation. Tell me, who gave you permission to attend our coven's gathering?"

"I did." A woman declared with a voice that rang with authority.

Two armed suits shouldered their way through the dispersing crowd. The humans bowed their heads and immediately moved out of the way. The remaining vampires in the group eyed the pistols warily before begrudgingly stepping off to the side. Senator Benson and her succubus counterpart followed in their wake. Benson wore a pair of gray business slacks. A white blouse peeked out from her gray suit jacket and she had her golden hair tightly wrapped into a clean French twist.

"What seems to be the problem here?" Benson inquired coolly.

Garcia and I stared at each other, stone faced and unmoving.

Dante jutted his jaw my way but kept his eyes on Ethan.

"Your guest here attacked Garcia for feeding." Benson went silent. Her lips tightened into a thin line. The suits stood beside her. Their hands came to their hips, only a breath away from their guns. Benson raised a slender brow. She pursued the following matter with great care.

"Was she following the treaty?" Benson inquired carefully.

Garcia bristled and shot Benson a murderous glare.

Astrid cast her an apologetic smile as the remainder of the crowd cleared out.

"Of course she was following the treaty." Dante snapped.

Garcia jabbed a finger at Benson before rounding on her.

"What were you thinking? Bringing a wolf to my coven's gathering without any warning? If we are going to work together there needs to be clear communication."

Benson offered her a perplexed frown.

"How peculiar. I figured you would appreciate me bringing a wolf to assist you with your political agenda. Did you or did you not claim that you were having trouble finding a wolf to help aid you in your cause?" Garcia struggled for words. "Did you not ask me to help you prove to the local pack that your intentions were pure?"

Everyone had evacuated the premises and a tense silence impregnated the night. The chirping of crickets pierced through the night air.

Garcia's face puckered.

She replied hesitantly, choosing her words carefully. "Yes, but–"

Benson bulldozed on, cutting her short.

"Do you not recall telling me that all the local packs have declined your invitation to the coven's gathering?"

Garcia's face soured, as if she had just swallowed something she didn't agree with. "Yes but a little notice would have been nice." Garcia replied crisply.

Benson's face tightened and her lips pressed into a thin line.

She gestured towards Ethan. Her expression remained somber.

"This is what I have to work with, Garcia. The local pack hates you with a passion. Thankfully, he happened to show up on my doorstep only hours before the party. You may feel free to ask him if he'd be willing to be your public example, proof that you're more than willing to welcome werewolves into the vampire community after the war."

She paused and gave Garcia a pointed glare before looking my way. I inclined my head in acknowledgement. I had to be honest, I did not like Benson very much but I had to hand it to her. The woman had a pair of brass balls. Ethan's eyes bounced from Benson to Garcia and then back, following their debate.

"Proof that you mean no harm to him or his associates. However, I must confess. The possibility of gaining his assistance now is unlikely, thanks to your uncerimonious ways."

Astrid watched the whole ordeal silently. Her expression remained unreadable.

Ethan on the other hand frowned and then shifted his weight.

"What is your people's problem with wolves anyway? If you even think of saying I smell like a wet dog I will literally bite you."

Benson scowled in disapproval.

"Mr. Matthews." She demanded, her voice sharp as a whip.

"You will do no such thing. Please refrain yourself from speaking."

She then turned to me with piercing ice blue eyes.

"Miss Adams, care to explain why you are attacking the head of the local coven?"

I just realized then that it wasn't a rhetorical question. I hadn't expected the tables to turn so quickly. A satisfied smirk pulled at the corner of Dante's lips. My nails dug into the palms of my hands. I wanted to rip that smug little smirk off of his perfect little face.

"She was attacking an innocent person. He was nearly drained dry and was at the brink of death. What else was I supposed to do, stand by and watch him die? We don't do things like that from where I come from."

Frank shifted his weight.

Astrid watched me with an intense curiosity.

"Where do you exactly come from anyway?" Dante asked imperiously.

He opened and closed his fist, testing the newly healed tendons.

I shot him a testy glare.

"Wouldn't you like to know?" I commented dryly.

Astrid rubbed her temples and let out an irritable sigh.

"Will you two knock it off? Look, let's be honest. Garcia was feeding off of a blood servant, not from some random bloke off the street. She wasn't violating the contract at all. Lexi here just attacked based on pure instinct." Senator Benson looked at me quizzically, her face remained stern and controlled.

"Both of you take a seat." Benson said as she inclined her head towards the patio furniture.

Ethan silently obeyed. I on the other hand did not. I wasn't going to be scolded for doing something I thought was right.

"I'll stand thank you." I replied stiffly.

Everyone's eyebrows shot up in surprise.

"It wasn't really an option." Benson replied with a curt nod towards the patio chair.

"Take a seat." She repeated, her voice cold as steel.

I grumbled sourly to myself and flopped down onto the patio furniture.

"Obviously you aren't from around here. Where you come from I do not know. However, we are a community of structure. Here we have rules and regulations. Carmen fed off of a blood servant. He was a willing participant and signed a contract saying that he would donate his blood for the vampire coven in exchange for some of theirs. In addition, he is compelled not to breathe a word about the supernatural community to any human soul. Think of it as a blood donor for vampires. If he happens to get too low they feed him their blood to accelerate his healing. Becoming a blood servant does not make you a victim. It is a mutual transaction between both parties. The blood servant gets a taste of the vampire's speed and heightened abilities in exchange for donating his or her blood."

Senator Benson studied our faces for clarification before continuing.

"I invited you to this gathering because I need Ethan's assistance. However, I cannot have you running amuck attacking important people within the community, especially if they are following protocol. It is a disturbance of the peace and will not be tolerated. Under no circumstances should our community be revealed to the public. All supernatural identities must remain a secret from the human population. In order to do so our behavior must be impeccable. Do you understand?"

I mumbled something beneath my breath before offering her a begrudging nod. If anymore outbursts were to happen it would not be in my favor. Ethan's forehead wrinkled with concern.

"What do you want with me anyway?" He asked, Lily with suspicion.

Garcia set her jaw and looked away.

Benson shrugged and gave him a congenial smile.

"It is simple really. We need your help easing the tension between the wolves and the vampires. Many supernatural creatures have gone missing as of late. As a community we are going to have to work together to get to the bottom of it."

Garcia's face twisted with anguish.

"They didn't take just any creature, Lily. They took Anna." She hissed.

Dante chewed on the inside of his cheek. His eyes burned with pure hatred.

Anna Johnson...why did that name sound so familiar?

Then it dawned upon me.

"Wasn't she the one we saw on the missing person's poster earlier today?"

I had blurted out loud before thinking.

Everyone's gaze turned onto me.

So much for laying low and not drawing attention to myself.

I silently cursed myself for my impulsive behavior.

Dante spat.

"Yes, Anna. She has been missing for a while now."

"She was Carmen's secretary" Astrid explained with a polite smile.

"Sweet little thing,.." Frank mused aloud with a troubled frown.

"What do you care anyway?" Dante asked, his crisp accent dripped with acid.

I shot him another testy glare but didn't take the bait. I had already bested him once and he was twice my size. He was probably still sulking from getting his ass kicked by a little skunk. Serves him right, he had it coming to him. It was only natural for him to sulk. Boys will be boys I suppose.

Ethan rubbed at his chin. A thousand thoughts danced behind his emerald eyes.

Benson glanced at a sullen Garcia, who happened to be staring pointedly off into the dark forest with her arms crossed.

"Will you be willing to help us?" Benson asked in earnest.

"We need someone your age to feel out the local high school. Anna was last seen near the high school premises before she went missing." Astrid pressed.

The vampires remained uncomfortably silent.

Ethan rubbed at the back of his neck.

"I suppose Lexi and I could be of some assistance." Ethan mused aloud.

"In exchange for a ticket back home of course." I added.

"Yes, in exchange for a ticket back home." Ethan agreed.

"Consider it done." Benson declared

Dante cursed beneath his breath.

Garcia let out a disgusted snort.

"You have got to be kidding me!" She said as she gestured towards me in a flourish of frustration. "If you plan on letting that *thing* into my coven you can think again."

Frank averted his gaze.

Astrid stiffened. "Are you too proud to ask for help Garcia?"

Garcia scowled at me, her brown eyes were as cold as stones. The firelight cast shadows across her sculpted features, making her expression dark and menacing. I contemplated on nicknaming her the Black Widow but then thought better of it. Something told me she wouldn't react kindly to that name. I opened my mouth to retort but she cut me off, with a voice of steel.

"Look, we don't know who or what you are capable of. Don't take this personal but we don't openly welcome another species into our coven without investigation. Last time we did that we ended up at war with the wolves."

Ethan bristled around the edges, the corner of his eye twitched.

"Alexis and I are a team. We work together. If you want me then she comes with the package." He ground out through gritted teeth.

Astrid watched Ethan. Her eyes were speculative.

Frank studied the ground as if it held the world's greatest secret.

Dante ground his teeth and stared into the dancing flames.

Benson's look transformed into an expression of concern.

"Then Alexis needs to come clean with who and what she is or the possibility of finding Anna Johnson is lost."

I tensed. My hands tightened into little fists. I could hear my heart pattering anxiously within my chest. Should I tell them what I am? What would happen if I did? Would they still help us find a way back home if I didn't come clean? Probably not. I mean, I did just attack the head of the vampire coven. So I assumed she wasn't in the most gracious mood. If I didn't tell them then I'd have to lie. Lying would leave me vulnerable. I can't use my magic on someone if I lie to them. And I was not good at telling half-truths or being ambiguous like a member of the Shadow clan.

My stomach twisted and turned, tying itself in knots. Tension hung in the air, building with each passing second. I exhaled slowly and tried to capture time. I suppose honesty was the best policy in these types of situation. Knowing my luck they'd probably figure out eventually anyhow. I'd rather that Astrid and Benson hear it coming directly from me than Frankie. I sucked in a breath, filling my lungs with the hot summer night air. "I'll cut you a deal. I'll tell you what I am and will also help Ethan coax the local pack to do your bidding if promise that you'll still help us find a way to get Ethan and me back home."

CHAPTER 7

I STARED up as the school towered over me. The building's large bay windows reached a story high and curved out to overlook the school's entrance. Pristine glass doors with metallic silver handles waited for our approach. Rusty red brick drank in the light of the morning sun as we walked towards the building's entrance. Clean and crisp landscaping complimented the front of the yard. Little trees popped up from circular pods of dirt that were surrounded by white cement.

"Welcome to Ferndale Hill High, the home of the Hawks" Astrid purred as she spread her arms out before her.

Ethan and I exchanged looks of concern.

What on earth did we get ourselves into?

We have seen fortresses before but they were regarded as castles, not high schools. According to Astrid each room within this building housed at least twenty hormonal teenagers who were placed under the watchful eye of one mortal adult. *How was that even possible?* The school itself had training grounds but instead of preparing their young for warfare they were used for extracurricular activities commonly known as sports.

I found the concept quite amusing. *Why would one use all this space for play instead of training? Did they think kicking balls back and forth was more important than preparing their youth for any danger?* I had asked Astrid if this school had used any type of punishment and if so were they cruel or unusual. With a grim reply she simply said standardized testing and detention. Ethan sucked in a breath and tugged the sleeve of his backpack closer to his chest.

"Well I guess it's all or nothin' eh?" Ethan said with an air of confidence .

Meanwhile, he clutched his orientation paperwork tightly in his right hand.

"I feel like we're signing up for the army or something." I murmured breathlessly.

"Oh quit being so overly dramatic. They don't even have ROTC here." Astrid replied.

Her amber eyes sparkled with amusement.

Ethan's face twisted with confusion.

"R O T C?" The words formed funny sounds in his mouth.

"Yes. ROTC. Reserve Officer Training Corps." She replied in a matter of factly tone.

Her clicking black heels led us towards the entrance.

Sometimes I wondered if Astrid even realized we came from another realm. Just the night before we had discussed Ethan and I's native history and the origin of Gaia on Garcia's patio. You'd think me attacking the head of the coven and the events thereafter would have been somewhat memorable. *Apparently not.*

Astrid looked different. I couldn't quite put my finger on it. She looked younger than what I had remembered. Today she wore her hair in two pigtails. Black curls cascaded down a designer t-shirt. She wore a snug pair of hip huggers, black heels and red lipstick. Had she changed her appearance specifically for this mission? Kitsune weren't the only ones known to change their shape. Succubi could change their appearance too. Kitsune rather, use their shape shifting talent more so to play pranks while succubi used theirs to hunt.

Frank quietly trailed behind us with his hands in his pockets. His expression remained sullen and thoughtful. Meanwhile, an athletic display case greeted us at the entryway. Our sneakers squeaked against the speckled linoleum floor. I inhaled. Fresh paint and floor wax flooded my nose as I dragged my fingertips along the pale brick wall. Burgundy lockers were lined up in rows off to our left, the ground beneath them a dark gray carpet. A petite woman sat at miniature office desk in front of the stairs.

"This is Miss Anderson, our attendance secretary." Frank began.

"She's in charge of all the paperwork you use when you sign in or out of the school." Astrid added.

Frank flashed Anderson a congenial smile as he pressed us forward.

"Miss Anderson, I don't believe you have had the pleasure of meeting our two new exchange students Ethan and Lexi."

Miss Anderson gave us a polite nod. She was a woman in her late forties. Her chestnut eyes were hidden behind a pair of spectacles. Sandy blonde tresses with streaks of gray framed her face and ended at her chin. Ms. Anderson adjusted her spectacles and gave us a honeyed smile.

"No I don't believe I have. From where about do you come from?"

I froze. Ethan fidgeted. Together we glanced at Frank and then at Astrid, searching for some sort of answer. *From where about did we come from?* Would it be appropriate to say we came from Gaia, the realm of the supernatural? Senator Benson's foreboding face loomed in the back of my mind. Her sing song voice echoed in my head, reminding me that secrecy of the supernatural race was of the utmost importance. The idea of Garcia separating my head from my spine was another thought that discouraged me from speaking. Astrid shifted her weight.

The corner of Frank's lip twitched as he struggled to come up with a reply.

"Wales. Alexis and Ethan come from Wales."

Miss Anderson's eyes lit up like a light bulb.

"Oh how exciting. Please tell me, what is your favorite thing about Wales? I always found the British Isles fascinating."

Frank's relief was almost palpable.

"What is my favorite thing about Wales?" I asked with a hint of uncertainty.

Miss Anderson nodded expectantly, eagerly waiting for my reply.

How the hell was I supposed to know? I've never been to Wales before.

I paused for a minute. Certainly Frank didn't mean we came out of the stomach of a whale did he? *Couldn't he have picked something more attractive? Out of all the places we can come from we have to come from the belly of a whale?*

Astrid forced a smile.

She reached over to give me a side hug and spoke through her teeth.

"Yes Lexi. Please do tell us what is your favorite thing about Wales."

I struggled to come up with something to say.

Ethan simply shifted his weight.

Astrid pinched the back of my arm, jolting me back into the present.

Ethan cleared his throat and forced out a throaty chuckle.

"Yes, um, about Wales. The weather is fairly nice." He rocked back and forth on his heels with a stupid grin on his face.

Miss Anderson raised a brow.

Astrid and Frank were not impressed.

"Um yeah. Anyway we should probably get these two back to orientation." Frank said.

"Yes, let's." Astrid said as I rubbed my arm.

"Orientation is just up the stairs and to the left. The staff will be able to assist you with anything you need. I hope you had a great summer Frank, it is so good to see you."

"Thank you, Miss Anderson."

"We really have to work on your social skills.." Frank murmured quietly.

Astrid had already left us with Frank and Miss Anderson. *So much for sticking together.* I thought dryly to myself. Frank and Miss Anderson exchanged pleasantries before heading upstairs. Straight ahead was the main office, encased in glass. The orientation sign directed us to the right, towards the cafeteria. Pillars of stone held the two foot story ceiling up into the air. Sunlight filtered through the bay windows and mixed with the dome overhead lights. Fluorescent and natural sunlight lit the room. Masses of students swarmed around tables like ants at a picnic. A mixture of strong perfumes, body odor, sweat, pheromones, fresh paint and freshly waxed floor overwhelmed my fox senses.

Multiple different forms of conversation bounced off of the speckled linoleum and burgundy brick walls. A sentry of lockers stood off to the left. Groups of students meandered in and out of their aisles.

"Sweet Inari. What in Gaia's name is going on here?" I whispered to myself, eyes wide with wonder.

Someone called out Frank's name.

Our heads turned in unison. Frank cringed and mumbled something sour underneath his breath.

A tall man with sandy hair and a square chin approached us. A brown clipboard rested loosely in his right hand. He wore black baggy training pants and a loose fitting shirt. A silver whistle bounced against his broad chest. His white sneakers squeaked against the speckled floor as he approached.

"Frank! You haven't aged a day." The man approached from behind and clapped Frank on the shoulder. His blue eyes twinkled with delight. "It might be your senior year but it's never too late to join the team."

A tight smile tugged at the corner of Frank's lips.

"Mr. Huizenga, what a pleasure. Still having trouble getting people to join the team?"

Mr. Huizenga let out a gruff sigh and ran one of his large hands through his hair.

"The football team is off to a rough start. However, that's usually the case every year. Out with the old in with new I suppose."

Huizenga rubbed his jaw. "Who are your new friends?"

He had gestured towards me and Ethan. Frank began to introduce us when a thick Italian accent suddenly interrupted him from afar. Sweet mother of Gaia, it was Garcia. May the goddess of good fortune look kindly upon our souls.

"Oh Frank darling! I am so glad that you were able to get the kids started." Garcia cooed affectionately as she approached. Her black heels clicked briskly against the polished floor.

I narrowed my eyes.

Ethan perked a brow.

The three of us exchanged looks of bewilderment.

Who was she calling kids anyway?

Garcia wore a black dress with a white business jacket. She had twisted her glossy hair into a tight bun. Within seconds she dove in like a hawk and swooped us up into a tight bear hug.

"What in Gaia's name?" I began to sputter.

She squeezed tighter, promptly cutting off our air supply

I squeaked. Ethan choked and Frank's eyes watered.

"Oh, I am so sorry my dears. Did I hug you too hard?" Her voice dripped with feigned innocence.

Huizenga flashed us an apologetic smile as he rubbed at the back of his neck. Something told me this was going to be the orientation from hell.

Garcia reached down and pinched our cheeks between two perfectly manicured nails

"I am so glad to see my wittle exchange students." She cooed.

Huizenga cast us another sympathetic smile.

Meanwhile, Ethan and I stood there, baffled.

She tugged us close and hissed her own endearments into our ears.

"I swear if any of you screw this up I will gut you all and eat your liver for dinner."

My mouth snapped shut. She pulled away and flashed us a honeyed smile. Mischief sparkled behind her eyes. A slack jawed Ethan gawked at her with a horrified expression. This lady was off her fucking rocker.

Mr. Huizenga shifted his weight awkwardly to one side and cleared his throat.

"Well, hello Miss Garcia. It is a pleasure to see you again."

She facial structure deadpanned. Thankfully her back was to him, lest she shatter his attempts for useless pleasantries. So the little human wanted to make small talk, what's so wrong with that anyway? Garcia gave me a solid pat on my cheek before straightening to her full height. She schooled her expression and turned around.

"Indeed, it has been a pleasure Mr. Huizenga." She replied crisply before wrapping a possessive hand around each of our shoulders. "Unfortunately these two here a lot of catching up to do. They can meet up with you after they are done."

Instantly, she began steering us towards the office encased in glass.

Humbly Ethan and I obliged, knowing public confrontation was not a logical option.

Frank stuffed his hands in his pockets and trailed behind.

After last night's demonstration I learned that Garcia didn't appreciate people questioning her in public and when they do she has a tendency to throw things. I on the other hand prefer to keep my feet on the ground. The last thing I wanted her to do was go bat shit crazy and fling me across the hall like a rag doll. What was her deal with Mr. Huizenga anyway? Ethan glanced back at Huizenga's shrinking form as we got further away.

"Not much of a fan, eh?" Ethan inquired casually.

Garcia's face soured at the very implication of being friends with the man.

"The man is insufferable. He's constantly doting and never knows when to shut up."

I grimaced at her reaction.

"A bit harsh don't you think? I mean it's not like he can help it. You are vampire after all and are built for making human men all googly eyed. Right?"

Garcia scoffed at the very idea of catering to the needs of a lowly human.

"All I am saying is you should be patient with him. Maybe give him a chance?"

A small smile tugged at Frank's lip.

Did his eyes just twinkle with amusement?

Garcia let out a regal snort.

"After you've lived as long as I you learn that some things aren't worth the time. Keep your eyes out for principal Lemmings, little fox. Once you see him I want to know what you think."

She hustled us through the glass doors and into the office. Two students were already at the front desk, waiting for assistance. The student ahead of us had a glossy black hair intricately woven into a French braid. She wore a canvas messenger bag, white capris and a brown top that complimented her bronze skin. The other was a tall girl with long blonde curls that cascaded down the small of her back. She wore short shorts and a designer t shirt that hugged her torso. She looked our way. Sky blue eyes met mine and then lingered on Ethan. She reminded me of the Barbie doll in the commercial I had watched earlier this morning. She and Barbie shared many similarities, high cheekbones, a skinny nose, baby blue eyes, flawless skin and lips the color of pink frosting.

Frank nudged Ethan with his elbow and whispered.

"Careful now, don't go around attracting the eye of Olivia Gaines."

Ethan's face crinkled with concern.

"Who is Olivia Gaines?" I mouthed.

Frank snorted and merely shook his head.

"One of the most popular girls in the school. Ruthless, but popular. She also happens to be dating a brute named Andrew Brown, the football team's quarterback. I'd stay clear if I were you."

Barbie fixed Frank with a vexing stare.

Had she heard what he had said?

Frank returned the gesture.

A tiny prickly sensation crawled up my spine.

Then again, Barbie held Ethan's gaze a little bit longer than I liked.

It was then that we were promptly greeted by one of the three receptionists.

"Good morning ladies." Garcia's cool reply ripped me back into the present. Polite pleasantries wasn't her style. She placed one hand on each of our shoulders and tugged us close to her side. One set of pristinely manicured nails had dug themselves possessively into my shoulder. "These two are my new exchange students. They will be placed under my care. I still need to fill out the paperwork for them to attend this school."

One of the receptionists nodded and headed into the back room while the other assisted Barbie. My stomach dropped and my body went cold. I felt like I had just been dunked into a bucket of ice water.

"Your care?" I hissed. *What did she mean her care?* There was nothing caring about her. Garcia was crazy if she thought I would willingly stay in the same room as her let alone live under the same roof. I tried to voice my opinion but Garcia's nails pinched my skin while the receptionists weren't looking.

"Ow!" Barbie turned around and looked at me.

I wanted to rip out her pretty little curls and set them on fire.

"Is everything ok Alexis?" Garcia asked me innocently.

All the while, her eyes remained on Barbie.

Ethan chortled quietly. I shot him a murderous glare. My hands curled into little fists. Everyone was watching me now. They were waiting to see what I would do. I thought about creating an illusion where she would be engulfed by a fiery pit of hell. I smiled at the thought of her burning alive. Instead, I bit back all of the colorful words I could possibly say. There was no point in making a scene. I guess imagining all the things I'd like to do to her will have to suffice for now.

"Nothing, I must have something in my shoe." I growled begrudgingly.

A tall man with stocky features and broad shoulders stepped out of the principal's office. He wore pin striped shirt, black dress pants and a pair of wire rimmed glasses. His black dress shoes scuffed against the carpet. He inclined his head towards both Frank and Garcia before pulling off his spectacles.

"Mr. Marino, Miss Garcia."

They returned the gesture. "Mr. Lemmings."

His piercing brown eyes swiveled over us.

"Are these new recruits?" He asked gruffly with a tight lipped smile.

Mr. Lemmings was in his forties. He had a square jaw, close set eyes, a rectangular shaped face with bushy eyebrows, a widows peak, and a receding salt & pepper hairline.

"As a matter of fact they are. They will be staying with me this year." Garcia replied primly.

His brown eyes glittered with curiosity. "Well isn't that something."

Lemmings tucked his glasses into his front pocket and leaned in with an open hand. "Welcome to Ferndale Hills. I am the principal Mr. Lemmings. It is a pleasure to meet you." His soft hand gave me a firm shake.

You can tell a lot by someone's hands and their handshakes. This was a businessman. His shake was not too hard nor too soft but just right. He also did a lot of writing and was right handed. You could tell by the callus on the side of his index finger and the nodule on the outside of his pinky.

Something about him tickled my interest. He smelled like oil and steel but stank of cigarette smoke and dog. I didn't see anything mechanical about him. His hands were as soft as silk and I could not find a single fiber of dog hair on his shirt.

Reluctantly, I shook his clammy hand. His brown eyes swiveled from Ethan and I to the crowd outside the glass windows. He sighed.

"Well I suppose I should be out there greeting the other students."

He paused, allowing his penetrating brown eyes to swivel over us once more.

The hairs on the back of my neck prickled.

"Stay out of trouble folks." Within seconds, he exited the door with a sense of purpose. Garcia finished scrawling her fancy penmanship across the last paper. After a few paperwork exchanges here and there we too were heading out the door to get our schedules. A moment of silence had built its' way between the four of us.

Something told me Garcia and Frank weren't telling us the whole truth nor were they keeping us in the loop. *Why did Garcia want us to give her input on Lemmings? What was Anna doing at this school anyway? How many people were truly missing?*

I cut through the silence with a hint of ice.

"What exactly is going on here Garcia?"

Garcia's nose wrinkled with distaste.

Frank grimaced at my tone.

Did I speak too loudly?

Garcia stole a glance around before urging me towards a less populated area.

"Keep moving you silly little girl. We are not going to stop in the middle of the main walkway to have such a detailed conversation. Such things should be done in private. Secondly, you will address me as Miss Garcia when we are in public."

Ethan and I raised our brows as she shooed us to a more discreet location.

"Paranoid much?" Ethan pressed.

Frank did not reply to the jab, nor did Garcia.

"The main goal here is to fit in Lex.." Frank said as his eyes surveyed our local surroundings. Casually, he leaned against the wall as if it were a demonstration.

Garcia looked around for anyone eavesdropping in on our conversation.

"I know I am not your mother." She hissed.

"That's for sure." I replied vehemently.

Ethan gave me a look that screamed *knock it off*.

Garcia ignored me intentionally.

"For that very reason you are expected to call me Miss Garcia. By doing so you will be following proper etiquette. Do I make myself clear?"

I flashed her a petulant glare.

Her penetrating stare bore into my very soul.

Frank chewed on the inside of his cheek.

I wanted to say some other things that were probably not within the realm of proper etiquette. However, I thought better of it. Ethan sucked in a breath and attempted to ask the same question in a different way.

"So, Miss Garcia, what is exactly going on here? There has been some lack of communication. We feel as if you're leaving us out on a limb. No one told us you'd be coming and we were kinda taken by surprise. Besides, we know nothing about this case and so far Mr. Lemmings seems to be pretty legit."

A flicker of pride danced across her eyes.

"My my, little wolf, you're catching on quick."

She paused and looked me over with a hint of disdain.

"Unlike your counterpart here." She added dryly.

I opened my mouth to protest but she continued to speak over me as if I didn't exist.

"Last night was a catastrophe, mainly on Frank's part."

Frank grimaced in reply.

"I said I was sorry.."

"If he hadn't let you in, none of this would have happened. Thankfully, we were able to amend the situation by the use of your services. However, people have been going missing Lexi. Not just *normal* people if you get my drift. Now the elders have already been on edge, understandably so. People they care about have gone up in smoke. However, that lack of communication between Frank and I is what broke the camel's back. Now shit has hit the fan."

She ground out each word with deadly precision.

Yes, as a matter of fact we did know shit had hit the fan. Me attacking the head of the local vampire coven had caused a commotion. Garcia's authority had been publicly challenged and now she was zooming the scope in on me in order to keep me in line.

"As a consequence Frank is in charge of teaching you how to fit in. He may be nearly as old as I but I truly believe that this will be an excellent learning opportunity for him. We need answers, Lexi. We don't need lip.Get on board or get out. Whatever happens I want you to keep one thing in mind."

She leaned in dangerously close. Her breath came out hot but her tone was icy and flat.

"Lillian Benson has agreed to appoint me to oversee this task and make sure that Frank coaches you and Alexis on how to fit into this world. Fitting in is survival here. If you dare to even step *one* toe out of line I will consider killing you. There are other lives at stake here, please keep in mind that your actions may affect the lives of hundreds of people around you." She paused and narrowed her eyes into menacing little slits.

Frank shifted his weight.

Ethan held his breath.

I schooled my expression.

"Do I make myself clear?" She hissed.

We both mumbled "Yes Miss Garcia."

She straightened and flashed us a charming smile.

"Now as for your mission. I want you to scope out this entire school. If there is so much as a peep of information on a missing person's case I want to know about it. Anything out of the ordinary I want to know, even if it is a speck of dust out of place. Kapeesh?"

Reluctantly, we nodded.

Her face softened into a satisfied smile.

"Good, now I need to get back to work. Run along now. We will talk more during dinner time" She gave us a wink and shooed us away before scurrying off to do whatever head vampires do best in their spare time. I watched her as she sauntered away in her fancy heels. Ethan let out a breath of air and Frank's shoulders eased.

"That was close." Ethan whispered as soon as she was out of view.

"Yep. I about shat me-self." I said as I rubbed at my arms, trying to rid myself of Garcia's deathly chill. "How much you wanna bet she has supersonic hearing skills like some bat or something?'" Ethan grimaced. "Let's just assume she does and get bloody on with it."

"Is she always this crazy?" I asked Frank.

Frank shook his head.

"You have no idea." He grumbled sourly.

Just then, a shadow flickered in the corner of my eye. I turned but no one was there. I couldn't tell what it was but I could feel another person's presence. Anxiety scampered up and down my arms like a thousand ants. I turned around to see Astrid standing next to us. I nearly jumped.

"Hey you guys, how was it?" She asked with a brilliant smile.

"Swell, it was just swell." Ethan grumbled.

"That is if you count getting a verbal lashing from Carmen Garcia as swell." Frank mumbled.

A sheet of sympathy coated Astrid's face.

"Yeah, I figured. That's why I watched from afar."

We all flashed her needled glare.

"Really?" I deadpanned.

Astrid brightened and flashed us an apologetic smile.

"On a positive note, I took the liberty of grabbing your schedules for you."

Frank arched a brow.

"Don't we have to pick up our schedules in person?"

"Aw come now Frank, you know I have my ways." Astrid replied with a mischievous grin.

I wonder if Frank knew Astrid could shape shift.

"Oh, Alexis don't forget you have English with me."

She gave me a flirty wink before sidling up to Ethan. His body stiffened as she leaned in.

"Ethan, *baby*, I am not so good at math. Will you do the honor of being my tutor?"

She batted her eyelashes at him. Her voice came out husky and low.

He gaped at her, clearly struggling for words.

"Math, huh?" A hot flush began to creep across his cheeks.

"In exchange I can teach you other things..." Astrid said coquettishly.

She ran a slender finger down his broad chest.

He turned a deep crimson.

"That is if you will allow me." Astrid added shyly.

The poor boy was going to spasm if she didn't stop. He gurgled with nervous laughter and scratched at his rusty curls. He turned rosy each place she touched.

I think I was going to get sick.

"And what type of things are you offering to teach?"

Could he be that dense?

Frank watched the whole ordeal with an pained expression.

She paused and leaned in closer. Her lips hovered over his ear lobe.

"The art of poetry." She whispered and smiled smugly as she pulled away.

Relieved, Ethan took in a breath of fresh air. His posture had eased.

"Sure sounds like a plan. However, I can't really promise how much help I will be when it comes to math. This is all sort of a new thing for me if you get what I mean."

I rolled my eyes. "Alright, come on you two love birds let's get a bite to eat."

Ethan's cheeks flushed.

"Works every time." Astrid announced triumphantly.

"Love birds? Who, who said we were love birds?" Ethan stammered.

I shook my head and walked away, not giving him a chance to defend himself. I nearly ran into a disgruntled Barbie. Steely blue eyes bore into me. Golden tresses framed her heart shaped face. I got a good whiff of her scent. Distressed pheromones filled my nostrils with the smoky scent of rage, the musky smell of lust and the acrid smell of jealousy. Most of all she smelled like jasmine and wild wolf.

Thoughts danced around inside my head. *Could Barbie be a wolf?* Surely we weren't the only supernatural creatures in town. Were we? Garcia did mention that there was a local wolf pack. Could Barbie be a part of the local pack? If so, how many wolves were we dealing with here? Secondly, how would they react to Ethan being on their territory? Barbie glowered at Astrid then at me then at Frank. Before I could ask she spun around without a word and stalked away like a disgruntled cat. She left the spicy smell of hatred and irritation in her wake.

"What's got her panties all in a knot?" I asked with a perplexed frown.

Frank let out a low whistle. "Uh oh, you've attracted the wrathful eye of Olivia Gaines."

Astrid released an impatient sigh. "What did you do this time?"

"What's up with her, anyhow?" Ethan asked, purely bewildered by the whole ordeal.

Astrid snorted in disgust. Apparently, she wasn't a fan.

"She's one of the most revered people on the cheerleading squad. I don't see what her problem is. She has the body of Barbie and the legs of Angelina Jolie. Her father is rich and everyone fawns over her. What does she have to be so angry about anyway?"

The sudden change in Astrid's aura made me shift my weight. Her aura had transformed from a jovial rosy pink to a brewing stormy purple. Something told me that Astrid and Olivia had a history. What it was I had no idea and I wasn't too keen on finding out. Instead I shrugged. "Maybe she's jealous?" Ethan offered.

"Does it really matter?" Frank added.

"Regardless, I'm one hangry fox, let's get some grub."

CHAPTER 8

THE MORNING BELL CHIMED, letting everyone know that we had five minutes left to get to class. Clearly no one cared. Not one person attempted to leave the heavily congested hallway. The jocks stood down the hall, the cheerleaders gossiped in the corner and a group of nerds gushed about some new game console in the middle of the walk way. Bleary eyed, I squeezed myself between several bodies.

Didn't they realize I was trying to get through? Setting a few of them on fire with my magic was tempting. However, I imagined Garcia frothing at the mouth and I had thought better of it. Maybe Frank was right, maybe I should have drank some coffee this morning. Currently the latest gossip was centered on a recent missing person's case. The poor bastard went missing during his summer vacation and hasn't popped up since. I needed all the info I could get and my exhaustion was proving to be burdensome.

I inched passed the local youth group. I didn't think they'd appreciate a fox demon raining on their prayer parade for some guy named Jacob Parks. I tiptoed past a group of Goths. Who diligently stared daggers into my back with their black kohl lined eyes. One of the girls chomped on a piece of gum, like a cow chewing the cud. She pointedly blew a bubble and then popped it between her teeth as I passed.

I flashed her my most winning smile.

"Beautiful day, eh?"

She scowled in disgust.

Sweet Inari, my sarcasm was going to get me in trouble some day.

After much ado, I managed to stumble into the chemistry lab just after the tardy bell rang. Discreetly, I tiptoed to a spot in the back of the room. Maybe no one had seen me come in? Ethan and Frank slipped in shortly after. Thankfully, the teacher was nowhere to be seen. So, I took the opportunity to gather some intel.

"So, what's the scoop on Jacob Parks?"

Frank opened his mouth but a Hispanic girl with bronze skin and a black braid whipped around in her chair. The scent of rosemary and sage rolled off her in waves. It was the girl from the office visit during orientation. Her hawk-like eyes met mine.

"You mean you don't know?" She hissed incredulously.

Frank's mouth clicked shut.

Hawk Eyes scrutinized me with her scornful gaze.

"I'm surprised you haven't heard. It's not like he hasn't been missing since July 18th."

"You don't say?" I replied sardonically.

"Yes, it's been plastered all over the news."

"Since July, huh?" I inquired flatly.

Frank stiffened in his chair.

Hawk Eyes' face twisted with impatience.

"Did you not hear what I had just said?"

"Oh I heard you, loud and clear."

I shot Frank a prickly glare.

He sunk further into his seat.

Ethan however did not react in kind.

"Did you know about this?" I asked, purely aghast by his reaction.

Ethan blinked. "Well, yeah. Frank brought me up to speed on the way here."

Hawk Eyes scrunched up her nose.

"She's not from around here, is she?" Hawk Eyes asked.

I forced a smile but was showing more teeth than I was hospitality.

"I am Lexi, and you are?" I asked through gritted teeth, straining for patience.

I made it a point not to extend my hand but she ignored the gesture.

Her hawk-like eyes took me in, analyzing me from head to toe.

It was as if she were appraising my intelligence.

I flashed her a tight lipped smile.

"Alexis, this is Selena Rodriguez." Frank replied.

By this rate I was fuming.

"Did it just happen to *slip* your mind?"

Frank sighed as he flopped into the chair next to me.

"No, I never got a chance." He replied.

He had ruffled the back of his head, black hair stuck up every which way.

"Hello Selena, my name is Ethan."

He reached out his hand.

Selena pursed her lips, her expression remained thoughtful.

Hesitantly, she took his hand and shook.

I mumbled something about insufferable know it alls beneath my breath.

A moment later the TV in front of the room crackled to life. The morning announcements began. Two cheerful teenagers materialized on the screen to greet their fellow students. One of them just happened to be Olivia Gaines. Today she wore a sweater that had the word PINK in all capital letters. Her blonde curls were piled high into a messy bun on top of her head.

"Welcome back Ferndale Hawks!" She said with a pearly grin.

Her male counterpart chimed in with a charming smile of his own.

"I don't know about you, but it looks like we're off to a great start for the new year."

"You bet, John." Olivia said.

She went into great detail about the weather and listed different events that were being held after school before ending with, "and most importantly, the cheerleading tryouts will take place this Friday on the football field. Be there or be square!"

Olivia finished with a wink before handing it off to John.

"It's that time of the year folks! Tryouts for men's soccer begin this week. Mr. Huizenga will also be holding a tryout session for those who are interested in joining the Ferndale Hawks football team. Both will be happening this Friday after school. We also are beginning the local canned food drive for the homeless. All proceeds and offerings need to be dropped off at the main office and will directly go towards God's Kitchen. Make sure you put your homeroom teacher's name on each can so you can win points for a pizza party. Now an important word from our principal Mr. Lemmings." The screen switched to an image of Mr. Lemmings standing in front of a solid backdrop.

"Good morning Ferndale Hawks. I want to tell you how much I appreciate your time and how excited I am to start this new school year. As most of you know we have lost someone very dear to our school. The Parks family and friends have created a video of thanks for all the condolences that they have received and have asked me personally to play this slide show in his memory."

Mr Lemming's image faded out. The screen went black. There was a moment of silence then images of a charming young man with bright blue eyes and a mess of brown curls began popping onto the screen. He had a smile that crinkled the corner of his eyes. Some images showed him in a red and white football jersey as he high fived a team member. Others showed him dressed up in a tux that complimented his broad shoulders.

Mr. Lemmings spoke as old images faded and new ones began to appear.

"Jacob Parks was a blessing to this school. He actively served in our community and his church. Some days he would work at God's Kitchen, other days he would spend time assisting the Humane Society. His dream was to become a youth pastor. He is survived by his mother Mrs. Colleen Parks and his father Mr. Jonathan Parks. He played a significant role in the school community."

"He was an active member of drama club and helped Ferndale Hawks make it to their second state championship on the football field. Most of all he was loved by many and had a huge heart. The Parks family want to extend their gratitude for all your kind words and condolences. Before we begin class I would like all teachers to hold a brief moment of silence. Thank you for your time and have a wonderful day."

The screen flickered off.

The room remained silent and tense, like the air was tightly wound around a wire and was going to burst at any moment. Suddenly, the classroom doors burst open. All eyes turned to glare upon the intruder.

"So much for a moment of silence." I muttered beneath my breath.

A handful of students murmured in agreement. In walked a heavy man in dress slacks and a frumpy white lab coat. A set of watery blue eyes hid behind a pair of black glasses. The thick lenses magnified his eyes into large orbs.

"Good morning class." He drawled, each word dripped with boredom.

He slapped a packet of papers down in front of me.

"Take one and pass it down." He mumbled.

He had a nasally voice and a pale complexion.

Moments later he waddled up to the whiteboard and wrote MR. DINKLE in all caps with a squeaky red marker.

"My name is Mr. Dinkle. If your schedule says Chemistry, room 203 then you are in the right place. If not, then I suggest you leave."

"Well, I'll take that as my cue." Frank said as he drew back his chair and left.

A snicker bubbled up from behind but it was me who was given Dinkle's deadly glare.

The laughter belonged to a flinty eyed boy with a buzzed head.

"Turn to page two on your syllabus." Dinkle said, each word came out as a low monotone whine. With great effort he circulated the lab like an overweight vulture searching for prey. He droned on. "In chemistry you will be working with different elements. It is necessary to come to class prepared. You are required to bring your textbooks to each class session."

My eyelids drooped and my attention fluttered.

The lack of feeding was catching up with me.

His lifeless voice eventually lulled me to sleep.

Later, Ethan nudged me awake.

I snapped up and wiped the drool off my face.

"What? What did I miss?" I sputtered as I hastily rubbed the sleep out of my eyes. Selena shot me a dirty glare as the other students filed out of the room.

I frowned. *Great*, looks like I am on the teacher's pet's hit list.

Apparently sleeping in class was a felony. Then again, back at home my sensei would have rapped my knuckles if he had known. So I should have assumed the same rules would apply here as well. Live and learn I suppose.

Ethan's eyes twinkled with amusement as he tapped at his chin. "You missed a spot."

Hawk Eyes on the other hand was not amused.

I flushed and quickly swept the drool off my chin.

"Oh nothing much. He went over safety protocol, classroom expectations, late homework policies" Ethan's voice drifted off as he used his fingers to list off the multiple things I had slept through. I gave him a menacing scowl. By the time he was done Ethan had ran out of fingers. Hawk Eyes managed to swing her backpack over one shoulder. Her flinty brown eyes met mine.

"In Ethan's defense and more so for my own, I highly recommend you read over the safety portion for this class. If you're not careful you could really make a mess of this place. I'd hate to have you blow up the whole school or have you end up dying because you ate something poisonous."

Her expression became methodical before she offered me a glass of brown liquid.

"I was saving this for later but I think I can manage."

My eyes narrowed into little slits.

"What is this?" I inquired with great suspicion.

Hawk Eyes offered me a perplexed frown. "Coffee, of course."

Frank had offered me the same thing that very morning. *Damn him and his damn coffee*. The very idea of coffee made me think of Frank. When I thought of Frank then Garcia came to mind. It was then that their lack of communication came to the forefront of my mind. The very thought of it just pissed me off.

"What's so great about coffee anyway?" I replied sardonically.

"Coffee is not only a natural stimulant but it increases one's focus and ability to stay awake. Not to mention it decreases your chances of getting Parkinson's, diabetes and liver cancer."

I grumbled something foul beneath my breath and snatched the bottle out of her hand before stalking off into the congested hallway.

Screw him, the humans and their damn syllabi. Why didn't Frank or Garcia inform us about Jacob Parks? Then again, he did tell Ethan but why not me? Something was telling me there was more going on than what we were being told. Secondly, who has the time to read a syllabus anyway? I had better things to do then research how to mix two liquids together for a chemistry class. Besides, I highly doubted that I would be blowing anything up anytime soon. I mean, it's chemistry, how hard could it be? You mix a little of this and that and it changes color right?

"What's her problem anyway?" Hawk Eyes asked.

Ethan chuckled and shook his head.

"That's Lexi for you." He replied with a lopsided smile.

I unscrewed the cap and guzzled. A rich chocolate elixir of icy delight trickled into my mouth. *We will be done with this investigation in no time and soon we will be heading back to Mount Kyoto through some rift. Until then, appeasing a crazy ass vampire and a meticulous selkie will have to do.* A shudder of satisfaction rippled through me. So this is why humans enjoy coffee. With a satisfied smack of my lips I discarded the glass bottle into the recycling receptacle and went about my day.

A few classes later I zig zagged across the school grounds twice. By evening I would have the legs of an amazonite warrior. Panting, I stumbled into history class just before the tardy bell rang. Mrs. Patterson quirked her brow as she took in my haggard state. Frank merely chuckled. In the meantime, the scent of rosemary and sage tickled my nose. My stomach clenched once I recognized the scent signature. *Please don't let it be the all-knowing Selena Rodriguez.* I turned around groaned. Sure enough there she was standing there observing me like a hawk. I figured I'd nickname her Hawk Eyes. Meanwhile, I struggled to keep my books from spilling over.

She crossed her arms and arched a brow.

"You do realize you can put your books in your locker right?".

"Oh thanks Captain Obvious and where am I going to find the time to do that?"

I snapped sarcastically, books still teetering.

She shrugged her shoulders and feigned a sense of empathy. "Oh I don't know, possibly between classes? There is a reason we have a five minute passing break."

I had a feeling that Selena was going to end up being an insufferable know it all. I was tempted to give her a little zap but remembered the all too keen image of Garcia tossing me across the room like a rag doll. Instead, I behaved myself and took a seat. One day I told myself, one day I'll get an opportunity to tell her how I really feel but today was not that day.

Mrs. Patterson dove into her own lecture about classroom expectations and homework policies.

Frank slipped me a tissue. I eyed him with a quizzical expression.

"Just in case you have a repeat of what happened earlier." He whispered

His gray eyes flashing with humor.

I narrowed my own.

Figures, Ethan couldn't keep his trap shut if his life depended on it.

A smug smirk tugged at the corner of his mouth.

So, Frank wanted to play. No matter, I'd show him. This time I'll endure and stay awake for the whole class period. The table wiggled underneath the consistent pressure of Hawk Eyes' hand as she hastily took notes on each topic. I leaned over and whispered wickedly into her ear.

"Hey Hawk Eyes, what are you writing over there, a diary?"

She scowled. "My name isn't Hawk Eyes."

She ground the tip of her mechanical pencil into the paper.

"Sure it is. You watch everyone like a hawk. Now you do realize you are practically rewriting the syllabus, right?"

She narrowed her eyes.

"Now who is Captain Obvious?" Frank elbowed me in the side.

I tried to protest but he inclined his head towards Patterson, who happened to be heading in our general direction. She casually walked our way while continuing to teach. Patterson was a petite woman of Asian descent with high cheekbones and thin tickle-me-pink lips.

She wore a pair of black dress pants with a gray button down short sleeved shirt. Her onyx eyes scanned the classroom like an eagle in search of prey. She glided across the floor, graceful as a cat, her expression calm and poised.

Frank studied the board diligently as she approached.

Hawk Eyes remained hunched over her notes.

Patterson slipped me a note as she passed. She moved like liquid. The scent of fresh pine, eucalyptus and lavender rolled off her in waves. The smells made my heart clench. Memories of running through Mount Kyoto's forests tugged at the back of my mind. I could almost recall the cool dirt squishing between my toes.

The teacher's fancy penmanship brought me back to the present. It read *please pay attention during class* in big black bold font. Frank's eyes danced with laughter but he kept on writing. Hawk Eyes shook her head in silent disapproval.

A hot flush rushed through my cheeks. I looked up only to see the back of Patterson's silver-streaked black hair, wound up in a tight bun. Two black hair sticks held it firmly in place. She continued to teach but kept a watchful eye on me.

Later on Astrid entered the room. The dress she wore accentuated every curve of her body. The sweet scent of peaches and honey filled the air. Silently, she offered Mrs. Patterson a white slip of paper. Patterson accepted the slip with a nod. All the girls and boys watched the succubus intently as she slinked into her seat. She offered me a demure smile.

Near the end of class Hawk Eyes flashed me a satisfied smirk. So far my first day in modern high school was not going so well. On a positive note, I managed to stay awake for the whole class period. *Go me.* The bell went off, signaling the end of fourth period and the beginning of lunch. My stomach growled its approval.

Students buzzed about the cafeteria like little bees in a hive. One of the lunch ladies ushered the line quickly through the checkout lane while other ladies with hair nets and gloves prepped the food. Various fragrances alienated my nose. Harsh scents of bleach peeked through the smell of spilt milk, fruit, melting greasy cheese, body odors and heavily applied perfumes. I grabbed a plate.

The plate had little compartments for different food groups.

Maybe the designer had thought the cafeteria food would taste better if it didn't touch. Something told me that was not the case. I glanced over a boy's shoulder and caught a glimpse of what they were serving only to see shriveled up chicken nuggets, shiny red apples and a mess of mushy broccoli and noodles. My assumptions were correct. Each helping was splattered unceremoniously on to the styrofoam lunch tray.

Slowly we inched down the line as lunch ladies slapped alien substances onto our food trays. Some of them made smacking sounds as they plopped onto the plate. After much ado, I walked away with one mushy blob of broccoli, a pile of limp spiral noodles, five shriveled up brown nuggets, one shiny rock hard apple and an icy carton of chocolate milk.

A strange thought occurred to me as the apple rolled around in its own little compartment. What would happen if I were to accidentally throw this apple? Would someone die if it happened to hit them in the head? I frowned at that possibility and made a mental note to speak with Garcia about our food options later this afternoon. Frank waved me over to his table. Happily, I obliged. Ethan nodded to me as I approached. He had stuffed his mouth with a bunch of chicken nuggets and was having some trouble chewing. Poor thing.

"Slow down you dolt or you're going to choke to death"

"But I is so haanngry" He protested with great difficulty. "An' we only haf twenty minutes tah eat" I joined them and looked at Ethan's plate. I saw only two nuggets and a jiggly mess of overcooked broccoli and noodles on his plate. This wasn't good. Werewolves have a high metabolism and need a lot of protein to satisfy their carnivorous side. A jiggly mass of overcooked vegetables and mushy noodles wasn't going to cut it. Yep, we were definitely going to have to talk to Carmen about our food options.

"It sounds like you have a high metabolic rate than most people. You should pack some snacks and munch throughout the day. It will maintain your metabolism and keep your organs functioning properly."

Hawk Eyes' familiar scent signature invaded my nose.

I groaned.

She cast Ethan a reassuring smile.

Ethan returned the gesture.

The hairs on the back of my neck prickled. My inner fox snarled with contempt. If she thought she was taking my friend she had another thing coming.

"Well if it isn't Selena Rodriguez, the know it all. What would we do without you?"

My voice dripped with sarcasm.

Her nose wrinkled and her eyes narrowed into little slits.

"*What's your problem anyway?*"

I bristled and violently stabbed my fork into my food.

"You. You are my problem, you and your big words. You have this annoying habit of butting in on everyone's conversation. No one asked you and no one cares what you think."

Her brown eyes blazed and her jaw tightened with rage.

"Well *excuse* me for your lack of vocabulary." She snarled.

Frank rubbed at his temples and took in a deep breath.

"Alright you two, that is enough. Let's start off on a new slate. Shall we?"

Selena and I exchanged daggered glances. We both stood our ground. Forget starting off on a clean slate. I thought bitterly to myself. Neither of us wanted to apologize. With that thought Frank frowned.

"Ok let's give it a go." He prompted.

"Selena this is Lexi. Lexi this is Selena."

There was a pregnant pause. The air between us thickened. Neither Selena nor I had made an attempt to move. Frank's gray eyes grew stormy. Ethan watched the whole ordeal as a silent bystander.

"This is where you shake hands." He pressed.

Without blinking I held Selena's gaze. I proceeded to rip off a top of my chicken nugget with my teeth and chew slowly. Ethan glanced at me then at Hawk Eyes before strategically popping another chicken nugget into his mouth. *Smart.* Maybe he thought if his mouth was full we wouldn't expect him to talk or take sides.

My fox tail twitched with agitation and swished to and fro beneath the layers of my human illusion. Something deep inside nagged at me. A memory of some kind. It was faint but I recall my father's gruff voice, reminding me to keep my friends close but my enemies closer.

Astrid approached from behind, shattering my reminiscence.

"Hey sorry I'm late. The librarian needed help shelving books at the media center." Her sing song voice cut through the tension like a hot knife through a cold stick of butter. Her scent signature engulfed me, filling my lungs with peaches and honey. My shoulders relaxed. Calming pheromones gushed forth from her aura, drowning the tension that hung in the air. Leave it to the succubus. When things got tense she'd call out her handy dandy endorphins to calm everyone down. Astrid slipped into the chair next to Ethan.

"Any news on Jacob Parks?" She asked.

A glimmer of hope flickered across Hawk Eyes' face.

Frank raked a hand through his hair.

"No not that I recall. All I know is that Jacob lived on the same street as me before he disappeared." He paused and then his eyes widened. Hawk Eyes leaned in, listening hungrily. "Oh! He did complain about something before he disappeared. I remember him saying he felt like someone was following him. He thought he was being stalked by some of the girls from the football fan club. It made sense at the time. We didn't write it off as important because his last couple of touchdowns had carried the football team into the state championship. When things like that happen the fan girls seem to go haywire."

Astrid nodded once, but her expression remained thoughtful.

Hawk Eyes chimed in, her brown eyes burning brightly.

"There has been some word of a strange van driving around town. Jake mentioned something about that before he disappeared." Her eyes cast downwards as she looked at her food. She had barely ate. "Anyway, I gotta head to the library before lunch is up. Promise me you'll let me know as soon as you find some leads?" She pressed, a hint of desperation colored her tone.

"Sure no problem." Astrid replied with a reassuring smile.

She sighed as soon as Hawk Eyes left.

"Poor thing, I feel so bad for her." Astrid murmured.

"Why?" Ethan struggled to ask with a mouth full of food.

"Jake and Selena were really good friends. They went together everywhere. Selena partly blames herself for his disappearance. She believes that Jake would have never disappeared if she went with him to the grocery store the day he went missing. She too lives on the same street."

I frowned and fidgeted with my fork. A little flame of guilt burned through my chest. Maybe I shouldn't have been so hard on her. What would I do if Ethan ended up disappearing? The thought twisted a knife into my heart.

Frank pushed away his tray, leaving his food untouched.

"Look, it doesn't do anyone any good to play the blame game."

His calm voice dulled the tension that was building up inside me.

"Besides, it wouldn't have mattered if she went with him or not. Jacob Parks was part of the local werewolf pack here at Ferndale High. He shouldn't have needed Selena's help in the first place."

Realization dawned on me, blossoming like a flower.

"That's it!" I exclaimed as I snapped my fingers together.

Astrid, Frank and Ethan all looked in my general direction.

"Anna Johnson was with the vampires and Jacob Parks was a werewolf." I observed aloud.

"And your point is?" Frank asked, half annoyed by my outburst.

Ethan wrinkled his nose. "Hang on Frank. I think she's onto sumthin'."

I frowned. "Don't you get it? If there's anything we should know by now it is that they are targeting the supernatural community. Everyone that has gone missing is related to or is a supernat."

Astrid's amber eyes narrowed into slits.

"*Great*." She muttered sullenly to herself. "We not only have to avoid catching the public's eye but we now have to avoid getting snatched up by super nat kidnappers? How on earth do we plan on pulling off something like that?"

"All we can do right now is worry about fitting in so we aren't the next ones to disappear. Do any of you have a plan?" Frank asked as he plucked a piece of fuzz off of his apple. Leave it to Frank, the voice of reason and logic. He was right though, we already had a problem that needed fixing. "Besides, Carmen will have my head if we don't come up with some ideas."

Ethan let out a snort and waved a hand at Frank.

"Don't worry about it big guy. I gotta plan."

Astrid and I perked a brow.

"And that would be?" I asked him casually.

A smug smile crept across his face.

"It's simple. I'm gunna try out for the football team."

Astrid choked on her chocolate milk.

"Have you even played football before?" She rasped.

Ethan frowned, purely offended by the implication. "No but it can't be that hard. What do you plan on doing princess? Do you even have a plan?"

"Poor wittle Ethan. No need to get defensive now." I cooed.

He shot me a testy glare.

He tends to get sensitive when his ideas are shot down from the sky.

"As a matter of fact I do." She replied imperiously.

His eyebrows shot up to his hairline. "Oh really?"

"Yes, *really*." She flashed Ethan wicked smile.

"I plan on working in the media center as the librarian's assistant."

Her amber eyes went all misty and her voice got husky around the edges.

"It is an honor to make sure books are properly taken care of."

Frank gagged on his food.

"Alright! Let's move on before you undergo a nerd-gasm." He said as he thumped his chest to prevent himself from choking.

Ethan snickered. Astrid rolled her eyes at the boys and began violently picking her food apart with her fork. I paid no heed to their little squabble. My eyes watched Barbie from afar. She was a wolf. I knew that for a fact by her musky scent signature. Regardless, people would gravitate around her like planets around a sun. Even boys took on the courage to meet her gaze, despite her wolf heritage. If anyone could fit in it was her. *What was her secret?* Was it her perfume? Her clothes? Her hair?

"Hello? Earth to Alexis."

Astrid waved her hand in front of my face, pulling me back into the present.

"Hmm?" I pulled my gaze away from Olivia Gaines and turned to look at Astrid.

"Do you have a plan?" I looked back at Barbie.

A small smile tugged at the corner of my lips. "Yeah, I think I do."

CHAPTER 9

A SHRILL WHISTLE echoed across the stadium. An army of disgruntled boys in padded football gear began charging the metallic life sized dummies with full force. Salty sweat and thick perfume hung heavy in the air. The girls and I stood shoulder width apart, practicing our formations and cheers. Our white sneakers contrasted sharply against the track's red asphalt.

Burgundy ribbons tickled my cheeks as I clapped along to the beat of the cheer. Astrid insisted that I wear them. In the meantime, wheezing football players jogged behind us. Ms. Mulder shook her head and brought the whistle to her lips. She gave it a short blow and signaled for us to stop. We froze. She wore a white tennis skirt, a lavender polo and white sneakers.

"Alright ladies! We are going to try a pyramid exercise. This will test your balance and coordination. Part of cheerleading is being able to work with one another and making sure that you flow smoothly during your presentation."

She paired us up in groups of six. I had been paired with a stout brunette, whom I happened to nick name Brownie, a pair of twins with smooth skin as dark as chocolate, Hawk Eyes who was formerly known as the all-knowing Selena Rodriguez and last but not least

Barbie. Who happened to act like a dictator diva in a skirt. Barbie waved in my direction.

"Alright, shortcake, you're on top." She demanded as she flicked blonde curls over her shoulder.

My heart nearly stuttered to a stop. "Excuse me?"

The corner of her eye twitched.

What did she mean by on top? I figured that I'd just do a few turns here and a few claps there then be on my merry way. Isn't that what cheerleading was all about? No one mentioned I'd be teetering precariously on top of an unstable pyramid made up of several hormonal teenage girls. Garcia was going to have my head if I screwed this one up.

Hawk Eyes and Brownie got down on their hands and knees. One of the twins joined them. Barbie and the twin's sister hopped on. I froze. A hot flush bubbled through me. Maybe if I stood still they wouldn't see me. One could only hope, right? Barbie flashed me the evil eye.

"Well get on with it now! We don't have all day. You're on top." She demanded tersely.

I sucked in my bottom lip. A sense of uncertainty blossomed within me.

What if I fell? Would anyone get hurt? Would Garcia have my head for making a scene? Barbie tipped her chin and narrowed her eyes.

"You do know how to do a pyramid formation don't you?" She inquired imperiously.

Each word dripped with extreme irritation.

The twins' expressions twisted with sympathy.

Hawk Eyes scowled profusely.

"You know you don't have to be so rude about it." She hissed.

Barbie let out a snarky snort and tossed her hair. "Oh, can it, Selena."

Brownie grimaced beneath the girls' weight.

"I don't mean to rush, but it's getting awfully uncomfortable down here.."

I puffed up my chest and took in a deep breath. Here it goes. It's all or nothing I suppose. Garcia was *so* going to have my head. Maybe she would throttle me. I wondered if it would hurt? A nervous titter tickled my throat.

Then I barked out a laugh.

"Sure I know what a pyramid is." I said with feigned confidence.

Technically I wasn't lying. A pyramid could be a shape or a building. I mean, how hard could it be? In all honesty, I wasn't lying and if I were then any magic that I planned on using against Barbie would have been halved as a result. That wasn't a chance I was willing to take.

Barbie bubbled with irritation, her voice came out as sharp as a whip.

"Well?" Barbie growled.

The twins began to hum what I recently had learned was the Jeopardy theme song. Everyone joined in unison. It was then that I realized I have been spending too much time watching too many of the human's game shows and should probably reconsider what I do on my spare time here on planet Earth.

"Well, here goes nothing!" I crowed.

I climbed onto Hawk Eyes' spine and pushed myself up using Barbie as leverage. Barbie teetered, Brownie buckled beneath the uneven distribution of weight. The girls trembled beneath me. The pyramid swayed ever so slightly. There was a pause. A brief moment of silence as the pyramid stilled. Then Brownie's knees gave out first, the twins second and then Barbie's.

"What are you doing?!" Barbie shrieked.

The pyramid's formation shuddered and we tumbled to the ground like a deck of cards. My stomach dropped. A twin smacked into the concrete. Hawk Eyes groaned. Brownie moaned. Something crunched. Barbie squealed. The coppery scent of blood tinged the air.

"I am sorry, I am so sorry." I apologized profusely.

"What in the world happened? Is everyone ok?" Ms. Mulder asked as she rushed on over. Barbie cast me a murderous glare as she held a hand to her gushing nose.

If looks could kill I'd be dead.

She flared up with the spicy scent of rage.

"Okay?" She snarled, her eyes blazed with rage. *"Does it look like I am ok?"*

I debated on answering that question but I figured it was rhetorical.

So much for trying to fit in.

I grimaced as she jabbed a finger at me.

"Shortcake over here doesn't know how to balance her own weight." Barbies accused.

"Her name is Lexi, I'll have you know." Hawk Eyes replied hotly.

My jaw nearly dropped two feet. *Was she seriously trying defend me?*

"You sure get worked up, don't you?" One of the twins said.

"Oh shut it, you babbling half wit." Said her identical counterpart.

Meanwhile, Ms. Mulder cradled Barbie's face as she fussed over the blood.

My mouth snapped shut.

"I said I was sorry." I mumbled apologetically.

"No one cares what you have to say." Brownie grumbled.

A sheet of hot embarrassment crept across my cheeks.

Hawk Eyes arched a brow at Brownie.

"*Really* Alice? Was that *really* necessary?"

Mulder's mouth twisted into a dissatisfied frown.

"Now girls, simmer down. It was an accident. I do not want to hear anymore about it. Do I make myself clear?" Mulder interjected Her voice was stern as she dabbed at Barbie's face with a balled up handkerchief. The rest of the girls held their breath. Tension clung to the air. We stood around the two in a tight circle. It just occurred to me, I happened to deface the most popular girl in the entire school. What an excellent way to begin the school year. A man's deep baritone thrummed through the thick silence. "What's the problem here ladies?"

We turned to see Mr. Huizenga approaching the crowd, his gate calm and steady. He smelled like clean cut cologne and mint. The girls parted for him. A pack of panting boys did their stretches in the background, dripping with sweat. Ethan's emerald eyes loomed over Barbie and then wandered to me. He cast me a quizzical expression. I simply bit my lip and shrugged. Mr. Huizenga kneeled in front of Barbie. Brownie whined and rubbed her butt.

Hawk Eyes simply rolled her eyes.

GONE MISSING

"Oh you're fine. Quit being such a hypochondriac."

Brownie flashed her a scathing glare.

"She has a broken nose." Mr. Huizenga declared solemnly.

The boys behind him shifted their weight and exchanged uncomfortable glances.

A hushed murmur spread through the group like wildfire.

He rose and dusted off his knees.

"You should take her to the office and call home. She will need to sign an accident report."

Ms. Mulder sighed and helped Barbie stand up.

"Alright sister, let's get you to the office so you can call your mom. Ladies we are going to call it a day before any more people get hurt."

Mr. Huizenga went off to pack up some of the football gear a few yards away.

We all watched Ms. Mulder and Barbie disappear around the stadium.

Brownie was the first to speak once Barbie was out of earshot.

"Oh my God. You broke her nose!"

I grimaced at Brownie's outburst.

Hawk Eyes mumbled something about manners.

One of the twins simply shook her head. "Could you be any louder, Alice?"

The other sister clucked her tongue in sympathy.

"Girl, you better watch your back. Olivia Gaines can be rough."

I let out a derisive snort. "Bah! It's not like she'll hunt me down or anything."

The twins exchanged looks of concern

Something told me otherwise.

The curly haired twin looked both ways before she continued, her voice hushed.

"I don't think you understand. In fifth grade she put gum in Alice's hair for spilling something on her dress. The gum wouldn't come out so they had to chop it off."

Brownie nodded in sullen agreement.

"Took me three whole years to grow it back.." She confessed.

Cold chills shot down my arm as I took in her glum expression.

The boys had finished packing and were coming on over to get the scoop on what happened to Olivia. My stomach curdled.

For the sake of Inari! Was nothing private around here?

Hawk Eyes made a pshaw noise between her lips.

"Oh ignore them. That happened a long time ago and things have changed. Next time balance your weight instead of throwing it all around."

One of the boys from practice let out a disgusted snort as he and his cronies approached us. He had his hair shaved close to his scalp and flinty brown eyes. It was the boy from chemistry class.

"Or maybe she shouldn't eat so much next time." He paused and scrutinized me with his piercing brown eyes. A smug smile curled at the corner of his lips. "I am surprised Miss Mulder would put a whale like you at the top of the pyramid. I mean come on, what was she thinking?"

I grimaced, I may be curvy but I didn't think I was fat.

A few of the boys shifted and murmured in hushed agreement. Their scents tickled my nose, filling my lungs with the smell of oak, musk, a hint of wolf and most of all submission.

Were these boys part of the local wolf pack?

Ethan flashed him a dirty glare.

Hawk Eyes gnashed her teeth. "That was a bit uncalled for and you know it."

One of the curly haired twins straightened flipped her hair over her shoulder.

"Hey asshole, just because she has a curvy figure doesn't mean she's fat."

Her sister elbowed her in the side.

"Do you even know who that is?"

Curly snorted with disgust. "He may be the best lineman on the football team Jayda but that doesn't give him any right to call a girl fat."

"Yeah, you got some nerve." Brownie grumbled in agreement.

So much for keeping a low profile and staying subtle. I managed to break the most popular girl's nose and piss off the biggest bully at Ferndale

Hills all in one sitting. *Go me.* Buzz raised a bushy brow and crossed his arms.

"And who asked you pork chop?" Brownie's face twisted. In Buzz's defense Brownie was a little bit on the hefty side but that didn't give him a right to call her pork chop.

Ethan stepped forward with a foreboding frown.

"Andrew, that's going a bit too far." He warned.

His voice came out low, his tone unyielding.

Buzz's posture stiffened at Ethan's challenge.

The boys in the back shifted their weight. One of them elbowed the buddy next to him and tilted his head towards the scene. They all watched, waiting for Buzz's reaction. Buzz simply shrugged.

"What's it to you? It's not like you're dating her or anything."

His beady eyes glittered as they bore into Brownie.

Brownie shifted her weight.

Some of the boys in the back mumbled in agreement with one another.

I frowned. Who were these blathering idiots and what the hell was this guy's problem anyway? Hawk Eyes let out a derisive snort as she pushed her way to the front. She now stood in front of Buzz, only inches from his face. He towered over her as she jabbed her tiny finger at his chest.

"You got a lot of nerve. You know that? What makes you think you're so great?"

Each word dripped with venom.

He leaned in. Her face hovered inches from his.

Her face hardened, soft lips pressed into a thin line.

"I am so sick of slime like you, who think beauty is set to one specific interpretation. Most of what Lexi has is muscle anyway. Who are you to define her full potential? All you know about a woman probably comes from a magazine!"

Tension crackled between them.

I watched in stunned silence.

Buzz's upper lip curled into a severe snarl.

"No one cares what you think you dirty little spic."

Brownie gasped. The twin's mouths dropped

I wasn't entirely sure what he meant but I assumed it wasn't good.

"Look that's no way to talk to a lady." Ethan began but Hawk Eyes interrupted him with a hiss. "What did you just call me?"

The earthy glow of her aura had flared into a burnt orange.

Buzz's cronies stopped laughing and exchanged looks of concern.

Had they just realized the girls were closing in?

The boy's behavior screamed with submission. They must have been the betas and Buzz must have been in the lead. Buzz repeated himself. He took the time to enunciate each word clearly.

"Did I stutter?" He replied, his words dripped with acid. "I called you a dirty little spic." Within seconds Hawk Eyes whipped her arm back and slapped him across the face. Her hand made a cracking noise.

His head knocked back from the force.

Time slowed. I held my breath. The girls inched closer. Buzz prepared to swing. His gang prepared to pounce, ready for the command. I grabbed Hawk Eyes by the collar and gave her a good yank. Ethan stepped up and restrained Buzz by tugging his hand behind his back into a hammerlock.

"I wouldn't if I were you" Ethan said, his voice chilled.

"She hit me first, it's only fair!" Buzz sputtered in his grasp.

"Make a move and I'll snap your limb." Ethan warned.

Some of the boys inched forward.

Ethan simply flicked his wrist.

Buzz let out a pained gasp.

Immediately, they stopped in their advance.

Hawk Eyes struggled beneath my hold, lunging like an enraged cat. A string of profanities flew from her mouth as I struggled to keep her still. The twins jumped in to assist. "I am of Mexican heritage you racist prick! If you're going to insult me then do it right!" Needless to say, we were in an interesting predicament. I wondered if this was what Garcia meant by causing a scene.

If that was the case then what sort of consequences would she have in store for me? It wasn't like I was the one jumping around screaming like a crazed lunatic. Then again I did break the most popular girl's nose. Not on purpose of course, but still maybe that had amounted for something.

Huizenga's booming voice yanked me back to the present.

"Alright you two break it up! Playtime is over!"

He walked towards us, his fists balled tight. He stopped and crossed his burly arms over his broad chest. Hawk Eyes stiffened once Huizenga approached. Ethan released Buzz's arm. Buzz cried out in pain.

"What on God's green earth has happened here?" He demanded.

His blue eyes pierced ours, willing us to speak.

Hawk Eyes wilted with guilt. We released her. She stared at the ground.

All eyes were on me.

A nervous titter tickled at the back of my throat.

Quickly I swallowed, forcing it down.

"Well you see sir. Buzz here was calling me fat and-" Huizenga quirked a brow. Buzz grumbled underneath his breath, something about his name being Andrew. I found it prudent to ignore him at this point. Hawk Eyes stepped forward.

"It was my fault Mr. Huizenga. I'm the one who threw the first hit. You see, Andrew here was insulting Lexi. Instead of coming to you I thought I could handle it myself. I tried backing Lexi up. He called me a name.." Her chin dipped with shame. "Instead of handling it appropriately I lost my temper and slapped him across the face. Mami taught me better than that, and I take full responsibility for what I did."

Hawk Eyes rubbed her arm and dug her toe into the earth.

Brownie jutted her jaw and chimed in.

"Thankfully Ethan was here to stop Andrew from punching her in the face."

The twins nodded in agreement.

Ethan stood in complete silence.

The boys had scattered to go gather their things.

Mr. Huizenga eyed Ethan with approval and flashed Hawk Eyes a scolding glare.

I stepped forward and cleared my throat.

"In Selena's defense Andrew did call her a dirty little spic."

The group grimaced in unison.

Huizenga scowled in Andrew's direction, his expression became stony.

"Alright. You three are coming with me. The rest of you are going to take your things and wait in the lobby for your parents." Silently we complied.

My imagination ran rampant inside my head. *What if Garcia felt like I started this whole mess on purpose? Would she blow me up or skewer me with a fork at the dinner table?* Yes despite her being a vampire we still ate dinner at the dinner table. I could only imagine all of the possibilities that waited for me at home. Maiming was at the top of my list. My heart stopped as I stole a glimpse at Ethan.

What would she do to Ethan? He interfered with a human confrontation, with physical force. Then again he had taken control of a situation that could have gotten out of hand. All the while, he exuded a sense of calm. The very thought of it made my heart flutter anxiously inside my chest. Despite all the possible outcomes he protected me. I flushed. Even his teammates looked at him differently, now with a sense of reverence.

Could this have helped him get closer to the local pack? Half of the boys smelled like wolf and all of the ones who had backed up Buzz in the beginning were wolves. If that was the case then maybe I wouldn't get throttled after all. I could only imagine Garcia bursting with pride. A tendril of pleasure blossomed within my center. My stomach flipped as I recalled the way he moved with such speed and fluidity. I replayed the image over and over inside my head as I stole a glance his way.

Was this still the scrawny, hot tempered pup I used to rough house with when I was young? Over time he must have grown into a muscular predator. His emerald eyes met mine through locks of red hair. A small smile pulled at the corner of his lips.

I flushed.

Quickly, I turned my head towards the wildflower field on my right. Maybe if I looked at the field long enough he would forget I was looking his way.

When we approached the school Mr. Huizenga took Buzz, Hawk Eyes and Ethan into the glass office to interrogate them further. Hawk Eyes offered me a weak smile before disappearing into the room. I held a lot of respect for her. She didn't have to help but she did. Nor did she have to step forward or take responsibility for what had happened. Buzz had gotten what was coming to him and she should have left it at that but she didn't. She just had to take responsibility for her actions. Nor did Ethan have to intervene but he did. If he hadn't Hawk Eyes would have been hurt.

A bitter taste filled my mouth. A trickle of guilt slithered through my core, writhing and uncoiling like a poisonous snake. Why couldn't I be like that? Why was it so hard to take responsibility for my own actions? Would things have gone differently back at home if I didn't throw a fit about marrying Noah? Would my homeland still be at war if I actually stepped in and intervened? An incessant toe tapping brought me back to the present. I turned to confront the source of noise only to meet the piercing gaze of Carmen Garcia herself. I froze.

"We need to talk." She said, her voice forebodingly silky smooth.

Silently, I followed her.

"Care to explain what went wrong?"

A chill rippled down my spine like ice water on a hot summer day.

I managed to keep my heart rate in check but a nervous titter escaped my throat.

"Oh you know, some stuff." I paused and quickly added "Some normal stuff of course." Technically I wasn't lying. Teens are normally hormonal and they have a tendency to disagree with one another.

Garcia held my gaze as she waited patiently for me to continue. "Spill."

I groaned. "Alright. Alright. You take the fun out of everything."

She arched an expectant brow, clearly unamused.

I told her everything. When I finished she simply stood there.

"I see." She turned and proceeded towards the office.

Thunderstruck I stood there for a brief moment before trailing after her.

"Wait! You're not mad?" You're not going to throw me or something?"

"Why in the world would I do something like that?" She replied, her was voice rich with Italian undertones.

I grimaced and offered her a helpless shrug.

"Oh I don't know, because you seem to like throwing things? I caused a scene and a fight broke out because I drew attention to myself."

She held her hand up to silence me.

"No you just made a mistake. Making a mistake is different from causing a scene. You fell. Hawk Eyes is lucky Ethan was there to stop that boy from punching her in the face." Her voice turned to ice. "I would have dealt with him in a different manner."

I blinked. "So you aren't going to kill me?"

Garcia smirked. Her chocolate eyes danced with amusement.

"Not today little fox, perhaps at a later date?"

I released a breath of air.

Mr. Lemming stepped out of the glass office.

"Ah Miss Garcia I am glad you're here. Might I have a word?"

Garcia offered him a tight smile. "Of course, Principal Lemmings."

"Please, come to my office so we can speak privately."

"It would be my pleasure." Garcia replied graciously.

Together they walked into the back room. He opened the door for us. It was a small office. In the corner sat a house plant the size of a miniature tree. In the other corner sat a tall bookcase with a vast collection of books. The scent of oil and metal teased my senses as we entered the room. Ethan sat on one of the three chairs in front of Mr. Lemming's desk. We each took a seat. His mossy green eyes held a somber expression. Garcia and I took the seats next to him.

"What seems to be the problem here Mr. Lemmings?" Garcia inquired innocently.

Lemmings sighed as he rubbed at his stubble.

"Ethan here has violated the school policy by physically handling another student."

Garcia crossed her legs and casually leaned back in her chair.

"Oh?" She feigned ignorance.

"Yes, he physically handled another student during an altercation on the football field."

Garcia nodded and frowned.

"I see, that's strange. Because I am under the impression Ethan was intentionally preventing another student from committing assault on a young teen."

She let the words hang there.

Mr. Lemmings licked his dry lips.

His caterpillar eyebrows furrowed.

"Yes but we have a no touching policy on the school premises."

Garcia arched a slender brow.

"You would have rather Ethan stood by and let this little snot pummel a young girl in the face?" She replied crisply. "I must say Mr. Lemmings, I am concerned."

Mr. Lemming's broad forehead wrinkled as he struggled to come up with a reply.

"No, I mean, not really, but we can't have students physically restraining others."

Garcia shouldered her purse and began to rise.

"I see, well I cannot assure you that Ethan will stand aside when students are in harm's way. Regardless, I will speak to him about intervening in such situations once we get home. In the meantime I request that your staff are more attentive to the environment around them."

Mr. Lemmings folded his large hands diplomatically.

"Miss Garcia. I am well aware that Ethan is new to this school. Regardless of his status he needs to follow the protocol of this school if he is to go here. In the handbook it is clearly written that we have a no bullying or harassing policy. As a consequence for violating one of the school's policies he will be attending an in house suspension."

Garcia offered him a calculated smile.

"Yes, and I assure you this matter will be brought to the super superintendent's attention."

Mr. Lemmings blanched at Garcia's cool reply.

"You have a good day now, Mr. Lemmings."

Together we left the office. Garcia led the way, leaving a path of silence in her wake. Her brown eyes blazed. A cloud of tension crackled all around her. Ethan shuffled along with his hands in his pockets. His eyes remained downcast as Garcia stalked ahead. We made it to the parking lot. Hot summer air engulfed us in its muggy embrace.

"Well that went well." I said cheerily, more so to lighten the mood than anything. No one responded. So, I tried again. "On a lighter note is it just me or does Mr. Lemmings seem to have a fascination with the supernatural? I mean really, the Vampire Forensics: Uncovering the Origins of an Enduring Legend? What about his book on When Werewolves Attack? Is this guy serious?"

Garcia chortled with mild amusement.

"Humans." She mumbled bitterly to herself.

"No I am serious. He has a vast collection of books on his book shelf that pertain to the supernatural. We should really look into that." Ethan grunted. I nudged him playfully with my elbow before we climbed into Garcia's Escalade. "Oh chin up. I am sure Buzz is getting his fair share."

Ethan mumbled darkly through gritted teeth. The intensity of his green eyes reminded me of a stormy ocean. "No, Andrew is not getting his fair share. They believe he is the victim of this whole ordeal. He's walking off with a free pass. Selena and I are the ones who get an in house suspension while that prat roams free."

Garcia remained tight lipped, her mouth was pressed into a thin line as she started the engine and began to drive.

"Aren't you going to say anything?" I asked her.

Her Egyptian eyes looked at us through the rearview mirror.

"If this so called "Buzz" wants to cry wolf then so be it. We will just have to show him what it really means to cry."

A sly smirk curled at the corner of her lips.

An excited chill shivered down my spine and off we went.

CHAPTER 10

"SHH! Make it quick, we are running out of time!" I whispered urgently while teetering precariously on my toes. I had no idea that being on the lookout could be so exhausting. Frank eyed me carefully. My stomach bubbled with excitement. He hesitated. The anticipation was killing me.

"*Just do it already!*" I hissed.

He sucked in a breath and held it.

"Do you really think this is a good idea?" He asked.

His gray eyes wavered with uncertainty.

I nodded and he bit his lip.

"What if we get in trouble for it?"

I waved him off and flashed him a winning smile. "Bah, you worry too much Frank. Take it easy for once. You're a vampire for goodness sake. This will be fun! I am sure if we hurry up no one will notice."

Frank's gray eyes clouded with worry.

"Well, if you say so..." He mumbled and then reluctantly threw Mrs. Puffins, Mr. Dinkle's boa constrictor, into Buzz's locker. Together, we slammed the door shut before she could slither away. I figured we were doing the damn thing a favor anyway. All she did was sit in her cage and do nothing all day. By doing this she would at least get some sort of exercise. We stalked off stealthily to our next class, making sure to avoid any cameras on our way there. Thankfully, Astrid took the time to identify each one.

Over the last couple of days I've managed to slowly corrupt Frank. Each day he toes the line with me and assists me in my devious ways. Then again, Garcia herself appointed me in charge of making Buzz's life a living hell at school. Happily, I obliged. The missing person's case died down a bit. Jacob Parks was nowhere to be seen and now the latest gossip was centered on Ethan. Apparently everyone in school thought he broke Buzz's arm all because Buzz came to school in a sling the day after the incident had happened. Somehow I think that was one of Garcia's doing. Astrid squealed in delight when she learned that I broke Olivia Gaines' nose. She even agreed to try out for the musical with me. Which had failed miserably.

Apparently, my singing skills are subpar. I guess that sort of thing happens when your voice can break glass. *Go me*. Thankfully, Mr. Smith was kind enough to tell me all the slots were taken and had no more room on the theatrics team. But we all know it's because I made Tommy Lee Jone's ears bleed. Later, Frank and I met up at the cafeteria. I sat down next to Frank who idly poked at his food with a fork.

"Yo, what's up doc?"

I didn't even bother going through the cafeteria line. Garcia and I discussed our options when it came to food. In the end, I had opted for cold lunch.

"Oh nothing much." He mumbled half-heartedly.

Frowning, I nudged him with my elbow. "So who killed your puppy?"

He chewed at his chapped lip. "I've got a lot on my plate right now."

I tried a different angle. "How is the new job going eh?"

Frank grimaced as he rolled a few shriveled peas around with his spoon.

"Horrible, absolutely horrible."

"What's so horrible now?" Ethan asked as he plopped down next to me.

I scooted over giving him plenty of room.

"My new job at my McDonalds." Frank replied.

Ethan flashed him a perplexed frowned. "You're workin' at a burger flippin' joint? Aren't vampires supposed to be filthy rich or somethin'?"

Frank groaned as he dragged a hand down the side of his face.

I gagged on my turkey sandwich.

Frank's stormy eyes shot me an icy glare. "Technically we don't flip the burgers at McDonalds. Regardless, don't remind me. I am not the greatest cook."

Astrid's laughter tinkled as she appeared behind Frank.

"I think you're confusing Frank with Edward Cullen, hun."

She slid her tray onto the table and sat down next to Frank.

Ethan scrunched up his nose. "Edward Cullen?"

"It's some stupid book reference." Frank grumbled as he fumbled with his sloppy joe. "Enough about me, how has the whole football gig been doing since you finished that argument between you and Drew?"

Ethan cast his eyes downward and shrugged.

"Not great really." He mumbled.

Frank patiently waited for an explanation.

The turkey sandwich turned to paper in my mouth.

It was Ethan's turn to start playing with his food. It wasn't like him to not eat.

"I don't know. The guys have been acting weird ever since I made a fool of Andrew the other day. They used to be all about Andrew and now they are all buddy buddy with me. I don't understand it. It almost makes me feel uncomfortable. Should I really trust them if they are so quick to switch sides? Now Andrew hates my living guts. He won't even speak to me. I preferred being the outsider and having my own space. Now they are all up in my business. It's almost like I am the center of attention and I am on a big stage." He pushed his food around and frowned. "It's weird."

Frank raised his brow and looked at Ethan expectantly.

Silence stretched out and Astrid tinkled with musical laughter.

"I can't believe you are complaining, love."

Ethan pursed his lips. "They're smothering me, why shouldn't I complain? A man needs his space and all that jazz."

Frank rubbed his temples and slowly shook his head. "You don't get it do you?"

I tilted my head, things were getting a bit interesting.

"Get what?" I had asked, in complete bewilderment.

Frank looked at me like I was from another planet so Astrid took over.

"I don't think Ethan understands that there are a bunch of were-wolves on the football team. Nor do I think he realizes that he won them over by challenging their alpha. Andrew was their alpha, well temporarily since Jacob's been gone, so now they look up to him as their leader."

She eyed Ethan flirtatiously and leaned in to whisper in his ear.

He stiffened in response, he never dealt well with Astrid's magical touch.

"So maybe you should use all that jazz to your advantage eh?" She ran a playful finger along his arm. Her pink aura swirled around his in a tantalizing gesture. "I suggest you get started with leading. Girls tend to like men who are in charge, if you get what I mean" She wiggled her eyebrows and gave him a wink.

Ethan flushed. "So that explains the smell.."

Astrid frowned. *"Excuse me?"*

Uh oh. I thought. *She probably thinks he is referring to her scent.*

Quickly, I jumped in to intervene.

"Don't get the wrong idea, Astrid. Ethan never grew up with a pack or around any other werewolves. He's probably referring to their scent signature."

Astrid's shoulders relaxed. "Got it. Now enough about that. The homecoming dance is next week. Are any of you going?"

I shrugged my shoulders. Homecoming wasn't really something that interested me. Unless I could get away with setting one of the trash cans on fire and causing mass chaos. However, I didn't think Garcia would approve of such brash behavior.

"Oh I don't know, what about you Ethan?"

He smiled brightly and struggled to speak through a mouthful of food.

"Yeah. I am bringing Olivia Gaines. You?"

My fork clattered onto the table top.

Astrid's spoon nearly missed her mouth but Frank just kept on chewing.

"I am sorry can you repeat that?" Astrid asked stiffly.

"I am bringing Olivia Gaines."

I busted with laughter, nearly choking on my own food.

"You, with Olivia? Ha! You are joking right?"

Frank methodically chewed his food, making it a point to not say anything as Astrid shot Ethan an icy glare. His attempts of not being noticed failed miserably as Astrid gunned him down with questions him.

"Did you know all along?" She asked, her voice tinged with accusation.

Frank shrugged. "Yea. I was there when she asked him. I don't see what the big deal is anyway."

She pouted, glossy lips reflected the fluorescent light.

"And how long ago was this?" She asked imperiously.

Frank let out an exasperated sigh. "I don't know! Why do you care anyway?"

"What's it to you anyway?" Ethan asked. "It's not we're *dating* or anything."

I sucked air through my teeth. "Ooh, wrong answer buddy."

"I need to go." Astrid rose, her back was straight as a board.

She stalked off with the predatory grace of a cat. We all watched her bang the lunch tray hard against the trash can. I winced as she threw it haphazardly into the dirty pile. Her black hair swished with each step. In seconds she rounded the corner and disappeared. We all exchanged glances with one another and indulged in a brief moment of silence.

"What's her problem anyway?" Ethan asked with a frown.

"Who knows she's a woman, can't say really." Frank mumbled.

Thoughtfully, I tapped my finger against my chin.

"Uh, maybe it's because you are taking Olivia and not her?"

Ethan let out a miserable groan.

"I but I don't even like Olivia. She's the one that asked me!"

"Yeah, don't mention that to Olivia bud."

A shrill scream shattered the cafeteria's cheerful chatter. Buzz rounded the corner sprinting at full speed. Hawk Eyes rushed towards us. She skidded to a halt.

"What on earth is happening Selena?"

Ethan asked as she bent over gasping for breath.

"Mr. Dinkle's snake escaped his cage!"

Frank blinked, while I feigned innocence.

"It's a her." Frank replied flatly.

Hawk Eyes gaped at Frank. "Does gender specification really matter right now?"

"Oh really?" I inquired coyly. A satisfied smile tugged at the corner of my lips but I quickly schooled my expression into one of mild curiosity. I smirked as I watched a terrified Buzz jump up onto one of the lunch room tables. "How tragic."

Mr. Dinkle's brown boa constrictor slithered across the linoleum. She stopped only inches away from Buzz's table. He screamed like a little girl. *How the man became a leader of a werewolf pack was beyond me.* Silence engulfed the cafeteria as all eyes locked on Mrs. Puffins. Olivia's fork slipped from her grip and clattered onto the table top. Mrs. Puffins let out a hiss and the crowd went wild.

Everyone began to scream and scatter. Food went flying towards Mrs. Puffins, girls shrieked in complete terror. Most of the boys gave Mrs. Puffins a wide berth while others climbed onto table tops. *So much for acting all manly.* I thought smugly to myself. Some even oohed and ahhed when Mrs. Puffins coiled herself around the table legs. The intercom chirped and Mr. Lemming's gritty voice spoke over the noise.

"Miss Alexis Adams please come to the main office. I repeat Miss Alexis Adams please come to the main office." Frank shot me a private smile as a handful of frazzled teachers sprinted towards the cafeteria. *Well I'll be damned, I was wondering how long it would take till they called me in. Personally, I had hoped that they wouldn't call me in during the show but duty calls.* I let out a satisfied sigh and proceeded towards the main office.

One of the secretaries gave me permission to head through the narrow hallway that led to Mr. Lemming's office. I rounded the corner and slipped in without a word. I figured with the door being open it was free game to enter. "Hello?" I called out into the silence.

No one answered. Dusty sun beams swirled down onto an empty office chair which happened to sit in front of a mahogany desk flooded with paperwork. Silence enveloped the room. I could hear the muffled voices of the secretaries up front. Curiosity tugged me towards the desk. A scientific magazine named *The Wonders of the Supernatural* sat on top of a picture.

So my suspicions were correct, Mr. Lemmings really was into sci-fi. Maybe someday we could discuss vampires and werewolves. I took a peek at the picture. My stomach dropped. It was a photo of Jacob Parks. Next to him sat a picture that belonged to another missing person's case. Anna Johnson's soft smile stared back at me. A notebook sat wide open, weighing the photos down like a paper weight. *What in Inari's name was going on here? Why would Mr. Lemmings even keep these snapshots in the first place?* I leaned in, struggling to read Mr. Lemming's pinched handwriting which read the following.

Subject A: Jacob Parks, suspected of taking on wolf-like characteristics and emanating wolf-like behavior on June 28th 2016 during an altercation with Subject B and an abnormally large dog. Both Subject A and Subject B were collected shortly afterwards for study. The cause for attack was unknown. Subject B: Anna Johnson displayed similar behavior after displaying critical scratches and bite marks. Subject B did not survive transformation. Tests have been administered upon Subject A. Subject A is still under observation and has healed rapidly at an exponential rate.

A pair of muffled voices rounded the corner. Hushed whispers increased as their footfalls neared. I held my breath. My heart thundered within my chest. Droplets of perspiration blossomed along my forehead. Icy panic trickled through my veins. *What if they walk in on me in Mr. Lemming's office?* My stomach twisted at the possibility. Electricity tingled across my fingertips.

Quickly, I twisted the veil of air around me like an invisibility cloak. I inched my way towards the door and peeked around the corner to see Mr. Lemmings in a black and purple pinstripe shirt holding a steamy mug of coffee. He reeked of steel, oil and old cigarettes.

"I don't care John" Lemmings snarled. "Even if she did steal your snake. It is too early. All we can do right now is investigate. Besides you have no proof. As of right now we have a tangible lead on Matthews. All you have is speculation and a strong dislike towards Alexis Adams. Ethan Matthews is our primal focus at this time."

Mr. Dinkle bit his lip.

I held my breath as I inched along the wall.

"I agree that there is something strange about Mr. Matthews. No normal boy should have been able to restrain Andrew Brown the way he did. But sir, the lab is currently working on subject A. Don't forget subject C keeps escaping. Do you really think it is wise to collect more specimens?"

A floorboard creaked beneath my weight.

Damn it, I knew I shouldn't have eaten that extra cookie during lunch.

Time froze, but my heart hammered away. I took a shallow breath and held it.

Silently I prayed the sound hadn't given me away.

The two men paused and turned towards me.

Mr. Lemming's caterpillar eyebrows furrowed with suspicion.

Mr. Dinkle wrung his hands as Mr. Lemming's beady eyes searched for the source of sound. His dark brown eyes pierced through me. He paused and frowned.

Did he see me? He couldn't have, could he? I had warped reality using my magic. *Surely he couldn't see me through my webs of illusion. Then again, there was a chance that he had, all he had to do was peer through the veil of trickery with an intense desire to see the truth.* Tension hung in the air. My lungs burned.

"We will do whatever it takes to better our society through the use of science, John." He said before slowly dragging his eyes back to Dinkle.

Dinkle licked his lips.

"But sir, what about the media? They are already hot on our trail. There has been so much focus on the Park's boy and Miss Johnson."

"Well, until something major happens we will just have to lie low now won't we? Anyway, you best go. Miss Adams should be here any moment."

Reluctantly, Mr. Dinkle nodded and waddled away. Lemmings stepped into his office and closed the door. I pressed my lips tightly together as I watched him waddle away. *What in hells bells was going on here? Should I enter Mr. Lemming's office, or should I run? Surely if I ran, Lemmings would suspect something.* He did announce my name over the intercom, so complete ignorance would be hard to feign. I sucked in a deep breath and released the veil. The electrical tingle faded from my fingertips.

Miles well, I figured I'm screwed anyway. I rapped a nervous hand against the wooden door.

"Come in." Lemmings called out in his gruff voice.

I wiped my hands onto my jeans before twisting the knob. It was icy cool beneath my clammy fingertips. I poked my head through the doorway, to see Mr. Lemming's writing. The light reflected off of his receding hairline. The evidence of his crime was nowhere to be seen. The very idea of it infuriated me.

"Have a seat." He said without looking up.

"You called?" I inquired as I sprawled myself along one of the seats like a lazy cat.

"That I did." His words scratched effortlessly along the paper.

"So what's this about, Mr. Lammings?"

He set his pen down and folded his hands underneath his chin.

"It's Mr. Lemmings, Alexis. Now let's be honest with each other here."

A nervous titter escaped my throat. "Honest about what?"

Mr. Lemming's narrowed his furry brows.

"Can you explain to me why a boa constrictor is in my cafeteria?"

I flashed him a cordial smile, but in reality I held my breath.

"Now why would you ask a question like that?"

If he asked the right questions then I would have to answer. Being a kitsune had some cons. For instance, I cannot lie and if people know my true name then they have a powerful influence over me. That was not an option, especially after seeing that paperwork. Mr. Lemmings raised a brow and began to speak again but a shrill alarm screamed through building. I practically fell out of the my chair. The alarm loudly pulsated above us. Mr. Lemmings frowned.

"What is going on?" I shouted over the screaming alarm.

"It is a fire alarm. Either someone pulled the alarm or there is a real fire. No matter, we'll discuss this later. Come now Miss Adams we need to go outside. Go follow everyone else outside and meet up with your sixth hour class."

Apparently, according to school protocol is normal to silently walk down the hallway in a single file line when your school is on fire. I couldn't comprehend why. If there truly was a fire wouldn't people be running to the nearest exit? Instead, lines of students trickled out of the double doorways like fish through a stream. The students spoke to each other in hushed voices in order to avoid a scolding glare here and there from their teachers. We received a brief visit from the men who fight fire and then were given permission to head back inside after waiting twenty minutes in the cool September air. Apparently, someone thought it funny to pull the fire alarm.

One of the teachers shooed us into a group. A pair of girls next to us got into an excited conversation about homecoming.

"Alright people, stick together, that's it, good."

I grabbed a disgruntled Astrid by the arm.

"Whoa, slow down there chica. What's got your panties in a knot today?"

A curious Hawk Eyes sidled up next to us.

"It's because Ethan asked Olivia to homecoming instead of you, isn't it?"

Hawk Eyes gasped. *"No way, why?"*

Astrid's eyes glittered gold for a brief moment.

Thankfully no one noticed but me.

"Who knows?" I shrugged.

Astrid snorted. "He can ask whoever he likes. It makes no difference to me."

Ethan slipped in from behind.

"Who can ask who to what?" He inquired with mild curiosity.

Astrid stiffened and her cheeks went pink.

I rolled my eyes and smirked. "Nothing, Ethan."

However deep down inside I am sure he had heard. He was a werewolf after all. If he could locate where we were via our scent within this large mass of people then I am sure he could hear the conversation between us three girls.

"Anyhow, enough about dance drama I got something really important to tell you guys."

Hawk Eyes leaned in her eyes hungry for gossip. "What is it?"

I debriefed them about what I saw in Mr. Lemming's office. I left out the supernatural tid bits. I decided I'd fill Astrid and Ethan in later on those, once we were in private. However, I did mention Lemming's interest in Ethan.

Hawk Eyes was stunned into silence.

Ethan frowned, clearly bewildered. "What would he want with me anyhow?"

I shrugged my shoulders. "No clue, he knows your strong and must realize you have some special abilities. How am I supposed to know? All I know is that you need to watch yourself and lay low if at all possible. Speaking of which you should probably be with your class right now. I'd hate to have them find out you've been missing." Ethan gave me a brief nod and off he went. Hawk Eyes watched us with cool calculating eyes. Twenty minutes later Miss Mulder wrangled us all up and lead us back into the classroom.

"Alright folks. Before I begin the lesson I would like to go over a brief announcement. The school is in need of a newspaper club. I will be hosting the club and as of right now I am currently taking any applications. We are in need of at least five participants to make this club successful. Please notify me by Friday afternoon if you are interested."

Hawk Eyes' small hand whipped into the air.

Ms. Mulder smiled pleasantly her way. "Yes Miss Rodriguez?"

"Ms. Mulder the three of us are interested in applying for the newspaper club. Can we talk about it after class?" Astrid and I flashed her the death glare for not including us in this decision.

"What? I thought it would give us good intel." Hawk Eyes replied softly through a forced smile so only we could hear. I assumed the smile was more for the teacher than for us. *Damn her and her feigned innocence.*

Ms. Mulder nodded, extremely pleased.

"I will see you after class then." She turned and began to write on the whiteboard with her squeaky black marker. "Now that's settled please open your books to page 322. We will be learning about sonnets today. By the end of next week you will be creating your own sonnet."

Olivia sighed with misty eyes.

"How romantic. Maybe Ethan will be able to write me one. What do you think Astrid?"

Astrid forced a pleasant smile but her eyes glittered dangerously.

"Maybe he can work on fixing your nose first. Try focusing on one thing at a time love."

Olivia huffed and turned around.

Astrid twirled a lock of hair around her finger as she read about sonnets.

I shot Hawk Eyes a menacing glare as soon as Ms. Mulder turned her back.

"Dude, what happened to asking us first before signing us up? I am tempted to say no just to spite you."

Astrid carefully watched Ms. Mulder as she made her rounds. "Lexi has a point you know. Why wouldn't you give us a heads up first? We are your friends after all. Did you think we wouldn't have listened to you?"

Hawk Eyes bit her lip and waited till Ms. Mulder's back was turned before replying.

"I was afraid that all the positions would fill up or that you guys would say no. Finding out what happened to Jacob means a lot to me. I figured if we were on the newspaper club then we could ask questions without it drawing as much attention."

She twiddled her thumbs and mumbled an apology.

"Well, you do have a point. We could probably cover more ground work if we were able to ask questions without drawing attention." I mused aloud.

Hawk Eyes' face brightened.

"You really think so?"

Astrid licked her finger before turning another page.

"Hmm, would it be possible to terrorize other students through the use of writing?"

Hawk Eyes her suspiciously. "I mean we could have a gossip column if you really wanted to. Who do you have in mind?"

Astrid shrugged, her expression remained nonchalant.

"Oh I don't know, someone like Olivia Gaines or Drew?"

In seconds, Astrid had my full undivided attention.

"Is it possible to get dirt on her and make a story?"

Hawk Eyes rubbed her chin, her expression remained thoughtful.

"I am sure we can find dirt on anybody. As long as we are subtle we could probably even publish something on "said" dirt."

Astrid and I eyed each other. A sly smile spread across our lips.

"If that's the case then count us in."

CHAPTER 11

THE COOL AUTUMN breeze tickled my cheeks. Cheerleaders bounced around on the red asphalt like a bunch of crazed rabbits.

An announcer's voice boomed across the stadium.

"Give some applause for the Ferndale Hills marching band!"

The crowd roared with excitement. Our opposition on the other hand did not. We sat tightly together, packed like sardines in a can. The stadium lights clicked on as purple clouds loomed over the setting sun. Red and white uniforms marched onto the field armed with shiny musical instruments.

I squinted my eyes against the setting sun's glare.

"They look like a bunch of little musical ants down there."

Astrid chuckled and held her hand up.

"Just wait and see." She replied with a smile.

The crisp September air tickled the back of my neck, filling my lungs with the smells of popcorn hotdogs and chips. Moments later, the band sprang to life. Music buzzed through the stadium. The percussion kept the tempo. The players twisted and moved in synchronization. The band shifted as one, each step precise. Together they used their bodies to make different patterns. The beat tingled through my veins, urging me to dance. I favored the ones with the spinning flags and enjoyed watching them twist and turn in their ceremonial dance. Almost more so than watching the football players smash into each other. Rough housing has always brought back special memories of home. Back at Mount Kyoto the local kits and I would wrestle for sport. Even Pa would join in on the games. Sometimes he would let us ride around on his back when we were young.

The announcer's rumbling introduction pulled me back into the present.

"And now, to announce your runner ups for the homecoming king and queen!"

Drumsticks clattered in anticipation. Cymbals clashed. The band broke out into a jazzy song. Three different couples strolled onto the football field. I nearly choked on a popcorn kernel. *Well I'll be damned.* Olivia Gaines and her evil counterpart Andrew Brown were the first couple to saunter down the center of the football field. Andrew wore a white tuxedo, almost a size too big. Olivia wore a slinky black dress that accentuated every curve of her body. She had her blonde curls twisted into a French twist, exposing her long neck. The expression on her face was tense. Together they strode side by side, their arms intertwined.

Hawk Eyes strode in from behind in an elegant blue evening gown that glittered like the stars on a hot midsummer night. She glided across the football field with her arm tucked into Frank's. He wore a freshly pressed tux that complimented his broad shoulders and fit him just right. He walked down the center of the football field with predatory grace. Shortly afterwards some joe schmo and his average jane doe walked down next. Who they were I did not know. Nor did I care. All three pairs lined up front and center. The cool September breeze rustled through Frank's wavy black hair as we waited in anticipation for the announcement.

"Let's get a drum roll!"

The drums began to roll. I bit my lip. Astrid gnawed on her fingernail. Her other hand squeezed my knee tight. The tips of her oval fingernails dug into me like little daggers. She wanted Hawk Eyes to win, badly. Silently, I did too. Despite her *Miss Know It All* tendencies, she was still a good friend. One of the student council members jogged up to the announcer and handed him a white envelope. Excitement flushed through me as we waited in great anticipation.

"Your homecoming king and queen for 2016 are..." He ripped open the envelope and the cymbals crashed. "Olivia Gaines and Andrew Brown!" We tensed as everyone else burst into applause. Some whistled, others hooted and some hollered their approval. A shadow of disappointment flickered across Astrid's face. Together we sat in stunned silence.

A few hours later, white Christmas lights dimly lit up the dance floor. Who would have known that a few lights here and there could change the ambience of the entire school. Contemporary music echoed against the vaulted ceiling of the cafeteria. The place vibrated with noise and reeked with heavy perfume, sweat, and spicy sex pheromones. A huge homecoming banner hung loosely between two large pillars. Girls hung all over guys like syrup on pancakes. I observed the couples dancing from afar and kept my distance.

I can't believe I let Astrid pull me into this. *It's going to be fun*, she said. *We're going to have a great time*, she said. *You won't make a fool of yourself*, she said. I was re-considering my decision making skills. Was it really worth trying dresses on for several hours for this dance? So far, not so much. Back home Pa taught me many things. He taught me how to wrestle, fight and cook but he did not teach me how to dance. That was a mother's affair. Sure, I was aware of ceremonial rituals but I knew nothing when it came to wooing a man. So I stood back and observed from afar.

Astrid stood by my side with one hand on her hip, surveying her surroundings. Black kohl lined the rim of her almond shaped eyes and flicked up at the corners of her smoky eye shadow, giving her an exotic flare. Today she didn't wear her winged spectacles. Despite not wearing her glasses she still glided across room with the grace of a predatory cat. Her scarlet lips curled into a confident smile. Seduction rolled off of her in waves. Every now and then I caught a student or two staring at the body of my best friend. She was a succubus afterall, and this was her domain. The cafeteria boomed with life force. Living energy hung in the hair like a foggy haze. She closed her eyes and took in a deep breath, sucking in tendrils of energy into her nose. When she opened them her eyes glimmered like liquid amber.

"Hungry?" I wasn't referring to the Applebees we just ate. She shook her head with a smile. The place was filled to the brim with emotional energies. Even I was getting a high off of the human's life force. "No, quite full actually." I glanced at her for a second and realized her complexion had a healthy glow.

"Are you feeding right now?"

Astrid gave me a playful wink.

"Why wouldn't I be? The room is overflowing with emotion. Excitement, angst, happiness and jealousy, they are all here. Why do you think I love football games so much? I don't have to be naughty to feed Alexis. I feed off of emotional energy including but not limited to lust. Succubi feed off of a person's life force. Our emotions are filled with our desires, wants, and dreams. They are the force that drives our spirits. I take a human's emotion and absorb it into me. Lust and desire just happen to be more filling."

Oddly enough, I understood what Astrid meant. Kitsune also have similar ways of feeding when it came to consuming a human's life force. However, we were not limited to consuming only human life force. I too was feeding off of the human's chi. We could also feed off of the earth's life force. Regardless, if we are not careful we could cause harm to the environment and to the people that surround us.

Someone from behind cleared their throat. We both turned to meet Ethan's emerald gaze. He loomed over us in his black tuxedo. He had pinned a white Canna lily to his lapel. A mess of rusty red curls fell into his face. His green eyes reflected the soft glow of the glittering white Christmas lights. My jaw nearly hit the floor. *Ethan in a suit? Who would have known he could have looked so good?*

"Good evening ladies." He smiled. His eyes danced with amusement.

"Well aren't you a little charmer." Astrid replied with a languid smile, her remained expression reserved. She stared off into the distance, as if something in the crowd had caught her attention. A flame of pride swelled within me. I nearly burst at the seams as I put a hand over my heart and feigned a sniffle

"Aw, my wittle Ethan wooks all grown up!" I reached out and pinched his cheek.

He slapped my hand away and directed his full attention towards Astrid.

Clearly, I needed to work on identifying silent social cues.

His eyes were on Astrid and Astrid only.

"Astrid, would you care to dance with me?" Ethan asked, as he extended his hand in invitation.

She turned to look at him. Wisps of black hair fell in her face.

"What about your date Mr. Matthews?" She inquired coyly.

He offered her a non commital shrug.

"We're not really an item Astrid. I keep trying to tell you that but you won't listen. She's the one who asked me. I think it's more for image and everything. She hadn't paid me any mind until that thing with Drew happened. I figured it'd be rude to decline her offer after she went through all that trouble to ask." He shifted his weight restlessly and ran a hand through his hair. "Besides, she's with Drew right now getting her homecoming court photos taken for the yearbook."

A small smile tugged at her scarlet lips. Her expression softened.

Oh no, if he thought he could steal my sidekick he had another thing coming. I scrambled into action, desperately trying to prevent the possibility of being the one stranded at the high school dance.

"Hey! What about your whole we girls need to stick together speech? Oh and don't forget the whole sisters before misters." I even made quotations in the air to emphasize my point.

Astrid offered me an apologetic smile. "Sorry Lex."

Ethan chuckled and took her hand. His body posture eased.

"Don't worry Lex. I'll bring her back. I am sure you can fly solo for just one song."

I rolled my eyes and yanked a candy bar out of the side of my dress. I tore the wrapper off with my teeth.

"Well you owe me." I grumbled with a mouthful of chocolate. "Like REAL big. Now go before lady Godzilla finds you." I shook the bar at them. *"Well go on now, get"*

Ethan flashed me a boyish grin.

I shooed them away.

He snatched up her hand and off they went. A wistful smile tugged at my lips as I watched them from afar. They swayed to and fro like two sheaves of wheat in the summer breeze. On second thought, maybe this was worth enduring two hours of dress shopping. Nevertheless, I went off in search of the closest snack bar.

All hell had broken loose while I was stuffing my face with chips and soda. Polite etiquette has never been one of my specialties. Besides who can turn down the irresistible crunch of barbecue Lays? Yowling and shouting had erupted through the cafeteria like two cats fighting in an alley. Someone shrieked.

"You think you can just march on in here and take someone else's date for a joy ride?!" I pushed through the crowd to see Olivia straddling Astrid as she clawed at her neck. Rage twisted her face, muscles pulsated and popped along her jawline. Astrid slapped at Olivia's thrashing hands. I sucked in a breath.

Anytime now Astrid should just pop up like a daisy. Moments had passed and she still had not arose. *Come on Astrid*. Dread tugged at my stomach, filling my insides with ice. I frowned. *Something was wrong, she shouldn't still be on the ground. Why wasn't she getting up?* My brain buzzed with questions. Astrid gasped for breath as she feebly clawed at the hands around her neck. Her body oozed with calming endorphins. I am assumed she was trying to calm Miss Kitty down. On the other hand, Olivia had gone berserker kitty on her ass and wasn't having it. All the while, An awestruck Ethan just stood there, completely dumbfounded. Girls never fought over him like this back at home. The crowd lulled softly with excitement.

I flashed him the death glare.

"Don't just stand there Sherlock, do something!" I hissed.

Meanwhile, everyone else just stood around and watched.

Ethan burrowed his hands into his hair.

"What do I do?" He stammered.

His green eyes swirled with distress. Frustrated, I threw my hands up into the air.

"How am I supposed to know? You got her in this mess. Now you get her out!"

Olivia howled as she banged Astrid's head against the speckled linoleum. Astrid's eyes began rolling into the back of her head. It was then that realization dawned upon me. *She didn't want to risk exposure, that was why Astrid wasn't fighting back.* Olivia's pheromones shifted from human to wolf. Olivia's fingernails began to extend and her face elongated ever so slightly. Thankfully, she had taken down her hair and it had hid most of what was happening.

"I am so sick of you! Why do you have to be such a skank!? What makes you think you can just steal my date?! I swear. You ruin everything Astrid!"

The crowd bristled with excitement. A soft hush rose amongst the onlookers. *How could everyone just stand around at a time like this? Why wasn't anyone doing anything?* I cursed beneath my breath. *God damn werewolves and their stupid anger management issues.* Silently, I begged Astrid to whip out her wings and claws but we both knew she had to lay low. Jordan Takahashi, the omega of the werewolf pack, closed his eyes and tried to console Liv with his magic but nothing happened.

"She's not responding to my presence.." Jordan murmured.

He reached out to her but she slapped him away.

"Go, away!" Olivia screamed.

An awestruck Jordan backed away.

"I am trying everything here Ethan.." Jordan stared at her in complete bewilderment. The rest of the pack exchanged uncertain glances. It was the omega's job to calm any wolf's nerves. Their primary duty was to create a calm atmosphere for their pack. Their very presence ensured stability. If Olivia wasn't responding to Jordan's magic then something was severely wrong. "Why isn't she responding? Nothing seems to work!"

"Ugh, quit standing there stammering like a buffoon." I snarled at Ethan and smacked him upside the head. "This is your domain, so take control of the situation already!"

Jordan reached out to Olivia but she smacked him away.

This was his opportunity to work with the wolves as a team. Olivia was a member of the pack and was on the brink of shifting. Several of the boys from the football team looked to him for guidance. If he didn't take control now then the reality of werewolves would be revealed to humanity as a whole this very night. Both Garcia and Benson would surely have our heads. The crowd began to chant.

"Fight, fight, fight." A concoction of scents filled the air as the impending chaos built. The smells ranged from musty uncertainty, sickly sweet panic to peppery excitement. I sucked in a breath, the heavy cloud of emotions filled me with life. Understanding bloomed across Ethan's chiseled features. His expression turned to stone. His wavering gaze transformed into cool determination. Within an instant, he began dishing out commands. I recognized that most of the crew were from the football team. Ethan had to shout over the crowd's chant for violence in order to be heard. His voice came out rich and firm.

"Takahashi." Ethan announced.

The slim boy of Asian descent looked up.

"Go grab a teacher to help break up this fight."

"You think that's a good idea, boss?" One of them asked with a sense of uncertainty.

Ethan on the other hand, appeared unperturbed. Normally an omega would remain present during a situation as this but for some reason his powers weren't working.

"He's quickest guy on the team. The rest of you will just have to reign yourselves in."

Ethan dipped a chin towards the Anderson twins.

"Boys, get yourself into position. We're going to put this bitch in her place." His eyes were a blaze. I couldn't necessarily blame him, she was nearly exposing the whole team on an account of female rivalry. "You three! Push back the crowd, we're going to need some space."

Everyone took their positions.

Ethan sucked in a breath. "Everyone ready?"

Zach and Zander Anderson cracked their knuckles.

"Better now than never eh?" Zander said with a grin.

Brad, Jared and Drew grabbed a few friends and began using their barreled chests to press back the crowd. The majority of them were linemen after all so the job shouldn't have been too difficult. Meanwhile, Zach, Ethan and Zander did their best to pull Olivia off of

Astrid. No matter how hard they tried she kept slipping away. Zander yelped and ripped back his hand.

"Bloody hell, she bit me!"

Zach peered at brother's throbbing hand.

"Damn mate, she drew blood."

A feral snarl escaped Olivia.

"Lexi, a little help here would be great." Ethan demanded.

The crowd pressed against Brad, Jared, and Andrew. They insisted that they see what was going on. I sucked in a breath of air and slowly began to inch towards Olivia. She whipped her head in my direction. I stepped back as the eyes of a wolf met mine. It all made sense now. I recalled the conversation Frank had with us earlier. I remembered him commenting on how Buzz was the head of the young werewolf pack. Olivia must have been his main squeeze because she too was a wolf. Due to her strength she must have been the alpha female of the group. Maybe that was why only Ethan could only keep a good grasp on her because now he was considered the lead wolf. All her attempts to woo him, were they just meant to keep her at the top of the pack's hierarchy? Did she have any feelings for him at all? A mixture of uncertainty twisted within my core.

Electricity tingled across my fingertips. My heart hammered like a frantic hummingbird trapped inside a cage. Perspiration dotted my forehead as I gathered the energy around me. The air stilled, time slowed and outside influences twitched ever so slightly as I played with the possibilities of different illusions. *Should I warp time? Should I create an illusion to help this pass off as a normal lovers quarrel?* Regardless, something had to be done. Astrid couldn't take on her true form without causing an apocalyptic uproar amongst our classmates. My knees shook and sweat trickled down my back. Stopping time with this many people for a long period would not be an option. Already my strength was beginning to wane, calling forth energy for masses of people can be quite exhausting.

Sticky blood trickled slowly from my nose. I sucked in a breath of air. Just a little bit longer, that's all it would take. My fingers trembled as I twisted time to a complete stop. I slowly pieced the situation together so Olivia's movements appeared less supernatural and more humanly possible. Illusion, after all, was a Kitsune's greatest specialty, so was the shifting of time. I tweaked the speed of her swings and turned the volume down on her screams so the brawl would be less noticeable. I altered reality, making her appear more like a human and less like a wolf. Quickly, I released the rest of the crowd and gasped for air, focusing my illusion mainly on Olivia. Music shattered the silence and the liveliness of the crowd snapped back to life. Now they chanted in unison. "Fight Fight Fight!" Sweat continued to trickle down my back now at a normal rate. My nose continued to bleed.

"Easy tiger. Everything's going to be ok" I spoke soft and slow as I inched forward. It was official. Astrid owed me big. I was about to take on tiger lady by myself. I knew I should have watched more Discovery channel but alas there are only so many hours in one day. I bit my lip as I took another step closer. Each muscle in my body wound tight like a string. Olivia's head snapped up. Frosty eyes the color of ice blue glaciers stared up at me. Her glossy lips drew back as she let out a wolfish snarl.

"You can't have him!" She growled and leapt towards me.

I ducked. A black shape blurred across my vision, slamming full speed into Olivia, taking her down. Together they rolled and tumbled as they slid across the floor. It was Frank. The crowd broke apart. She thrashed and howled under his grasp. He pinned her to the ground as she arched beneath him. Stray strands of black hair fell into his face. His forehead wrinkled with concentration. Selena quickly followed, her clacking heels in quick pursuit. Black curls fell into her round face.

"Alexis" She puffed for air. "What did you do and why are you bleeding? We came as soon as Frank heard the noise."

Frank wrestled with Olivia, doing his best to subdue the beast. His gray eyes glowed with silver. It took me a moment but I twisted the veil around him, allowing me the ability to adjust the way others were able to perceive his appearance. *What could I say? Illusions are what kitsune do. Maybe I'm good for something after all?* Something made me wonder what Garcia would do or say in a situation like this.

"Selena, get them out of here!" Frank ground out each word through a set of gritted teeth. Ethan bent down and scooped up Astrid into his arms. Selena tugged on my arm. No way was I missing out on the party. If Frank needed any help I was determined to back him up.

"Go on without me. I am covering for Frank."

Selena bit her lip. "Are you sure?"

I set my jaw and nodded as Ethan carried Astrid away.

"Absolutely. If you find any teachers send them our way."

Selena nodded and ran off after Ethan. Olivia's brutal strength began to diminish. Her face took on a less angular appearance. Most importantly her frosty eyes faded into their normal misty blue haze. Her body trembled, glistening with cold sweat. Feebly she twitched under Frank's iron grip.

"Frank. Back off." I said.

His stormy eyes watched me warily.

"No." Tufts of black hair fell into his chiseled face.

"I said back off. She's not a threat anymore." I replied, my tone level.

"What makes you so sure?" Frank asked as he continued to maintain his grip.

He pressed his lips tightly together, eyes cold as flint.

"Because you are hurting her."

Olivia took shallow breaths. Seconds ago she was a raging like a lion and now she laid beneath Frank like a brittle leaf. All the strength had leaked out of her. Her hair fell in wet ringlets across her pale face. High cheekbones took on a gaunt appearance. The pack magic must have pushed her to the edge. Her need to protect her alpha had pressed her to the breaking point but what would have caused her to lose control?

Jordan's magic should have helped subdue her. Had someone slipped something in her drink? Was that why she hadn't responded to any of the Omega's cues? It was the Omega's job to soothe members of the pack. The pack magic gave him that advantage, so why hadn't it worked? There was a commotion in the back.

Teachers began splitting up the crowd.

"That's enough. Alright. Alright, back it up!"

Frank rose and dusted off his tuxedo. The smell of oil and steel tickled my nostrils as business shoes scuffed against speckled linoleum.

Figures, I should have known. If any assistance were to come it would have came late. Reluctantly, the crowd parted for Mr. Lemmings as he approached. The rustling crowd grew silent.

"Everything ok here, Frank?" Mr. Lemmings asked as he raised a bushy brow.

His brown eyes scanned the room, taking in our surroundings.

Frank's mouth tightened. "Yes sir."

Mr. Lemmings tilted his head as he took in Olivia's appearance. His expression remained curious and mildly perplexed.

"I seem to think otherwise. Don't you Miss Adams?"

My heart stopped. I froze.

"Frank here was helping Olivia calm down. You know good old high school drama."

I jittered with laughter and flashed him a winning smile.

Lemmings frowned. His face hardened.

"The security footage seems to say otherwise Miss Adams. I'll take it from here. Mr. Marino and Miss Gaines you are coming with me."

I cringed. His tone was not diplomatic. Without another word Lemmings swiveled on his heel and left. Frank and I exchanged wary glances. We all knew what really happened. Someone or something had pushed Olivia to her a raging point. What that was we did not know, but I intended to find out. Regardless, Lemmings wouldn't have taken what we would have said into consideration anyway.

Frank pulled Olivia up to her feet but she wilted against his chest like a flower on a hot summer day. Her knees buckled with each step. My stomach twisted with disgust. If anyone could win an award for the being the biggest drama queen it'd be her. Earlier her aura blazed out of control. She even had the strength of ten men. Now it flickered faintly like a dying flame. Could she have been crashing from a significant high? Sure her life force had been weakened significantly but surely she could still walk on her own? *Couldn't she?* Or had she spent all her energy on her fit? She did almost shift into her wolf after all. I frowned.

What in the world had set her off earlier anyhow? Could the history between her and Astrid been so sour that it would provoke her to chance a transformation in public? If so, what had happened between them that made their relationship go bad anyway? What had made her so angry that Olivia would lose control over her wolf? I knew many werewolves were temperamental by nature and angered easily. I have even heard stories about people losing control of their wolf but I hadn't actually seen it until now. I flipped my cell phone open and put Garcia on speed dial.

"Hello?" Garcia replied, her voice sharp as a whip.

"We got a problem." I briefly explained what had happened. Silence ensued. I held my breath for what seemed like hours. *Wasn't she going to say something?* Several different scenarios rolled through the back of my head. I checked the phone and placed it back to my ear.

"Hello?"

"I'll be there in five." Her voice came out forebodingly crisp.

Then there was a click.

CHAPTER 12

THE NEXT DAY Frank didn't come to school, nor did Olivia. Truth was they both had received a suspension. However, rumor has it they both had been hospitalized. Gossip about the fight on Saturday had spread across campus like wildfire. Naturally, it had blown up to epic proportions. Thankfully no one had mentioned how Olivia's eyes shifted from the color of a blue summer sky to a frosted lake. The glacial gaze she gave me that night still sent shivers down my spine. Nor did they happen to notice the shift in her facial structure from human to wolf. If that had been the case I am sure Garcia would have had our heads by now.

Astrid and I sat next to each other in the lunchroom. She wore bandages on her arms to hide what should have been superficial scratches from Olivia. None of the humans needed to know that she healed at an exponential rate.

"I am telling you she is not human!" Astrid said in a hushed whisper.

I snorted. "No shit Sherlock."

I glanced both ways before leaning in.

"Why didn't you go all demon lady on her ass?"

Astrid glared at me, her amber eyes were liquid lava.

"And get exposed? Are you insane?"

I rolled my eyes and ripped off the head of a dinosaur chicken nugget with my teeth. "It would have been better than being Miss Kitty's scratching post." I grumbled sourly.

"Look, I tried to calm her with my pheromones but she wouldn't take it. I am telling you she isn't human. It was like an animal had taken over her brain."

I cast her a dull eyed stare. Astrid was right, Liv wasn't human but it was not my place to say. I too had my own secrets. Besides, Astrid was a smart cookie. She'd eventually find out on her own.

"I don't suppose spitting in her face was part of your pheromone ritual?" I replied mildly.

Astrid's lip quirked with mild amusement.

I raised my brows, unamused. It was a look I had inherited from my father. One quite similar to the one he gave me when I tried to bull shit my way through something. She hid a smile behind the milk carton as she drank. Moments later she smacked her lips in satisfaction before crinkling the cardboard in her hand.

"No, but I am sure she deserved it." She replied, her eyes glittered with laughter.

She tossed the refuse onto her lunch tray.

I frowned. Something nagged at me from before.

"What happened between you two that would make her risk going furry in public?" Astrid cast me a sideways glance and opened her mouth to speak. Before she could finish Ethan plopped down next to me. Takahashi slipped in next to him.

He flashed me a cheerful smile. "Good morning ladies!"

Ethan took my chin tenderly within his calloused hand, paying no heed to the fact that he was interrupting a private conversation, and inspected my face with great care. I tried to break free but Ethan let out a low growl.

"Lemme see." He rumbled.

I froze for half a second.

"What happened Saturday night Lex? You were bleeding."

I averted my eyes and tried to look away. His emerald gaze held mine.

"It was nothing." I mumbled.

Ethan continued to stare at me, unfazed. His forest green eyes were clouded with deep thought. "We have been friends for a quite a bit of time. If you think you can lie to me then you got another thing coming."

"Maybe she tripped and fell?" Takahashi chuckled at his own joke.

I was not the most graceful person in our group, I'll give him that.

Ethan gave him a glare, obviously unamused.

Jordan cleared his throat.

"Or not." He replied submissively before taking great interest in his carton of chocolate milk. My relationship with the wolves has improved significantly ever since Ethan stepped up as alpha. However, boundaries were still being drawn and Ethan made it clear that my well-being was not something to joke around about.

"Don't lie to me Lex." Ethan pressed.

I fiddled with my flimsy spork. Suddenly beheading dinosaur chicken nuggets didn't sound so appetizing anymore. "Look, I took on a bit more than I could chew. I haven't really mastered mass illusions and Saturday had called for that."

There was a pause at our table.

A few moments later Hawk Eyes stalked up and slammed her tray on the table.

"Out with it." She snapped at all of us. Her hawkish brown eyes pierced through me specifically. I gaped at her. The rest of the gang exchanged bewildered glances. She threw her hands up into the air. "What are you people, some sort of demon spawn?" She growled in exasperation.

The accusation made my heart twist. My mouth went desert dry. *Demon spawn?* Each word punched a hole in my chest. I knew it was coming sooner or later but I didn't think so soon. Regardless, I wasn't ready. I didn't think the words would hurt, especially from *Miss Little Know It All*, but it did. I figured she of all people would respect me for what I am. Little did I know that she would despise me for what I was instead. Astrid shot to her feet. She began to say something but Hawk Eyes cut her off with the wave of her hand.

"Please don't treat me like I am stupid. I need to know the truth. I am your friend and you owe me that much."

The environment at our lunch table grew still.

"What the hell is wrong with you?" I sputtered.

She stabbed a finger at me. "What the hell is wrong with me? Nothing is wrong with me. To hell with you, Lexi. You are the one who is not human. How dare you play me for a fool, especially after calling me a friend? I saw you Lexi. You stopped time."

She turned and began jabbing a finger at Astrid.

"And you! Don't get me started on you. Olivia had torn you to pieces and today you come to school without a scratch on you! Normal people would flinch when someone bumps their wounded arm in the hallway but not you! And you have the audacity to try to cover up what is going on? Do you realize there was another mauling this weekend? Did you even have a clue? Things are happening at Ferndale Hills and I want the truth damn it and I want it now."

We all sat in silence and stared at her.

Ethan fumbled with a wrapper.

Jordan traced an index finger along the logo on his milk carton.

Astrid pursed her lips.

I tried to speak but nothing came out. My mouth remained dry as cotton.

The air crackled with tension.

Astrid licked her lips and looked away.

Ethan's gaze fell to the floor.

Hawk Eyes threw her hands up into the air.

"Fine!" She said venomously and snatched her tray up. "If you want to be that way then fine." In seconds she stalked away.

The rest of the day dragged on like a snail on a hot summer day. English class was especially boring. Miss Mulder cleared her throat and did her best to grab her student's attention. In the meantime, I watched the leaves dance and twirl outside. Autumn had painted the trees with the colors of fire. Hot sun kissed my cheeks as it filtered through the classroom windows. Fall was such a fickle thing. One day hot, another cold. I pondered upon the meaning of it all. Everything around me was dying. How could death be so beautiful yet so tragic? Speaking of death, Hawk Eyes the murderer of friendships came crashing through the classroom doors. I scooched further down into my chair. Maybe if I slouched she wouldn't find me. It was worth a try right? They say if you make yourself appear smaller people are less likely to notice you.

Silently, she stormed up to her assigned seat, which happened to be next to mine. *Yay me*, I thought bitterly to myself as she plopped down into her seat. She trained her stone-eyed glare on the whiteboard ahead. The air around her crackled with tension. My stomach flip flopped and twisted like a ball of snakes. Should I say something? If so, what would I say?

Oh by the way I am a fox demon, Ethan's a werewolf and Astrid is a succubus. Oh and don't forget Frank, who happens to be your boyfriend, is a vampire but don't worry he's a vegetarian so everything's going to be ok. However he, Ethan and I belong to a coven which happens to be ran by a crazed vampire lady named Carmen Garcia. Who by the way has extremely expensive taste and has a tendency to throw things, mainly people. Oh and if I were to tell you I was a kitsune the crazy said vampire lady would probably take my head.

No biggie right? Psh. Let's be honest, she'd probably wonder which crazy crackers I was eating.

Regardless, I had to try to mend the situation between us. Hawk Eyes happened to be one of my friends and lately those were hard to come by among the human race. An awkward silence had spread between us. Usually she'd update me on the latest gossip or she'd brainstorm how we could make the homecoming incident newsworthy. Obviously that wasn't going to happen. I hardly doubted that any of that would have gone well anyway. The inside of my mouth turned into sand as I thought of things to say. I licked at my dry lips only to come up with the lamest topic imaginable.

"So the weather is nice isn't it?"

Yep. Leave it to me, the weather lady, to try to salvage an extremely awkward conversation. I mean seriously, the weather? *What was I thinking?* I waited to see if Hawk Eyes would send some of her own storm clouds my way. A nervous titter threatened to crawl out of my throat. She gave me a stiff nod. I glanced at Astrid, desperately waiting for some sort of assistance. *Was she just going to leave me hanging?* Her amber eyes locked with mine. I held my breath. *Any day now Astrid, any day.* She opened her mouth. My heart leapt.

She was going to back me up after all.

Her expression softened.

"Lexi, love. I think you need to give Selena some more time."

I face planted into the table and let out a miserable groan.

A sheet of flaming hot chagrin blazed across my cheeks. *So much for I got your back.* I thought bitterly to myself. Girls in this realm are so damn fickle. Quickly, I averted my gaze towards the scenery outside. I'd do anything to keep them from witnessing me blushing. *What in the world was I thinking anyway?* Astrid was never the type to go in guns blazing. She always favored subtle craft and perfect timing over impulsive decisions. These were two things I didn't have. I just had to keep pushing. I just couldn't leave well enough alone, now could I? No, I had to get answers.

"Playing the silent treatment eh? What are we now, two? Can't we have a civilized conversation like two normal human beings?"

I watched Hawk Eyes's jaw tighten out of the corner of my eyes.

Her pen faltered for a brief moment.

I smiled smugly to myself. "Not so tough now after all now are we?"

Quickly she regained her composure as she continued to grind words into her planner. Her expression remained cool and aloft.

"Normal human beings don't stop time and civilized people do not lie to those they claim to be friends."

Groaning, I let out an exasperated sigh. "Oh come off of it already."

Miss Mulder cleared her throat and clapped three times. Everyone went silent. Some watched us, waiting to see if we would ignore Miss Mulder's cue. I sulked silently in my corner while Astrid doodled in her notebook. Hawk Eyes continued to carve words into her planner with her pen.

Something outside caught my eye. It was a man and a woman. They were arguing in the parking lot. Both wore a white lab coat that hung down to their calves. She was upset about something. The wind rustled through her black hair. The faint smell of tea tree oil shampoo drifted upon the autumn breeze. He wore a strong cologne. She threw her hands up into the air before stalking towards the white van. He said something and she muttered something under her breath before yanking the passenger door open. She hopped into right hand side of the vehicle and slammed the door shut. Miss Mulder pressed on.

"By next week you should be studying the Salem Witch trials with Mrs. Patterson. And since Halloween is coming up soon I thought it'd be fitting to begin our unit on The Crucible. The Crucible also happens to be about the Salem witch trials. We will end this unit just before Thanksgiving break. I figured it'd be perfect since the Puritan culture also plays a significant role in both the Thanksgiving feast and within the Salem witch trials. Now let's get into your presentation groups. Presentations will begin on Thursday and will end on Friday. I have put a time slot up on the board and you are free to sign up at your leisure."

The students bustled with conversation as they scooted out from their chairs and began to seek out their team members.

I turned to Hawk Eyes and Astrid.

"Isn't it great that we will be learning about magic?" I asked.

Hawk Eyes scowled and ripped a piece of paper from her notebook.

"We won't be learning anything about magic." She grumbled as she crinkled the page violently between her fingertips. "We will be force fed our nation's biased opinions about magical users. It won't even scratch the surface of magical history."

Oh God, sure enough here comes out Miss Little Know It All. I rolled my eyes. I'm surprised they haven't rolled out of my head by now at the rate it was going. Figures, she'd skip out on a civilized conversation but will only speak if she can spew out useless facts as an alternative. Useless facts or not it was still an opportunity to fill in the awkward silence between us. I couldn't pass this up so I swallowed my pride and took the bait.

"And how would you know about magical history anyway?"

Her fierce eyes met mine. "Because I am a witch."

Without another word she snatched her things and stalked off. My fox tail bristled beneath my human guise and snapped back and forth with agitation.

Astrid merely blinked in surprise.

"What the hell?" I growled through gritted teeth. "She has the gall to yell at us for not telling her what we are but she just now comes clean about being a witch?" My blood boiled hot inside my veins. "Isn't that a bit backwards?"

Astrid watched Selena warily. She was slow to reply.

"Mm, we will just need to keep an eye on that one now won't we?" She mused aloud.

Her facial expression remained calm as a tranquil lake on a quiet summer's night. The hairs on the back of my neck prickled with rage.

"How can you just stand there cool as a cucumber? Doesn't this bother you?" I sputtered with bewilderment.

Astrid adjusted her winged spectacles before looking back at me. "Could that have been the reason why she knows you stopped time? Because she is a witch?"

I paused. Confusion fuzzed the edges of my rage.

I hated it when people answered a question with a question. *Why couldn't people just talk normal to one another? What was so hard about having a one on one conversation with another person? Why did everything have to be so damn cryptic?* Then again, could that have been the reason why Hawk Eyes knew I stopped time?

I pondered this.

"I mean, is that even possible?" Astrid continued, wondering aloud.

I shrugged my shoulders. Uncertainty uncoiled within my belly, filling me with doubt.

"I suppose so. I mean, it would make sense. I hadn't mastered the time stopping technique so its elusive qualities could have easily been witnessed by another magic user."

Astrid frowned and rubbed her chin. She paused. A parade of thoughts danced behind her eyes. Suddenly she changed the topic, giving me the verbal cue that we would discuss this topic later, somewhere more private.

"Want to stay after school and watch the boys practice for their last game?"

"Um, sure I don't see why not?" I replied, a bit thrown off but the change in tactics.

However, as of right now I'd do almost anything to get in a distraction from what had just happened.

CHAPTER 13

ASTRID and I leaned our backs against the bleachers. Together we watched the boys scramble around on the football field. It was an Indian summer. The crisp October air tickled our hair but the afternoon sun kissed our cheeks with heat.

"I am going to miss the warm weather" I said wistfully.

Astrid nodded absently "Yeah me too."

Her amber eyes were locked on Ethan.

A moment of silence drifted between us. "Lexi?"

I opened one curious eye and peered at her. "Yeah?"

She watched Ethan with a distant expression.

"How long have you known Ethan?"

I too watched him. Buzz tripped and fell. Ethan paused and offered him a helping hand. Effortlessly he pulled him up and they continued their drills.

"Well we were practically littermates. What do you wanna know?"

A faint smile flickered across her lips. "Everything."

Her sweetening scent had peaked my interest. *Did Astrid have a thing for Ethan? If so, for how long?* I looked back at Ethan. The boy I had grown up with had grown. His once scrawny legs were now built with muscle. Baby fat had thinned out to reveal an angular face. His soft green eyes had grown sharper, more keen and aware. *Was there something worth looking into?* A vision of Ethan taking Buzz down appeared in my head. Fingers of warmth tickled my stomach.

Huizenga's shouting jolted me back into the present. His voice echoed across the stadium. I leaned back against the cold bleachers and gathered my thoughts. Puffy white clouds floated across an azure sky. For a brief moment I studied the horizon, only to see off in the distance a group of boisterous geese flapping their way towards the south.

"Well, he enjoys fishing, hunting, wrestling and horse play. However, do not be mistaken by his appearance. He may look young but he is old, very old. Centuries in fact." I tilted my head back and watched the puffs of clouds drift by. "In Gaia the wolves don't age as quickly as they do here. Also, when a werewolf shifts on a normal basis he tends to age much slower than his human counterparts. Regardless, we grew up together under the same roof just outside of a human village on Mount Kyoto. He is both a brother of mine and a loyal friend." I closed my eyes. A small smile pulled at the corner of my lips. "He is well known for being kind, funny and hard headed. He is slow to anger compared to most wolves but I think that his best trait will always be his loyalty. He may come off all tough but that's not necessarily the case. He's actually pretty sensitive. In the end he is a great friend."

A chuckle tickled the back of my throat.

"One time he played a prank on my betrothed. The asshole had insulted my mother. I was so enraged I could barely contain myself. So in the middle of the night Ethan helped me sneak fleas into his bed. The poor bastard couldn't stop itching for days!"

Astrid watched me, her amber eyes danced with curiosity

"What did your mother say when she found out?"

I stiffened. I wasn't expecting her to ask me that. The question itself had startled me. Each word cut into me like a hot knife. Everyone knew, well, everyone on Mount Kyotom but we weren't on Mount Kyoto anymore. I looked away, hoping she couldn't see the emptiness in my eyes. "She never did."

My mother had died giving birth to me but Astrid didn't need to know that. Not now. I knew she hadn't intended any harm. Nor did I want her to feel bad for asking. Silently, I picked at a piece of lint on my clothes and looked up to see her watching me with concern. *Had my voice cracked? Or did my aura shift in color?* Understanding had dawned on her face.

"I won't get to meet your mother, will I?"

It was more of a statement then a question.

I flashed her a weak smile and shook my head no.

Her amber eyes burned with an intensity.

"I am sorry. I didn't know." She said in a hushed whisper.

I shrugged. "Don't worry about it. I've learned to cope."

Astrid bit her lip and rolled a pebble between her fingers. "And Ethan's family?"

I twirled the string of lint between my fingertips.

"Pa had told me his parents had a heart of gold but in all honestly I don't know. I never had the honor of meeting his family. They died in the war." My voice drifted off as I watched the boys do their drills. Astrid remained respectfully silent. Her gaze fixed itself on the football field. There was a long pause before she spoke again.

"You want to go back home don't you?"

I nodded my head. "Of course."

"How do you suppose you'll get there?"

"I was hoping Garcia would help us find a rift after we win over the werewolves and get to the root of all these local disappearances."

Slowly, she kicked her feet back and forth. A pensive expression stole across her freckled face. "Do you think he'll be able to win over the other wolves? You know, the ones who stood by Drew?"

A sigh escaped my lips. "Who knows? All I know is that his love runs deep. He is as gentle as any werewolf comes but he does not tolerate hate and stands for what he believes in. He is extremely protective over the ones he cares for. He also has a tendency to be very inclusive. Most importantly, he knows that respect is earned, not given. I think all of these attributes will give him an edge over Andrew. I guess we'll just have to see."

I popped a piece of popcorn in my mouth and chewed.

There was a pregnant pause.

"Lexi?"

I turned to look at Astrid.

"Do you love Ethan?"

I gagged on a kernel and barked out a laugh.

"Excuse me?" I sputtered, completely stupefied.

"Absolutely not! I mean come on!" I scrambled for answers. "I practically consider him my sibling!" Quickly, I looked away so she couldn't witness me blushing. I mean sure I found him attractive. I have considered the possibilities. However, if I were to mention any of these things then Astrid would have been crestfallen. A look of relief washed over her face. Huizenga blew his whistle.

"Oh look, what do you know, practice must be over. Let's go see what they're up to." Instantly, I hopped off the bleacher and took my chance to escape. The guys were stripping off their gear as we approached. Some of them guzzled from their water bottles while others dumped water over their heads. Astrid and I watched with great appreciation.

"I still can't believe the last game is next week." Zach announced.

Ethan tousled his wet hair with a dry towel. When he did the muscles around his shoulders rippled. I quickly averted my gaze. Heat surged into my cheeks.

"I wouldn't worry too much about it Zach. We'll do fine as long as we work as a team. Speakin' of which, hey Drew come on over and get some of this purple Gatorade. It tastes great!"

Buzz made it a point to sit alone.

Was he still sulking from something that happened months ago?

Ethan flashed a friendly smile at his sulky team mate.

"Nah, I'm fine, thanks." Buzz replied curtly.

How charming. I thought to myself.

Ethan had tried including Buzz, regardless of what has happened in the past.

Zander simply stretched and rolled his eyes.

"Oh please don't tell me you still have a stick up yer ass about what happened between you and Ethan earlier?" He spoke in a thick Australian accent. "Seriously mate. Why do yeh still got yer balls in a knot anyway? That happened in August. It's been a whole month and a half. Quit yer bloody sulkin' and come join us. If you didn't look it I swear I'd mistake yeh for some gurl."

Buzz bristled like an enraged cat. "Why you.."

Brad, a burly gentleman with a mess of brown hair and Jared, his corn rolled counterpart both stepped in to assist the boys from hurting themselves.

Brad gave me an apologetic smile as helped separate the two.

"Alright you two break it up." Jared announced.

"Honestly the both of you are bickering like a bunch of girls in heat." Brad added.

"Yeah, we only have one more game so pull it together!" Jared finished as he peeled the two apart.

Leave it to the linemen to try to break up the fights between the boys.

Ethan clapped them both on the back with pride.

"They have a point gentlemen. We need to make sure we're working together. I want no fighting boys. We are on a team and Andrew is a part of this team as much as you are Zander. We are a pack. It's time we start actin' like it eh? Drew will come on his own time. All I ask is you give him time. Understand?"

Ethan eyed Zander carefully as if silently challenging him to speak.

Andrew simply sulked.

Zander on the other hand, locked gazes with his alpha. A moment of tension passed between them. Ethan's eyes blazed with finality. *Was Zander seriously going to brawl with Ethan right here and now on the school premise?*

Jordan, the omega of the group, simply closed his eyes and let his magic take hold.

Eventually, Zander relaxed and looked away.

He grumbled something foul beneath his breath.

Zach clapped his twin brother on the back and gave him a toothy grin.

"Hey now, ya know we'd do the same thing for you big guy."

Zander shrugged his shoulder away from his fraternal twin.

"Yeah, yeah I know."

Jordan wiped the sweat off of his face with a towel. He was small but quick as a whip. Sweat lathered his hair making the thin black strands stick up every which way. "So, we still on for tomorrow night?"

Jared, formerly known as the giant, itched at a spot between one of his black cornrows. The makeshift jersey stretched thinly across his barreled torso.

"Sorry, I have to look at a college tomorrow. You know, being a senior and all." He replied, his tone was laced with disappointment.

Ethan flashed him an apologetic smile.

"No biggie Jared. We'll keep you informed on what's goin' on. Anyway, great job today you guys. I gotta head out. A friend is picking' me up from practice and I gotta go get some stuff from my locker." He exchanged a few five highs and headed our way.

"Put a shirt on now would you?" I hissed with heated cheeks.

Lean muscles rippled once again as he lifted the gym strap over his head.

He waved me away.

"I will, you prude, once I get to the school. Astrid you don't mind do you?"

Astrid tilted her head and watched with great appreciation.

"No, no, not at all. You take as long as you like." She replied with a wicked grin.

Embarrassed, I dragged a hand down my face.

Together we hiked up the hill towards the school.

"So what's happening tomorrow?" I probed, eager to change the subject.

He let out a frustrated sigh as he raked a flustered hand through his wet hair.

"The full moon is coming up. We gotta find a place to stay that night, and soon."

I arched a brow at him.

"Why not use the woods in your backyard?" Astrid suggested.

I cringed at the very idea of having a pack of werewolves running around wild in our backyard. The other half of me wondered what Garcia would say. I could only imagine the look on her face when Ethan brought the idea to her attention. What would she throw next?

Ethan bit his lip. "You think Garcia's gunna take well to that suggestion?"

"It's their land after all. Besides, if Carmen wants to mend the relationship between the wolves and vampires then she will do whatever it takes. She's already taken you under her wing in order to prove that she's serious about the well-being of the werewolves. Using vampire land as a safe haven for wolves during the full moon would be the perfect olive branch."

Ethan tapped his chin thoughtfully.

"You know, I think you're onto something'. I've been searching for a chance to bond with the pack. Things have been shaky after the whole ordeal with Andrew and all. A moonlight run through the woods on Saturday night would be a perfect opportunity. We need something private. Somewhere that we can hunt without causing' any trouble."

We stopped short to see Olivia standing at the top of the stairwell. She froze mid step when her blue eyes met Astrid's. She clutched her paperwork tightly against her chest. Astrid stepped forward and shifted her weight. Her pink aura rippled with red irritation.

"Good afternoon, Liv. Fancy seeing you here when no one else is around."

Olivia's jaw dropped.

A smug smile cured at the corner of Astrid's scarlet lips.

"Your face, your body." She stammered.

"There are no scratches. Thank God you are healed but how?" She paused and her blue eyes widened like saucers. She brought a shaky hand to her gaping mouth. "You didn't receive the taint did you? Please don't tell me you have received the taint."

Panic oozed from her pores. My heart ached for Liv, I could only imagine what was going on inside her head. Benson recently informed me that passing the taint to a human without their consent is against werewolf law. She also mentioned that a mere pack member couldn't legally transfer the taint even if the human wanted her to. To do so would be considered a felony. Such actions would result in severe punishment and maybe possibly death. Only clan heads were given the legal right to transform humans into wolves.

Even so, there is a lengthy process. It was no longer simply a bite.

In fact, all interested parties would have to take an assessment to see if becoming a wolf is a good fit. If not they would be declined the opportunity and compelled to forget about the werewolf community. That's where the vampires came in handy. After approval the human would then have to arrange a meeting with a clan head to go over the conditions and expectations of becoming a pack member. During that meeting the human would be counseled on the risks of becoming a wolf. Even then the clan head has to get approval and support from the national werewolf board before beginning the ceremony. Besides, most of the people who sign up don't make it through the first full moon without dying. Now according to Benson there were cases like Ethan where the humans are born with the wolf gene. In these circumstances the children are mentored at a young age on how to control their wolf.

Confusion twisted Olivia's face as she babbled incoherently.

"I didn't mean to-" Astrid cut her off with a wave of her hand.

"You know I never got the chance to return the favor for Saturday night."

Her amber eyes glowed with glittering specks of gold.

"Your eyes" Olivia sputtered.

Astrid flashed her a sardonic smile.

"They are glowing gold." She stepped back. "You aren't a werewolf and you don't smell like a vamp. What are you?" There was a creaking and a series of snapping. Wind swirled around Astrid, whipping her hair around her face. The flesh between Astrid's shoulder blades separated and a pair of leathery wings broke through the back of her shirt. They stretched and flapped. Shreds of cotton fluttered to the floor. Power rippled off of Astrid in waves. Her muscles sharpened and became more defined. Her hair and the hem of her skirt fluttered softly to the beat of flapping wings. I reached out to touch them but Astrid slapped my hand away. Her golden eyes remained locked on Olivia. A long black tail slithered out from underneath her skirt. It hung low, flicking back and forth like an agitated cat. Her golden eyes glittered and a pair of small ram's horns protruded from her skull.

"Funny you should mention that." She bent her knees and shot up into the air with a flap of her leathery wings. "Because I am neither!" She shot towards Olivia. Her fingernails stretched, into sharp talons.

Sweet mother of Gaia. Astrid was going to kill Olivia right here and now. Where was the popcorn when I needed it?

"Was that hit worth it, Liv?" Astrid taunted as she dove in.

Olivia tensed. "I don't know what you mean.."

Astrid's eyes flashed with gold.

"Oh don't play coy with, Miss Gaines. We knew you took a hit."

"How did you…" Olivia sputtered.

"We could smell it on your breath.." Astrid continued.

When she meant we, she must have meant her and Frank.

"Liv, what does she mean by this?" Ethan asked, completely baffled.

"Your little *cheerleader.* Has been a *naughty* girl." Astrid hissed.

"I was only trying to ease up.." Liv began.

"Oh save it for the choir." Astrid snarled as she took a swipe.

Liv let out a feral scream and ducked.

Ethan shouted at the two of them. "No! Stop!"

He tossed his gym bag off to the side and sprinted after them.

"You just couldn't resist, could you?"

Astrid began as she twisted a hand.

"Just had to have it all, didn't you Liv?"

A gust of wind simply flung Ethan out of the way.

"You hate me that much, do you? Well, now here I am!" Astrid swiped Olivia across the chest with her steely talons. Her golden eyes blazed with rage.

"You always get what you want and you never have a care in the world!" Olivia screamed.

"You think it's easy being me, Liv?!" Astrid shouted back as she shredded through Olivia's things. Little bits of paper twirled to the floor.

I watched the whole ordeal in stunned silence.

"That's enough, both of you!" Ethan tried to break them apart.

Astrid swung again but Olivia slid to the left and pounced.

"Do you know how hard it is to keep up a front, to act like everything's ok?!" Olivia demanded as

she landed on Astrid's back and began ripping at her hair. She clung onto those horns for dear life like a bull rider clings to a bucking bull. "Do you even comprehend how hard it is to compete with you?!"

"Haven't you realized you got friends? You pompous little *bitch*?"

Astrid twisted and screamed as Olivia sank her fangs into one of her wings.

"You aren't alone, Olivia. Why can't you just see that?" Ethan began.

Olivia flew into a pillar and slid down into a crumpled heap. Astrid sauntered after her. Her heels clicked briskly against the polished floor. Each step echoed throughout the cafeteria. Blood trickled down her wing, lacerations on her face began to knit themselves together.

"You don't realize how much of a nuisance you are to me, do you. You may be top dog in your pack but to me you are nothing but a little fly. *Understand*? I will not stand for your incompetence any longer. I want to make one thing clear. The only reason I didn't fight back on Saturday was because it would have exposed myself and my friends."

"I am sorry.." Olivia began as she lay there in a crumpled heap.

"Sorry doesn't cut it, Liv. You lost control. You exposed yourself to the humans. Now they might know what you are. Not only that but you may have exposed Frank as well because he had to restrain you. You may even end up revealing Ethan and the rest of your pack. Regardless, I will not let you pull them further into this mess."

"But I love him and you were going to take him away!" Olivia shrieked.

Vehement hatred darkened Astrid's face.

"You don't know what love is!" She snarled back and twisted her hand

Flames sprouted from her palms and swirled around her fingertips.

"Astrid..." Ethan began.

"You are just some sniveling brat who does whatever it takes to get what she wants!"

Sweet Inari, Astrid was about to torch the place if she wasn't careful. How were we going to clean this up? Burnt schools aren't easy to hide. Senator Benson would have to pull a lot of strings if things got out of hand. Surely heads would topple. I imagined myself without a head and wondered what I'd look like. For a brief moment the image was amusing.Then it dawned on me that this could possibly become a reality if

Astrid wasn't careful. Icy dread washed down my spine. I sputtered into action.

"Astrid don't!"

I tried to grab her attention but she was inches from letting go. I sucked in a breath. Electricity trickled throughout my fingertips. Needles of pain shot through my body. I still hadn't recovered from Saturday's endeavor. Something told me that this was going to hurt. I gave the veil of time a good yank.

The veil of time around Astrid and Olivia thickened, making their movements seem as if they were moving through a pool of molasses. Seconds later, Ethan pushed his way in between them. Astrid came to a halt. I gasped in a sharp breath of air and released. Everything clicked back into real time, moving at a normal pace. I was left with a pounding headache.

Ethan puffed for air as he stood there between him with his arms extended. "Enough!" He shouted with outstretched arms. "Both of you need to stand down!" Astrid arched an eyebrow at Ethan and then burst with cynical laughter.

"You are commanding me to stand down? What am I your little pet dog?"

Fire crackled between her fingers.

Ethan huffed and puffed from the exertion.

"No but Olivia is one of *my* wolves and she is my responsibility." Ethan snarled.

The glacial blue eyes of Olivia's wolf glared belligerently at Astrid.

Ethan cast his glowering gaze Olivia's way and she flinched.

He jutted his chin in Olivia's general direction.

"If you kill her then you will create an even bigger mess for us to clean up. What the hell were you thinking exposing yourself like that in a public place? You're lucky you didn't break anything. Now get a hold of yourself!"

Astrid frowned. They glared at each other silently. Ethan didn't waver. His emerald eyes glowed with the gaze of his wolf and he stood his ground. I held my breath, waiting in anticipation to see what would happen next. Begrudgingly Astrid rolled her eyes. The fire between her fingers fizzled into nothing.

"Fine. Have it your way but she had it coming."

Her dragon wings snapped closed and folded themselves neatly along her spine. Her wings, horns and tail slowly disintegrated into ash and drifted away. Leaving tendrils of curling smoke in their place. A curtain of glossy black hair tumbled down her back, concealing the tears in her shirt. The glowing gold specks in her eyes flickered and faded to a honeyed brown.

Ethan bent down to offer Olivia a hand.

"Look, there's no need to try to tackle everything on your own Liv."

Olivia scrambled to pick her things up off of the floor. Shame shadowed her expression

Her eyes remained downcast.

"I am sorry." She mumbled. "I lost control on Saturday. I apologize for my behavior. It's just, I was so mad! Astrid always has a tendency to outdo me in everything. When she's around I don't seem to have a chance. I just want to belong. Then I saw her with you–" Pools of frustration welled up in her eyes. "I really wanted you to like me Ethan. I just wanted to feel like I belonged. Drew isn't that great of a person but at least with him I feel like I had a place in the pack. I was his mate, his alpha partner. I love him, really I do–" Her voice turned bitter. "But you don't feel the same way as I do, do you? I feel so torn. Please tell me you care for my well-being." She looked up at him. Her eyes glistened like blue sapphires in the rain.

Ethan frowned and chose his words carefully.

"Olivia. I do care for you and I will do whatever I can to support you.. but I want you to understand that this feeling only goes so far. I care that you were a part of the pack and I still do want you to participate in the pack. However, I need you to understand that I cannot care for you in the same way you care for me." He knelt down onto one knee and cupped her face. "What you are feeling is confusion. Two alpha males have switched places and you don't know where to turn. I can help you with that, yes but not as your mate." He looked into her eyes. Her watery gaze held his. "I am sorry that I agreed to go to the dance with you. I feel that it may have led you on. I need you to know that I care for you but I cannot love you the way you want me to. Nor can I accept your offer as a mate. I feel that you want to be with me more so because I have a position of power now and Andrew does not. That cannot be helped, it's a fact you're an alpha female and I have taken the alpha male's place. Your mind will heal with time. Regardless, my heart belongs to another and you are not her. If you can respect that then please join us. If not then I am going' to have to ask you to leave the pack."

He released her and rose to offer her a hand up off of the ground.

She sniffled and bit her lip.

"I-I gotta go." She stammered and quickly got up. "I can't be here right now."

In seconds she pushed through Ethan and ran down the stairs.

"She needs to held accountable for her actions." Astrid began.

"Now's not the time Astrid." Ethan warned.

"You are just going to let her get away with what she did?" Astrid pressed.

The hackles on my neck began to rise. The feral glare of Ethan's wolf peered through his emerald eyes.

"I will deal with it accordingly. When I see fit, Astrid."

He spun around on his heel and stalked off to his locker.

A sullen Astrid trailed behind.

I let out a breath of air. All tension seeped out of my shoulders.

"Well. That went well now didn't it?"

Ethan shot me a deadly glare. "Can it Lex. I don't want to hear anything from you."

"What? You're not seriously trying to blame this on me are you? How was I supposed to know Astrid was gunna go bat shit crazy?"

Astrid's amber eyes burned holes into my back.

Ethan banged his palm against the locker. It released under the pressure. His green eyes blazed with fury. "No that's not the problem. The problem is you just stood there! You didn't help, you didn't try to contain the situation. How am I gonna explain this to Garcia anyway? Oh by the way Benson's assistant had a tantrum and went demon child on a member of the local wolf pack? Do you realize what sort of position you've put me in, Astrid?"

Astrid's spine straightened and she lifted her chin.

"You can tell her that the bitch got what she deserved." She replied smugly.

Ethan rested his head against his locker in pure frustration. Rusty curls tumbled into his face.

"Why do you suppose she's so obsessed anyway?" I grumbled sourly.

"It's puppy love." Ethan mumbled against the cool metal. "When a new alpha takes over the other wolves have to adapt, each one does so differently. She is trying to bond but she is still so young and does not know how. She's mistaking the attractive pull of pack magic as love more so as a form of power."

Ethan let out another frustrated snarl and banged his forehead against the locker door. His hands curled into tight fists. "*Sweet Inari*, I should have seen it coming. Her need to protect, her desire to please. I should have known this would have happened. *Damn it!*"

"What on earth are you talking about?" I asked, purely perplexed by his behavior.

Astrid let out an aggregated sigh. "Don't you get it Lexi? He's an alpha now. Drew is not. Olivia was the alpha female, so naturally she'd be attracted to him."

I frowned and pursed my lips. "Yes that makes sense but wouldn't she know how to control herself by now? I mean she's in her teens."

"It doesn't work that way Lexi." Ethan replied with a growl. "Liv's been bitten. She has to be taught control."

Astrid let out a cynical snort. "The PCP didn't really help either. Lowered inhibitions and all."

"PCP?' I asked.

"You know, drugs?" Astrid replied with an arched brow.

"Why would she need drugs?" I inquired with a frown.

"Liv has been under alot of stress. She's the most popular girl in school. Her father's a nut job about her grades and she's a fucking werewolf for Christ sake. Why wouldn't she crave drugs?"

"Well that's not going to fly as long as I am in charge." Ethan slammed his locker shut and stormed down the hall.

Silently, we shuffled after him and stepped out into the cold October air.

Dusk painted the sky with deep purples and blues. The setting sun dipped deep into the horizon. Together we took a seat on an empty bench in front of the sparsely populated parking lot.

"Frank should be here any minute now." Ethan mumbled as he rubbed his neck.

Off in the distance I heard a muffled thud and a few bumps. The soft pounding came from a white van. Strange, the vehicle's make and model was similar to the one I saw earlier in our English class.

"Hey, you guys did you hear that?" I had asked.

Ethan lifted his head. "Hear what?"

I pointed towards the parking lot. "There's a thumping sound in the parking lot."

Their brows raised. *Figures, they'd think I had gone crazy even though I am the one who has the hearing of a fox.* Sure, Ethan had great hearing but his ability was diminished by his human form. The thumping sound continued.

Curiosity won me over. I inched my way over to the van. *What's the worse it could possibly be?* I had thought to myself. The clunking got louder. My heart skipped a beat. I inched closer. My hackles stood on end. I held my breath. My stomach flip flopped in anticipation. *What was it? Could it be a dog?*

I was fifty feet away, now twenty. The thumping stopped. I paused. My pulse pounded inside my head and my muscles stiffened. *What if the thing broke through the back doors of the van and attacked me?*

The headlights clicked on. I backed away from the blinding lights. The engine roared to life and the van pulled forward. The driver revved his engine. His speed increased but he didn't change in direction. *He was heading straight towards me!* Hot adrenaline coursed through my veins but I was frozen in place. Someone grabbed me by the arm and wrenched me away. It was Ethan. He smelled of pine trees and mint. Concern swam in the depths of his green eyes.

"You shouldn't stand in the middle of the street Lex. Are you okay?"

I closed my mouth and gave him a trembling nod.

Twenty minutes later the street lights clicked on. They filled the abandoned parking lot with their golden glow. If the crickets weren't killed off by the October frost I swear they'd be chirping right now. Astrid twirled a piece of hair between her fingers. Ethan fidgeted with his gym bag strap. I bounced my leg and glanced around. The parking lights buzzed in the background. One flickered on and off.

"This isn't like Frank. He's never late."

Ethan groaned as he dragged a hand across his face.

"I wonder what is taking him so long?" Astrid mused aloud.

"Should we call? I mean, it's getting late.." I suggested.

A few more moments passed before Ethan whipped out his cell.

"That's it. I'm giving him a call." Ethan grumbled sourly as he punched Frank's number into his phone. It rang once, twice, three times. Cold trails of uncertainty snaked up my spine. Usually Frank answers on the first ring if not then the second. Together we held our breath and hovered over the phone. The phone clicked.

"Frank?" Ethan asked.

There was a crash then a shout and then a scream.

"Frank? Frank is that you?"

Another crash answered. Something shattered. Muffled voices argued with each other.

"Frank? Are you ok?!" Astrid shouted into the receiver.

Scratchy noises replied and then a gruff voice that had answered the phone.

"Sorry, Frank can't come to the phone right now. He's a little busy."

There was a click then silence ensued. We all stared at the phone in shock. Ethan frantically dialed again but the phone went straight to voicemail. The sickly sweet scent of our fear hung in the air.

CHAPTER 14

I BREATHED a sigh of relief as I shuffled into the kitchen. Exhausted, I yanked open the fridge and grabbed a jar of blood before plopping onto the living room couch with a groan. Sure enough, Boots, our house cat, meowed incessantly as she pattered around the corner. *Damn cat*, I thought sourly to myself as she weaved in and out of my legs. I never really considered myself a morning person. Regardless, I only had a few minutes to myself before I had to pick up Ethan from practice. Bleary eyed, I popped the top off my mason jar and took a long sip from the bloody cocktail. I gave my lips a satisfied smack.

"It's been one of those nights Boots." I muttered miserably more so to myself then to the cat. I paused and bent down to scratch the base of her tailbone. Her spine rippled between my fingertips. They say animals can understand humans. Sometimes I wondered if that pertained to vampires too. I'd like to think so.

"You wouldn't believe who visited me in my dream last night. It was the one and only indecisive Mrs. Smith and her crotchety old husband Dan. This time she couldn't decide what burger she wanted or even if she wanted a burger in the first place. Then of all things she couldn't decide how she wanted it cooked and when I cooked it her ass of a husband had accused me of cooking it wrong. We literally had a ten minute argument on how to cook a cow!"

Boots let out an indignant meow as she slammed her forehead against the side of my calf. I muttered some indecent things beneath my breath. I was utterly perturbed.

"I may be a vampire but damn it all I know how to fry a wretched hamburger. I am a few centuries old after all. One would assume that I have obtained the ability to cook, wouldn't they?"

Boots coiled herself around my leg.

I let out a disgusted snort and shook my head.

"Humans. They can be such fickle creatures. A little black around the edges hasn't hurt anyone, now has it?"

I took another swig from the Mason jar. Something rustled outside. I frowned, with a pop of air I was at the bay windows. There was no need to hide what I was within my own quarters. I was in one of the coven's house after all. In fact, we were in a community filled with supernatural creatures. I wiggled a finger through the venetian blinds and peered around with a careful eye. Some would say I have an eclectic sense of paranoia. However, I have hypothesized that one can never be too careful in the modern age. Humans tend to be nosey creatures and to make matters worse many of them had access to advanced technology. I frowned. Nothing was there. Crisp October air whistled through the barren trees but nothing seemed out of place. I took a peek beneath the veranda. *Still nothing.* Maybe it was the dry leaves scuttling across the walkway?

A canister crashed through the kitchen window and landed on the floor with a solid clunk. Shards of glass tinkled across the tile. Another scowl tugged at the corner of my lips. Well that was odd. I followed the hissing sound. Within seconds I made it to the doorway only to witness what appeared to be a swiveling can of tear gas. *Who in their right mind would own tear gas in a community like this?*

Then it hit me. *Could it be the police? Did they know what I was?* Surely, the locals had thought I was weird but Lexi, Ethan and Astrid had had been careful not to reveal my true identity to the public. None of the humans that reside in this town should even know that vampires exist. Cold sweat prickled at the nape of my neck. I frowned at the swiveling canister of smoke

If someone had thrown it into the kitchen then I could easily throw it out, right? The possibility was quite likely. I bent down to retrieve the spinning can but the deadly white gas blistered my skin. I hissed in agony and withdrew my hand. I stared at the thing as if it were a venomous snake. *What sort of contraption would cause such a thing?* Something else crashed through my living room window and landed on the wooden floor with a hiss.

"*Seven hells.*" I muttered dubiously beneath my breath.

I could have sworn tear gas didn't blister the skin.

The air around me grew heavy. I leaned back and took a peek.

Sure enough, a second canister swiveled around in a circle, spewing gas every which way it went. An acidic vapor crept along the hardwood living room floor, as it's smoky fingers sought out its prey. The white smog engulfed me, filling my lungs with flame. Blood leaked from my tear ducts and left my eyes as dry as desert sand. Molten blisters sprouted along my skin. The fog seared my vision, making it hard to see. *What sort of concoction would do such a thing?* Frustrated, I let out a blood curdling scream. My fangs snicked into place and deadly talons extended from my fingertips.

A cacophony of noises took place all around me as I cradled my face within my trembling fists. Someone had kicked in my front door, while another shouted orders from the kitchen.

"Subject D is on the move!" Someone shouted.

"The silver nitrate isn't holding him down." A woman replied.

"Surround the perimeter!" A man urged.

"Go, go, go! Don't let him get away!" The voice was indecipherable. They were all around me, now. The images of their bodies spun around the room. I stumbled towards front door, my muscles moved like jelly, but a man stood in my way. He had appeared from the smoldering mist. I couldn't make out his face. Details were fading in and out of the foggy haze. Despite my snarl, he refused to move. So, I threw him across the room. His body crashed against the wall then landed with a thud.

The copper undertones of blood stirred the beast within. The desire to feed burned through my veins. I tried to make a run for the back door but a woman met me halfway. She had raven black hair that flowed to her hips. She held a firearm within her quivering hands. She commanded me to stand down, but I couldn't speak. My mouth watered at the sight of her pulsating neck. Sickly sweet fear oozed off her in droplets of sweat. I licked my lips. Her white skin smelled like honeyed milk. The beast within me screamed for a sip. It would only be a tiny taste. I was healing at an unnaturally slow rate… besides all we'd need is one drop. One drop wouldn't hurt. I swallowed. It took every ounce of willpower to keep the beast at bay.

Meanwhile, the smoldering mist enveloped me with her deadly embrace. My flesh was smoldering and blowing off in flakes. The desire to feed coursed through me, making it hard to think. I did not hear the gunfire but my vision went white from the pain. A silver bullet ripped through my chest.

In a matter of moments I had her throbbing pulse between my teeth. I bit down and drank deep. Hot blood gushed into my mouth. She let out a frightened scream. The firearm landed on the ground with a solid clunk. The beast within me shivered with delight. I cursed myself for being so weak. *Come now Frank, you couldn't contain yourself? A little gas here and a gun shot there never hurt anybody.* Animal blood should have sufficed but it couldn't compare to the divine nectar of human life. The fear of death had overcome me. My beast purred while everyone shouted in a frenzy. "He's not going down!"

Ashamed, I tore at her neck. I had lost myself within the lust for blood. Meanwhile, her life force vibrated through me. Her flailing arms grew feeble beneath my grip iron. Time had stilled, muscles and flesh began to knit. The gas smoldered every piece of skin it had kissed. Then something pricked between my shoulder blades, my neck and then my calf. I let out a savage hiss.

Searing pain sprouted within my back and spread through my veins like molten lava through a dry forest. I was in a state of delirium. Dazzled, I plucked a feathered dart from my jugular and rolled its needled tip between my fingertips. Dazed, I swayed. The room began to spin. A lab coat shoved his way between me and the ones with weapons.

"No! Stop, or you'll end up killing the specimen!"

He stood there, arms wide open.

I turned, my mouth opened. I tried to scream but nothing came. The woman's limp body fell to the floor with a sickening thud. Tears of regret trickled down my cheek. The room around me spun. I worked my lips but nothing came out. I stumbled forward. Everyone tensed but my muscles buckled beneath my weight. Down, I fell in a crumpled heap.

Needles of fright stabbed into me. *What was happening to me? Why couldn't I move? Why weren't my muscles cooperating? Why couldn't I coordinate?* The human's blood should have healed me. The beast within me snarled with rage. Full flight or fight mode was kicking in on pure instinct. My breath came out in shallow pants. I had forgotten I didn't need to breathe. Waves of panic washed over me. *Can't move... can't.. can't move. Why..where..*My vision tunneled. Then everything went black.

"We need to get him out of here before anyone sees."

"But what about Martha?" One of the others asked.

"She's as a good as dead if you ask me."

"Are you crazy? We' can't just leave her here."

"We can and we will. We got what we came for didn't we? Now it's not our fault Martha got in the vamp's way. The boss told us to grab the specimen and leave without being seen. We've done that now it's time to go. Now help me get him into the van."

Someone gripped my ankles and gave them a good yank. *No, no, no, no.* Desperately, I dug my talons into the wooden floor. My cell phone rang. Someone answered it. I let out a scream. Something fell. Then everything went blank.

Moments later, maybe hours, a car door slammed. Bleary eyed, I opened my eyes. It was dark and everything was fuzzy. My vision flickered. The cabin stank of old blood and cigarettes. I tried to cover my nose but I couldn't move. Two people sat up front. They muttered indistinctly between themselves. Their voices went in and out like a faltering radio station.

"You think he's going to make it?" One of the passengers had asked.

"I don't know." The driver replied. "You gave him three shots of silver nitrate Nigel, when he should have been only able to handle one. For your sake I hope he does, if not then the boss is going to be *pissed*."

"What else was I supposed to do?" Nigel replied incredulously.

"You were supposed to give the silver nitrate a chance to settle in the bloodstream before shooting again. You mindless twit."

"How was I supposed to know? He wasn't going down..." Nigel grumbled to himself. "I can't see what the Boss would want with a blood sucker anyway."

"He said something about a serum but who knows, maybe the man is a loon?"

Their voices went in and out. Everything was a jumbled mess. My eyes fluttered and everything went black. Hours later, I awoke on the cool concrete.

A nearby faucet dripped incessantly in the background. My nerves grated with each splashing drop. Bleary eyed, I lifted my head. Dizziness overwhelmed me. The room tilted and spun. Sharp twangs of pain ricocheted through my brain. I looked up only to see bars, lots and lots of silver bars. My blood turned to ice. *No, no, no, no, no, this is just a dream, it has to be a dream.* I flung myself at the bars. *Maybe if I hit hard enough they'll break?* My skin sizzled against the silver's embrace. My vision went white. Electrical pain jolted through me. Enraged, I let out a blood curdling scream. Burnt flesh filled the air. I collapsed to the ground in a crumpled heap. Unconsciousness had taken over me.

My eyes snapped open. Two people were in the middle of a conversation a few feet beyond my cell. I remained still as stone as I analyzed my predicament. Brute force had gotten me nowhere earlier. My smoldering skin served as a solid reminder of that. I cursed myself for letting my emotions get the best of me. *Maybe if I lay as still as a stone they won't notice I am now awake?*

I stole a glance at the blurry bars that surrounded my cell.

My stomach roiled with panic.

Quickly, I closed my eyes, desperate to quell the nausea that rose up within me. *Breathe Frank, just breathe....*Thankfully the light wasn't on or I may have wretched from its intensity. Someone said something in a language I did not know. Maybe Russian? No, no it was definitely French. Then footsteps disappeared along the hallway. Something metallic let out a huge groan before slamming shut. A long stretch of silence ensued.

I shivered and clamped a shaky hand to my clammy forehead.

Silently, I cursed. All my thoughts were a jumbled mess. Someone must have done a number on my head. *Just think Frank, just think...* I recalled images of breaking vases, shattering windows and claw marks. Then there was lots and lots of gas. Things were starting to make sense. I peeked at the bars. Then it clicked. The gas had the same effects as silver, just like the dart. I tried piecing everything together. *Had they been able to break down the molecular formula of silver and bottle it up as a form of gas?* I found the very idea of it baffling. I mean... that could explain the pain and why my skin had burned when it made contact with the gas, Silver was a purified metal after all.... and it didn't react well to the undead or anything supernatural...A hushed conversation picked up between a woman and man.

The woman sounded awfully familiar while the man reminded me of a well spoken man off of BBC News.

"Do you think they'll let us out?" She asked.

"No, probably not." He said.

"That's not fair though!" She sniffed.

"Life's not fair love. Get over it." He replied, his response clipped.

"The full moon is only two days away." She whined.

"Yep that seems to be the case, poppet."

"Do they really expect me to shift in this tiny little box?"

"For the love of God, *will you put a sock in it already?*"

She let out a haughty huff.

"Frank, Frank are you awake?"

I opened one eye. The shadow of a man sat across from me. I could have sworn he was in his early twenties, maybe late teens. He had a familiar musky smell but I couldn't place where I had recognized it from. Due to the silver nitrate I couldn't quite make out his features beyond the haze. All I could tell was he sat upon his cot with his spine against the cool concrete wall. He had one arm propped up on his knee and the back of his head tilted back with a weary groan.

"Honestly woman, enough with the bloody waterworks. Crying

isn't going get you anywhere love and even you know it. So do us all a favor eh and shut up."

He had a crisp cockney accent that was cold as a winter's wind and when he spoke it was with a double dose of venom. The familiar voice crackled with frustration. It belonged to a woman but I couldn't remember who.

"Do you think he's going to wake up?" She asked.

The shadow gave a complacent shrug.

"Don't know. Don't care." He said.

The woman let out a choked sob

"How can you be so nonchalant?! Aren't you worried about getting back home to your family?"

The shadow let out a spiteful snort as he plucked a piece of lint off his hospital gown.

"I don't have family..not in these parts anyway."

"Oh never mind! Frank, Frank, are you still there?" She began again.

"Stars and stones woman! Where else would he be?"

Maybe if I play dead they won't notice me

I closed my eyes and laid still as a stone.

"Frank are you ok?" She tried again.

"Will you just give it a rest woman?"

My eyes fluttered open. My vision adjusted to the dark.

"Olivia? Is that you?" I asked, with a hint of uncertainty.

The gentleman stepped closer to the front of his cage. A saucy smile spread across his face. "Well I'll be damned. The poor bloke is alive after all. Didn't expect you to be waking' anytime soon." His mismatching eyes pierced into me. One was a brilliant sky blue and the other a sea foam green.

Olivia gasped with delight.

"Frank is that really you? Are you ok?"

I let out a weary groan.

"Yes it is me. I am as well as I'll ever be I guess. They got you too I take it?"

Olivia let out a pitiful laugh and flashed me an empty smile.

"Yes, I suppose they did."

I frowned as I worked the muscles loose in my jaw. "But how?"

Olivia managed to give me an empathetic shrug.

"How am I supposed to know? I had a mishap with Ethan and Astrid and then the next minute I remember being pricked in the back with some sort of dart. A few hours later I woke up here with a hell of a hangover."

She paused for a moment and bit her lip.

"Oh... and don't let me forget. They have Jake too...."

She tilted her head towards the second cot on her right.

"He bunks with me but they have him out for testing."

She stepped forward to grip the silver bars but then thought better of it. Limp blond curls clung to her tear soaked face.

"I thought you were as good as dead." She whispered hoarsely.

"I was afraid they had gotten you." The bottom of her lip trembled.

The man across from me rolled his eyes.

"Well thankfully I am not..." I said.

My thoughts were still a bit hazy but things were becoming much more crisp and clear.

The man's eyes glittered with humor as I pushed myself up from the cold concrete.

"Well aren't you a crispy critter?" He was referring to the third degree burns on my skin. I pulled myself into a seated position and took a quick inventory of my surroundings. To my right, a thin bed frame hung from the wall. I also caught a glimpse of an open privy and an exposed sink.

"You're in a cell..." I observed aloud.

It came out more as a clueless statement then a redirection.

"No shit, Sherlock." Olivia grumbled.

Bright Eyes' condescending gaze slowly scanned me from head to foot then back up again.

He grunted and perked a brow. "Not very bright, now are you?"

Within seconds I was a few steps away from the silver bars.

"Thankfully, no one asked you." I replied with a snarl and flashed him my fangs.

He returned the gesture with a sardonic smile.

"Well don't you have a bit o' kick left in you, eh?" He frowned and gave me a thorough look over. "Damn, you must be knackered! They shot you up pretty good I might say. Bloody hell, you even got the shakes and everything'. I am surprised you didn't overdose."

The sudden movement made my head spin. I stumbled and rubbed the space between my eyes with trembling fingertips. My stomach twisted with horror. *What in the world has gotten into me? Normally I have more control than this.*

"What has happened to me?" I rasped. "My whole body, it burns..."

His eyes crinkled with amusement. "You newbies are a trip, you know that right?"

The little energy that I had left was disintegrating. His mismatched eyes glittered with life. His long fingers curled around the bars but the silver did not bite his skin. *Why hadn't the silver affected him? What could he possibly be?* I glanced at the shackles around his wrists. Our captors had taken special precautions with this one and I wanted to know why. Calico eyes pierced into me.

He leaned in, hungrily feeding off of my distress.

"Well that's the beauty of it, isn't it?" He hissed. "They shoot you up with some drugs and then you go limp. Some people say it is like liquid fire. It burns through your veins and drains you dry. They say when you wake it feels like you were hit by a semi." He paused and then let out a dramatic sigh. "Ah, but I guess it's to be expected. That's what they use to subdue vampires after all."

My blood began to boil.

"That is what you are, is it not?" He asked.

His sneer made me want to rip out his throat and drain him dry.

"Do you ever shut up?" I clipped.

He barked with laughter. "I am afraid not, mate."

Bright Eyes smoldered with pleasure. My knees buckled with fatigue. Something told me he enjoyed taunting me. In fact, if I didn't know any better I swear he was getting some sort of fix off of my negativity. *Could he be feeding off the very essence of my rage?* I made a feeble attempt to ignore him. Maybe, just maybe he might go away. Olivia bit her lip.

"It will pass Frank. It's the side effects from the silver nitrate." Olivia said.

"Yeah, Frank. Whatever you do don't touch the bars." Bright Eyes jived.

Olivia tried but I ignored her meek gesture of kindness. Whatever they shot me up with made my skin itch and boil. Instead, I focused most of my attention mainly on Bright Eyes.

"So are you a vampire then?" I inquired with an incline of my head.

The thought of possibly being related to this creep made my stomach roil. The probability was very unlikely, but you never know. Some vampires over the years have developed more of a tolerance for silver. The silver still had hurt but with time they became more acclimated to the pain. Usually those vampires were extremely old.

Bright Eyes' smooth features twisted with disgust. "Not bleeding likely!"

His response was too quick, I bristled at his tone.

"You got something against vampires?" I asked.

Olivia frowned. "Why does it matter what you or Frank are?"

Bright Eyes ignored her and lifted his chin. "You vampires have piss poor luck if you ask me. You'd think with the whole superhuman speed thing you'd be able to dodge a bloody silver nitrate dart for fucks sake." Bright Eyes paused and examined me with a thorough eye. "Poor sod, I betcha you didn't even see it coming'."

By now I was seeing red. I snarled and threw myself up against the silver bars.

"What do you even know about vampires anyway?" The metal scorched my skin.

"Enough!" Olivia shouted over the chaos.

"We all need to get along, despite our differences!"

I breathed heavy and held my burnt hands to my chest.

"Oh that's rich, coming from the most self-centered and judgmental girl from the school campus."

Olivia's face twisted with pain. "What in the world has gotten into you?"

My stomach clenched with shame.

"You were one of the kindest souls I had ever had known. Usually you're so calm and collected. I've never seen you get so agitated and angry before."

A twang of guilt shivered through me. I could see the stormy gray glow of my eyes in the reflection of her somber gaze. She was right, usually it took a lot of time to get me to this point... some invisible force was unraveling the small amount of sanity I had left. *Could it be the silver?* Bright Eyes threw his head back and laughed.

"It's the dart love, it makes 'em more irritable if you know what I mean."

A million questions buzzed through me. I wanted to ask him how the silver nitrate worked. Would it come out of my blood stream? Were the effects permanent?

The latch to the steel door clicked.

"Quick, pretend to be asleep." Olivia hissed beneath her breath before diving beneath her covers. For a brief moment I was blinded by the harsh light from the hallway. Soon after a beefy man with a large hunting rifle stepped into the light. He had eyes of steel and skin as brown as tanned leather. A petite woman in a lab coat followed in his wake. Her black high heels click clacked briskly against the cold concrete. On her nose perched a pair of square spectacles. She wore her hair in a tight bun. She cast a wary glance towards Bright Eyes.

"Careful with zat one, Theodore. Zat is the thing that choked Jonathan and stole the keys to its cell. He is a tricky one and has a tendency to escape."

Her French accent dripped with disdain.

Bright eyes returned the gesture with a congenial smile.

"Well good mornin' to you too, love." Bright Eyes crooned amicably.

His hands hung loosely from the silver bars.

She let out an indignant huff before stalking off towards my cell.

She approached slowly and when she spoke her words came out hushed.

"Ello there cherie, my name is Marie. Please don't be afraid, we just want to get to know you."

I eyed the gun warily. "Where am I and why am I here?.."

She tinkled with laughter. "You are here to help better the world with science of course! You will learn how important you really are all in good time."

Her petal pink lips curled into a honeyed smile.

"Come with me cherie, no struggling now."

I snarled and threw myself at the bars.

Olivia flinched but remained curled up in her illusive fetal position.

"Why am I here Marie?!" My voice came out as a menacing growl.

Marie gasped and stumbled back.

Within a flash Theodore had his rifle trained on my chest.

I gripped the bars, my skin sizzled with heat. Searing pain blazed through my fingers and palms. This time the burn was to be expected but I refused to show them my pain.

"Stand down..." Theodore warned. His finger hovered over the trigger. The rifle was too far away to grab. Theodore stood there, waiting expectantly. I glowered up at the barrel that was now trained on my head. A tumultuous mass of emotions tumbled around inside my head. Bright Eyes watched the whole ordeal with silent amusement.

Stupid, stupid, stupid. I had let my anger get the best of me.

How could I be so stupid? I couldn't be much help if I were dead, now could I?

Reluctantly, I withdrew my hands. Curls of smoke rose up from my blistering skin.

Bright Eyes snickered and shook his head.

"Tut, tut." He clucked. "You should have listened when she told you not to touch the bars, mate. They coated them with silver. Blimey, you think you could just bust outta here without any troubles? Weren't you paying any attention? The place is loaded. Like I said, you vampires have piss poor luck."

Marie frowned and adjusted her glasses.

"I see we caught you at a bad time. I am sorry zat you are upset."

She took her glasses off and rubbed them clean.

Her voice shook with a tinge of regret.

"We mean you no harm, cherie, but we must take extra precautions just in case. I am sure you understand. You can come with us peacefully." She inclined her head towards Theodore and his rifle. "Or... we can provide the encouragement needed." Theodore stared at me, his gaze as cold as steel. The rifle's barrel didn't waver.

CHAPTER 15

"SOMEONE MUST HAVE TAKEN HIM." Astrid said in a hushed whisper.

Ethan gaped at the phone, dumbfounded.

Icy dread blossomed within my core.

What did she mean someone must have taken him? Frank was a stuffy old vampire. Who in the world would take a bloody vampire anyway? More importantly, who had that type of manpower? My insides twisted with restless uncertainty. Was I seriously struggling with the idea of Frank being gone? What has gotten into me? When I first stepped into this world all I had cared about was playing pranks and getting back home to my clan.

Had I taken a liking to Frank? I thought the only person I had cared for was Ethan. Sure, I had taken a liking to Astrid but Frank wasn't someone I thought I'd be worried for. I simply had thought of him as a boring vampire who constantly played by the rule book. My first priority was to get back home. Was that even possible? What if Carmen couldn't find a rift to get us back? Cold sweat trickled down my spine.

If I couldn't get back then I couldn't marry Noah. If we didn't marry then the peace treaty between our two clans would be broken. If that was the case then I wouldn't come home to a family at all, now would I? The Shadow Clan would just gobble them up now wouldn't they? Who would make up my clan then? I stared down at my open palms. A sense of hopeless gnawed at the back of my mind. *Was it possible to start fresh here on earth?* If so would Ethan, Frank and Astrid make up my new clan?

I thought back upon what Frank had said when we first met. In order for us to get you back to your family we have to work together. I recalled the memories Frank and I made together and remembered the prank we pulled on Buzz.

A sliver of warmth unfurled in my belly. I remembered the time he protected us during homecoming. He had risked a lot that night. *Did that mean we were family?* Maybe I wouldn't be able to make it back to Gaia. Even if I could it wasn't guaranteed that I'd make it back in time in the first place. Maybe I had a new pack and maybe Frank was a part that. If that was the case then we were family, not by blood but by kinship. And families worked together. If that was so then I had to make a choice. *Would I help find Frank or would I focus primarily on getting home?* A few moments passed.

I thought of the times I had let Pa down and how I ran away. Disappointment unfurled within my core. I had let my people down in exchange for my own gain. Knots of guilt tangled at my core. *How could I have been so selfish? Why couldn't I look past my own selfish ways?* A few seconds later a tiny seed of hope blossomed within me. Then it occurred to me. Maybe, just maybe this would be chance to do something right. I paused. I'd be taking a risk a huge risk. I hated taking risks. I may have missed my chance to help Pa but I haven't missed my chance to help Frank. *Would it be worth it?* Only time would tell. I was torn between confusion, uncertainty and hope. *Why couldn't anything be easy?* Another moment passed and begrudgingly I pulled out my phone.

"I can't believe I am doing this." I grumbled as I punched Garcia's number into my phone. Normally, Astrid would have done this but her phone was dead.

"This better not come back to bite me in the ass." I rumbled beneath my breath.

Ethan's brows furrowed with concern.

Meanwhile, Astrid bit her nails.

"What are you doing?" Ethan asked.

I pinched the bridge of my nose. "I am making a choice, Ethan."

Ethan's brows arched. "A choice?"

"Frank's our friend and I suppose that makes him part of our pack now doesn't it?"

I replied sourly, straining for patience.

Ethan rubbed at his chin. "Yeah, yeah I guess it does, doesn't it."

Astrid hugged herself tight as she paced silently back and forth.

Garcia answered. Her voice came out tight and clipped.

"Make it brief and to the point, Adams."

"Frank has been taken."

There was silence on the other end. I checked the screen.

"Hello?" I asked with uncertainty.

Garcia's voice was filled with icy restraint. "Are you sure?"

I rolled my eyes.

"Of course I am sure." I snapped.

Astrid chimed in. "Do you really think Lexi would be calling you if she wasn't?"

Carmen cursed beneath her breath.

"Astrid, call Lily. A cab will arrive in ten. We'll rendezvous at the house in twenty."

Then there was an abrupt click.

"Right. See you then." I mumbled as I stared at the blank screen. She had hung up.

I turned to Astrid but she was already on the phone pacing to and fro as she debriefed Senator Benson on Frank's current situation. Ten minutes later a cab pulled up to the curb and rolled to a stop.

"I call shotgun!" I said, shooting up from my spot on the bench.

"Whatever" Ethan mumbled numbly as he tossed his gym back into the trunk.

Astrid rolled her eyes and silently shook her head. I tugged the passenger door open only to be greeted by cloud of stale air and cigar smoke. Coughing I tried waving it away.

"Having second thoughts Lexi?" Astrid teased.

"Are you making an offer?" I inquired.

Astrid made a show of contemplation and then shook her head. "Nope! I'm good."

I narrowed my eyes at her as she scooted in next to Ethan. *Was it just me or did she happen to sit real close?*

The driver let out a wet cough and hacked a wad of spit into a used Speedway cup.

"Welp. Get in. Haven't got ol day ya know."

He flashed me a yellow grin and rubbed the spittle off of his beard. I sucked in a deep breath. *Well here goes nothing,* I thought to myself and slid gingerly into the cab's passenger seat.

"Where to lil' girl?"

I rattled off the address while nervously fingering the collection of bills deep within the pocket of my pants.I was nervous about him spitting on me, more so than having to dip into my stash. Who knew what type of germs roamed the face of this planet, anyhow? Clouds of white cigar smoke hovered thickly in the air. *Did this vehicle even meet state standards for transportation?* Thoughtfully, I crinkled the thin paper bills between my fingertips.

My thoughts drifted back to Frank. *Was he okay? What were they doing to him? Did he end up becoming subject D in Mr. Lemming's studies? Why was Mr. Lemmings studying the supernatural anyway? Who were the guys in the white lab coats that I had seen earlier today? Was it even Mr. Lemmings that took him? If so how can he possibly capture a vampire as old as Frank?*

Millions of questions buzzed around my head like little flies around a pile of shit. I glanced into the rear view mirror and caught a glimpse of Ethan. He sat rigidly in the back seat. The muscles along his jaw popped. Astrid silently rested her head on his shoulder. Worry etched her visage as she stared off into space. Tension hung in the air like great big storm clouds, making it hard to breathe, think or feel.

A numb feeling of loss trickled through me. First I had lost my land to the shadow clan, then my life to Noah, my people and homeland to the portal, and now I had lost Frank. A lump of anguish tightened within my throat. Salty tears welled up in the corners of my eyes. I swallowed, trying to force the lump down. Silently, I stared into the side view mirror, willing myself to count each tree that passed by. I couldn't cry. Not now. Not when Frank needed me. I let out a derisive snort. *Who was I kidding?* I'd probably run away. I'm such a coward. Anger flared through me. For once in my life I gotta do something right. I gotta make a change. I got to stand and fight. I can't keep running, not when people needed me. Silently, I vowed I would make them pay. I would find them and make them pay. Something bright caught my eyes. It was the gleam of the SUV's headlights.

A black SUV pulled up behind us. We took a few turns but the SUV tagged along. Its' blinding headlights pierced through the darkness of the cab. My heart fluttered within my chest. *Were they following us? Should I mention something to the gang?* Perspiration bloomed from my pores. My heart thundered. The urge to run burned through me. I bit down on my cheek and willed myself to stay. The driver next to me puffed out a ring of smoke from his cigar.

"Nice trick you got there." I said, more so for a distraction than idle conversation.

"Yep" He replied gruffly, clearly not interested.

His beady eyes never wandered from the road. They hid beneath his scruffy brows and hovered above his bushy beard. Suddenly, I didn't feel so bad about giving him monopoly money for his fare. If Ethan knew he would object profusely. *But what Ethan didn't know couldn't hurt him right?* We wound down street and pushed passed the pine trees. The black SUV continued down the road, leaving dead leaves swirling in its wake. Silently, I had criticized myself for being overly paranoid.

Swirling police lights flickered through the forest.

The shadows of officers wandered around the building on the top of the hill.

I signaled the taxi to stop near the base of the driveway.

"Right here will do just fine, thanks." I said.

No need to advertise what was going on to an unknown bystander.

The taxi lurched to a stop.

The driver eyed me suspiciously.

"Whatcha got goin' on up there girly girl?"

"Wouldn't you like to know." I teased.

"How much?" Ethan asked.

He rubbed at his scratchy beard.

"That'll be thirty dollars squirt." He opened his hand, waiting hungrily for his fare.

"That much?" Ethan asked, with a perturbed frown.

"Sorry lil duck. Gotta' make a livin' if ya know what I mean." He hacked out a wad of tobacco and spat it into the Speedy cup.

Astrid simply grimaced in reply to the human's disgusting habit.

He wiggled his fingers expectantly. "Cough it up now, haven't got all day."

Immediately, Ethan began to fish for his wallet.

"An extra twenty for the trouble." He dipped his head towards the swiveling police lights waggled his furry brows. "I don't wanna start anything, if you know what I mean."

Ethan began to argue but I just shoved the wad of bills in the driver's hand.

"Whatever. Keep the change." I said.

The greedy driver's eyes widened in surprise.

"Lexi, how did you get..." Ethan began but I was already getting out.

Little did the driver know that I had just handed him a wad of illusionary bills. Who knew a handful of Monopoly money could go such a long way. I guess anything was possible with a little bit of magic. I wondered if the illusion would suffice. According to the driver's greedy gaze and the way he snatched the money out of the air confirmed that my illusion was sufficient enough. Little did he know the bills would only appear real for so long. *Serves the geezer right,* I thought bitterly to myself.

Ethan snatched his stuff from the hatch.

Meanwhile Astrid slithered out of the backseat like a languid snake.

Ethan frowned as the taxi drove away.

"Lex, where did you get all that cash?"

"I didn't." I replied and off I went.

"Lexi, you tricky little fox!" Astrid teased.

I flashed her an evil grin.

Ethan's face twisted into a confused frown. If I were to tell him I think he'd have a fit. Together we hiked up the gravel drive. The rocks crunched beneath our feet as we climbed the winding driveway. Off in the distance a photographer clicked away with his camera. The flash lit up the crime scene like strobe lights on a dance floor. The light revealed trails of blood on the front yard and broken glass. A handful of officers waltzed around in navy jackets. The coppery scent of blood tinged the air. The sickly sweet smell of fear and perspiration quickly greeted us as we neared the house. We took refuge within the brush.

"The place is crawling with uniforms." Ethan mused aloud.

"You got anything up your sleeve Astrid?" I asked.

Astrid adjusted her winged spectacles. I wondered if that had helped her see our predicament a bit more clearly. She shook her head in disbelief. "It's not like I can charm people by the dozen or I would. This many people would be difficult, even for me"

I bit my lip as I watched an older police officer lead a younger officer towards the outer border of the yard. He murmured something into the younger officer's ear and the younger nodded in reply. The older officer gave the younger one a pat on the back before walking back to the house.

"Hey Lex, why don't you just work your magic?" Astrid asked.

Ethan eyed me warily as I silently weighed my options.

Should I tell her? Or should I let her find out on her own by leaving everything to chance. Then I thought of Selena and remembered how angry she was at me for not saying anything to her about my abilities. It was then that I decided truth would probably be a better option.

"I can't, not this time anyway. If it was under different circumstances I might have been able to, but even doing three is risky. Usually I can cloak one person at a time for an extended period of time. However, tonight that's not the case. Saturday took a lot outta me. We are bound to get caught and I can't afford to lie."

Astrid arched a brow and waited for me to explain.

I released a patient sigh.

'If I lie to someone my ability to use magic against them would be cut in half."

"In other words, if we get caught it will put Lexi in an awkward situation."

Ethan explained with a congenial smile.

"And the likelihood of that happening is quite high." Astrid observed quietly.

"I don't suppose you could use your succubus ju ju juice without exposing yourself could you?"

Astrid flashed me an apologetic smile and shook her head.

"No, I am afraid not. My seductive powers are more influential when I am focused on people who are within close proximity of me."

"The placement of the officers are too spread out." Ethan mused.

"Correct. I can however physically take on twenty humans, regardless of proximity but in order to do so I'd have to take on my true form." She offered the two of us a sheepish smile. "As you already know from previous experience, my true form is more useful for other things, those things being more violent in nature and all."

Oh do I ever.

Last time I saw Astrid in her true form she was kicking Olivia's ass. I hardly doubted Senator Benson would appreciate Astrid throwing her police officers across the yard like rag dolls. Ethan's chuckle broke the comic scenery playing out inside my head.

Quickly, he cleared his throat when Astrid shot him a dirty glare.

"Yeah um, about that. I am sure they'll approve of your horns with Halloween coming up."

Astrid smirked and rolled her eyes.

"Oh sure. You should talk wolfman. I doubt they'll mistake you for Grandma from the Little Red Riding Hood story either." She brought her hands to her face and spoke in a mockingly high pitched voice. "Oh grandma what big eyes you have. Oh no grandma what big teeth you have!"

The eyes of Ethan's wolf flickered into his gaze and he flashed Astrid a wolfish grin.

"Better to see you with my dear."

He teased and waggled his eyebrows at her.

Now it was my turn to roll my eyes. "Alright, alright both of you hush."

Someone cleared their throat behind us. We all froze. Panic shivered down my spine. The back of my hairs prickled as we slowly pivoted on our heels to look up. Behind us stood the junior officer, full frontal with his arms crossed. Umbrage shadowed his visage. I scrambled for the right verbiage but Ethan nudged his way to the front. The police officer eyed him warily

"Good evening officer. We are here to seek an audience with Senator Lily Benson. Would you kindly point us in the right direction?"

Leave it to Ethan when it came to pleasantries.

If it were me I would have just jumped over the yellow tape.

The officer lifted his chin and eyed us carefully, especially me.

Was he literally sizing us up?

I returned his sizzling glare. The skin around his eyes tightened with irritation.

"This is a crime scene. Public access is forbidden. I was given specific orders not to allow anyone access. Now run along, kids."

I arched my brow at and shifted my weight.

Well isn't he Mr. Captain Full of Himself?

My mouth opened before common sense could even possibly take place.

"Look, don't know who you're calling kid but we are here to contribute to the investigation. We aren't asking to jump the yellow tape, lieutenant. We simply have information that may help speed things up. So be a dear, cut the crap and get to the point."

Junior scowled. "I don't appreciate your tone.."

"Nor do I appreciate your attitude." I quipped back. I suppose I was the reason he was getting so incensed. But honestly, someone had to get this prick off of his high horse.

"Lexi." Ethan began, pure warning colored his tone.

Ethan only managed to grimace as I plowed on.

"No, screw pleasantries. Frank is in trouble and Junior here won't even give us a chance to speak when we even have a recording of the kidnapper's voice. We don't have time for this shit." Junior's hand began slinking closer towards his gun as I pressed forward and rambled on. The scent of honeysuckle tickled my nose but I disregarded it. The shape of a woman slinked up from behind. She wore a form fitting business skirt and a black cardigan jacket. "So are you going to at least tell your boss that we have some important evidence to take into consideration? If not-"

Astrid shoved past me.

"Ma'am! Do not step any closer or I'll have to-"

Astrid ignored his threat and my dirty glare.

"Miss Garcia! Can we get a little assistance here?"

Carmen Garcia straightened her blazer as she stepped into the light. Black business wedges crunched into the gravel. Her silky black hair was pulled up tight into a gibson tuck. The swiveling police light cast blue and red shadows across her angular face.

"What seems to be the problem here Officer Thomas?"

Junior's spine straightened at her sudden appearance.

"Mr. Po po here- ouch!" Astrid had pinched my arm and Ethan discreetly elbowed me in the side. Garcia flashed me the death glare. The fires of hell danced behind her eyes. My mouth snapped shut. It was obvious she didn't want me involved. So, Astrid took over instead.

"What our dear friend Alexis is trying to say is this *prestigious* officer won't let us pass." Her husky voice dripped with honey. She emphasized on the word prestigious and smiled cordially at him. Junior's eased beneath her sex laden stare.

How typical, the man was like putty in her hands.

A satisfied smile curled at the corner of Garcia's scarlet lips.

"Could it be due to Miss Adam's insolent nature?"

Astrid simply shrugged and I glared.

"Let us pass Carmen" I snarled.

"Or I swear..." I left the threat hang between us.

"Or you'll what?" Garcia hissed.

"Honestly Miss Adams, there's a lesson to be learned here. You're more likely to get things done if your words are more like honey and less like vinegar."

I looked pointedly at Ethan waiting for his support.

Instead, he averted his emerald gaze. "She has a point you know. You can't just barge in here spouting off insults and then expect people to work with you."

I bristled with irritation.

How could they be arguing about this when Frank was missing?

"Point taken, now can we get a move on already? We don't currently have time to analyze my verbal etiquette."

A statuesque Garcia arched another slender brow. She turned to the office but her expression remained cool and unreadable.

"We do appreciate your help lieutenant. They are with me you can let them pass."

Lieutenant Narcissist sputtered, purely taken back.

"But Miss Garcia. I was given specific orders not to allow any access to the public."

The depths of her black pupils expanded and bled into her chocolate irises until they were as black as a coal cave on a starless night. Dazzled, the officer started to stare. When she spoke her voice came out as cold as a winter's kiss.

"Now be a good boy and let them pass. If anyone asks then you refer them to me."

Junior's grip on his firearm loosened voluntarily.

The woman was a damn snake charmer and he was the snake.

Solemnly he nodded and his shoulders sagged in resignation.

"Let them pass, they are with you. Got it." He replied dully.

Garcia smiled smugly and patted him on the cheek. "Now that's a good boy."

The officer's shoulders relaxed and his hand fell away from the gun.

"Please do come in." He said pleasantly and temporarily removed the tape to allow us passage. I eyed him dubiously before ducking under the yellow tape.

"*Bloody hell*, what in the world did you do to him?" I whispered once we were out of hearing range.

An amused Garcia eyed me out of the corner of her exotic Egyptian eyes.

"I compelled him to do my bidding. I don't suppose we share that same trait?"

I grumbled sourly to myself. "If I had the power to oogly eye someone into my bidding then I wouldn't be in this position now would I?"

"Perhaps not." Garcia replied with a sigh. "Come now, this way."

Astrid ran a playful finger down my arm. Her touch left a trail of goose pimples in its wake. I shivered as an instinctual need began to flower inside my core.

Damn succumbing and their tantalizing ways.

She flashed me a coquettish smile.

"Oh don't pout Lexi. I can teach you the other ways to compel men."

Ethan's cheeks heated slightly as he quickly averted his gaze.

A small smile crept across Garcia's scarlet lips.

"That'll be for another time my dear. Let us focus on the matter at hand, now shall we?"

Garcia announced grimly.

Our laughter died out as soon as Carmen Garcia swung open the door.

I sucked in a sharp breath.

"Oh my God." Astrid gasped.

"No way…" Ethan breathed in disbelief.

CHAPTER 16

A FLURRY of violence had taken place here and it had riddled the room with disaster. Shards from a shattered lamp were strewn across the floor. Slash marks marred the overturned furniture. Swirling police lights peeked through the cracked blinds, peppering the room with flashes of red and blue. Stale blood tickled my nose. Wind whistled through the broken bay windows.

Tattered curtains swayed hauntingly in the breeze. Sickly sweet fear, peppery rage, stale sweat and coppery blood clung to the air, making it hard to breathe. The right side of the living room wall was smashed in from impact. Below it lay a sheeted corpse with what appeared to be a broken neck. Claw marks created grooves within the wooden floor panels. Whoever they belonged to had been dragged outside against their will. *What in hells bells was going on here anyway?*

Among it all stood Lily Benson, like a beacon after the storm. She was as still as the photo markers in the room. Maybe she could sort all this out and figure out what happened. Only time would tell. She scoured the crime scene with calculating eyes. Her slender figure stood over a broken lamp. She wore a navy suit jacket and slim dress pants. Her blonde hair was pulled back into a tight ponytail, revealing a face as calm as a frozen lake. She may have had excellent control over her appearance but her scent signature told me otherwise.

The faint smell of papyrus hinted that she was scared. The musky undertones explained that she was worried and the peppery addition to it all implied caged frustration. Silently, Carmen drummed her nails impatiently against the side of her leg. Off to the side two men in black suits stood at ease. Their hands were clasped in front. Not a hair was out of place. Benson stirred the silence with her empty words.

"What do you suppose happened here?" She inquired, stiffly.

Astrid hugged herself and Ethan rubbed a hand along his jaw.

"Definitely a struggle, that's for sure." Ethan murmured.

I sucked in a deep breath and closed my eyes. Various scents danced across my palate, filling my mind with multiple possibilities.

"It sounded like an ambush over the phone." Astrid whispered hoarsely.

"There was no other way they could have taken him."

Garcia bent down and ran her slender fingers along the grooves within the floor. Latex gloves hugged her manicured hands.

"There are fingernail grooves along the wood." She murmured softly. "He must have tried gripping the floor so hard that it left marks." Her expression remained thoughtful but her voice was tense.

One of the suits stiffened.

"Ma'am you are the touching evidence. Please step back."

"Is that really necessary?" Ethan inquired.

"She has as much invested in the investigation as you." Astrid began.

My hackles prickled with irritation.

Garcia's eye twitched but I managed to cut in before she could speak. "What seems to be the problem anyway? You're just standing there and Mr Paparazzi has already taken pictures of the crime scene or he'd be in here by now. At least Garcia is attempting to figure out what had happened while the rest of you jokers just stand around like a bunch of ass hats."

The man opened his mouth to argue but an incensed Benson flashed him a regal glare and held up her hand.

"Miss Adams that is quite enough!" She replied, her voice as sharp as a whip.

Her eyes flicked over to the guard. His mouth snapped shut.

"Carmen is here to help. I have personally called upon her for assistance. She can work with the evidence in whatever way she sees fit. Owens, your services are not needed here anymore, you may be dismissed."

Owens tensed for a brief moment before bowing his head.

"As you wish, Senator Benson." He managed to flash us a scathing glare before stalking out of the room. A murderous Garcia returned the favor by staring daggers into his backside as he left.

Benson's eyes glittered with calculation.

"So what do you think went on here?"

Garcia fingered a piece of cloth and sniffed.

"Do you really want my honest opinion?"

For a brief moment Senator Benson chewed on the inside of her cheek.

"I think he was kidnapped." Garcia announced without the slightest hesitation.

"How can you be so sure?" Benson began carefully and then quickly added. "This can easily be just a scuttle between two vampires. If that's the case I am not going to call in favors or resources when he can just waltz back in a few days later. You of all people should be able to understand that. We need to consider all the possibilities here."

Garcia scowled as she rolled the cloth between her fingers.

"Frank wouldn't disappear. Not without giving me a heads up first. Besides he's well liked within our coven's community. Why would anyone want to attack him? Besides he is as almost as old as me. Do you honestly think a vampire as old as me could be taken like this?"

"Is it possible that someone does not agree with your political tactics and has decided to use Frank to get to you? You did adopt him as your own, did you not?"

Garcia shook her head and handed the cloth to her colleague.

"Frank's historical connection with my kin is irrelevant. Anyone in my coven knows better than to mess with what is mine. In addition, this fabric here does not have Frank's scent on it. Nor does it have a smell that I recognize."

Benson reached for the cloth with tentative fingers. She analyzed it with a thoughtful expression before dropping it into a plastic bag. A thousand thoughts danced behind her eyes. Doubt wrinkled her brow.

"Even vampires have different scents Carmen." She replied, her tone pretentious. "Besides, what makes you so sure that this wasn't a struggle between two vampires? You have been advocating for the werewolves. Your coven isn't the only one that knows this. Nor are they the only ones that have expressed a concern about integrating the wolves into vampire society. You should have assumed this would have caused tension within the vampire community." Realization flickered behind her eyes and she pursed her lips.

"Were you not prepared for a possible uprising?" Benson asked, her tone was almost accusatory.

Garcia's aura and the skin around her eyes tightened.

Together, Astrid and I grimaced.

Everyone could sense the room going tense.

Ethan merely brought his fingers to his brow and shook his head.

"Here we go again.." He mumbled bitterly beneath his breath.

Garcia tilted her head in a reptilian like manner, all human features were forgotten beneath a curtain of cold disdain. Thankfully, Garcia hadn't heard his commentary. She had zoned in all her attention on Senator Benson.

"Are you suggesting I am the cause of Frank's disappearance?" Garcia inquired coolly.

Astrid and I exchanged looks of concern.

Meanwhile, Ethan watched the whole ordeal with a placid expression.

The air within the room thickened with tension.

Senator Benson simply shrugged, her expression remained cool and aloof.

"I am not necessarily saying it is your fault. All I am saying is that you could have taken some precautions that could have prevented this from happening. Both you and I know how volatile vampires can get."

Garcia closed her eyes and pinched at the bridge of her nose. She was doing her very best to maintain her composure. However, the smoky undertones of rage rippled off her in waves. Mentally, I began counting down the seconds it would take before she started throwing things. *Didn't she realize Garcia was a ticking time bomb?*

With great discretion, I began to inch away. I made a valid point to put as much distance between the two of us when things like this happened. Being launched across the room was the last thing I needed right now. Silently, I roamed the room, trying to take in as much information as I could before shit hit the fan. There had to be some sort of answer here, besides the act of violence.

"Being a leader requires you to evolve. The war between werewolves and vampires happened *centuries* ago. Discord between our species has only proven to be fatal, not helpful. So it's obviously time for a change."

Garcia replied as the skin around her eyes tightened. Purple veins threatened to surface along the corner of her eyes. Each passing moment her voice increased and her tone sharpened "However, my political movements are not what is in question here, especially since it was you who suggested that we should unite our species in the first place."

Garcia jabbed a lacquered fingernail at Senator Benson's chest.

Each word dripped with venom. Her restraint wavered as if it were hanging from a thread.

"*Your* leadership skills and *your* ability to uphold *your* promises are what is under scrutiny here. I signed this treaty under the inclination that *you* would keep our existence from being revealed to the human populace here at Ferndale Hills. Ever since then everything has gone wrong!"

Ethan watched the whole ordeal with a bored expression.

Meanwhile, calming pheromones rolled off Astrid in waves.

"And for the love of God Astrid if you don't quit I swear I'll rip those pheromones from your very soul and eat your corpse for dinner." Garcia snarled.

Astrid swallowed, any attempt at reconciliation through sorcery was now gone.

"You insisted that we unify our species and coexist cohesively with one another. You even told me that if we united our two species then both species would be safe. You gave me your word and now Frank is gone. So my question is are you going to own up to your promises and follow through? Or are you going to hide behind your body guards like the little coward that you are."

Senator Lily Benson stiffened at Carmen Garcia's accusation.

Astrid nibbled on her nail.

Ethan stood still as stone.

"Here it comes." I grumbled sourly to myself.

Thankfully, neither of them had heard me. Senator Benson's spine went rigid. She reminded me of a rooster puffing up her chest. In Benson's defense, Garcia had wounded her pride.

Astrid shifted her weight.

I searched the room. Something nagged at the back of my mind. The scent was off but I couldn't put my finger on it. I stepped closer to the sheeted corpse. The guard's eyes flicked from Benson to Garcia then back to Benson as if they were a pair of volleyballs in a high school tournament.

Benson bristled with indignation.

"How dare you talk to me in such a manner! You have no right to speak to me like this!"

Purple veins trickled out from the corners of Garcia's eyes. Yellowed fangs unhinged themselves from her upper jaw, making a clicking sound. She threw her head back and laughed. Black liquid pooled into the whites of her sclera, turning her eyes into obsidian jewels.

The guard's heart rate quickened.

"I have no right to speak to you in such a manner?" She hissed.

What little control Garcia had over her pent up frustration had unraveled.

She flashed Benson a condescending smile and let out a regal snort.

"Come now Lillian. Who are you to lecture me on speech? You are not my boss and I am by no means your subordinate." Her Italian accent lilted as she spoke.

The remaining guard stiffened. He hadn't paid me any mind. He was too worried about the two creatures who were arguing in front of him. I had wondered if he even knew Senator Benson was a Selkie. Benson's fingers twitched. The moisture in the air grew heavy, making it harder to breathe. Water was Benson's specialty. If there was water then she had the upper hand.

Regardless, his hand inched towards his firearm. The gesture had made me assume he was not aware of Benson's magical presence.

Perhaps he didn't know Benson was purely capable of handling the situation herself. His heart thundered behind his ribs like a frantic humming bird inside a cage. His pores leaked with the sickly sweet scent of fear. His terror peaked Garcia's interest. Her inky black eyes swiveled to the source of terror. Her predatory gaze gripped his. A smug smile pulled at the corner of her scarlet lips. Onyx eyes glistened, reflecting the red and blue police lights. He froze, enraptured by her glamour. Her lacquered nails lengthened into sharp talons.

"Leave us" She hissed. "Forget everything we had said."

His body relaxed and his face went slack.

"Yes mistress." He whispered, glassy eyed as he drifted towards the door.

Benson's expression purpled.

"You can't just compel my guard to leave."

"Would you rather me rip out his throat?"

The guard's terror had only intensified the situation between Senator Benson and Carmen Garcia. Garcia had made the right call. Ethan crossed his arms and bit down on his thumb. His steady gaze watched the two supernaturals warily. Him stepping in would only make matters worse. He knew that, so did I. Astrid didn't even bother. The tension in the room had doubled. Their energies crackled in the air. The hairs on the back of my neck prickled with unease. The only option we had was to bite our nails and sit tight. My instincts told me things were going to get ugly fast if this conversation kept going in the same direction as it had. Regardless, something caught my eye near the sheeted corpse. I crouched down. Black hair had pooled out from the sheet's protection. The conversation between Garcia and Benson rose and fell in the background.

"Let me be clear, Lillian. I never was and never will be your subordinate. When I had signed the treaty I had signed it as your partner, as your equal. Not as your subordinate. In return you promised me and my coven safe passage in this city as long as we followed the local protocol and regulations. You also had promised us security if we served as your muscle to help keep the supernatural community in check. However, I don't feel as if you are holding up your end of the bargain. Frank is missing and you are hesitating on helping him."

I fingered the silky tresses and brought one to my nose.

The familiar scent of tea tree oil tickled my palette.

Benson snorted and rolled her eyes.

"Oh don't be ridiculous Carmen. You are making a big deal out of something that is probably nothing. Right Ethan? You of all people should know. The wolves have scuffles and sometimes they seek an area of seclusion to cool off."

"I am making a big deal out of nothing?" Carmen inquired tightly.

Ethan straightened and rubbed at the back of his neck.

When he spoke his words came out calm, steady and reserved.

"In all due respect Senator Benson, I don't agree."

"Oh?" Benson inquired with arched brows.

Her expression demanded a further explanation.

"The ones who came into this room in the middle of the night were not members of the undead. The scent signatures are human. Besides, Frank never showed up to pick me up from practice. When I had called he didn't pick up. Instead, we heard a scuffle in the background and some stranger answered the phone. Shortly afterwards his phone had been shut off."

I peeked under the sheet. My stomach twisted as the scent of death flooded my nose. A familiar face stared up at me. *Could it be the woman from the parking lot?* Her frosty blue eyes were glassy now with the reaper's kiss. Horror twisted her bloodless face. Panic had froze her blue lips into a silent scream. Her head laid at an awkward angle. It appeared she had died of a broken neck. *Had Frank broke her neck in a futile attempt to escape?*

Maybe this had been the clue I was looking for all along. Her lab coat smelled faintly of latex gloves, surgical steel, cigarette smoke, stale blood and urine. Frank had either scared the living piss out of her or her bowels had released shortly after she died. Each clue screamed scientist. I dropped the sheet and stood.

"Ethan's right." I said with a sigh. "Someone took Frank and I don't think he's coming back. It's time I come clean with what I found at the school."

I tugged off the powdery gloves and stuffed them in my back pocket before raking a nervous hand through my hair. The two women paused. Together they turned to look at me, intentionally waiting for me to continue.

"Something's going on at the school. Lemmings has notes on the supernatural in his office." I looked at Garcia and chose my words carefully. "They got Anna. Or they *had* anyway. She was attacked by an abnormal dog. They took her for observational purposes. I assume they wanted to see if she would change but she didn't survive what they had called the transformation. Jacob was at the scene or so it is implied because they captured him too that very night. The one that did the attacking got away."

Benson's brow wrinkled with concern.

Garcia became still as stone.

My voice drifted into nothing. I glanced down, desperately trying to keep the conversation flowing, and nudged the woman's corpse with my toe. "I have a feeling Jane Doe here might be the missing link to all the disappearances at Ferndale High. She and her partner were at the school earlier today. They were arguing about something. About what I don't know what. Regardless, they were driving a white van. Parks had mentioned being followed by a white van before he disappeared and a white van just happened to show up on the school premises a couple of hours before Frank disappears? I mean come on. What are the chances of that being a coincidence?"

I shifted my gaze to Astrid more so for self-preservation than anything else.

She gave me a helpless shrug. I was hoping she' throw me a bone over here, maybe help a sister out? What was she supposed to do? Protect me from the foul wrath of Carmen Garcia?

Pft, Who was I kidding.

"You haven't thought to tell any of us this until now?" Garcia asked, her tone was acrimonious.

I paused and shrugged my shoulders helplessly.

"I wanted to make sure my suspicions were true before bringing the subject up."

Garcia arched a brow.

"Are they?" She asked icily.

Confusion muddled my thoughts. "Are they what?"

"Your suspicions, are they true? Has Frank's disappearance provided you with enough data to come to that conclusion? Or should we wait till Astrid disappears too."

Her wintery words stabbed into me like jagged icicles.

Guilt gnawed at my stomach as I stared down at the lifeless body before me.

"I am sorry, this wasn't what I had intended to happen."

I lifted my eyes to Ethan. His wolf watched me intently behind his emerald gaze. He had chosen to be silent. Normally he would have came to my aid by now but I assumed he was taking his time to process all the information I had just gone over.

Had he too thought I had put him in danger?

I prayed for the alternative. He used to strike first then ask questions later but then again that type of mentality had altered somewhat since he assumed leadership of the pack at Ferndale High. Or maybe his wolf was struggling with the dead corpse in the room. The body hadn't been dead for very long and the smell of fresh death must have been excruciating for him. He was a werewolf after all. The desire to eat what was in front of him must have been overwhelming. I tried to reach out again.

"They are interested more so in you Ethan. They want you as a specimen. What that means I don't know. They made it sound like they were doing some sort of study."

He bowed his head in acknowledgement.

"I am aware" He replied quietly.

He tucked his hands into his pockets made his way over to the body. His expression remained reserved but thoughtful. He crouched down and inspected the body with meticulous care. I bristled with irritation.

Why wasn't he saying anything?

Sure he had already known and I had told him about it earlier. However, he used to be a man of many words. *Why was he holding back? Why hadn't he intervened? Was it because he now had a new pack to look out for? Was he really taking his role as Garcia's peacekeeper seriously? Sure she was using him to help unify the two species but what about me? Wasn't I part of his original pack?*

Then it hit me. It wasn't about me. I wasn't the only one he had to protect anymore. He had a whole community to look after now and a reputation to uphold. Nor were we the only ones at stake here. We had Astrid, Frank, Selena and the wolves to worry about. Any wrong moves and their lives would be at risk. Silently I cursed myself for my own stupidity. A hot flush of frustration burned through me. *Why hadn't I come to that conclusion earlier?*

Astrid lifted her chin in an act of defiance.

"You can't possibly be blaming Lexi for Frank's disappearance."

Garcia's face hardened. "I am"

Astrid stared at a silent Benson and a thoughtful Ethan.

"You can't be serious!"

She gestured towards the upheaval in the living room.

"How could she have known that something like this would have happened?"

"She couldn't have." Benson reassured her. "However if she had revealed this information sooner then perhaps Frank would still be here."

Ethan cleared his throat and brushed his hands off onto his jeans.

He rose, slowly. "Well one thing is for sure. We aren't doing Frank any favors by just sitting here. All we can do is move forward. There is a strong possibility that these are the same people that took Jacob. In the past Selena had mentioned that Jacob complained about a white van shortly before he disappeared. Selena would know because they were close. If Lexi's right then, this woman is associated with the missing person's case that we're trying to solve. From what I can tell her scent signature implies medical field or lab work. Judging by her appearance I am leaning more towards lab work."

Astrid lifted her head and pulled her fingernail away from her mouth.

"Lexi, do you think these might be the same people who had taken Jacob?"

I shrugged my shoulders and rubbed at the back of my neck.

"Possibly. I really don't know. They could be the missing link that links all of this together. All the stories align. Frank and Jacob were taken by a white van. I witnessed a white van that had something thumping inside it and now Frank is gone."

Ethan and Astrid exchanged knowing glances. We all had discussed Jacob's disappearance with Selena at the lunch table but we never really came to any specific conclusion as to what had happened to our classmate.

Benson took in the crime scene with great consideration.

Her expression remained thoughtful and poised.

"That explains Frank and Jacob but what about Anna? She is human, so how would she fit into all of this?" Benson murmured thoughtfully to herself.

"Isn't it obvious? Anna Johnson was working with the vampires. If I am not mistaken I believe she was Garcia's secretary at the time of the disappearance."

Garcia's posture had turned from defensive to thoughtful throughout the duration of our conversation.

"You are not mistaken." She replied silkily out of the corner of her mouth. She gave me a sidelong glance. "However, I do not see how her responsibilities as secretary would have anything to do with her disappearance"

Ethan practiced the art of patience as he rubbed a hand along his jawline.

"But it does though, especially if you used her to deliver a message to Jacob's pack. The disappearance took place when there appeared to be a disagreement between Jacob Parks and another wolf. According to Lemming's notes she simply happened to be at the wrong place at the wrong time."

Benson tapped a pen thoughtfully against the side of her leg.

"Perhaps, that may be the case but how do we figure out what is going on? Who do we bring to justice and what can we do to prevent this from happening again?"

An idea blossomed inside me and festered until I couldn't hold it in any more.

"What do you guys think about witches?"

Benson's eyebrows shot up in surprise.

Garcia gave me a sidelong glance.

"Hear me out. I think I have a plan." I said.

CHAPTER 17

BANG, bang, bang! Astrid rapped on the door with her bare knuckles. I breathed heat into my hands and rubbed them vigorously together. A cold chill hung in the air. Autumn's breath glazed the bushes with frosty kisses. Clouds of steam escaped our lips as we patiently waited for someone to answer the door. Astrid banged again. Someone spoke Spanish off in the distance. *Bang, bang, bang!*

"Just a minute!" a voice called out from the hallway.

"Quick, cover the peephole." I murmured to Astrid.

The last time we did this Selena looked through the peephole and then refused to acknowledge that we were freezing our asses off on her doorstep. The curtain facing the front yard swished. Selena's face pushed against the window pane. Quickly, I twisted the molecules around us to create an illusion. The doorstep appeared to be empty. Astrid rolled her eyes and banged again.

I bit my lip as the locks unclicked. *Would she turn us away? Would she take the time to hear us out? Or would she just slam the door in our face.* I guess there was only one way to find out. The door opened a crack and then Selena's head popped out. Her face twisted in confusion. Cooking spices rolled off her in waves.

"Hello?" She called out dubiously, her brown eyes searching.

I lifted the veil to reveal the two of us on her doorstep. She gasped and took a step back. Her scent signature spiked with fear, turning the sweet rosemary into bitter lime. Hatred singed the air, filling the space beneath the veranda's awning with the smell of burnt garlic.

Astrid offered an apologetic smile.

Selena's face fell almost instantly. "Oh it's you."

"I am so glad to see you too." I replied with forced cheeriness.

I flashed her a smile that was more teeth than anything else. In reality, I wanted to strangle her. However, Benson had stressed the importance of being diplomatic. I suppose it would be smart to take her advice into consideration, considering she was the senator and all that jazz. Selena rolled her eyes before trying to slam the door in my face. Thankfully, Astrid slipped her foot between the door and its frame.

"Go away!" She hissed.

"Not until you hear us out." Astrid insisted.

Selena murmured something beneath her breath.

A shrill ringing exploded inside my head with the flick of her hand.

"Son of a bitch!" I gasped and pressed my hands to my ears.

Astrid must have experienced the same thing because she cursed and leaned into the doorframe for support. Her foot still remained firmly wedged between the door and the frame.

"Please let us in Selena." She rasped painfully.

Selena's face hardened. "Why should I?"

Astrid's eyes flickered with gold. "Because Frank is missing and we need your help."

I panted, desperately trying to stop the ringing within my head.

"Oh really? Is this another one of your ploys?"

"Mija, what is going on out there?" Someone's footsteps echoed down the hallway. Selena's face flushed with dread. "Nothing, Mami!"

She flicked her fingers and the ringing stopped.

Astrid slumped against the door frame in relief. A round face peeked out from behind Selena's shoulder. It belonged to a petite woman in her forties. She had bronze skin like her daughter and wore her black hair in a messy braid. She penetrated us with her hawk like eyes as she silently wiped her wet hands onto a white dish towel.

"Who are your friends, Mija?"

Selena stiffened. "They aren't my-"

I flashed the woman a brilliant smile. "What a pleasure to meet you. You must be Mrs. Rodriguez. Selena has told us so much about you."

The woman's eyebrows disappeared into her hairline.

Selena shot me a deadly glare.

Astrid chuckled. From her oozed warmth and happiness.

"Good things of course. Mostly about your food. Your tamales are amazing!" Astrid added.

Mrs. Rodriguez flushed with pleasure when she looked upon Astrid.

"You are too kind. Please do come in, the two of you must be freezing out there on the step, yes?"

Selena narrowed her eyes contemptuously.

"I'd prefer to watch you shiver uncontrollably from the comfort of our home."

Mami flashed her an angry glare.

"I am not asking you nicely, I am telling you. Do you think money grows on trees niña? Who do you think I am, Edison? You are letting all the heat out you stupid girl." Selena tried to protest.

Mama Rodriguez cast us a tight lipped smile.

"Will you excuse me and mi hija?"

We both nodded. She grabbed Selena by the ear and pulled her into the hallway.

"Mami!" Selena protested but Mami slammed the door behind her.

A brief conversation in the form of Spanish took place behind the door. Their hushed voices rose and fell in rapid succession then there was a cracking and a moment of silence.

Moments later, a scowling Selena opened the door.

"Mami urgently requests that you come in and demands that I apologize for my rude behavior." Selena announced glumly, as she rubbed tenderly at the pink handprint on her cheek. Begrudgingly, she opened the door wider for us to pass.

A sense of satisfaction kindled inside me.

"Don't mind if I do." I replied smugly and stepped right in.

Astrid silently shook her head in disapproval before trailing in from behind.

A mixture of cooking spices mingled in the air. We followed a stiff Selena down the long corridor. Wooden floorboards creaked beneath our feet as we neared the kitchen. The scent of corn, roasted meat, paprika, toasted garlic, sautéed onion and melted cheese strengthened as it danced across the air, dazzling me with waves of hunger.

Family pictures decorated the wall and at the end of the hallway stood a white table. On the table sat a vela candle of a woman with flowing robes. From it flickered a flame. The candle light swayed to and fro, illuminating a crucifix that hung on the wall above. We passed the kitchen where Mami bent over the counter. Irritation wrinkled her brow. Silently, she kneaded the dough furiously between her gnarled fingers. We inched our way past the opening to the kitchen and towards the stairway. Selena slid her hand along the railing. Together we climbed the stairs and stopped just outside of her bedroom doorway.

"Are you going to help us or not?" I demanded in a hushed whisper.

"Well that depends." Selena mentioned mildly as she glanced down the stairs to check if her mother was listening before shoving us into her room. Quickly, she shut the door and began casting wards along the cracks. Astrid threw her arms up in frustration.

"We don't have time for this!" She hissed.

Selena shot her a deadly glare.

"Mami doesn't know what I am or what you are for that matter and I intend to keep it that way. You came to my house asking for my help. So we're going to play by my rules. Comprende?"

A flash of gold flickered across Astrid's eyes. Silently, Astrid ground her jaw but she didn't argue. In the meantime, Selena clicked on the radio so her mother couldn't hear our hushed conversation over the music.

"I want the whole kitten caboodle. No lies, no beating around the bush. I want to know everything, are we clear?" Selena asked.

Her eyes bore into me.

A sense of uneasiness blossomed within my core turning my blood into ice. *Was it really a good idea to tell her what I am? What if she was working with the people who kidnapped Frank?* A flush of frustration rushed through me. *If that was the case and she really was working with the scientists then Jacob wouldn't be missing now would he?* He was her closest childhood friend and confidant after all. *Why would she turn them in? What would she have to gain anyhow?* Then there was Garcia and Senator Benson. I had sworn an oath to keep the supernatural a secret from the human community. Was Selena even human? She herself openly admitted she was a witch. So how do witches fit into this equation?

My eyes drifted to Selena's hands. *Would she do the smack down on me if I didn't tell her the truth?* If Selena really wanted to she could easily broadcast our conversation across the world with this realm's level of technology. She was livid with me after all. Either way I was screwed. If the public found out about magic then Garcia would have my head and if I didn't fess up then Selena would have my skin. After Selena had used her powers on me I figured it would not be in my best interest to lie. If I were to lie I'd be helpless against her.

Astrid rolled her eyes. "Enough with the bull shit. Lexi's a Kitsune and I am a succubus. Now are you going to help us or not?"

Selena jutted her jaw. "Prove it." She replied, her tone icy.

"We don't have time for this. Frank could be anywhere right now." Astrid snarled.

I held up a hand to silence her. Normally I would have agreed but in this case something in me had clicked. Garcia's words reverberated in my head, use honey instead of vinegar.

"If Selena is going to help us then we owe her the truth. Especially if we consider her to be our friend." The words felt foreign in my mouth as they came out. "If you wish to see my true form then there's no going back. You must promise to keep this between us. There's a whole community we're putting at risk here. Understand?"

She arched a brow.

"Fine. So be it." Selena replied imperiously.

Her almond shaped eyes held mine, silently challenging me to continue at my own risk. The tension in my shoulders had eased and I released my breath. Who would have known that I could be so being diplomatic? I guess it wasn't that hard after all. *Go me.*

"Astrid. I need you to make sure she doesn't scream."

A devious sneer curled at the corner of Astrid's mouth.

"With pleasure." Her voice came out as a sultry purr.

Selena snorted in disbelief. "If you think you can get me to scream.."

One moment Astrid was behind me and the next she was beside our friend. A flicker of fear danced briefly behind Selena's eyes but she stood her ground. I took a deep breath and leapt head first with arms outstretched.

Selena readied herself to strike.

Instead her mouth dropped in complete awe.

The illusion that encased me within my human form unraveled. Black fur sprouted from my legs and arms. Russet fur prickled from my elbows and knees on up. White tufts coated my stomach and chest as the clothing around my body disintegrated. My hands shortened into paws. Muscles contorted in some areas and elongated in others in order to adhere to the skeletal structure of a fox. My mouth lengthened into white muzzle topped with auburn fuzz.

Thin black whiskers sprouted from my cheeks. My button nose transformed into the wet black nose of a fox. I landed onto the ground with a soft thud. My bushy red tails swished to and fro. Their white tips twitched as I sat back upon my haunches. I yawned, revealing a set of razor sharp teeth. Golden eyes stared up at a shocked Selena. I waited expectantly. The black tips of my ears swiveled as I took in the miniscule sounds of the house. I could hear the clacking of Mami's knife against her cutting board. Astrid shifted her weight and cracked her fingers.

"Are you ready for round two?" She asked, purely amused at the whole situation.

Selena just gaped at her, in complete bewilderment.

"Round two?" She asked hoarsely.

I chuffed in mild amusement.

Two hours later we were sitting at the dinner table eating empanadas in Selena's dining room. Mami had to leave for work and her father had been out town.

"So a Kitsune is a fox spirit. Your main powers revolve around illusion but fox spirits have a tendency to work with elemental magic. In fact, your specialty is electricity?"

I nodded and stuffed some more empanadas in my mouth.

"So, your father helped you a lot with illusionary magic and that is why you are able to maintain a human form. But you can't lie to people without it hindering your abilities. And you are here because?" Her voice trailed off.

I pushed a piece of empanada around with my fork and swallowed. The buttery crust melted on my tongue. "Well Ethan and I accidentally ran into some portal that spat us out into this realm. I am trying to get back in time for the wedding. Thankfully, Senator Benson has agreed to help us as long as we assist with the investigation but it has been a real hot mess."

Selena's brows shot up in surprise. *"You have a fiancé?"*

I rolled my shoulders in a simple shrug. "Can't be helped."

"Get this." Astrid began with a mischievous grin. "They have an arranged marriage. It's supposed to be some cute pact between their two tribes to keep the peace. Is that crazy or what?"

A mystified Selena just stared at the two of us in complete disbelief.

"Not to mention, she's two hundred years." Astrid added.

Selena's eyes widened in disbelief.

"Oh stop it Astrid, you're going to overwhelm her."

Astrid let out a cynical snort.

"Oh hush, Lex. It's not like I am three hundred years your senior."

"Three hundred years?" Selena whispered.

I offered her an apologetic smile.

"Yeah, anyway his name is Noah. He's a complete ass."

I stuffed another empanada into my mouth and shivered with delight.

"Oh shit, did I forget to mention that Ethan's a werewolf?"

Selena merely groaned.

"Now, now, don't forget. I'm a succubus that works for the government." Astrid reminded her with great cheer.

"Yes, yes, who isn't aware of her family heritage and together you and Senator Benson are trying to maintain the secrecy of the supernatural community from the human race." An exhausted Selena rubbed at her forehead. "Frank's a vampire, you're a fox, Ethan and Jacob are werewolves and Astrid's some secret agent trying to save the world. That's a lot to take in."

"Yep that pretty much sums it up." Astrid said cheerily.

"We tried to warn you, Selena." I said..

Selena's brow furrowed with concern.

"It's Hawk Eyes to you Missy."

CHAPTER 18

GOSSIP CRACKLED through the hallway like wildfire in a dry forest. Watchful eyes burned into our backs as we passed through. A thunder cloud of smoky rage, tart excitement and musky confusion hovered over our peers. Hushed whispers wisped in and out of our hearing range. Ethan and I exchanged wary glances. We had picked up snippets of different conversations but neither of us had liked what we had heard.

Aren't those the new kids from Wales? Some person inquired.

Aren't they the ones who hung out with Frank before he disappeared? Someone asked.

Wait a second, isn't he the one who stood Olivia up at the dance? Another accused.

I grimaced at the accusations but Ethan remained unperturbed. Lately, he had developed a strong front when it came to emotional expression. *Could it be due to the pack?* They say wolves shouldn't allow emotions to get the best of them. Then again, assuming leadership probably meant he needed to be on his best behavior. Regardless, we both sought refuge in the chemistry lab. Maybe if we entered quietly no one would take notice.

No harm in hoping right?

Wrong. A soft hush flooded through the lab once we stepped in. Buzz and a few of his friends, including Takahashi, lifted their heads. They watched us warily as we took our seats. A snide sneer curled at the corner of Buzz's mouth. His brown eyes glittered with calculation.

"Well, well if it isn't Ethan Matthews." Buzz tilted his chin in defiance.

The fluorescent lighting reflected off of his sandy brown hair. Ethan's shoulders tensed but his face remained placid as a lake on a midsummer night. *Wolves.* I thought bitterly to myself. *The last thing we needed was a fight for dominance right here in the chemistry lab.* Little did he know, I was a fox and I had teeth too. Punishment or not, I was more than willing tag team them despite Garcia's warnings. I could feel the flick of my tails beneath the layers of human illusion. Like Ethan, I too had to keep my emotions in check, lest my barriers melt away. I flashed our adversary a pointed glare.

"Can we help you?" I replied through gritted teeth.

Takahashi rubbed a hand along his jaw and lowered his gaze. It was a dismissive gesture. He was the omega of the pack and wasn't prone to stirring up trouble. Technically an alpha's enforcement didn't apply to him but he was just submissive by nature. It was an omega's job to step up to the plate to help soothe the pack whether the alpha willed him to or not. Takahashi just happened to be in the wrong place at the wrong time. Hawk Eyes shifted uneasily in her chair. Buzz leaned back and propped his elbows on the back of his chair. A humorless smile curled at the corner of his lips. *What the hell was his problem anyway? Didn't he know it was rude to stare?* His stony brown eyes focused on me alone.

"As a matter of fact you can." He replied coolly.

"Let's start by you telling me where is my girlfriend is." He began.

He didn't blink. In fact, his eyes screamed with challenge. I flashed him a smile that was more teeth than anything. If he thought he could bully me into submission he had another thing coming.

"That's rich. Don't you mean ex-girlfriend?" I quipped back.

"Last time I recall Olivia had dumped you for Ethan." I continued.

A low growl rumbled deep within Ethan's throat.

"You're not helping, Lexi.." Ethan began.

Buzz's smile thinned and the corner of his eye twitched. I wasn't in the mood to play nice. If he wanted a verbal bout we can have it right here right now. It was now Jordan's turn to step in. He approached the tension with great care. Calming pheromones rolled off him in waves.

"It's been brought to our attention that Olivia has gone missing." Jordan announced.

My heart skipped a beat, despite the tension my shoulders began to ease.

The mask of indifference around Ethan's face cracked with surprise.

"Missing?" Ethan inquired as concern creased his brow.

"Yes. Missing." Buzz enunciated each word clearly. His voice was sharp as a whip.

Ethan glanced at Takahashi with searching eyes, waiting for some sort of explanation.

Jordan only lowered his gaze and respectfully looked away.

"I am not too keen on the details." He admitted.

Buzz leaned forward, watching me intently.

His wolf peered at me through his hungry brown eyes. "It just so happens to be that Olivia was last seen fighting with Astrid. Who happens to be *your* best friend. So it is only natural that we assume you know where Olivia is, yes?"

The very question caught me off guard.

Ethan bristled and flashed Buzz an icy glare.

His aura rippled with rage.

Musky scent patterns altered from cautious to protective in a matter of seconds.

"Lexi and Astrid may be friends but that doesn't mean they are responsible for Olivia's disappearance. You do realize that, right?"

His own wolf met Buzz's gaze. Each word rang with challenge.

The crowd around us murmured with excitement.

A muscle in Buzz's jaw pulsed. The tension between the two had escalated. Buzz had once been in line to become alpha when Jacob disappeared but Ethan had won that position over before he could cement his leadership. Buzz has had a chip on his shoulder ever since.

"How can you be so calm?!" Buzz shouted.

Jordan kicked it up a notch with his calming juju juice.

"Would you knock it off already?" Ethan hissed.

"Sorry Boss. Just doing my job." Jordan replied with an empathetic shrug.

Regardless, he didn't back down when it came to offering his pack emotional support.

"Gotta love omegas." I commented with a dry smile.

"Andrew, why are you so upset?" Ethan asked, completely befuddled.

"She's probably off fuming somewhere.." I mumbled with a roll of my eyes.

"Olivia was supposed to be with you that night. Instead of watching over her you waltzed off with Astrid and now she is gone!"

Bewilderment wrinkled Ethan's brow.

"Don't you feel partly responsible for her going missing?" Buzz accused.

"Andrew.." Ethan began.

"She left the school that night in a frenzy because you had kicked her to the curb and no one has seen her since. Are you trying to tell me you don't feel any anguish for what had happened between you and her?"

Frustration twisted Ethan's perfect features into a tangled mess.

"Now that's enough!" Ethan snarled

"It's not like they were dating or anything!" I sputtered with indignation.

"That's not the point." Buzz replied. His voice was acidic.

"Look," Jordan began with an apologetic smile. "What I think Andrew is trying to say is, when you take a girl to the dance you stay with her during the dance and keep her safe. You don't go off with someone else."

My eyebrows shot up in surprise.

Never in my life have I seen a wolf on the lower end of the totem pole speak up to his alpha in such a direct manner. All the while, Jordan delivered the message with great reverence and remained dutifully docile in his approach. Buzz however, jabbed an accusatory finger within Ethan's direction.

"Maybe if you kept an eye on her then she wouldn't have disappeared."

A few of the girls grumbled in agreement. One of them snorted with disgust.

"How humiliating" One of the girls murmured.

"She's probably devastated." Another replied in the back.

"Poor Olivia, I'd want to disappear too if my homecoming date threw me aside for another girl."

Hawk Eyes frowned.

"It's not like he meant to hurt her feelings." She replied defensively.

They shot her a murderous glare.

Instinctually, she wrapped her arms around her center.

I licked my lips.

Hawk Eyes wasn't there the other night when Olivia confessed her feelings for Ethan. Nor was Buzz. *Had he known what had happened? Was that what had fueled his rage? Or was it because he truly cared for her.* Thankfully, Ethan shot her down or else Buzz may have challenged him to a duel for leadership. In Olivia's defense, I too would have probably crawled into a hole and disappeared. Especially if my crush told me he wasn't interested. A wave of pain danced across Ethan's face once he began to realize what had happened. All anger had melted away. Guilt rolled off of him in waves.

My heart broke at his expression.

"I didn't mean any harm. I didn't think Olivia would take it the wrong way. She was yours after all." He replied softly, his expression downcast. He looked down at his hands, searching for some sort of answer. Something told me Buzz didn't understand where Ethan was going with this. Normally a wolf would display a sense of ease if potential competitor backed down from their mate. Instead he had stiffened and his scent patterns had changed.

The wolf in him glowered up at us.

"She was mine from the beginning and she always will be." Buzz replied.

"But that's not the point." He continued.

"The point is I trusted that you would take care of her. You didn't and now she is gone."

A shadow of guilt crept across Ethan's face. His aura had shifted from a fiery red to a depressing blue. The hairs on the back of my neck tingled. I didn't like what Buzz was trying to do. When I spoke each word came out like daggers of ice.

"Did it ever occur to you that Olivia wants nothing to do with you and because of that she may be avoiding you altogether?"

Hawk Eyes clapped a hand to her gaping mouth.

"I mean, can you blame her? I sure as hell can't."

Several people in class murmured in shock.

Ethan ran a hand through his rust colored curls.

"No, he is right. I should have at least checked up on her. I should have made sure she was alright but I didn't and now she is gone. She and everyone on the team are part of my responsibility. As head of our group it is my job to keep everyone safe. There are no room for any excuses. I made a mess of this and it is my job to clean it up."

Andrew's shoulders relaxed some.

I stared at Ethan in disbelief. *What happened to my carefree friend? What was this garbage about responsibility anyway? Since when did he fully accept the local wolves as his own anyhow? He didn't owe anything to anyone.* The old Ethan would have brushed this off with a laugh. *Was he seriously taking Buzz's thoughts into consideration?* This was absurd, especially after the way Buzz had treated him in the past. *Why would he even comprehend considering Andrew's point of view in the first place? Has he gone mad?* Before I could reply the doors to the classroom swung open. Mr. Dinkle entered the classroom with an armful of paperwork. All eyes turned to watch the teacher as he waddled up to the front of the room.

"Ah Mr. Dinkle. So good of you to join us." Buzz announced icily.

"Care to update us on the missing students?" He added.

Jordan simply sunk deeper into his chair with a submissive sigh.

Dinkle stiffened. Buzz may have accepted Ethan's grievance but he clearly wasn't satisfied. He waited for an answer as he tapped his mechanical pencil impatiently against his desk. A sea of whispers gurgled from the back of the room. Some students complained while others nodded in agreement with Buzz's bold inquiry. Who could blame him? He had been the only one with enough courage to ask the question that was on everyone else's mind in the first place. Dinkle plopped the paperwork onto his desk with a supine sigh.

"Mr. Brown you are well aware that I am not at liberty to discuss these matters with the student body."

Ethan looked concerned.

"Does that mean you know something but aren't allowed to tell us?"

Dinkle licked at his lips. His bored façade wavered slightly. Buzz joined Ethan and tilted his head. His brown eyes glittered with suspicion.

"Yeah." He drawled with a predatory smile.

"What are you trying to hide anyway?"

Our fellow students exchanges looks of uncertainty.

Meanwhile, Dinkle's mouth tightened.

His frog-like eyes flicked from Ethan to Andrew then back again.

"I am not hiding anything." He replied, his tone casual. "It's just not up for discussion and that is final. Now open your books to chapter eleven."

A maelstrom of complaints bubbled across the room. Students shifted in their chairs. Dinkle's frog-like eyes darted to the left then the right. The jowls along his cheeks quivered. The sickly sweet smell of fear tickled the air. Beads of sweat blossomed above his lip.

Hawk Eyes stroked a calm hand along her braid.

"If you know where Frank might be then you should tell us. Miss Garcia considers him to be a brother and you know how tight she is with the press. We'd hate for you to lose your job for withholding any pertinent information that could lead to his discovery."

My lips curved into a humorless smile. *"Boy, wouldn't that be a shame?"*

I couldn't help myself but comment. To see him squirm beneath the pressure gave me great delight. In the meantime, Dinkle's eyes bounced anxiously between all four of us like a frenzied tennis ball, ready to implode beneath the pressure of the student body's complaints.

"Enough!" He shouted over the tsunami of complaints.

Everyone went silent.

He took a breath and adjusted his glasses.

"Like I had said, I am not at liberty to discuss political matters with the student body. Those discussions are meant to take place at home. Today we will be learning how to create a smoke bomb using potassium nitrate and sugar. Now open your books to chapter eleven."

Buzz glowered up at Dinkle.

"This is bullshit." He snarled and slammed his textbook shut.

Our classmates recoiled in shock.

Dinkle's face purpled. "Mr. Brown that is no way to address a teacher!"

His jowls quivered with rage.

Buzz shot up from his seat.

His chair legs screeched across the linoleum floor. Everything in the room went still.

"Where do you think you are going young man?" Dinkle sputtered in exasperation.

"Sit down this instant!" He demanded.

Dinkle's confidence deflated beneath Buzz's steely glare.

"Sorry teach, if you can't ensure my safety then you sure as hell can't make me stay."

He thrust a bunch of books into his bag before stalking off.

"I'll be back once this school has its priorities straightened out."

Buzz flicked a haphazard salute to the class but didn't bother to look back. Hundreds of eyes watched him as he went. A wave of restless whispers traveled across the room.

"Did he seriously just mouth off to a teacher?" One of the students asked, aghast.

"Dude has some balls." One of the boys grumbled.

"Where does he think he is going" The girl behind me asked.

"Is Dinkle really going to let him leave after the way he behaved?" An awestruck student replied.

Ethan frantically threw his stuff into his pack as Dinkle helplessly wrung his hands.

I watched him with a raised brow.

Hawk Eyes cast him a questioning look.

He offered us an apologetic smile. Rusty curls fell into his emerald eyes.

"Sorry-I'll explain later." He replied breathlessly before racing out after his friend.

A soft hush quelled over the restless classroom. Students silently exchanged wary glances. Seconds lengthened into what had felt like years. The awkwardness of the situation increased with each passing breath. A bewildered Dinkle stood at the front of the room, dumbfounded as he stared at the door ahead. Normally, I would follow in Ethan's wake but I found the possibility of Dinkle revealing himself quite intriguing. The man was under a lot of pressure and I wanted to see if he'd break.

Was it possible that he knew where they held Olivia and Frank?

He most certainly knew where they held Jacob. So I didn't see why not. Anticipation crawled up and down my arms like an army of ants. The muddled scents of Andrew's frustration and the confusion of my peers had left a funny taste in my mouth. I didn't take comfort in the fact that I found the mass of chaos tantalizingly intriguing. Being amused by dark humor was a Shadow clan thing. That wasn't necessarily a road I should venturing right now. In result, I desperately tried to change the subject.

"So that went well, eh?"

My insides shriveled beneath everyone's blank stares. Apparently I was the only one who had a sense of humor around here. *Go me.* Someone had to know when to laugh, right? Or not. Hawk Eyes cast me a sidelong glance. Who would have known my attempt to lighten the mood would have backfired? Little did I know, that my attempt wouldn't break the silence but would only direct the attention towards me instead.

I cleared my throat and forced a smile that was more teeth than cheer.

"So how about those smoke bombs?"

A composed Dinkle rubbed at his chin with a chubby hand.

His froggy eyes narrowed into tiny slits.

"Yes, about those smoke bombs." He eyed me suspiciously before droning on.

"You will need sugar and potassium nitrate." His tone didn't change.

The tension in my neck unraveled once everyone's focus was on him now instead of me. I leaned back and devoted my attention to the squirrels outside. Beside me Hawk Eyes scribbled furiously away at her notes. Then it occurred to me. *What if the scientists reveal the identity of the supernatural community to the human race? What would happen then? Would everyone be able to coexist like the squirrels did with the humans? Or would there be a civil war?* The idea itself sent shivers down my spine. Surely everyone would be able to get along, right?

"Hello? Earth to Alexis?" A bronze hand waved in front of my face.

The familiar sounds of unzipping backpacks awoke me from my stupor.

"Next time we will focus on creating smoke bombs in class. Till then read chapter twelve."

I stretched like a cat and let out a languid yawn.

Poor Dinkle, didn't he realize no one was listening?

Hawk Eyes snorted with disgust and silently she shook her head.

"What?" I demanded incredulously.

Did I happen to say that out loud?

Lines of disapproval etched her face.

"You should take your education more seriously." She replied with a stern scowl.

My eyes about rolled out of my head.

"Spare me." I grumbled beneath my breath.

Hawk Eyes had a tendency to rant about the importance of education. If she had heard my sullen comment she would have given me a solid knock upside the head. Thankfully, for my sake, she didn't. Dinkle glanced our way. He drummed his stubby fingers along the side of his leg. His forehead creased with irritation.

"Let's be honest here. When am I ever going to need potassium nitrate?"

Dinkle cleared his throat. "Ladies, class is over and if you don't head out now you'll be late to wherever you need to be."

Hawk Eyes cast him a sheepish smile. "Right then. Let's be off."

He regarded us with gall, eagerly waiting for our dismissal.

Together we headed for the door.

"Textbooks are meant to be read, not slept on." She prattled on but I wasn't listening.

Something wasn't quite right. My instincts were urging me to stay but what for? I glanced behind. A shifty-eyed Dinkle kept glancing at the clock as he fidgeted behind his desk. His polliwog eyes flitted from one student to the next. I frowned. My intestines writhed with uncertainty. *What was he up to anyway? What in the name of Gaia would make him want us to leave so badly?* Against my instincts, we exited the lab.

"Speaking of textbooks are you still joining me in the media center for lunch? Our group project on the Salem witch trials is about due and we are severely behind."

I grimaced. Hawk Eyes didn't have a clue or an inkling that something had gone wrong.

"Well that all depends. I may have to request a rain check."

Hawk Eyes stiffened and flashed me a murderous glare.

"On what grounds?" She replied, her tone sharp as the bladed edge of a serrated knife.

"On personal matters." I replied with a conciliatory smile.

She watched me, stone faced. Clearly, she was unamused.

My smile twitched into a grin as I backed away. Mischief danced in my eyes. "Speaking of rain checks, would you be a pal and let Ethan know I won't be able to make it to math today?"

Her expression boiled.

"What do you mean you won't be in class today, Alexis?"

I boomed with laughter and gave her a reassuring wave with my hand.

"That my friend will be discussed at a later time."

Her hawkish eyes narrowed into little slits.

"Lexi..." She rumbled dangerously.

"Thanks! Gotta go, bye!" I flicked her a friendly salute and veered away.

Selena was in hot pursuit. I delved into my core, withdrawing the energy I needed for conjuring. Magical energies rippled and spiraled down my arms like electrical snakes. I grabbed a hold of real time and twisted the molecules around me into a cloak. Atoms sizzled along my palms.

Magic dripped from my fingertips like wet paint. I tweaked my surroundings to my advantage, painting illusions here and there to help ensure my invisibility had taken place. Hawk Eyes sprinted after me. We passed several classrooms along the way.

Lady luck was on our side because we didn't make a scene. Thankfully, passing period was over and everyone had left for class. The last thing we needed was a list of memories for Garcia to wipe clean from the minds of our peers. Hawk Eyes was gaining on me. In fact, I was counting on it. It's not easy to explain how doors can move on their own accord. Thankfully, due to Hawk Eyes' perusal I didn't have to. I yanked on the door and slipped into the room.

I nearly crashed into a wooden cabinet but managed to twist out of the way without making a single squeak on the freshly waxed linoleum floor.

Chemical bottles peeked out from the glass paneling. Multiple smells leaked out from the wood, despite its study build. Hawk Eyes stormed into the room a split second later than I, shouting my name. Dark energies crackled around her.

She nearly ran into a workstation with cedar cabinets and black counter tops. Several of them were scattered around the back of the room. I gave her a wide berth and tip toed along the wall's service bench. She glanced around the room, her hazel eyes aglow with the fires of hell. *Note to self, don't piss off Selena.* If I wasn't careful she would likely take after her mother and crack me upside the head with her shoe. A startled Dinkle slammed the phone onto the receiver. He shot up from his desk, red in the face.

"Miss Rodriguez! What is the meaning of this?"

Hawk Eyes skidded to a halt. I choked back a laugh. Glee trickled down from my head to my toes, filling me with hot delight. Her stony gaze met mine. I flashed her a wicked smile and waggled my brows. Her mouth parted in protest. I pressed a finger to my lips and inclined my head towards a bewildered Dinkle. He hadn't known I entered. For all he knew it was just her and him in the room. Realization dawned upon her face. The fires of hell faltered behind her gaze. She had the gift of sight. That was how she discovered I wasn't human. As of right now she could see me but Dinkle couldn't. *Would she be silly enough to insist on announcing my presence?* The last thing she needed was a visit to the looney bin. So she stumbled for some sort of recovery instead.

"She's not here." Hawk Eyes murmured in disbelief.

He adjusted his glasses and scowled. "No. She is not."

Disgruntled grooves creased his forehead.

A hot flush colored her bronze cheeks. She swallowed. "I apologize, sir for my rude behavior. I thought she came in here. I must have made a mistake."

His expression softened and he waved her off with a pair of chubby hands.

"Very well child. Off you go. I'd hate for you to be late."

Selena cast me a meaningful look before slipping out, leaving me to fend for myself. If looks could kill, I certainly would be dead. Dinkle rushed over to the door. I stumbled out of his way. Frantically, he locked the classroom door shut and hurried back to the phone. I wove through the row of desks as I approached his workbench.

Cluttered paperwork was strewn haphazardly across the countertop. Books teetered precariously in a pile off to the side. The corner of a keyboard peeked out from the bottom of a coffee stained grade book. I crept closer, praying that the floorboards wouldn't creak beneath my weight. He smelled like the sludge on the bottom of a coffee pot and old cigarettes. Despite my body's protest, I leaned in. We needed answers. If I had to fight off the stench of this human's flesh then so be it. His clammy hands fumbled with the receiver.

Shaky fingers jabbed themselves into the dial pad. *Why was he in such a rush?* I hovered closer, willing the papers beneath me to stay still. It was better to have Dinkle move each item himself than risk being discovered. So I made sure not a speck of dust was out of place. He drummed a beat against his leg that only he alone could hear. Little drops of perspiration dotted his balding head. A voice picked up on the other line. Palpable relief smoothed out the creases in his forehead.

"Hello?-Oh thank God it's you. We have to stop this Paul. I am serious. The students are starting to get suspicious. We're bound to get caught if we continue! An outbreak almost occurred in the classroom today."

I strained my ears. A crackly voice came from the phone.

"Don't be such a worry wart John. No one is going to find out. Besides it would be unproductive if we were to stop the experiments right now. We actually have a female werewolf now! Do you know how hard it was to find another female wolf after the first one had died?"

Dinkle's mouth dropped in shock. "Miss Gaines is a wolf?"

My blood turned to ice and my stomach twisted with dread. Claws of frustration tore through me. They had another wolf before Jacob and now they had Olivia too?

Scornful laughter crackled from the receiver.

A shiver worth a thousand scurrying spider legs rippled down my spine.

"Yes! Miss Gaines is a werewolf. Were you not there for the security footage?"

"You mean the security footage after the dance?"

"Yes!"

My heart nearly shattered. *Stupid, stupid, how could I be so stupid?* Little did I know about the security cameras and their ability to capture the supernatural on screen. *Why didn't I think of that during the dance?* I should have done better, then again I hadn't realized or even thought that my illusions wouldn't be captured on screen.

"Yes, well... I saw it but... I figured there was some sort of glitch on the computer screen."

"Well it wasn't. I have tests to confirm it. Who would have thought we'd find another female wolf on campus, let alone a vampire? The preparations for some more testing are taking place as we speak. Soon we will be able to measure the height of their pain tolerance."

"You kidnapped Miss Gaines?" Dinkle asked, completely awestruck.

"Oh come now Jonathan, you can't really call it kidnapping when she isn't a kid.

My stomach twisted with hate. It took everything within me to contain myself.

"I figured you would be excited John, I mean in a matter of days we will learn if vampires are stronger than their werewolf counterparts."

My chest tightened with pain. I couldn't believe what I was hearing.

Did he think we were just cattle?

I leaned in, desperately trying to glean as much information from this conversation as possible.

Dinkle twisted the phone cord around in his hands and licked his lips.

"How are you going to do that?" He inquired, his voice quavered just slightly.

The voice on the other line grew impatient.

"By having them fight each other under observation you idiot. How else would I be able to do it?"

My mouth went desert dry.

I brought trembling a hand to my lips.

Fight each other? Had this man gone insane?

Dinkle nearly dropped his phone. He scrambled to get the handset tucked back under his ear.

"But they are just kids!" He sputtered. "Isn't that considered cruel and unusual punishment?" The voice on the end simply scoffed. "Don't be silly John. Cruel and unusual punishment only applies to human law. These things aren't human, John. They are monsters. When are you going to get that through your thick head?"

Pain flickered behind John's blue eyes. Molten rage bubbled up inside me. We may be different but surely that didn't meant we were monsters. The man on the other line cleared his throat. The sound dragged me back into the present state of mind.

"We will discuss this later on a more secure line. I have a meeting with the school board in ten minutes and it is imperative that I arrive on time."

He paused and his voice took on a more foreboding tone.

"Remember our arrangement, John. It's too late to back out now and you know that."

John let out a defeated sigh then there was a click on the other end.

Disgust slithered through me, filling my veins with poisonous hate.

How could they let this pompous asshole be the school principal? Didn't they notice students were disappearing under his care? White hot fury coursed through me. *Who gave him the right to play with other people's lives like this anyhow?*

I dug my teeth into the side of my cheek. I had to keep calm. If I made a sound then everything I accomplished here would be for nothing. The desire to scream clawed at my throat but I did everything I could to contain myself. I bit down on my tongue, willing myself to breathe.

Multiple thoughts and ideas buzzed around inside my head. On a positive note I figured out Frank was still alive. On a not so positive note we did not know where they held him, Olivia or Jacob Parks. Lemmings had mentioned something about werewolves being on campus.

Did that mean that most of his subjects had come from the school itself?
Was that why all the students had gone missing? Only time could tell.

Dinkle slumped in his chair and fumbled hopelessly through his grade book. Bags of exhaustion hung from his eyes. I frowned. *Didn't this guy have anything better to do besides work?* I couldn't stay much longer. I was pulling energy from my very own core in order to keep the illusion of invisibility going. Eventually, I would run out. It was only a matter of when. He had to at least eat, pee or sleep sometime, right? Speaking of food, a Jimmy John's sandwich sat at the corner of his desk. It oozed with mayo. The tantalizing smell of crisp lettuce, roasted bacon and ripe tomatoes sent a gurgling pang of hunger through my intestines.

Dinkle froze.

I licked my lips. His head whipped in my direction. I sucked in a deep breath and held it. His blue polliwog eyes darted to and fro, searching for the source of sound until they landed on me with a sense of cold certainty. *Well damn.* So much for being covert. I thought bitterly to myself. He paused, then squinted. My heart had stuttered. I had forgotten to breathe. Apprehension froze me in place. *Could he see through my guise?* I was only using illusive magic after all. My fingers tightened around the threads of magic. Mystical energies surged through me. Droplets of cold sweat trickled down my spine. He swiped a chubby hand towards my face, blindly grasping for the source of noise.

I stumbled backwards but managed to catch myself before crashing into his bookcase. He leaned in further. I gathered up my tails and held them close to my chest. My heart thundered like the hooves of a thousand race horses. I pressed my back tight against the wall. He inched closer. His breath stank of old cigarettes and stale coffee. His body trapped me between the bookcase and his desk. I had nowhere else to go. Terror gripped my chest. I took in a shallow breath.

A sharp knock shattered the silence.

Dinkle bristled with irritation.

"Who is it?" He snarled.

A muffled voice called out from the other side of the door.

"Mr. Dinkle, is that you?"

John grumbled sourly behind his breath.

He paused once more and stole one more dubious glance my way before waddling towards the door. My shoulders sagged with relief. Seconds later, the chakra in my solar plexus sputtered, sparked and cramped. The fluent flow of magic from my chakra to my fingertips faltered. A wave of terror washed over me. *Had it been that long already? Surely I couldn't have ran out of magical energy that fast. Not yet.* I yanked on the mystical tendrils that weaved through my veins. Sure enough each pull took more effort. I cursed.

Damn, damn and double damn. If it wasn't one thing then it was something else. If I wasn't careful then my illusion could unravel and everything I had accomplished here would be lost. I was running out of time. The magic within my core was almost spent. I should have known I wouldn't have been able to hold an illusion this complex for that long. Mentally, I cursed myself for my own stupidity.

I glanced to the left then the right. There was nowhere to hide. I contemplated squatting behind one of the student workstations but surely Dinkle would find me on his way out. I tiptoed after him. Desperately, I tugged the molecules closer to me, trying my best to maintain the illusion of invisibility. Maybe if I was lucky I could slip out before he could notice. One could only hope, right? Dinkle cracked the door open to reveal a panting Hawk Eyes. My hammering heart leapt into my throat. A flood of hope rushed through me. Sweet Inari, here came the cavalry.

"Boy I'm sure glad you're still here." She gasped between breaths. "I forgot to grab a study guide for tomorrow's quiz. Is there any way I can slip in and get a copy?"

Dinkle frowned and puckered his lips. His face reminded me of a disgruntled bulldog. He looked at her thoughtfully. Wisps of black hair floated around her head in a wild disarray. A long pause stretched out between them.

"Mr. Dinkle?" Hawk Eyes probed.

John shook his head before swinging the door open further.

"Yes, yes of course come in."

A curious Astrid peeked around Hawk Eyes' shoulder and looked in.

Her amber eyes searched the room.

Dinkle's brow wrinkled with suspicion.

"Is everything alright Miss Rodriguez? It isn't like you to forget these sorts of things."

Hawk Eyes twittered with laughter and fidgeted with her braid.

"Oh well, you know, um, I think it's the stress from the upcoming exams. I sort of forget things when I am under pressure." He held the door for her. She paused for deliberate effect and looked me straight in the eyes. "As soon as I get this study guide *I can get out of here.*"

She had said the last words with a sense of purpose.

Astrid and John exchanged looks of bewilderment.

I recognized that as my cue and dove out of the open doorway and into the safety of the hall. I sucked in a breath of clean air and kissed the ground. *Sweet mother of Inari, thank the Gods for friends!* A tickle crept up my throat, urging me to expel the chemical-laden air that my body had ingested, but I suppressed myself. If I were to make a noise now it would be game over. Dinkle raised a fuzzy brow.

"Are you sure you are alright?" He insisted.

She stuffed a wisp of hair behind her ear and flashed him a jittery smile.

"I am sorry. I suppose that came off as a little rude. You see I have a dentist appointment later today and I can't wait to get out of school early."

Dinkle gave her a suspicious frown as she rocked back on her heels.

"I see. Well come in, I haven't got all day."

She moments later, she emerged with a study guide in her right hand.

Astrid offered John an apologetic smile.

"Thank you sir. Selena can get sorta nutty over things like this."

He grunted in return and closed the door.

"Well that was impressive." I wheezed between choked breaths.

"Can it Lex." Selena snarled.

The magic around me flickered like a dying light bulb before completely sputtering out with a guttural effect. Thankfully, no one else was there to witness my flickering presence. Astrid's cat-like eyes watched me with a neutral expression, she appeared unfazed.

"Yes I must agree if I say so myself." Astrid commented coolly as she pushed her glasses higher up onto the bridge of her nose. "You know, Selena has quite a knack for acting, despite her honest qualities. Don't you agree?"

I chose not to respond.

Astrid was not at all pleased.

"I appreciate the flattery, Astrid, but I think I will stick with the student council."

Dinkle should have known. Selena would have never forgotten something like that. With a flick of her hand she toss the study guide into the trash.

"We on the other hand have other matters to discuss." She said pointedly.

Her flinty brown eyes bore into me like stone daggers.

"Specifically with Lexi."

I grimaced.

Astrid shook her head and clucked her tongue. "Yes, I do agree."

Together their eyes smoldered with disapproval.

I flinched beneath their molten glares.

"Bathroom. *Now*." Selena hissed and stalked off without another word.

Obediently, I followed.

Astrid simply shook her head and took the rear.

"Tut, tut, Lexi you've been a naughty girl." Astrid purred.

I had to dodge a few students to keep up.

"I can't believe you!" Selena howled as shoved the door open and stormed in. "You insist on doing everything yourself. How can you just go on a whim like that without keeping us informed? We are supposed to be a team."

She slammed open each bathroom stall while Astrid kept watch at the door.

"I still can't get over that trick of yours." Astrid muttered enviously to herself.

I rubbed a nervous hand along my arm.

"Easy you guys, I made it out ok so what is the big deal?"

Selena's pupils dilated. "You can't seriously be asking me that, can you? You risked exposure. Why wouldn't that be a big deal?"

"Don't kid yourself." Astrid scoffed, each word dripped with disdain. Flames of rage danced behind her cat like eyes. "You were running out of magic you bumbling baboon. Selena was the one who got you out safe and sound. *Not you.* She was the one who caught onto what was going on. She was the one who came up with the idea of going in and checking in on you. If she hadn't you'd probably still be in that room right now. What were you thinking?"

A sliver of guilt gnawed at my center but I quickly pushed it away.

Astrid did have a point, Selena did come to my rescue. Regardless, I didn't ask for their help and I could have made it on my own. *Couldn't I?* A little voice inside told me no.

Astrid's expression softened.

"Look. I get that you want to help Frank and we get that."

Hawk Eyes nodded in agreement.

"We're all trying to help you. Really, we are." Astrid continued.

"All we ask is that you let us in!" Hawk Eyes interjected.

Astrid held up a hand in request for silence.

Reluctantly, Hawk Eyes obeyed.

"Selena has a point. We're stronger together than apart. The last thing we need is for you to get caught up in this mess too. Besides, do you realize how devastated Ethan and I would be if we lost you?"

There was a moment of silence between us.

Astrid's amber eyes had lost all their hellfire. Only coals of disappointment, hurt and betrayal lay in their wake. My stomach roiled with emotions. A part of me felt that what I did was justified and another part of me felt that I wasn't. *Did I have the right to jump in on my own without informing them of my decision?* We did, however, agree to work as a team but if I had waited I could have missed out on an important opportunity. *Why couldn't they see that?* I cleared my throat and swallowed my pride before looking the two of them in the eyes.

"Look, I am sorry. I jumped on an opportunity without informing you. You're mad. I get it. However, I want to make one thing clear. Frank risked himself to help keep you safe Astrid. If I ever need to take risks I am going to take them, regardless of the consequences."

I stole a glance at Hawk Eyes.

"I didn't tell you because I figured you would be furious if I told you what I was going to do."

"Sounds about right." Hawk Eyes replied with a mollified smile.

"I felt like if I didn't act fast I'd miss out on an important opportunity. I am sorry you feel that I kept you out of the loop."

The two of them inclined their heads.

"Now keep in mind it was my full intention to tell you everything during lunch but I suppose I'll tell you now. We'll just have to go over the details with the boys later."

CHAPTER 19

LUNCH TRAYS CLATTERED in the background while classmates chattered amongst each other. A miasma of greasy cafeteria food, unpleasant body odor and harsh cleaning products overpowered my nose. Together we sat off in the corner, in a secluded area, at one of the round cafeteria tables. Astrid pensively swirled a finger through her hot chocolate while Hawk Eyes pushed her salad around with a fork. The two of them had willingly remained silent while I brought Ethan and his pack up to speed on Lemming's plans. After I finished there was a long pause. A million thoughts danced behind Ethan's forest green visage. Next to him sat the twins, Zach and Zander. Far off to the right sat Jordan. Buzz was nowhere to be seen.

"Aren't you forgetting something?" Hawk Eyes pressed.

"Like?" I had asked, clearly not comprehending.

Ethan cast a quizzical glance my way.

The twins also watched me with a keen interest.

Everyone waited expectantly for a reply.

"Oh you mean the part where she sucked her magic dry and risked exposure by getting herself locked up with Dinkle inside the chemistry lab?" Astrid inquired coyly as she twisted a piece of hair around her other finger.

Concern furrowed Ethan's brow.

I shot the two girls a dirty glare.

Astrid returned the favor as she licked the hot chocolate off of the opposite fingertip.

Damn succubus. I thought bitterly to myself.

The last thing I needed was for Ethan to worry about me.

Zach's eyes danced with curiosity. "Do tell." He mused.

Jordan's eyes darted from me to the girls then back again.

"That's interesting and all but what does this has to do with Jacob?" Jordan inquired with a frown.

I made a point to ignore him.

"I did what I had to do." I hissed through gritted teeth.

"Lexi..." Ethan began.

Here we go, not again. I thought to myself as I let out a miserable groan.

"How am I supposed to protect you if you run off on a whim like that?" Ethan asked.

I threw my hands up into the air. I had reached my boiling point. I knew where this was going and I wanted no part of it. I was sick and tired of people trying to look out after me.

"Look, I don't need your protection Ethan. When are you going to get that through your thick head?"

Astrid and Hawk Eyes exchanged wary glances

In the meantime, Astrid pulled out a book while Hawk Eyes took a great interest in her salad.

"She sounds pretty selfish if you ask me, mate." Zander said with a cynical snort.

My fingers tightened around my bottle of chocolate milk.

I cast him a sidelong glance. "Well thankfully he didn't ask your opinion, *mate*."

Zanders ice blue eyes narrowed into tiny slits.

"Easy you two." Zach crooned.

"The last thing we need is a supernatural outbreak here in the school cafeteria."

Ethan's scowl deepened. "Lexi.." He rumbled in warning.

I jabbed a finger at Ethan and returned the challenge with a menacing glare.

"Don't Lexi me, Ethan. You can't tell me what to do. I am not one of your wolves and you will do well to remember that."

Zach's brows shot up in surprise. "Feisty one isn't she?"

Jordan sunk lower in his chair and pinched his brow.

"Can we please just get back to the point?" Jordan whined.

Zander leaned forward. "No it's okay Boss. Lemme handle this one."

Ethan's lip curled up in a feral gesture. "No, you won't."

His scent patterns flared with male hormones. Jordan flinched.

This was clearly not the time to whip out his pheromones.

"Lexi is *mine* and no one is going to lay a hand on her. *Got it?*"

The scent of wolf rolled off him in waves.

I merely rolled my eyes.

"Mine this, mine that. Honestly, Ethan I think you're missing the point here." Astrid said with a sigh as she flipped to another page in her book.

Hawk Eyes, on the other hand, didn't even seemed fazed. Silently, she stabbed at her food in sullen silence. Her body language told me she had a feeling something like this would happen. Then again, territorial issues and testosterone flare ups happened to be a thing when you hung out with a group of werewolves. Zander's ice blue eyes bore into me like daggers but he didn't make a move to argue with his Alpha.

Jordan, however, was bursting at the seams with frustration.

"That's all well in good. Ethan likes Lexi. Lexi doesn't like Ethan." Jordan stated flatly. "Now can we get back to the point? What did you learn about Jacob? Is he alive? Is he okay? Do you know where he is at?" His voice twanged with a hint of desperation.

I took a moment to pause.

Something inside my chest wrenched. *Why had I not realized this wasn't about me?* Lately things have been a bit rough for the omega ever since his former leader had disappeared. I wasn't the only one that was missing a friend here. Apparently, Jacob was kind to Jordan and had a tendency to keep Andrew's constant need to antagonize at bay. Not having him around must have been devastating for Jordan. I stumbled for some sort of response.

"They didn't mention Jacob but I am assuming he isn't dead."

"How can you be so sure?" Jordan asked, his voice quavered with uncertainty.

I grimaced. I couldn't do anything to comfort him without lying. That was a risk I couldn't afford. Kitsune couldn't lie. If they did their powers would be significantly diminished against anyone that they had lied to. Such a risk would leave me exposed and vulnerable to any future attacks. I highly doubted Takahashi would try to hurt me but I wasn't willing to chance it.

Someone approached from behind but I didn't break eye contact with Jordan.

Eye contact was everything with the wolves.

"Look all I know is that they have Frank and now they have Olivia and that in itself should give us enough reason to break in."

"Then you can count me in." A voice announced from behind.

I turned to witness Buzz standing behind me. I frowned.

"I thought you hit the road." I replied, purely surprised.

Coals of hatred burned in his eyes.

"Ethan filled me in on what was going on during chemistry. Sounds to me you need all the help you can get." Anger twisted his pale face and his scent patterned flared with smoky rage.

"Besides if they have Olivia too then it's me who is going in to save her."

Zander chuckled and waved his comrade down.

"Now, now simmer down mate. Just because you want her to be your girl does not mean you get to call all the shots. You should know that by now, eh?"

Zach snickered softly in reply to his brother's response.

Zander managed to mimic his comrade's expression to a T.

"I'm gunna be the one that saves her." He mocked.

Zach and Zander collapsed into a fit of laughter.

The girls were unamused.

Hawk Eyes simply shook her head, while Astrid remained nose deep within her book.

In the meantime, Jordan frowned.

"Do you know how ridiculous that sounds?" Zach inquired.

Buzz's face turned purple with rage. I watched him with a new sense of curiosity. It was refreshing to see him in a new light. Who would have known this lug of a nut had a soft spot? Never have I ever experienced him showing a granule of kindness towards someone else. Sure Liv and him may have been dating, but I figured it was more for show than anything else. I found the idea of Drew being a considerate human being down right charming.

Zach sighed and flicked away a tear.

"Look, you're upset. I get it but if we're ever gunna get Liv outta there we gotta work together."

Ethan simply sighed and shook his head in silent disapproval.

"Would it kill you guys to show some ounce of sympathy?" Ethan inquired with an impatient sigh. A few moments later he began to rub at his temples.

A fuming Buzz took his place at the table.

"Can we please get to the point?" Jordan pressed.

Zach mumbled something around a mouthful of pizza.

"Sorry mate. It's in our genes." Zander said with a sympathetic shrug.

Zach paused and took a good at my plate. "Ey, you gonna eat that biscuit?"

I sighed and handed over my cookie. *Damn, Australians and their slang.* I thought bitterly to myself. Zander rested his chin on a balled up fist and flashed me a lazy smile.

"So how will you go about doin' this lass?"

I leaned back in my chair and folded my hands.

A cordial smile curled at the corner of my lips.

"It's simple really. We will just have to break into the school." I replied.

Zach's smile faltered, a piece of lettuce hung from his lips.

Hawk Eyes stared at me in complete bewilderment.

"Did you say break in?" Hawk Eyes asked, purely aghast.

"Yes, as a matter of fact I did. All we need is a car and a place to meet."

"Well, you can meet at my place." Jordan interjected.

"The parents will be out of town this week and I can make everyone food."

Zach swallowed and broke out into a goofy grin.

"Zander has ol' Molly. You think we could take a gander in that?" .

Zander's face twisted with disapproval.

"Oi, now why do you have to go off like that without askin' first?"

Zach flashed him his puppy dog eyes. "Pleeeasee?"

Zander scowled at his sibling. Everyone at the table held their breath. A long moment passed before he grudgingly let out an irritated sigh.

"I suppose we can use her just this once." He groused. "Especially if it means we can find dirt on Dinkle. We better find somethin' and it better be good."

Hawk Eyes sputtered in shock.

"You can't be serious. If we get caught we'll get expelled!"

I shrugged, my expression nonchalant.

"I am dead serious and the key word is *if* we get caught."

Hawk Eyes worked her jaw, disbelief twisted her features.

"The very idea of it is outright scandalous."

The thought itself must have horrified her. Hawk Eyes had a sparkling record and a high reputation for academic excellence. The very idea of breaking into the school filled her with dread. She had worked too hard to taint her academic reputation.

"Look, if we don't take this risk then we could miss out on some important information. Information that could lead to where Frank, Olivia and Jacob are. It's simple really. I mean we have Astrid here who can override the security system. If we approach the school discreetly and wear black clothes then everything should be fine."

I waited for Astrid's input but she didn't reply. I turned to witness her deeply delved into a book, unaware of the whole conversation. I elbowed her. Her forehead creased at the interruption and she lifted her head.

"Hmm? Oh yes, about that." She adjusted her glasses and focused on us. "The security system shouldn't be a problem. It's an easy fix really but it's all about timing."

Ethan groaned as he dug the heels of his palms into his eye sockets. *"How can you read a book at a time like this?"*

She blinked and wrinkled her freckled nose.

"What? Reading helps ease stress levels and at this current time I feel a tad bit under pressure, don't you? Would you rather me suck on your face instead?

Ethan simply shook his head. "No, probably not. Not now anyway."

Jordan cast a skeptical glance Astrid's way. "Is she for real?"

Ethan gave Astrid a thorough look over but she had already went back to reading her book.

A distant smile tugged at the corner of his lips.

"Yeah, she's for real alright. She's been known to hack into governmental facilities before. If anyone can do it she can." Ethan replied with a hint of pride.

Zach looked at Astrid with awe and inspiration.

He swallowed his food and then flashed her a goofy grin. "Cool."

Zander chortled and clapped Ethan on the back, snapping him out of his stupor.

"Alright mate. We'll take your word for it." He said with a grin.

Ethan's freckled cheeks flushed furiously.

Buzz frowned. His flinty brown eyes burned with determination.

"Now wait one hot minute. So Astrid can trip the alarms and mess with the school's security system. That's great and all but I am assuming that she will need to be in front of a computer to monitor the progress. If that's the case then how do we plan on getting into Dinkle's desk?"

"Aw poppycock, why do you have to be such a downer Drew?" Zander growled.

Hawk Eyes shook her head and rubbed her jaw in agreement.

"No, Andrew's got a point, Lex. He keeps the place locked up like Fort Knox and it isn't like him to leave a key lying about. What do we plan on doing once we get inside the lab?"

The boys nodded their heads and mumbled in agreement.

Ethan flashed the group a deceptive smile.

"Well that's what lock picks are for aren't they?"

Both Hawk Eyes and Jordan had exchanged frowns. Their eyes were full of misgivings. The twins however shared a pair of smug smiles. Buzz on the other hand watched his alpha with a sense of uncertainty. He wasn't convinced. The group itself hadn't considered Ethan to be of a criminalistic mind. Then again, he did hang out with me and it was me who held up a reassuring hand.

"Okay, okay. Let's answer Zander's question first." I said as I took a measured amount of peas and placed two of them on the table, a ways away from the tray. "Ok so these two peas will be Zander and Zach. They'll be parked off in the distance. We need a group of four to infiltrate the school grounds. One on the east side, another on the west and two to go in. Zach and Zander will drive the getaway car, sorry folks you're going to be all the way over here. We can't risk you being seen."

I pointed at my lunch tray.

"This is the school. Let's say this pile of mashed potatoes is Dinkle's room. Let's say the parking lot is over here." I indicated to an area on the table. "Hawk Eyes this is you." I placed a pea in the area I designated as the parking lot. "I need you and Buzz to check the perimeter. Make sure that the coast is clear and we don't have any people coming into the school or wandering around outside. When given the signal you'll walkie Zach and Zander to come pick us up."

I paused and looked at Zach and Zander.

"You'll have to pick us up from the street. It is critical that you keep the car in the shadows. If you get too close to the security cameras then the authorities may be able to identify your car. Meanwhile, Jordan will keep a watch on the phone. If we do get caught we need someone there to answer our phone call for help."

I turned to look at Ethan. His emerald eyes met mine. They held a knowing expression that was all too familiar. In the past we'd work together like this when pulling pranks. A smile tugged at the corner of my lips. This was going to be like old times only this time it was Dinkle and not Noah.

"Ethan is going inside with me."

Hawk Eyes fidgeted in her chair and furrowed her brows.

"Why can't I come too?" She asked in a waspy tone.

I paused and held up my hand. Once she stopped talking I continued.

"Look. I can only allow invisibility for one person and myself. I can only perform this illusion for a limited amount of time. Doing it for two people puts me on an even more limited time frame. Ethan and I have done this sort of thing before so he'll know what to do. He'll be the hallway look out while I pick the locks. You'll be my eyes outside. Understand?"

I tilted my head towards Zander. "So are you in or not?"

Jordan nodded his head in acknowledgement. "I'm in."

Buzz tilted his head. "I am in as well."

Zach spoke up before his brother could utter a word. Like a chipmunk, he had stuffed his cheeks with chicken nuggets. "Count me in too!"

"Bloody hell." Zander cursed and rubbed his temple with the tips of his fingers. "What happened to comin' up with some sort of decision together? I am yer brother after all. *Shit.*"

Ethan chortled and returned Zander's friendly slap on the back.

"Sorry buddy, unfortunately for you Lexi can be *very* persuasive."

Zander let out an exasperated sigh. "Count me in too."

Zach elbowed him affectionately in the side. Zander swatted at his brother's hand. "Oh come off it." He growled. His face darkened as he ran his fingers through his short sandy brown hair. "I suppose we really do have to use Molly won't we?" Zach swallowed the remainder of his food and gave him a toothy grin.

"Astrid's wheels aren't big enough to hold the five us, let alone you."

Astrid's amber eyes peered curiously over the top of her book. "Molly?"

Zach shrugged. "Molly is what we call our minivan."

Astrid pursed her lips. "Alright then, let's make it a date."

"We can meet at my place. Say, sometime early in the morning?" Jordan inquired.

Astrid flashed the twins a sultry smile as she got up to leave.

"See you then, boys" She said with a seductive purr.

Before they could respond the lunch bell chimed.

I leaned in and gave them a wink. "Oh, and don't forget to wear black!"

Then off we went.

CHAPTER 20

MOLLY'S HEADLIGHTS CLICKED OFF. Her engine purred softly as we pulled onto an unlit street. We crept through the darkness. Patches of dappled moonlight danced across us as we puttered down the road. Anxiety clawed at my nerves. *What if we got caught? Would we be stuck in cages for the rest of our lives like the criminals on TV? What would happen to us?*

A whirlpool of doubts, fears and questions swirled inside my mind. Silence impregnated the cabin. No one had spoken since we left the driveway. With each passing moment the tension intensified. So did my fears. I itched with the desire to shatter the silence. *What was I going to say? How was the weather? Who was I kidding? I mean it's not like idle chit chat would be appropriate right now. Or would it?* Now I was just babbling. My grip on my gloves made my fingers tingle. Buzz closed his eyes and leaned his head back up against Molly's window. Ethan rubbed his brow. Zach sat in the front seat while Zander drove the van.

Hawk Eyes exhaled and hugged her new jacket tightly to her chest. Ethan maintained a rigid posture as he fidgeted with his gloves. Thanks to Garcia we all wore matching black jackets, ski masks, sweats and leather gloves. When she heard about the raid she went on a buying spree. No complaints here, we needed all the help we could get. I personally felt like the ski masks were a bit much but Ethan insisted that our faces be covered in case we were seen. We were officially Ferndale High's criminal geek squad once we put on the matching headsets. Benson was the one who insisted that we wear them. Apparently they'll help ensure that our team's communication is clear but remains private. Leave it up to Senator Benson to provide the fancy gadgets.

Shadows danced across the van's cabin as Zander pulled to a stop beneath a scraggly tree. The clock read three am in bold red letters. We didn't see a single light and all the houses we had passed remained dark. He cut the engine. Hot ticking and popping noises shattered the silence.

"Everyone ready?" I indicated.

"Better now than never." Hawk Eyes grumbled.

Ethan gave me a thumbs up.

Buzz nodded.

"You betcha!" Zach grinned.

Zander only grunted.

I adjusted the headset and brought the mic closer to my lips.

"Operator. We have positioned ourselves. We will arrive at the designated location in ten minutes. Do you copy?"

Astrid's voice crackled over the head set.

"Copy, loud and clear. Notify me as soon as you arrive Commander."

Earlier we had come up with the cheesiest code names. Astrid had stressed the importance of using code just in case someone ended up stumbling upon our walkie channel. Reluctantly, we agreed. Ethan insisted on being called Wolf. Zach lovingly gave Selena the nickname Viper for her bad temper. Andrew begrudgingly accepted his nickname Buzz and I took the name Commander. Zander went by Aussie and Zach decided on Dingo.

Together we hopped out of the van and stepped into the brisk November air. Zach and Zander remained in the van. A cool breeze tickled my cheek as dry leaves scuttled across the concrete. The walk took a good ten minutes. We approached the parking lot. Our breath came out in heavy wet clouds. Lot lights beamed brightly upon the abandoned parking lot like beacons in the night. The school stood tall off in the distance like a haunted house on a hill.

Darkness engulfed the glass windows. Silver moonlight cast shadows across the school yard. Leaves littered the tree lined walkway. The barren saplings lifted their skeletal arms towards the glittering sky. Silently, we tiptoed from one shadow to the next until we were on the east side of the building. Ethan's steamy breath whispered into the headset.

"This is Wolf. We have reached the designated location, over."

My breath came out in misty clouds.

"When you open that door you will only have fifteen minutes." Astrid replied. "Once you are in the time will begin. The alarms will go off if you are even a millisecond over. It's critical that you get in and get out as soon as possible. I cannot stall for you, understand?"

"We understand." Ethan said as he adjusted the timer on his watch.

"This is Viper. The north perimeter is clear, ready for entry. Do you copy?"

"This is Buzz, the south perimeter is also clear."

"We don't see anything on the south end." Zach replied.

I could only imagine him peering through those obnoxious binoculars.

"We copy, over and out." Ethan replied, clear as a bell.

"The countdown will commence."

"Three." Astrid began.

I reached deep within my core until my fingertips tingled with magic.

"Two." I yanked on the molecules within the air and twisted them into a veil.

"One" The molecules stretched around us, forming a bubble of invisibility. "Blast off."

The lock unclicked. Ethan's timer chirped.

Together we rushed inside and sought refuge in the sanctuary of the shadows. Silently, we creeped down the corridor. Our rubber soles padded softly against the carpet. My heart thundered in my chest. Each breath came out short and sharp. Only one hundred more yards to go. We could do this. We had fifteen minutes to get in and get out.

We rounded the corner and slipped from one shadow to the next. "Commander, since the alarm has been tripped there will be a security guard on the premises to make sure everything is ok. You have ten minutes till he arrives."

"Great." My voice dripped with venom. "Just what we needed. "

I fumbled for my pick set as we approached the chemistry lab.

"Operator, would you mind unlocking Dinkle's door?"

I scowled at Ethan. *Why wasn't his heart rate accelerating? Why wasn't he dripping with sweat? How could he remain at ease in time like this?*

"Sorry sister, I can't. If it was controlled electronically I would, but it is not."

I wiggled my pick around but the lock struggled to move. Sweat trickled down my neck. The leather gloves soaked up the faint moisture in my hands. Silently, I thanked Garcia for her thoughtfulness. If it hadn't been for the gloves my hands would have slipped. After a few more seconds of gentle coaxing the lock clicked. Ethan brought his hand to his headset as I rushed in.

"We're in." He declared into his mic.

I glanced around the room. Chemical–laden air filled my lungs. Our sneakers squeaked along the linoleum. Cedar workstations were everywhere. A branch hung just outside the classroom window, its outline sent spidery shadows along the wooden cabinets.

"If I were a teacher who was up to no good where would I hide my dirty laundry?"

My fox like vision gave me the ability to sift through the darkness. Ethan however, skimmed the room with his flashlight. His wolf's eyesight was superb but his human form hindered its abilities. My eyes followed the rows of desks all the way up to Dinkle's cluttered table top. Ethan's beam faltered when it approached the desk.

"Hey, he doesn't seem to be the type to hide things out in the open. Let's try his desk."

He gave me a solid slap on the back.

"I'll cover the hallway while you investigate the desk."

"Sounds like a plan." I replied as I yanked at each drawer.

"Nine more minutes folks." Astrid crooned.

Perspiration peppered my neck in cold drops. My hands trembled as I tugged open each drawer only to reveal miscellaneous items like pencils, pens and sticky notes.

Hawk Eyes' voice shattered my concentration.

"This is Viper. The perimeter has been breached. There is someone pulling into the parking lot. It appears to be an officer. I await for further instructions."

The hairs on the back of my neck hackled.

"Damn it. I thought we had at least five more minutes until he showed up."

Ethan took control over the conversation.

I continued to rummage through Mr. Dinkle's things, desperately searching for some sort of clue.

"This is Wolf, responding to your request. Which parking lot is he pulling into?"

There was a significant pause before Hawk Eyes replied. Tension had built. I tugged on a locked drawer. My heart jumped at the possible prospect of finding something. "He has pulled into the west lot."

I knelt down and began picking the lock with shaking hands. Damn my worries, my fear, my nervous energies. *Damnable hands, why won't they work?* A few more seconds passed.

"Six more minutes to go." Astrid pressed, her voice tight with apprehension.

"I may have found something here. We need more time."

I bit my lip, practically willing the drawer to open with my mind.

"Time is something we don't have." Astrid hissed through the headset.

"The officer has officially entered the building. I repeat, the officer has entered the building."

I cursed when I heard Hawk's Eyes' quavering announcement. *Damn, damn and double damn. Why did he have to enter the building now? I thought we had more time than this. What happened to our solid ten minutes?* Sweat trickled down my cheek.

Ethan held his breath.

Zach scoffed. "Hold it together princess."

Zander clucked his tongue reprovingly.

"Ladies let's turn it up a notch, time's runnin' out."

My heart pattered furiously inside my chest like a frantic humming bird within a cage. My pick slipped between my sweaty fingers.

"Not helping!" I snarled as I wiggled the pick inside the lock's chambers.

"Wolf!" I hissed. "Get in here and work on a possible exit plan."

Ethan slipped back inside, quiet as death and lithe as liquid.

"There is no way we will be able to use the front door." I said.

I could hear footsteps off in the distance. Ethan sucked in a calming breath as he ran his hand along the windowsill edge.

"Don't worry we'll figure something out." Ethan murmured quietly.

"Our first priority is to stay calm." The perspiration on his neck and the quickening of his heart rate had said otherwise. I didn't argue. I held my tongue and ground away at the chamber. The lock finally clicked and gave way beneath my pick. Ethan's shoulders sagged and I exhaled in relief. We gave the drawer one final tug and it squealed open.

"Four more minutes, folks." Astrid announced over the headset.

We cringed. The footfalls came down our hallway. I frantically skimmed the drawer with my eyes. A few valuable things like a portable speaker, student cellphones and other electronics were scattered across the bottom of the drawer.

"Tick tock, ladies." Zander reprimanded in his damn Australian accent.

"Quit flapping your trap, Aussie." Buzz snarled over the headset.

"All unnecessary communication over the headset must desist immediately." Astrid replied hotly.

Someone called out to us from the hallway.

"Hello? Anyone there?"

Ethan's posture went rigid. My heart nearly exploded in my chest. Something in the back had caught my eye. Someone had stuffed a notebook in the back of the drawer. I snatched up the book and rifled through it with trembling hands. Dinkle's scrunched up handwriting scrawled across the pages. One of the paragraphs went into great detail about some experimental serum. My heart nearly leapt into my throat. Hot tears pricked at the corners of my eyes.

The security guard called out again.

"You aren't supposed to be in here. I know you're there. I can hear you."

Ethan and I shared wary glances. Thankfully, the door to the lab was closed.

"One minute" Astrid announced.

Ethan took in another calming breath. "Dingo, prepare for departure. Viper, Buzz, we will meet you at the designated location."

"Aye, Aye captain!" Zach trumpeted over the head set.

The footfalls grew closer, becoming clearer and more distinct.

"Commencing countdown at ten, nine...."

A beam of light danced outside in the hallway, searching for the source of noise.

The guard crooned into the night. "Come out, come out wherever you are."

His flashlight peeked into the chemistry lab.

We ducked out of sight.

Cold sweat dripped down my spine. The door handle jiggled. Thankfully Ethan had locked it before coming back in. Keys jangled. My heart thundered rapidly inside my chest like the wings of a frightened bird.

"Eight...." Waves of panic froze me in my place.

"Mercy me, Alexandria." Ethan growled beneath his breath. He grabbed me by my arm with a vice like grip and dragged me towards the window.

"Seven..."

He shoved me towards the window but I got stuck between the frame and the sill.

"Six..."

Oh sweet Inari, was I seriously going to set off the alarm with my fat ass hanging off the window sill? Please tell me there was a better way to go. Dread gnawed at my stomach.

"Five..."

The footfalls increased. A beam of light cut through the darkness in the room like a glowing light saber.

"Four..." Ethan jabbed his elbow into my side.

"Three...." I tumbled through the opening.

"Two..." My back bounced off the frozen ground, nearly knocking the wind out of me. I rolled out of the way and Ethan followed.

"One...." Ethan tugged the window shut with a soft click.

The lab door swung open to reveal a pudgy security guard.

"Zero..." We waited expectantly, but nothing happened.

Together, we exchanged looks of confusion. *Why didn't the alarm going off? Did the security guard have access to the school's codes?* The classroom lights flicked on to reveal a heavy man in a gray security uniform. The fluorescent light reflected off of his balding head. Beady brown eyes scoured the room.

We sunk further into the shadows as his flashlight skimmed over the courtyard. I pressed my back firmly against Ethan's chest. He wrapped a protective arm around my center. Together we held our breath. My lungs burned for air but I didn't dare take a breath lest the guard see the puff of air out of the corner of his beady brown eyes. Ethan gave my hand a firm squeeze.

"Hmm...well that's funny..." Astrid announced. There were a few clicks here and a pause there before she continued. "The guard must have overridden the alarms with his own codes. No matter. This actually works in our favor."

We exhaled as one.

I reprimanded myself for getting caught up in human emotions. I was a fox spirit after all. Sure, my human form needed oxygen to survive but the very idea of me wilting away inside a jail cell terrified me. Being caged was a Kitsune's greatest fear.

Stars glittered dimly in the dusty sky. The moon peeked shyly around a wispy gray cloud. Silently, I had thanked her for not betraying our position. Together we huddled beneath the shadows of the white pine. Minutes had passed but it seemed more like years. Ethan held me close to his chest. Warmth rolled off him in waves.

I frowned and looked down at the notebook that I had clutched so dearly to my breast. A sliver of guilt slithered through me. I had just broken into the school premises, illegally, and had stolen something valuable from a human. *What would Inari say if she knew what I had done?*

Would she approve? She was the guardian of all myobu. *I was myobu after all, wasn't I?*

I was raised as part of the celestial tribe, after all, and was born into a clan that pledged their fealty to the goddess. However, everything that I had done tonight went against the myobu code. Myobu were Kitsune that were meant to help and protect people, not sneak and steal. As of right now I could be considered just as bad as the Shadow Clan.

The very idea made me shudder. *How could Dinkle possibly be one of the good guys? Hell, he was a kidnapper that sacrificed another's well being for his own gain.* Then again, was it even my place to intervene?

My hold on the book tightened. Venomous hate coursed through my veins. Seeds of doubt blossomed within my stomach. *Surely our intentions were pure. Weren't they? We were after all trying to help Frank. Surely Inari, the goddess of good fortune and prosperity, would support our cause?* The chill of the November air had seeped into my bones.

"Damn kids." The guard groused to himself. His mustache twitched with irritation. Begrudgingly, he flicked off the lights before stalking out of the chemistry lab. His grumbling had forced me to focus on the present. His footsteps faded away. I strained my ears, desperate to figure out the security guard's location. Ethan had managed to leave the window a crack open. We didn't have the luxury of shutting it all the way. We feared the officer may have heard the window shut on our way out. A few more moments of silence had passed.

Viper's hushed voice shattered the silence. I nearly leapt out of my skin. "The perimeter is clear. Our friend has left the building. Now let's get a move on, it's freezing out here!"

We sat there in stunned silence. Moments later, a sheepish grin crept along my face. Within seconds, he snatched me up into a bear hug and twirled me around. Misty laughter escaped our lips.

I shook my head in disbelief. "I can't believe we did it!"

We gasped between bales of laughter.

Ethan settled me down onto the ground and gave me firm slap on the back.

"Well done, Commander. Now let's get the hell outta here before my berries fall off."

The black ski mask hid his smug smile but I could hear the mirth in his voice

I offered him a brief nod.

"Alright team.. This is Wolf, operation Waldo was a success. We'll meet you and Aussie at the designated location in five. Do you copy?"

Zach whooped in the background while Zander's smug voice played smoothly over the headset. "You betcha Boss."

I shook my head and smiled. After much sneaking around we had managed to make it back safe and sound. Molly purred off in the distance just beyond the abandoned soccer field. Zander had parked her among the shadows. Her black paint made it easy for her to blend in.

I clutched the notebook tightly to my chest. Exhausted, we tugged the slider door open and climbed in. Buzz and Hawk Eyes were already inside. She blew hot puffs of air into her hands and vigorously rubbed them together. She flashed us a chattering smile. Ethan pulled himself up and into the cabin of the van. Meanwhile, a coatless Buzz sat in the back seat with his eyes closed and his arms crossed. He had given his coat to Hawk Eyes for extra warmth. Zach's head popped up between the passenger seat and the driver seat. He tossed Ethan a clean towel. Ethan caught the towel in midair and raised a brow.

"It's about bloody time mate. What took you so long?"

"Next time you can try evading a security guard while I sit in the car with the heat on."

"Yikes." Zach grimaced.

He folded the towel neatly over the bucket seat before he sat down. I went to take a seat as well but Zander clucked his tongue. "Nah, nah now. Yer outta yer mind if you think yer going to sit on my interior with a bum full of dirt. Now be a good lass and get yer self a towel from the trunk."

Like most boys Zander loved his car. He didn't appreciate the thought of me staining his seats with dirt. I frowned.

Zander waved me off. "Well get on with it already! We haven't got all bloody day. Now go get a towel from the trunk."

I opened my mouth to protest but he waggled his finger at me.

"Nah. Don't be goin' there. Yer in my car, my rules."

Slack jawed, I looked over at Ethan.

He gave me a firm nod.

Zach shook his head with a smile.

I ground my jaw, I fought back the urge to smack that smile right off his face.

"Do as he says Lex. It's his car and we promised no harm would come to it."

Ethan had replied with an exhausted sigh.

Buzz's mouth quirked in amusement.

Begrudgingly, I stalked back to the hatch.

Zander continued to grumble about damn Americans and their lack of intelligence.

When I came back Hawk Eyes was hugging her coat tight to her frame.

"So did you find anything?" She asked as she shimmied her hands up and down her arms. Zander had the heat on full blast.

I tossed her Dinkle's beloved notebook. She caught it in midair.

"Looks like they're working on some sort of supernatural serum."

Hawk Eyes frowned as she thumbed through the book. Buzz peered over her shoulder. Ethan exhaled and leaned his head against the icy window. "I am just glad we found somethin' after doing all that. For a moment there I thought we were screwed."

Zach peered over the edge of his head rest, his sapphires glittering.

His expression was quizzical.

"Serum eh? What do they need a bloody serum for?" Zach asked.

I shrugged my shoulders to ease the stiffness in my joints. "Who knows?"

"Do you think he will find out?" Buzz inquired.

"Well I'm sure he'll notice the notebook has gone missing." I said.

"We made a point to keep everything looking as if it were before we came in." Ethan explained.

"Yeah, Ethan even locked the door. The security guy had to use his keys to get in." I added.

"So you don't think they will check the footage?' Buzz asked.

"Footage isn't going to be a problem folks." Astrid announced over the head set.

"I made a point to scramble the system by inserting previous footage from the night before."

Buzz's mouth mouth formed into an astonished O.

Selena's eyebrows furrowed as she sifted through the pages. "Hmm. Very strange."

Her thoughtful expression peaked my curiosity.

"What did you find?" I asked.

She rubbed thoughtfully at her jaw.

"Well if I am reading it correctly, it looks like they are trying to combine different talents and bottle them up into some sort of injection."

Zander took a turn onto a winding road.

"Sounds like some Frankenstein science project if yeh ask me." He said mildly.

Hawk Eyes pursed her lips but her expression remained thoughtful.

"It appears to be exactly that, only they're picking and choosing DNA strands instead of body parts. Here, have a look." She pushed the notebook towards Ethan. "Do these traits sound like they'd belong to a werewolf?" He clicked on his flashlight. His mouth gradually dropped as his eyes danced across the page. "High temper, shapeshifting into a wolf form, venomous bites, super strength, unnatural healing rates, chemical reaction to the moon, temperamental, superhuman speed."

His forehead wrinkled with comprehension.

"Yeah as a matter of fact this does sound like a werewolf."

He offered the notebook back to Hawk Eyes.

She dragged her finger along the following page.

"Superhuman speed, retractable fangs, sensitivity to sunlight, nocturnal tendencies, thrives on blood, hypnotic gaze and unnatural healing rates. These all sound like vampire traits." She nibbled on her thumb nail as I sat down next to her and looked over her shoulder.

"Huh, it looks like he circled what was a desirable trait and crossed out what he deemed as undesirable." I said as I peered over her shoulder.

Ethan ran his fingers through hair and looked up wearily.

"How do they know our weaknesses anyway? Do you think they used living vampires and werewolves a scientific experiments?" Buzz asked, utterly perturbed.

Ethan and I exchanged a glance. If that were the case then was Frank still alive? Or was he being impaled with silver as we speak?

CHAPTER 21

WE HUDDLED CLOSE TOGETHER within the evergreen bushes as we peered through the frosted window pane. Inside Mrs. Dinkle struggled with dinner. We could be celebrating our own Thanksgiving dinner at home beside our own fireplace. Instead of eating turkey we gnawed on snow in hopes of finding Frank's whereabouts. The only bird we'd be experiencing today would be our own goose flesh. Astrid's teeth chattered in agreement. Together our stomachs gurgled with hunger.

"How long is this going to take?" I whined.

"Yeah. We've been at it all day. Enough is enough already." Astrid groaned.

"Sh!" Ethan hissed. "You said you'd do whatever it takes to figure out what happened to Frank. This is the perfect opportunity to glean any useful information."

Astrid rolled her eyes and rubbed her mittens together. Her and I had shape shifted so many layers of clothing under our white puffy jackets that we looked like a pair of Michelin tire mascots. Wistfully, I had thought of Hawk Eyes. We had informed her of our plan but she had politely declined. She didn't think that her human body could withstand the freezing temperatures for a long period of time. Sometimes I wish I were human, if that were the case then I wouldn't be out here freezing my ass off. I would be inside, basking in front of a fire place.

What did Ethan think we could accomplish here anyway?

"The only useful information we have gleaned from Mrs. Dinkle is how to stuff a turkey." Astrid groused sourly. At least I was better off than her. I actually had an animal form that was built for this type of weather.

"We could have learned that from the food network channel in the luxury of our own home." I quipped back as I watched Mrs. Dinkle prepare her Thanksgiving dinner. So far she didn't seem to be enjoying it.

Two young boys zoomed through the kitchen. They almost barreled into her. One was older and than the other. They looked like brothers. The older boy laughed as he held a toy out of the younger one's reach. He had a slender form like his mother. The younger huffed and puffed. He had a heavier frame than his brother with his father's pudgy cheeks and his mother's beady eyes. I could hear them arguing through the window pane. The younger one's face twisted as he reached desperately for the toy the older one had.

"Give it back!" He yelped.

"Boys! Please stop fighting." Mrs. Dinkle pleaded with an exasperated sigh.

We ducked beneath the frosted window pane and hid beneath the shelter of the evergreen bushes as the older boy sprinted towards our window. He made a sharp turn towards the living room.

"Come and get it!" He called out, still clutching his brother's toy car. His voice drifted off into another room. Slowly, I peered into the kitchen window to find a weary Mrs. Dinkle with sagging shoulders. She leaned into the island for support as she pounded her fists against the dough with controlled frustration. Dinkle waddled into the room. He came up behind her and reached out to rub her shoulders. She pulled away.

"Whatever you are trying to do is not going to work."

His face screwed up with anguish.

"Eve, I am trying.. I am doing everything I can here!" He protested and then took a deep breath. "We should have the money soon or at least some of it…It's just taking them awhile to get it in."

She frowned and turned to peer up at him. Her hands were covered with flour. She checked to see if the boys were nearby and when she realized they weren't she continued.

"How much longer, John?" Her voice came out in an angry hiss.

"If we don't act quick we will lose everything and it will be all your fault!"

His thick glasses magnified his large blue eyes, making his guilt easily visible.

"I have done some thinking.." She said as she turned to the sink to rinse her hands.

"What about, Eve?" He asked, purely hopeful.

"I'll do anything, I swear." He stammered. "I am trying to fix this. I made a mistake and I know I screwed up."

Solemnly, she stared down the sink as she methodically wiped at her hands.

Her voice came out flat and emotionless. "I want a divorce."

He gaped at her with watery blue eyes. His jowls quivered as his mouth worked. For a moment he tried to collect his thoughts. He reminded me of a gaping fish, desperately trying to take a breath of fresh air.

"We are in a lot of trouble because of you...." She continued quietly. "We are about to lose the house. I got the eviction notice yesterday… I think it's best that I give you time to get things situated. Each time we get ahead you bring us one step behind."

Dinkle shifted uneasily from one foot to the other.

"Eve…" He licked his lips.

"I got an appointment with a counselor. I am working on getting better! Please just give me one more chance."

He reached out to her and she stepped away.

"No. You keep saying you are going to get better. It has just gotten worse ever since you started working with that new principal. He's a bad influence on you." She warned.

"You are sick John, you need help. It's going to take more than a psychologist to help you get us out of this mess. We need a quick fix or we will lose everything. You say gambling isn't a big deal and that you have control. If you had control then you wouldn't be dipping into your children's savings."

His stubby fingers rubbed fiercely at his brow as she prattled on.

"All of our life savings, your child's savings, our house, *it's all gone!* You just had to do it though. You just had to go to the casino with him and risk it all! Not to mention have started smoking and drinking again too. After ten years of sobriety!"

A frustrated Dinkle ran a hand along the back of his balding head.

"Eve, I've already told you it was nothing. It was just one drink. My boss wanted to discuss something for the school. Besides, I am telling you more money should be coming in from the side job he told me about."

His round face brightened. "It's going to be big. Just you wait."

Her horsey face twisted with uncertainty.

"I don't like him John. I told you that. I told you I don't want him hanging around but you keep insisting that he isn't a bad person. He hasn't helped you any and since you began hanging out with him more you have gotten worse."

John dragged his hand down the side of his jowl and let out an exasperated sigh.

"I feel like you're over reacting..." He grumbled.

She balled up her towel and threw it into the sink.

"You got till the end of next month to get things straightened up. Or I'm out."

She stalked away leaving him breathless.

Astrid and I exchanged looks of concern. Ethan's eyes remained locked on the inside of the house. A little flame of guilt kindled within the bottom of my gut. Maybe we had been a bit hard on him lately. We might have taken pleasure in teasing him at school but we never knew he'd have such bad luck at home too. I wondered if things would have been the same if we had treated him differently than we do now.

Ethan temporarily extinguished that flame when he clamped a hand to my mouth and dragged me back into the safety of the bushes. I tried to wrench myself free.

What in the world has gotten into him?

"Quit struggling and pay attention!" He growled softly into my ear.

"Look, Lex." Astrid whispered as she turned my chin towards the driveway.

The snow fell from the sky like a white curtain. Off in the distance a black hummer puttered its way up the snowy driveway. Snow and branches crunched and cracked beneath its wheels. The vehicle lurched to a complete stop about a few yards away from the garage door. We peeked through the natural openings that the branches provided. A blanket of snow covered the tops of the bushes and provided adequate cover as we huddled together for heat.

One of the car doors slammed shut and a man in a brown trench coat began trudging through the knee high snow to get to the front door. We dipped closer to the ground. Two others followed close behind. Their expressions were grim. Ethan gave me one of his green eyed glares and held a finger to his lip. I rolled my eyes.

Leave it to Ethan to think I would talk at a time like this.

Astrid held her breath and closed her eyes. Little did she know I had already wove magic through the air to help ensure we stayed hidden. Due to my low energy levels I couldn't do much more than camouflage us. I only had a small amount of energy to spare. Astrid and I would have to go hunting later tonight. Like her, I could eat food but we both lived mainly off of another's life force. My kitsune heritage gave me the ability pull energy from the earth and its natural elements but doing so usually caused damage to the environment around us. Regardless, I held my breath and willed my heart to stop pounding. The wind hissed through the pines and sent a spray of white in our direction.

The man cursed and clutched the coat tightly to his chest. The burst of wind rippled through the bottom hem, causing it to whip around in all directions. He climbed the stairs and shivered as he took refuge beneath the veranda. The other two pairs of feet stood a few feet away. We couldn't see their faces. The man on the veranda wore gray dress pants and shiny black shoes. I would have assumed he was some sort of business man or a person in a position of power. He balled up his fist and gave the door three separate taps. A few moments later Eve answered. Her skin smelled like flour and fresh soap. Her smile faltered. The excitement drained from her horsey face. Clearly, she had been expecting someone else. She flashed the man a cynical glare before her face transformed into an emotionless mask.

"I suppose you are here to see John?" She inquired stiffly with a hint of disdain.

From our vantage point we could only see her face and not the other man's. However the familiar scent of well-oiled steel and old cigarettes tickled my nose.

"Well happy Thanksgiving to you too, Eve. I have something to give to John if that's alright with you" Mr. Lemmings replied coolly.

My jaw dropped.

Could it really be him?

Why in the world was he here at Mr. Dinkle's house in the first place?

"Make it quick, Paul. We really don't have time today." She clipped brusquely.

"What's going on?" A nasally voice called out from the hallway.

"It's Paul Lemmings. He has some sort of delivery for you."

She wrinkled her nose at Paul and then pushed her way back through the hallway. John stuck his round head out of the door frame.

"How may I help you?" He asked.

Lemmings hooked a thumb towards the snowy landscape.

"Come outside and shut the door John."

John frowned.

"Just do it." Lemmings said with steely resolve.

John quickly opened the door and stepped under the veranda. His round frame took up most of the space. Nervously, he fidgeted with his hands.

"Shut the door.."

Obidently, the door closed with a quiet click.

Lemmings pressed something in his hand.

"I know things are tight for the holidays. You did an excellent job on obtaining more specimens for the lab." He said the word specimens as if it had double meaning. "As promised, the corporation has provided compensation for your hard work. This is your reward for following through on such short notice."

A hot flush of anger boiled through me. *What a wonderful treat.*

Money in exchange for an innocent life. I thought bitterly to myself. Our teacher is selling us to the wolves. Any guilt I had for mistreating him melted away.

Dinkle's grip on the package tightened.

"Thank you sir. I really do appreciate it." He replied breathlessly.

His large eyes gleamed with hope.

Mr. Lemmings gave him a brisk nod.

"Any news on the missing notebook?" Lemmings asked.

Fear snuffed out Dinkle's tiny flame of hope.

His face whitened. "No sir. No news." He replied uneasily.

Paul grunted in disappointment. "Well that's too bad. Thankfully we have more than one hard copy. Happy Thanksgiving John."

Dinkle nodded. "Happy Thanksgiving to you too Paul."

Paul carefully climbed down the icy stairway and limped back to his car. The two other men followed. We watched the hummer as it reversed down the driveway. Snow spewed from his tires as it accelerated away. Astrid and I exchanged wary glances. Sorrow gnawed at my gut and my heart dropped as Ethan's gaze met mine. His mossy green eyes were hard as flint. His expression remained cool and collected.

"Ethan?" I paused, afraid to ask.

He glanced back at me and waited expectantly for me to finish. I needed to hear his opinion. I needed to hear my own suspicions coming from someone else's mouth before I could accept them as truth.

"You don't think that was compensation for Frank's disappearance...do you?"

It took him a moment. I held my breath, praying my accusations weren't true. The wind hissed. His eyes drifted towards the snowy pines.

"I do.." He replied, his expression remained grim.

Astrid clucked her tongue reprovingly as she hugged her jacket close to her waist. "Garcia and Benson aren't going to like this one bit..."

CHAPTER 22

"I JUST DON'T GET IT." Buzz growled.

He tossed the materials haphazardly onto the table.

"Careful with that... It's glass." Hawk Eyes replied with a grimace.

Ethan licked a finger and whipped through the pages of his chemistry book.

His eyes glittered with frustration.

"We know why they took them, we even have a hunch on who took them but we can't seem to figure out where they are keeping them! I mean, we have most of the puzzle figured out but all we're missing is one piece."

I shrugged my shoulders and wrapped my auburn hair up into a tight ponytail.

"Hawk Eyes could probably do a locator spell. Easy peasy, right?"

Hawk Eyes bit her lip and looked away. "It's not that easy, Lex..."

Buzz let out a snort. "How hard can it be? You're a witch after all, aren't you? Just wiggle your nose like that one chick on TV."

Lexi grimaced and shifted her weight. "It doesn't work that way Andrew,.."

"What's the problem then?" I pressed.

"The problem is I don't know how, okay?!"

Concern washed over Ethan's face. "What can you do Selena?"

She gave Ethan a feeble shrug. "I don't know how to do much of anything to be honest...but I am good at healing... but that's about it though."

Buzz threw his hands up into the air.

"Great, just great. We have a witch that may have been able to locate Olivia's location but she doesn't even know magic. We're so *fucking* screwed. What were you going to do? Heal the scientist's boo boos?"

"Andrew. You aren't helping..." Ethan warned.

Selena's eyes glistened with shame.

Silently, she forced herself to look away.

"I am sorry..." She sniffed.

My heart dropped. I didn't want to see her in pain.

"Shh, don't apologize." I crooned.

Ethan offered her a broken smile. "Don't worry about it Selena. We'll figure something out. I am sure there's someone out there that can teach you the craft, right?"

Buzz's blue aura flared.

"What do you mean it's okay?" He retorted. "She's the only way we can find where they are at and she blew it."

I shot Buzz a murderous glare.

"It's not like she meant it." I snarled.

Hawk Eyes covered her face in shame.

My blood boiled with rage.

"I swear to God if she cries, so help me I will pummel you." I hissed.

I could feel my tails flick irritably beneath my human guise.

Buzz snorted and stuck out his chin. "I'd like to see you try."

His eyes danced with hate.

Within seconds, I closed the distance between us. All lab activities were forgotten.

Ethan shoved his way between the two of us. His red aura swirled around him like flames.

"That is enough from the both of you!" He snarled and bore his teeth.

Ethan's wolf peered through his green eyed gaze. His scent had changed. Testosterone rolled off him in musky waves. Buzz's yellow eyed wolf rose up to the challenge. I faltered in my haste. A sense of uneasiness subsided in my stomach. Buzz had to get his wolf under control or he may have to experience dire consequences. I was worried more so for Ethan's sake though.

If Buzz wasn't careful Ethan may have to take him out. Any person who couldn't control his wolf was considered a liability. Unfortunately, acts of feral behavior are a common thing among the wolves and they have to be dealt with accordingly. The majority of new werewolves don't even make it to their next full moon because they are more likely to have problems keeping their wild halves under control. Such issues led to uncontrollable shifting.

In the past that had led to bloodshed and the loss of innocent lives. As a safety measure they had to be eliminated. As pack leader it was Ethan's responsibility to exterminate any member that poses a threat to the pack's safety or the surrounding human community. *Was that an action Ethan was willing to take? Could he handle the heavy burdens of leadership?* It takes a special person to kill their own friend for the good of the pack. Someone from behind cleared their throat. We all turned to see a suspicious Dinkle standing there, waiting for some sort of explanation.

"What seems to be the problem here, Mr. Matthews?"

Buzz and Ethan fumbled for an answer.

Hawk Eyes sniffled and wiped at the corner of her eyes.

"We are just having a disagreement on who will put which chemical in first."

Dinkle raised a fuzzy brow, clearly he was unamused.

"I see." He drawled.

"I assume you have resolved the issue, Mr. Matthews?" He asked.

Ethan flashed Andrew a wolfish smile but it was more teeth than cheer.

"Yes, of course. We've decided to take turns, isn't that right Andrew?"

Buzz worked his jaw.

I held my breath.

His blue aura wavered beneath Ethan's glowering gaze. The air between them thickened with tension, but Ethan stood his ground. Pack magic rolled off him in waves. The mere essence of it was quite domineering. Eventually, the muscles went slack around Buzz's mouth and his shoulders slumped in submission. It took Buzz a moment to reply before he offered his alpha an obedient nod.

"Yes, we agreed to take turns. Everything is fine here, but we appreciate your concern."

Dinkle grunted his approval.

Together we watched him turn around and waddle back to his desk. Ethan released Buzz's collar. Buzz pulled away and rubbed a hand along the back of his neck. He cast a suspicious glance Dinkle's way.

"What do you think was in that envelope anyway?..." Buzz asked.

"It had to be money." I mused aloud as I scooped red powder into the following petri dishes.

Selena's lips puckered with concern. "You really think so?"

I shrugged my shoulders. "Well yeah, what else do humans desire as a reward? I mean it's not like it was a cookie or anything."

A playful smirk toyed at the corner of Buzz's mouth. "Who knows? As far as we know it could be. I mean, let's be honest here, does it look like Dinkle would turn down a cookie?"

We all turned to look at Dinkle as he took a large bite out of his tuna sandwich. White chunks of tuna spilled out of the end of the sandwich. They made thick plopping sounds as they hit the paper plate below. We winced as he licked the tuna off of his stubby fingers and smacked his lips.

"Yeah I suppose you have a point." Hawk Eyes replied with a resigned sigh.

"So... I've been doing some thinking..." I announced carefully.

Everyone turned their attention back to me.

"Yes?" Ethan inquired with practiced patience.

I twirled the spoon around thoughtfully in the air.

"Well we've been playing on the defensive lately. So why can't we play the offensive?" I replied as I grabbed the bottle of potassium chlorate from Hawk Eyes' hands.

She eyed me suspiciously. "What are you proposing that we do?"

The clear liquid splashed around inside the container as I set it onto the table.

"It's simple really. You can use me as a bait. Once I am caught you can follow them to the hidden laboratory." I flashed them a brilliant smile. "Pretty smart, eh?"

Hawk Eyes returned the smile with a blank stare.

Buzz rubbed his chin thoughtfully and nodded his head.

Ethan's freckled face twisted with fury.

"Are you insane!? That is the most ridiculous idea I have ever heard!"

Buzz held his hands up in my defense. "Whoa, whoa, hold on a minute here. I think she is onto something."

Both Hawk Eyes and I turned to look at him with some measure of disbelief. Was Buzz, one of the largest bullies in the school and my number one arch enemy, seriously trying to side with me just now?

Ethan bristled with indignation.

"Absolutely not!" He declared with a note of finality. "Besides, all you care about is getting Olivia back, regardless of the consequences. I am not going to have Lexi get caught up in the middle of this. This is *strictly* wolf business."

A flame of irritation blossomed inside my gut.

"Figures. You wouldn't ever allow me to take any chances if it were to put my safety at risk. Why do you have to be so damn protective anyway?"

Hawk Eyes touched my shoulder. Her hawkish features softened with concern.

"Easy Lex.. He is just trying to make sure you are safe. We all care about you and we don't want you to get hurt."

I let out a disgruntled snort and rolled my eyes.

"Please, it's not like I am a baby or anything. I can take care of myself."

Ethan flashed me the death glare.

Buzz ignored us and gave his alpha an acquiescent shrug.

"That may be true. I will do whatever it takes to get Olivia back. Nor do I care what it takes to get that done. However, let's be honest with ourselves, this has moved well beyond pack business and has become a community concern. For Christ sakes, they have Frank Marino now. Frank is not only a vampire but he is also one of Lexi's friends. Quite frankly, no pun intended, I feel she should have a say in what's going on and how to rescue him."

He hooked a thumb in Hawk Eye's general direction.

"But Sabrina the teenage witch isn't going to cut it. Even she told us she can't do magic. If Lexi is going to willingly offer herself as bait then I think we should take it."

Ethan began to open his mouth to retort but Buzz held up a hand.

"Now, hold on. I'm not saying she should go in without assistance. That would be stupid. All I'm saying is if we can put a tracer on her it might be a better alternative than doing nothing at all."

My heart swelled with hope. I now looked upon Andrew with a new sense of reverence. Could it be? Was it true that the largest asshole in the entire universe was taking my side?

Hawk Eyes simply sighed and shook her head.

"Buzz does have a point, it's important that I don't go alone. I'm sure Astrid can whip up some sort of tracer that would keep track of me. We can do this Ethan, just like we did last time but I can't do it alone." I begged, hoping he would see how much this meant to me.

I couldn't stand just sitting around while everyone else did the work. I wanted to be a part of something, something special. I wanted Frank to know that he just wasn't some means to get me back home. Instead, I wanted him to know that he meant something special to me, that I saw him too as a part of my family.

Ethan sighed and raked a hand through his hair.

"Honestly Lex, you can't even do a high school science experiment without something going wrong." My heart sank. Ethan wasn't going to give in. He wasn't going to let me participate. He was too scared that something might happen to me. The very idea of him not trusting me made my heart break. "At this rate you'll probably end up setting the school on fire. Now you think you can run a covert operation without being caught?"

I let out a disgruntled snort and snatched the bottle of potassium chlorate off the table.

"He's right you know..." Hawk Eyes mumbled.

Buzz pshawed. "Come on, it'll be fine. If everything works out as planned we wouldn't need to follow any bread crumbs. The captors would lead us straight to the lab. I don't see why you are so worried. She'll have a tracer on her. Astrid will see to that. Besides, we will be hot on their heels so nothing would happen to Lexi in the first place."

Buzz's enthusiasm quelled the kindling flame inside my gut.

"See? Even Buzz thinks it's a great plan. What could possibly go wrong? Besides I do not screw every single science project up."

Ethan and Hawk Eyes exchanged a side long glance.

I violently inserted the syringe into the bottle and began dispersing the potassium chlorate into the petri dishes.

"Honestly, what could possibly go wrong?" Ethan asked rhetorically. He shrugged his shoulders and directed his gaze towards the ceiling. "Oh I don't know... Maybe it will end up a total disaster like that time your homemade volcano wouldn't stop erupting."

Hawk Eyes nodded as she preceded to take notes.

"Mmhm, or maybe it will be like the time where you pumped the pig's lung up so much with air that it ruptured in class?"

"Or maybe you'll get caught and we won't be able to find you?" Ethan quipped. "Maybe you will get tortured or even killed?" Hawk Eyes added ruthlessly.

"Yeah, so what do you think could possibly go wrong Alexis?" Ethan inquired. His green eyes burned with concern.

A frustrated Buzz pinched the bridge of his nose. "So far it's the only plan we got. Besides, Lexi can take care of herself. She is a big girl, Ethan."

Ethan shook his head. His inner wolf shown through his eyes.

"The answer is still no."

My fox tails rippled with irritation.

"No one asked you Ethan. You've made your point quite clear."

"Well Sabrina?" Buzz inquired. "What do you think?"

Hawk Eyes bit her lip. I glared at her, waiting expectantly for her input.

She made sure to choose her words carefully. "I am not so sure Lex... I don't think it's the greatest idea. I mean... what if something terrible happens to you?"

I met her gaze with an intense silence. "I mean... um... obviously this plan of yours is possible." She quickly added. "But what happens if we can't follow you and figure out your location? What if the tracer fails?"

"Well I think the both of you are overacting." I grumbled sourly to myself as I sullenly began to squirt a generous amount of the potassium chlorate on the red powder. Hawk Eyes grimaced and took a hesitant step forward.

"Um... aren't you supposed to wait to add that?" She asked.

"It all gets thrown in eventually doesn't it?" I replied, sharply.

Ethan sighed and raked a hand through his hair.

"Look Lex... We will find someone who can teach Selena how to do a locators spell. There's gotta be someone here that knows how. We will find them and we will get Selena the tools she needs to get the job done. Regardless of what happens you will not be going in there alone. You hear me?"

Mr. Dinkle clapped his hands to grab everyone's attention. The glass syringe slipped out of my fingers and clattered into the generous pile of red powder.

"Now listen up everyone. It's now time to add the potassium chlorate to your petri dishes. Please follow along and listen carefully. You will-" A fiery cloud the size of a basketball erupted from my petri dish before it exploded. Smoke drifted to the ceiling. Everyone in the room gasped. Hawk Eyes quickly grabbed the fire extinguisher and thoroughly sprayed the area down. Mr. Dinkle gawked at me as he finished the rest of his sentence. "You will only need a very tiny amount of the red phosphorus and potassium chlorate. If you use too much you will create an explosion..."

I coughed and waved the smoke away from my face. The heat from the combustion had singed my brows.

"Um, professor. The red phosphorus wouldn't happen to be this would it?" I asked as I lifted a bottle into the air.

"Yes, yes it would be Alexis."

Before I could say anything the spigots on the ceiling began shooting out water onto our peers.

Ethan cast me a knowing look.

Water drenched us from head to toe.

Complaints shot through the room like wildfire. Everyone stared daggers in my general direction when Dinkle told us we would have to treat this as a real fire. A wry smile curled at the corner of Ethan's mouth but I returned it with a menacing glare. "Don't even start..." I warned.

Together we walked out of the classroom in a single file line.

CHAPTER 23

RUNNING HAS ALWAYS BEEN a hobby of mine. When I was a human I would use running to help clear my mind. If anything had bothered me I'd slip on my shoes and pound my worries into the forest floor. I loved how the air would fill my lungs up with the fresh taste of freedom. Sometimes I'd run the trails, less so now after I became a vampire. My vampirism took the experience to a whole new level.

Each movement, sound and scent had become heightened. The need to run became primal. The trails were no longer a necessity. The need to feed drove me and the pounding heartbeats of my prey would guide me through the forest. The thrill of having the cool wind whipping through my hair sent chills of exhilaration down my spine. The scents of pine, cedar, honeysuckle and wildlife would over power me. I could taste the smell each tree and enjoyed the dirt's gritty grip between my toes.

But here it was different. My muscles still burned and my body still glistened with sweat. However, the air here was stale. The lab lacked the powerful scent of fresh pine and cedar. Machines chirped instead of birds. Screens twinkled around me instead of stars. Gritty dirt was nowhere to be seen, instead my toes scuffed along the moving belt of a treadmill.

Regardless, I needed the activity. It had been almost a week since they let me out of that god forsaken cage. If I had to sit a moment longer I think I would have gone insane. The vitals screen lit up in front of me. The sticky electrodes tugged at the hairs on my skin. Baffled scientists hovered around me as they frantically scribbled notes onto their clipboards. Maybe they were baffled because I wasn't breathing. For some reason they found my lack of need for oxygen scientifically intriguing.

These things tend to happen when you're an undead creature living on someone else's life force. For some reason humans tend to fixate on miniscule things such as this. That's why it is so critical that we vampires pretend to breathe. Every so often we take a breath to give the illusion that we are human. Normally, I'd be gasping by now but the scientists had me hooked up to a machine that measured my oxygen intake. Faking would be practically pointless now. Besides, theater really wasn't my cup of tea.

"So there is no way that I can be transferred to a different cell." I clarified.

It was more of a statement then a question. The itchy sensation of irritation began to build within my chest. The possibility of having to spend the rest of my stay here across from Bright Eyes had frayed my nerves. The man was absolutely insufferable.

"Ah cherie.' Marie sighed as she made a few checks onto her clipboard.

"I don't see why you get so worked up around him." She replied.

I opened my mouth but then I paused. I choose the following words carefully.

"People who feed off of my emotions tend to bother me." I replied curtly.

I forced myself to continue looking straight ahead. Olivia herself had told me that Bright Eyes was like a vampire of sorts. Instead of drinking blood he fed off of the energy around him. Most of the time that energy included people's emotions. However, I didn't know if the scientists knew about all of his abilities. I wanted to keep it that way in case it would work in my favor.

She tinkled with laughter.

"Ah but zat's how he feeds cherie. You feed off of the blood of living creatures to maintain your existence. He feeds off of the emotions and life force of others to maintain his. In a way you and he are not very different. Try to collect yourself when you are around him."

So she already knew..so much for using information in my favor, I thought bitterly to myself.

Was there anything these people didn't know about?

Her gray eyes glittered with amusement. Marie and I had met shortly after I had been captured. She recently transferred from France to the United States to study behavioral analysis and to promote supernatural diplomacy. We didn't hit it off well at first. When we first met I had a short temper and very little patience.

This is to be expected when a vampire is suffering from the after effects of a silver nitrate dart. Recently, I had begun to take a liking to her. She was easy going and had taken the time to listen and interact with me. I never imagined how hard it would be to carry on an intellectual conversation in a scientific laboratory. I guess that is what happens when you are the specimen and not the scientist.

She, however, was not like the other scientists. She actually treated me with respect and cared about my well-being. She was one of the very few people I could hold up a conversation with. These were the things that I treasured dearly and dreaded the thought of losing. Bright Eyes however had a tendency to bring out the worst in me. I didn't want to hinder Marie and I's blossoming friendship with my negativity. Finding friendship here has already proved to be difficult. So, I quickly changed the topic.

"So where are we anyway?"

I made my tone nonchalant and casual, hoping she'd take the bait.

She paused for the briefest moment and gave me a sympathetic smile.

"Ah Frank, Even you know I can't disclose zat information."

My heart sank.

The timer beeped and the treadmill's pace began to slow. She went back to scratching a few more notes onto her clipboard. I scowled. The majority of the scientists dispersed after the timer had gone off.

Many of them, including Marie, wore flimsy masks and lab coats. Most of them were armed with nothing but pens and clipboards.

I glanced around only to see a two of soldiers armed with specialized artillery. They stood stiffly within the shadows of the lab's perimeters. They were motionless like statues, their hands remained glued to their weapons and their eyes stared straight ahead. Realization dawned upon me. *Did the scientists honestly believe I was some harmless pig? What made them think that they could strut around me with no protection?*

A sour taste filled my mouth. Sure there were some armed guards scattered along the perimeter of this room but why weren't the scientists themselves armed? All they had were writing utensils, clipboards and air filtering masks. What were they going to do, stab me with a pen? What made Marie so confident? What made her think that only two men could stop me from ripping out her throat? One of my most prized weapons were my retractable fangs combined with my supernatural speed, all of which I had intact.

I slid my tongue thoughtfully along the side of my canine. The rest of the scientists roamed around like lost cattle. There was no sense of organization whatsoever. I could easily take down two maybe three guards before getting shot. I toyed with the idea. In moments, I could transform my fangs into personal blades. It would only take seconds.

I could hear their hearts pumping loudly. Entranced, I watched the soft spot within her neck pulsate ever so slightly. The lulling beat of her heart bewitched me. I had not ate in days. The beast within me yearned for sustenance. My body boiled with need. I found my reflection in the metal stethoscope around her neck.

A tickling sensation spread out from my eyes. Purplish veins trickled out from their corners. Pools of darkness began to bleed into my gray irises, making my eyes pitch black. *No, no, no.... I can't I can't lose control. I can't let her see me like this.* Cold panic rippled down my spine like a thousand spiders. The beast within me sneered. *Come now...One bite shouldn't hurt. You only need enough power to knock out her out. Don't you want to escape?*

I paused for a moment and licked my lips. My canines lengthened into sharp points. The alluring beat of Marie's heart pulled me towards her. My sense of smell heightened. I could almost taste the scent of her cucumber melon shampoo. Her pale skin smelled like peppermint. Just beyond that I swear I could capture a hint of the sea. The possibility of gaining my own freedom was intoxicating. I leaned in closer.

I could do it... but what if my calculations were incorrect? What if it didn't work? What if I couldn't stop? What if I were to drain her dry? I paused and shook my head. That wasn't a risk I was willing to take. In the briefest moment she looked up at me from her square spectacles. She gasped and took a step back.

"Cherie, your eyes." She whispered with wonder.

"Sorry, it's a bad habit." Ashamed, I averted my gaze.

The purplish veins quickly receded from my cheekbones. The whites of my eyes returned. I returned her gaze with a cloudy gray gaze of my own. The spell was broken. I couldn't. She was my friend. I knew if I had started now I wouldn't stop. For now I would fight the hunger raging inside. Sweat trickled down my neck but I didn't bother to wipe it away.

"I am sorry, please excuse me." She stammered nervously and clutched her clipboard tightly to her chest.

A frown pulled at my lips as I watched her hurry away.

Someone from behind snorted in amusement.

I turned to see Bright Eyes leaning his back against a wall.

"Oh it's you." I grumbled sourly. "What are you doing here?"

He ignored my disappointment and flashed me a satisfied smile.

"You should have known she wasn't going to freely disclose the information of our whereabouts."

"And I suppose you do?" I inquired with a perked brow.

His eyes twinkled dangerously.

"Perhaps." He teased.

If anyone knew it'd be Bright Eyes. He had already escaped twice since I had arrived.

"Aren't you worried that I'll beat the information out of you?" I replied wryly as I cast him a twisted smile.

I had to give it to him. The guy had balls. I itched for some sort of extracurricular activity, even if it involved brawling. Fighting has never been one of my favorite activities but beggars couldn't be choosers in situations like this. According to my calculations, Bright Eyes may have some nifty tricks up his sleeves. He was after all well known for choking his captors.

He shrugged and gave me a lazy smile

"Not bleeding likely, mate. We had a vamp here before and through the use ol' experimentation they figured out your kind's weaknesses."

I crossed my arms over my chest.

"And what would that be?"

Bright eyes hopped off of the wall and took a step closer to me.

My muscles tensed.

His mismatching seafoam and ice blue eyes glowed dangerously. He stopped, his pale face only inches away from mine. He had a musky woodsy scent that reminded me of the pines back at home. Waves of power rolled off of his broad shoulders. He eyed me curiously but his expression remained grim. Little flecks of gold peppered his gaze.

"You see those holes in the walls over there?" He asked.

My eyes followed the direction in which he tilted his head.

I nodded when I saw the discreet openings in the walls.

"They release silver nitrate gas that'll knock you on your bloody ass. Think of it as pepper spray for vampires and werewolves. So before you go munchin' on the staff might I suggest you think twice?"

He arched a brow over his icy blue eye. Black hair fell in his face. A playful smirk tugged at the corner of his lips. He looked over me thoroughly, as if sizing up his prey.

"Unless you of all people want to be maced and then shot with silver? If so, then be my guest. I assure you that if that were to happen it would be well worth the entertainment."

Each word cut me like a knife.

Irritated, I clenched my fists but this time I took Marie's advice and didn't take the bait. I returned the smirk with a placid stare. Curiosity tingled within me. I remembered Lexi mentioning that other people were abducted and were viewed as specimens. However, I didn't know exactly what had happened to them. Then it occurred to me. *Could the vampire have been Anna?*

"What happened to the other vampire?" I asked.

I eyed the openings in the wall with curiosity. Come to think of it,

Anna was merely human but there could've been a chance they changed her between then and now, couldn't they?

Bright Eyes stared at the hole. A look of disgust tainted his visage.

"Silver got wedged inside her body and she died." His voice came out chilled.

I turned to look at him but he had disappeared. One moment he was there and the next he was gone. Then it occurred to me, had Bright Eyes just shown remorse?

CHAPTER 24

MY STOMACH GURGLED. Burning hunger coursed through my veins. Silently, I laid upon the lumpy cot within my cell. I managed to cocoon myself in the thin blanket that they had provided me. Olivia's cell was empty and Jacob was nowhere to be seen. I was surprised to learn that I had taken a liking to their company. Olivia was no longer the brutal bitch from Ferndale High that I once knew. The pain this place had provided must have humbled her and transformed her perspective. I'm sure the withdraws hadn't helped either. I had also came to the assumption that the fear of being alone must have encouraged her to rip off her cool exterior.

Jacob wasn't so bad himself, for a werewolf. I hadn't taken the time to get to know him until now. I also had an inkling his supportive personality may have also played a role in Olivia's new abilities to reach out to others in need. Regardless, their presence provided ample distraction from Bright Eyes. Due to this very reason, feigning sleep while they were gone had become a recent hobby of mine. Such activities limited the conversation between me and Bright Eyes. That in itself was something I was okay with.

I jolted up at the sound of a pattering heartbeat and lifted my head.

A beady pair of glowing eyes observed me from the darkness. They shined like polished rubies in the night. My gut growled in protest as the rat scuttled closer to my cell. Her toes scratched softly against the concrete. I licked my lips. My mouth was as dry as the desert sand. Her tiny heart fluttered within her fuzzy chest. Longingly, I watched, with hungry eyes. I was desperate for her to come closer. Despite my silent pleas, she continued to scamper by just beyond my reach. Sharp pangs of thirst prickled through my veins. Bright Eyes let out a hopeless sigh as he leaned the back of his head up against the cold stone wall.

"You've got to lay still if you want them to come to you. You can't pop up like a daisy each time they pass. You'll scare em' away."

He was right. I had to practice patience. Within time they'd build up a false sense of security. However, time wasn't something I had. My parched veins itched with need for fresh blood. If I didn't feed soon I'd start to shrivel. It had been weeks since Marie could sneak a blood bag in. I had once again sent my blood nurse away. I refused to drink from the human vein.

Hunting animals was an option but feeding directly from the human vein was not. I couldn't go back to that dark place in my life. *Why couldn't the scientists understand that?* I managed to confess my dietary needs to Marie shortly after she had witnessed my brief relapse of self-control.

Regardless, they kept sending me blood nurses. Each time I compelled them to leave. Resorting to the old ways was not an option. If I went there I may never be able to come back. Thankfully, Theodore wasn't present at the time and we were able to come up with some sort of arrangement. Earlier, she was able to slip in one or two blood bags a week but recently she hasn't been able to do so.

A metallic clicking sound woke me from my stupor. The rat squeaked with fright and quickly scurried away. Someone had lifted the outside arm bar with a clang. The door groaned as it creaked open. Silently, I cursed as the blinding bright light spilled into the darkness. Bright Eyes stole a glance out of the corner of his eye. A burly figure with broad shoulders and a barrel chest stood in the door frame. His shadowy silhouette stood in stark contrast.

My vision recovered quickly to reveal Theodore wearing a white lab coat, black shoes, white slacks and a black top. His chocolate skin soaked in the hallway's luminescence as his piercing eyes scanned the room. Marie's petite form poked its head out from behind Theodore's side. A visual confirmation was not needed. I recognized the faint smell of sea salt beneath the minty bite of peppermint lotion and knew the distinct clean crispness of her cucumber melon shampoo.

"Rise and shine!" Theodore bellowed as he strode into the room. He held a tranquilizer rifle against his right shoulder. The rifle was cocked and ready to go with the safety off. I assumed it was more for security purposes and protocol than for show. The man had muscles of steel and the body of a beast. In my opinion, he didn't need weapons to look scary. I had recognized his old spice aftershave.

However, I didn't' recognize the smell of jasmine that quickly followed. Bright Eyes must have realized its presence because he too sat up straight. His eyes attentive

The smell belonged to a slim Asian who followed Marie into the room. She too wore professional business wear. She donned a black pencil skirt, white button up blouse and black flats. Silky black tresses framed her oval face. Almond eyes rested delicately upon a set of high cheekbones.

She reminded me of Carmen. My heart twitched and a pang of sorrow twisted in my chest. I sucked in a breath of air. I wondered what she may be doing right now at this very moment. *Did she miss me? Would they ever find me here?* Only time could tell and I could only hope. Bright Eyes stepped forward and into the light. The sweet smell of desperation and hope lingered from him.

His skin had lost its pallor from lack of nourishment. Hunger had dulled his sparkling mismatched eyes. Earlier, he had been snacking off my hate. Lately, he had not been able to get a rise out of me. No rise meant no nourishment. I was too tired to care anymore. Maybe he was trying to see if he could probe something out of Marie. He let out a long whistle. Black hair fell in front of his angular face.

"Look who has come to visit us on this fine morning." His British accent dripped with honey.

The girl cast him a murderous glare.

A complacent smile curled at the corner of his chapped lips.

Triumphantly, he snaked his arms through the space between the bars and rested his elbows on the middle bar. Marie ignored his jibe and dismissed him with a wave of her hand.

"We aren't here for you, we are here for Frank." She replied coolly.

His eye twitched but her expression remained aloof.

"Aw come on Marie I am hurt! Where's the bleeding love?"

His voice was hot with sarcasm. She disregarded him with a snort. She knew his games and knew how he fed. He fed off of the emotional energy others and she wasn't having it. Neither was I. Nor was Theodore.

"Speaking of Frank, it is very important that you are done feeding within an hour."

She eyed me sternly.

"We cannot be late."

"*Great*, take the jail bait with you and come back in an hour."

I had replied with a derisive snort.

Bright Eyes chuckled quietly to himself. "We assure you there will be no need to wait because a feeding won't take place. The man's made up his mind, mate."

Marie's mouth tightened. She continued to speak with controlled patience.

"Bianca here has offered, out of her own free will mind you, to be your personal blood nurse."

Bianca cast me a shy smile. She pulled back the hair along the nape of her neck only to expose her pulsing flesh. Her skin glowed like white marble.

Crazed hunger rushed through me.

"God damn it Marie!" I cursed, on impulse my fangs snicked down into place. I nearly threw my chair in a fit of rage but it was bolted to the floor. My mouth watered in protest. Desperately, I tried grasping for control. Despite my attempts, I began to shift. My nails bit into my fists. Purple veins trickled out from the corner of my eyes. Shadows bled into my sclera. Little beads of blood blossomed from my hands. I stiffened and sucked in a calming breath.

"Absolutely not." I growled with eyes as black as pitch.

Marie's forehead crinkled with frustration.

"But you need to feed!" Marie protested.

I took a step forward but Bianca took a step away. Her heart rate had quickened, which only made matters worse. *How could Marie tempt me like this? Especially after all the things I have told her in confidence?* Within seconds I closed the distance between us and gripped the silver bars with my bare hands.

"You know the deal. Blood bags only. No neck, no live prey." I hissed in an inhuman voice.

Marie watched me with guarded eyes.

Theodore stepped back and with his weapon raised.

Bianca cried out as my flesh began to sizzle against the silver bars.

Marie held up a hand, her face remained blank and expressionless.

"Stand down Theodore.." Marie said, with the utmost calm.

He glanced uneasily at me then at her, then back at me with great uncertainty.

"I said stand down." She said sternly, hints of musical undertones laced her voice.

Reluctantly, Theodore lowered his weapon but still maintained a tight grip. Dots of perspiration peppered his brow. Bright Eyes watched with keen interest. My skin crackled and popped. The stench of burnt flesh filled the air. My teeth clenched beneath my grinding jaw. I held my hands there. The searing of my flesh sent ripples of clarity through my brain. The pain distracted me from the need to hunt and the need to feed, and brought me back to where I needed to be. Marie waited for me to finish before she continued. Her voice came out in soft musical undertones, almost enchanting like the crashing waves of the sea.

"Now, now, Frank there is no need to throw a fit. The authorities have cut me off from getting access to the blood bags. I am sorry but they won't support your dietary requests unless they have adequate proof zat it is necessary. I don't agree with their methods but this is the best zat I can do." She said bitterly.

A hint of distaste colored her tone. Glaring, I took a steady breath and lifted my scalding hands from the purified metal. Smoke billowed from my blistering palms. A sickened Bianca averted her gaze. My burning flesh must have been too much to bear. Theodore kept his gun trained on me. A shaky finger hovered over the trigger. Moments later, new grafts of skin began to regenerate beneath the bubbling blisters. If Bianca came any closer I may have ripped out her throat. I exhaled slowly.

"I will leave her here in case you change your mind" Marie continued, with bits of steel in her voice. Sorrow and rage glittered vaguely behind her calm façade. She paused and leaned in. Bits of sea salt and peppermint tickled my nose. Her voice dropped an octave or two. "But if you ever, I mean ever, throw a fit like zat again I will stake you myself. *Do I make myself clea*r?"

Bright Eyes' brows nearly disappeared into his hairline.

"A bit kinky don't you think Professor Rousseau?" He asked with a amused smile.

"*Can it, Kitsune.*" She replied in flinty French.

Inky darkness receded from my blackened sclera. *Kitsune? Bright Eyes was a kitsune? So that explained the scent.* Silently, I acknowledged her with a slight dip of my chin. She stepped forward with the key but my hand flashed out to cover the keyhole. The purified metal boiled my skin.

"She will remain outside the cage." I glowered through gritted teeth.

Marie paused.

Our gazes locked.

The tension began to build within the prolonged the silence. My skin continued to crackle and smoke. Theodore's gun remained trained on my chest. *I'll be damned if that girl is allowed in my cell. If they let her in I was guaranteed to lose control. Leaving body parts strewn across my cell was not what I had in mind for tonight's activities.* Bright Eyes watched us from afar with glittering eyes. His pallor had changed for the better. He must have been feeding off of the emotional turmoil. However, it wasn't enough. Skeletal fingers still dangled loosely from his hands.

Marie gave me a curt nod.

"As you wish, Francesco."

Then she left. The door creaked to a close. The arm bar clanged back into place and the room went dark. A sliver of yellow light peeked through the barred opening of the steel door. I frowned. I hadn't recalled giving Rousseau my full name. Nonetheless, I cast Bianca a sidelong glance.

She returned it with a defiant glare.

"I bet you are wishing you hadn't volunteered for this job. Aren't you?"

She rubbed her arm but never failed to meet my gaze.

"You don't scare me." She hissed.

"Oh, don't I?" I replied with a amused smile.

Has this girl ever seen a vampire in his or her true form?

Her heart thundered in her chest.

The better half of me assumed she had not.

Regardless, she straightened her spine and lifted her chin.

"Not one bit." She replied with stubborn defiance.

Bright Eyes snorted and shook his head.

"Tough one isn't she?" He glanced over her with amused appreciation. "Obviously you haven't seen his temper yet, love. "The yellow light danced off his cheekbones. The lack of nourishment made them more pronounced. "She sure is hell bent on feeding you. Honestly mate, are you going to turn a blood nurse away just like that? Have you gone bloody mad? You haven't ate in ages."

Inky darkness bled into the whites of my eyes.

"If I drink from her now I may kill her. There are reasons as to my madness."

Bright Eyes heaved a sigh and raked a bony hand through his unkempt black hair.

"Whatever you say Frank."

Bianca's almond eyes narrowed with irritation.

"I am still standing here I'll have you know."

I looked at Bianca. Bright Eyes fell into a moody silence. I let out a steady sigh. My shoulders relaxed. My fangs retracted back into my gum line.

"You aren't afraid of me?" My voice came out in a hushed whisper.

She set her jaw. Her eyes burned with confidence but her heart said otherwise.

"No. Not one bit." She was lying.

She put on a good façade but her body was giving me tall tale signs.

A charming smile spread across my lips. "Then come closer, little bird."

She glanced at Bright Eyes then me, then back at Bright Eyes.

He watched her warily, still scowling.

She took in a breath and held it.

Slowly, she inched forward.

"That's it. Easy does it." I crooned with a voice as soft as silk.

The scent of jasmine grew stronger as she approached. She stopped just in front of my cell. She had hazel brown eyes with a golden ring around the rim of her iris. Her thundering heart made me ache.

"Look at me." Her eyes met mine. They wavered with uncertainty. I could tell this was her first time. She had never been bitten before. She had a strong jawline, flawless skin, full lips and an oval shaped face.

"Listen closely, little bird."

She watched with keen curiosity. Her eyes were attentive and eager. My pupils dilated and my irises thinned. My voice came out in husky baritones, lilting and rising like music. Her pupils expanded and retracted, like that of an entranced cat.

"You will go to Bright Eyes over there and you will let him feed off of you. Think upon the most emotional moments in your life. Recall those emotions and relive them in his presence. You have my word that he will not harm you in anyway. You will fall asleep when you are fully spent. Do you understand?"

She nodded once and whispered "Yes. I understand."

Bright Eyes' mouth twisted in a feral frown.

"I don't need your bleeding pity." He hissed.

"I can make it on my own without help, thank you very much." His will wavered when she drifted towards his cage. *Ah, the handiness of compulsion. It is a beautiful thing, isn't it? It's going to take a lot more than this to break me.* I thought dryly to myself.

A amused smile tilted the corner of my parched lips.

"No need to pout, think of it as a good use of resources. Besides, you can pay me back once you break out of your cage. That is why they are not keeping you well fed, is it not?"

Bright Eyes glanced at me in disbelief then at the girl then back at me again.

"Well, in that case." He replied with a distracted nod. "I don't mind if I do.."

I turned away and tossed my ragged body back onto the lumpy cot. Exhaustion overwhelmed me. My muscles ached.

CHAPTER 25

PATTERSON ROAMED the room as she drawled on about civil rights. My heart skipped a beat when she passed. Beads of sweat blossomed along my hand as I struggled to keep the rodent in my pocket at bay. Earlier I had snatched a mouse from the fateful jaws of Mr. Dinkle's snake. I had seen her scurrying around in the bottom of Mrs. Puffin's cage. For some reason the better half of me thought I could keep her safe within the pocket of my hoodie. Regretfully, I had not realized the mouse would try to escape.

I suppressed a breathless giggle as her tiny feet skittered against my skin. Patterson turned to write something on the board and the mouse squeaked. The history teacher paused and narrowed her eyes. I sucked in a sharp breath. *Why of all times would it choose to squeak now?* I glanced down at my pocket. Perspiration bloomed along the back of my neck. *She couldn't have possibly heard the mouse from across the room, now could she?* I was sitting in the back row after all.

Besides, an undisturbed Hawk Eyes sat next to me, scribbling furiously away into her notebook. The table squeaked beneath the relentless pressure of her hand. *Hawk Eyes didn't notice my dilemma, so why should Patterson?* After what had seemed like centuries, the teacher finished writing her note on the board and commenced to circulating the room. Silently, I stroked the rodent's sleek brown fur and ran a finger along her scaly tail. Moments later, she managed to poke her head out from the safety of my sweater. Black beady eyes glanced curiously around the room.

Patterson's head, unexpectedly, popped in between us.

"Miss Rodriguez?" Patterson inquired.

I nearly tumbled out of my chair.

Where in the world did she come from anyway?

Quickly, I shoved the mouse back into the depths of my pocket.

Patterson eyed me dubiously.

She couldn't have seen, could she? Just to be safe, I scooted closer to my desk. Maybe, if I scooted close enough she wouldn't witness the mouse scurrying around inside the pocket of my hoodie. *One could only hope, right?*

Patterson arched a skeptical brow in my general direction. A wisp of black hair fell in front of her face. The rest of it remained tightly wound and pinned in place with two ornamental sticks. I froze, droplets of trepidation trickled down my back. She had to have known. *How couldn't she?* Besides, I knew that look from anywhere. I am such a goner, what was I going to do?

"Yes?" Hawk Eyes inquired as she tucked a strand of her own hair behind her ear.

Patterson briefly glanced my way before focusing all of her attention on Hawk Eyes. "Would you do the honor of meeting with me after school?"

Hawk Eyes frowned and pursed her lips.

"Of course…but… did I do something wrong?"

The crow's feet around Patterson's eyes crinkled with amusement.

"Oh no, no dear. I just have a matter of great importance to discuss with you."

Patterson flashed me a polite smile.

"Is everything alright Miss Adams?" She asked.

I returned the gesture with a nervous smile of my own as I discreetly struggled to keep the mouse contained deep within the pockets of my sweater. Hawk Eyes watched me with a sense of uncertainty. Her forehead wrinkled with concern. It was then the mouse had escaped my clutches and plopped onto the classroom floor.

I reached for her but she managed to scurry away, well beyond my reach. Patterson watched the mouse with a cool curiosity as it ran beneath a student's desk. A bewildered Zander shouted and shot up from his assigned seat.

"Ah bleeding hell, there goes a bloody mouse!" He yelped.

One of the girls dropped her pencil and let out a startled gasp.

"A mouse?!" Immediately, she hopped up onto her table, seeking refuge from the formidable creature. "Kill it! Kill it!" Another screeched.

Other girls squealed as the mouse zoomed past their legs.

Hawk Eyes and I watched in silent horror as swarms of shrieking girls hopped onto their chairs.

Mortified, I sunk further into my own chair and tried hiding my face.

Meanwhile, boys chased after the helpless rodent. They left tables and chairs upturned in their wake. Books soared across the room. Pens whirled past our heads. A maelstrom of papers were strewn across the floor. Jordan laughed with delight. Things were all well and good for him until the mouse decided to crawl up his leg. His face went white.

"Get it off! Get it off!" He shouted spastically.

Zander took a book and rushed to his aide. *"Hold bloody still, mate!"*

He hollered as he began frantically beating his comrade's leg with a history book. The mouse squeaked and cried with fright as it traveled up Jordan's pants. Jordan danced around in a circle, itching and kicking the whole way. He did one last kick. The poor thing twirled into the air and landed into one of the cheerleader's hair. She let out a blood curdling scream and clawed at her scalp.

"It's in my hair! It's in my hair!" She cried hysterically, snot and tears streamed down her face. The little guy finally scrambled out of the tangle of hair and shot across the room. Her beady eyes were wide with fright. Boys trampled each other in hot pursuit. Toppled table tops and chairs lay in chaotic disarray.

Patterson paused before attending to the chaos. She eyed me with a look of speculation. I sunk further into my chair. I toyed with the idea of melding myself into my surroundings.

Would such actions lead to exposing the supernatural race?

"On second thought, bring Miss Adams with you." Patterson added.

A confused Selena glanced my way.

I frowned. "What for?" I asked with a look of uncertainty.

Patterson flashed me a tight lipped smile.

"Why for detention, of course." Patterson replied dryly.

"On what grounds?" I sputtered in indignation.

Her eyebrows nearly disappeared into her hairline as a book flew past her head.

"For creating mass chaos in the classroom environment and for not adhering to the school's policies. It is forbidden to bring animals onto school campus without administrative permission."

She paused gave me a thorough look over.

"Unless, you have your approval papers? If so, hand them over."

She extended a hand and waggled her fingers, waiting expectantly for me to reveal the documents in question. I opened my mouth to protest but the words got caught in my throat. Selena's eyes had followed our conversation as they bobbed from Patterson, to me, then back again. Her lips pressed into a thin line but all the while she managed to keep her comments at bay. Defeated, I sighed and averted my gaze.

"No... I don't have any papers." I mumbled half-heartedly in reply.

"Then the decision is made." Patterson replied brusquely.

"Miss Rodriguez, will you make sure you and her arrive at the same time?"

Selena flashed her a disarming smile as she wrapped an arm around my shoulder.

"It would be our pleasure Mrs. Patterson." Honey coated each word.

She inclined her head in my general direction and gave me a side-long glance.

"*Won't it, Lexi?*" She offered me a murderous smile.

I spluttered in protest but she pinched my side.

Damn her and her teacher pet ways.

Patterson gave us both a brisk nod.

"Good. Now if you will excuse me I have a mouse to take care of."

Hawk Eyes shot me an accusatory glare once we were out of Patterson's sight. Lines of irritation etched her forehead.

"What!?" I replied defensively.

"Dinkle had put the poor thing in the cage with his snake!"

Her eyes narrowed into tiny slits. "You stole Mrs. Puffin's food? I mean, really?"

I threw my hands up in the air. "The mouse was going to get eaten alive by a boa constrictor what else was I supposed to do?"

Hawk Eyes rolled her eyes. "Oh I don't know, maybe leave the mouse where it's supposed to be and let nature take its course?"

Each word dripped with sarcasm. Off in the distance Patterson tried attending to her students. It was now my turn to roll my eyes. Someone squealed in the background, then another book flew past our heads.

"Let nature take it's course? Let's be serious here. If nature were to have taken it's course then Mrs. Puffins would of had to work for her own food. How is she supposed to survive on her own if she doesn't know how to hunt?"

Hawk Eyes jabbed a finger at me.

"Let's be honest here, Lex. You probably just wanted the mouse for yourself."

I shrugged. "Yeah? What of it?"

More pens, pencils, books and paper flew across the room.

Exasperated, Hawk Eyes dragged her hand across her face. "You're hopeless... absolutely hopeless. Mrs. Puffin isn't meant to live in the wild Lexi. She is a pet. You of all people should be able to understand that. Besides, the mouse isn't yours in the first place. You can't just take what's not yours. You know that right?"

Patterson took a deep breath and stood up straight.

"ENOUGH!" Patterson boomed.

Her domineering voice cut through the chaos like scalding blades through frozen butter. Everything in her presence had become hauntingly still. Zander stopped throwing books. Hysterical wails turned into choked sobs. Hoards of boys froze in mid stride, their eyes were wide with shock. A handful of girls cowered quietly in the opposite corner.

Regardless, their bodies were still as stone. It was as if her voice had commanded time. Everyone turned to look at the petite woman who stood at the front of the room. The students couldn't help but comply. She was intimidating for her size. She maybe stood five feet if anything. Never, until now, did she have to raise her voice. Despite her size, Patterson had an air of authority about her. Today she had taken a stance that exuded power. There she stood, spine straight, her feet shoulder width apart and her arms neatly folded behind her back, military style. In her right fist she gripped a fallen ruler.

Hawk Eyes closed her gaping jaw. Silently, I shook my head. You'd think it was the end of the world, all over a little thing like a mouse. Humans were so silly. The creature is more frightened of them then they were of it.

One of the students flinched.

"Do not move!" She commanded.

Everyone remained still as a statue.

Patterson approached the cowering mouse with great care.

"Mrs. Patterson, don't!" One of the girls had hissed.

Her green eyes were wide as saucers.

"It might bite you!" The boy next to her wailed.

Patterson shot them a deadly glare.

"Be silent." She hissed. "All of you are acting like a bunch of fools."

Slowly, she approached the rodent each step graceful as a cat. The creature trembled in her presence, entranced, like a gazelle caught within a lion's gaze. She scooped the trembling mouse up into her hands. The dismissal bell for fifth hour chimed. Students fidgeted nervously as they eyed their book bags.

"Now class, no one will be leaving this room until it is straightened up. And when you are done you will sit at your assigned seat with everything in place. I will be dismissing those who have their area clean and are sitting silently, ready to go. I suggest you begin."

She flashed me a cold hard stare and handed me the mouse.

"I suggest you take this with you before you leave. The life of any creatures is not to be dealt with lightly."

CHAPTER 26

HOURS LATER ETHAN, Astrid, Hawk Eyes and I walked down the hallway towards Patterson's room. It was ten minutes past dismissal and we were running late for our appointment. We had passed a few of stragglers on the way there but they had mainly stayed behind for after school activities. However, for the most part the school was hauntingly empty.

Ethan's jovial laughter echoed throughout the abandoned corridor.

"You let a mouse loose in Patterson's classroom? What in the world were you thinking?"

Hawk Eyes cast Ethan a dirty glare.

"That's the point, Ethan. She wasn't thinking." Her scornful gaze burned into the back of my head. I sighed and prepared myself for a lengthy lecture. "She needs to take her studies seriously. Or at least respect the fact that others are trying to learn."

"Here we go again..." Astrid grumbled beneath her breath.

"I know right? The woman is a complete fanatic!" I whispered back only to glance back at a vexed Hawk Eyes. She was staring straight at me, clearly unamused.

"Feisty one isn't she?" Astrid replied.

Ethan watched the whole ordeal with mild amusement.

"Did the mouse really go up Takahashi's pants?" Ethan inquired.

"Better yet, was it true that the rat flew into Anna's hair? Oh, I wish I was there to see the look on that broad's face!" Astrid said with a twinkling smile.

Hawk Eyes gave her a foul frown.

"Astrid!" Hawk Eyes scolded in a motherly tone.

"*Oh will you just lighten up already?*" Astrid snipped back.

Ethan choked back a laugh until Selena's hot gaze whirled in his general direction. His freckled cheeks flushed with crimson. His attempt to transform his laughter into a brittle cough had failed miserably.

"It's not funny, Ethan. Someone could have gotten hurt." Hawk Eyes groused.

A sheepish smile curled across his lips. "Oh come on. We could make this into the next story for the school newspaper. People will eat this up like candy!"

My smile faltered.

"Really?" I had asked with a hint of exasperation.

"What?" He spluttered, one hundred percent oblivious to the fact that he hinted at using my embarrassment for his own gain. *How could he assume that I'd be okay with that?* I flashed him a deadly glare. He shrank beneath my fiery gaze.

"Look, it's been awhile since we've had a good story. Who knows? Maybe this will increase the distribution rates for the school newspaper. If the newspaper appears to be popular then people will be more eager to participate in interviews and interviews could provide us with possible leads."

A disgruntled Hawk Eyes slapped a palm to her forehead and let out a weary groan. "Unbelievable..." She said with an exasperated sigh.

My blood was beginning to boil. I stared at him with a look of complete bewilderment. "So you'd display my greatest moment of embarrassment to the whole school in hopes for one measly gain?" I asked with a hint of accusation.

"Honestly Lex, I'm having some trouble understanding why you're upset. I mean, isn't mass chaos your thing?" Ethan asked with a perplexed frown.

"True, but still... I find it embarrassing. The mouse wasn't necessarily intentional."

I fidgeted with a piece of lint in my pocket and sighed.

Astrid rocked back and forth on the heels of her leather boots.

"Oh don't think of it as embarrassment, Lex. Instead, think of it as an opportunity."

Together, Hawk Eyes and I stared at her, dumbfounded. She deliberately adjusted her winged spectacles but we all knew it was a meek attempt to distract herself from the awkward silence.

"Besides, I think Ethan is onto something. The public enjoys humor after all and even more so drama. If everything goes as planned the papers will sell like hotcakes. When they do everyone will be itching to open up to us. Everyone and their brother and sister will want to offer information in hopes of getting some fame. Maybe, just maybe we can use that to glean information about Lemmings and Dinkle."

I hesitated and took a deep breath.

She did have a point after all. I had thought dryly to myself. Maybe I should consider this an opportunity. *What is the worst that could happen? Sure I'd experience a bout of embarrassment but would that be worth gleaning information that could lead to Frank?* Reluctantly, I took a deep breath and silently willed myself to stay calm. Her commentary had squelched my boiling veins but I was still offended at the idea that my own friends would use my own downfalls to their advantage.

"Still, I don't appreciate the idea of becoming the butt end of a joke."

I tried to focus on the enunciation of each word. Maybe if I slowed down and stressed how upset I was then they would understand. However, the rest of what I was trying to say came out in a rush. Each word seemed strung together.

"I may have made some mistakes but it was never my intention to set the school on fire. Nor had I planned on breaking Olivia's nose during the first week of practice. The last thing I need now is to be known as the mouse whisperer of Ferndale Hill. I mean seriously, what does a girl gotta do to get a break around here? Besides, shouldn't we be focusing more so on getting Frank back than on net sales? As of right now we should be focusing on how to find the lab but instead we're spending the afternoon in school detention."

Hawk Eyes frowned.

Astrid watched me with keen interest.

Even Ethan maintained an awkward silence.

Together, as a group they watched me expectantly. My face twisted with frustration. I was about to burst at the seams.

I threw my hands up in a gesture of defeat.

"Ok! I am sorry. Let me correct myself. *I will be spending after school detention* with Mrs. Patterson because I released a mouse into her classroom. Meanwhile, she'll chit chat with Selena over a cup of tea."

Hawk Eyes arched an imperial eyebrow.

"Who knew?" Hawk Eyes replied dryly. "For some reason teachers don't appreciate mice being let loose in their classrooms." She inclined her head towards Patterson's door and offered me a reassuring slap on the back. "Now come on Miss Woe Is Me. Let's get this over with so we can go find Frank."

I swallowed as she gave me a gentle push towards the door. My mouth was as dry as a desert's sand. The conversation between me and my peers had lulled itself into a soft hush. The quiet had only added to the tension. I sucked in a nervous breath and held it with great anticipation. Hesitantly, I took an apprehensive step towards the door.

I paused and then licked my lips.

"Honestly, I don't see what the big deal is." I grumbled sourly. "It wasn't like I meant to set the mouse loose in her classroom..." I threw a nervous glance over my shoulder towards my friends. I've never been in the throes of human punishment before. I wondered what to expect.

Hawk Eyes waited expectantly.

Astrid raised a pair of inquisitive brows.

Meanwhile, Ethan watched with a look of concern.

"We all know that Lex, but what is done and is done and now you got to take responsibility for it." Ethan replied with a conciliatory smile.

I twirled a lock of hair nervously around my finger.

"You don't suppose she'll paddle me like they did back at home do you?"

Astrid burst with tinkling laughter.

"Oh she'd do nothing of the sort! Besides, Patterson is much more creative than that."

My stomach tightened with dread. Back home Pa had gotten creative. Whips and paddles never seemed to work on me, so he'd use restriction of magic instead.

"You don't suppose she will use isolation…. Do you?"

He grimaced and offered me a sympathetic shrug.

"Even if she does it's not like you haven't survived it before. Besides, each moment we waste here is another moment away from finding Frank."

I sucked in a deep breath. If anyone could relate to my current predicament it'd be Frank. I wondered what it was like at the lab. *Was it lonely? Did he have friends? Was he feeling vulnerable?* Steeled with a sense of new resolve I stepped forward with a disgruntled sigh. "Well, I suppose it'll be better to get this over with now than delay. Time is of the essence and all that jazz."

I pushed the door open to reveal Mrs. Patterson's petite form with hawkish brown eyes. Classical music played softly in the background. A mixture of lavender and natural spices tickled my nose. In one hand she held a steamy cup of green tea in her other she held a bound book. *Could it have been a Grimoire?* I couldn't quite read the title. It reminded me of something in French, besides, the golden writing on the binding had faded away. Despite the wear, the spine remained strong. She slipped off a pair of reading glasses and flashed us a quirky smile. Gray wisps of hair escaped her tightly wound bun.

"Ah, Selena I am so glad that you could make it."

Her hazelnut eyes roamed over Ethan and Astrid.

Patterson's brow perked with interest. "I see that you have brought some friends."

Selena bit her lip and fidgeted with her hair.

"Oh yeah. I am sorry, they are my ride home. I hope that is okay? My mom wasn't planning on picking me up after school on such late notice. She has to work and all."

Mrs. Patterson nodded sagely.

"Better to walk in pairs these days, if I do say so myself."

The corners of her almond eyes crinkled.

"I suppose we will get this all done in one shot now won't we?"

We all exchanged glances. *What did she mean by one shot?*

Astrid wrinkled her freckled nose in confusion.

A befuddled Selena furrowed her brow.

Ethan shrugged with a perplexed expression.

"Please, come in." She beckoned us all in with a small hand. We followed her as she glided further into the room. History posters lined the walls. The white curtains were drawn. Slivers of golden sunlight peeked through the linen blinds. Sandalwood incense hovered in the air. I pulled up a seat in the front row. Meanwhile, Patterson clucked her tongue and shook her head in soft reprove. "Alexis you will be sitting in the back. I am afraid that there will be no cookies and tea for you my dear. You are in detention after all."

She turned to stroll up to the front of the room. I grumbled something sour beneath my breath.

She paused. Apparently she hadn't taken a liking to what I had to say. Stone faced, she cast me a sidelong glare. Stony brown eyes pierced into me, like tiny shards of flint. The silence held between us for what felt like centuries, until I shattered the it with a half hearted apology. It took a moment before she spoke but when she did her tone was as brisk as a cold winter wind on a snowy day.

"You will do the following reading on the Black Plague. After reading this piece you will explain how rats and mice can spread disease within the human community. You will then explain why it is important not to bring wild rodents into the classroom. This assignment will be signed by your guardian and returned to me by tomorrow morning before school begins. If the following expectations are not met then I will devise other consequences to meet your needs."

I returned her icy glare.

Her flinty gaze held mine. It took everything in me not to come up with some sort of snide remark. After a good moment, I begrudgingly complied. Her expression softened and she turned to my friends. She poured them all a cup of tea and began distributing shortbread cookies. Hot steam curled and twisted into the air. Once everyone had settled in she sat down and folded her weathered hands.

"Let's be frank and to the point, shall we?"

The group exchanged another set of bewildered glances.

A stretch of silence impregnated the room.

Patterson cleared her throat and began again.

"I know what you are Selena, and I am aware of what you need."

There was a slight pause in the conversation.

"And what exactly am I?" Selena proceeded cautiously.

She peered warily over the rim of her tea cup.

Patterson returned the gesture with a good natured smile.

"You're a witch, of course and a witch in dire need of training."

Patterson replied with a throaty chuckle. "I suppose your mother lacks the craft?"

I tensed. The hackles on the back of my neck rose.

How could she know that Selena was a witch?

I watched her warily out of the corner of my eye.

Ethan's brows shot up in surprise.

Astrid had nearly dropped her cup.

In the meantime, Selena had coughed up some tea. She took a moment to catch her breath while Ethan and Astrid exchanged wary glances.

Ethan's brow wrinkled with worry.

Patterson's face remained calm as pond on a still summer night.

"The very idea is outrageous.." Astrid mumbled as she brought the mug up to her lips. In the meantime, her expression remained guarded but her rosy aura had wavered with uncertainty. My fox ears swiveled beneath my human shell. I zoned in on the conversation taking place on the other side of the room.

Patterson's eyes crinkled with amusement.

"Don't be absurd, Mrs. Patterson." Selena replied as she relentlessly, gasped for air.

"Where in the world would you come up with a silly idea like that?"

Patterson's mouth curved into a knowing smile.

"I have my sources." She replied crisply as she sprinkled some herbs into her tea. She used her shortbread cookie to swirl the mixture around.

Ethan's mouth twitched once ever so slightly.

"Don't you think that is going a bit too far Mrs. Patterson?" Ethan asked.

He let out a nervous laugh. "I mean come on. A witch? *Really?*"

Patterson's nose wrinkled with distaste.

"You shouldn't speak out of turn Mr. Matthews. Especially if the conversation does not pertain to you. You are here as a guest, not as a participant. Please do not interrupt. This is a discussion between two witches. This matter does not concern wolves." Astrid's hold on her cup had tightened but her face remained impenetrable.

I gaped at Patterson. *Did she seriously just call him a wolf?*

Ethan stiffened. *"Excuse me?"*

He had feigned misunderstanding but we all knew she had said the word *wolves*.

Patterson frowned. "Don't play coy with me young man. I know what you are so there is no reason to deny it."

Ethan stiffened. "And what exactly do you propose I am?"

Patterson snorted and sipped her tea. "My dear boy you are a werewolf."

Astrid scoffed and let out a derisive snort. "A werewolf? Come now, we are in the 20th century. There's no such thing as werewolves, old woman."

Patterson's eyes narrowed into little slits. The green aura around her body flared slightly with indignation. "Don't be so naïve child. There are plenty of things that go bump in the night and Mr. Matthews happens to be one of them."

My pen clattered from my hand.

Who was this woman and what did she want?

Selena gaped at her in disbelief. The sweet smell of fear began to blossom from her pores. The air thickened. Astrid watched with hooded eyes.

CHAPTER 27

MY HEART THUNDERED inside my chest. *How could she possibly know? We were all so careful. So who could have told her?* The pen threatened to slip out from the grip between my sweaty fingertips. I managed to appear calm despite my increasing panic. I stole a glance at Astrid, who sat still as a stone. *How could she sit so still while every molecule in the air vibrated with tension?* Despite her attempts, she still reeked with fear. Thankfully, Patterson hadn't noticed. Beside her sat a fidgety Hawk Eyes and a fuming Ethan. The muscle along his jaw popped. The carnal need to protect, the primal desire to fight and the sole motivation to survive flashed through his emerald eyes.

Patterson's pheromones hadn't change. She did not reek with malice. Then again nor did Dinkle or Lemmings. Was it because they truly believed what they were doing was for the well-being of the world? Regardless, I did not detect any deceit nor the fruity rot of fear on her. In fact, her skin had maintained its subtle earthy tones and hadn't changed one bit. *Had she been oblivious all along to the emotional turmoil that was beginning to fester in the room?* I found the idea down right fascinating. Then again, Patterson was human after all.

Unlike my Kitsune counterparts, she could not smell the subtle shifts in pheromones. Little did she know that she was surrounded by a ring of agitated supernatural creatures. Nothing about her screamed supernatural. So how would she have known about Ethan's true identity? No one knew except Garcia, Benson, us and the local wolves. *So who were her sources?*

Regardless, my instincts screamed run but if I ran could the others keep up? I didn't doubt Ethan and Astrid's abilities but Selena was merely human. *What if we couldn't outrun Patterson? What if she really did work with Lemmings? What would happen to us? Would we be caught?*

My stomach twisted into a ball of knots. A bunch of scenarios flashed through my mind like reels of film. Images of us being caged up in a lab made my insides curdle. There was only one thing to do. We had only had one choice. We had to fight. I gathered currents of electricity within my hand and shot a crackling ball of energy towards Patterson's head.

"Ethan! Grab Selena!" Ethan threw his mug aside and pushed Hawk Eyes out of the line of fire. Liquid tendrils of green tea twirled in the air as the cup shattered against the classroom wall. Together, Ethan and Hawk Eyes tumbled to the floor. Their bodies rolled across the carpet. He held her close, taking as much as the fall as possible. My energy ball zipped past them but Hawk Eyes had cracked her head against a table on their way down. She groaned as she held her bleeding skull.

"Selena! I am so sorry. Please forgive me."

Ethan held her protectively in her arms as he tried his best to staunch the bleeding.

"Have you gone mad?!" Patterson roared above the chaos.

She bent her knees and made an x with her forearms. A magical barrier rose up and encased her within its protective shell. The tangled mass of electrical currents crashed into her shield. The crackling currents of electricity parted before the barrier like water against a stone. The momentum of the crash sent her sliding backwards leaving trails of ripped carpet in her wake.

"What on earth has gotten into you?" Patterson asked.

Lights popped and shattered. Shards of glass showered to the floor. The writhing electrical currents scattered and fizzled into nothing.

Astrid pounced, talons at the ready.

"We aren't coming with you without a fight!" She shouted.

An exasperated Patterson backed away.

"What on earth are you talking about child?"

Black leathery wings burst through the back of Astrid's blouse.

"And I am not a child. I am well over a hundred years."

Her amber eyes blazed with flecks of molten gold.

She pounced again." You're working with them. Aren't you?!"

Patterson gasped as she took a step back.

"Sweet Mother Mary and Joseph!" Horror etched Patterson's face.

"I am not working with anyone!" She said.

Astrid swiped.

Patterson stepped to the side as Astrid's claws cut through air.

Astrid screamed in frustration.

I sent another shot her way but missed. Patterson pushed her arms outward. A maelstrom of wind exploded from her, forcing us back. She twisted her hand and directed the torrent towards Astrid's center. The blast sent her spiraling backwards. Ethan bellowed her name.

Astrid grunted as plaster cracked beneath her spine. She slid down the wall in a crumpled heap. *So much for the help.* I thought dryly. What was I supposed to expect? Succubi were known more for their ability to seduce and transform than for their strength. An exasperated Patterson threw her arms into the air.

"My classroom is ruined because of you! A poster won't be able to cover something like that!" Tangled wisps of gray hair stuck up out of her bun in a disarray. Long bangs escaped and hung loosely to frame her face. Her eyes smoldered like burning charcoal. "Have you no respect for education?"

Patterson twisted her fingers. Gnarly roots and thick vines sprouted from the carpet. They slithered forward, blindly grasping and pulling Astrid into their embrace.

"Astrid move!" Ethan hollered.

"Go fight. Don't worry about me." Hawk Eyes mumbled groggily as she held her head.

"Leave her! Focus on the enemy at hand!" I snarled.

Ethan scooped Hawk Eyes up and gingerly laid her beneath the safety of a table. "Stay here." He whispered.

He turned and leapt towards Patterson. He arched through the air like an arrow as his body transformed from man to beast. His body lengthened. Clothing tore. Muscles rippled, bones cracked and popped as they realigned themselves. His human nose lengthened into a snout. Pink lips turned black to reveal human teeth as they sharpened into yellow fangs. Sleek black fur sprouted from his freckled pores. His deep cry morphed into a throaty growl. He dived towards Patterson with a feral snarl and snapping jaws.

A commanding voice cut through the chaos.

"Enough! All of you!" An unexpected icy torrent of water blasted Ethan backwards. He bounced across the floor and slammed into a wall with a yelp. His wolf sprawled unconsciously across the floor. Black fur dripped. His mouth hung open, his pink tongue lolling.

I stepped forward.

Patterson shifted, readying herself for my next move.

"I said that's quite enough!"

Thick spears of ice torpedoed towards me. The jagged points of ice caught me by the collar of my shirt. My stomach lurched as they yanked me back. Seconds later, I was pinned to the wall. Breathless, I wiggled for freedom. Senator Benson stepped forward. Her golden hair was pulled back tight in a French twist. She wore a pinstripe blazer and black dress slacks. Her blue eyes glittered like frozen sapphires.

"Oh no you don't." Benson warned with a twist of her hand.

Instantly, the spears wedged themselves further into the plaster.

"When I say stay, you stay." She snarled with distaste.

A mystified Benson paused as she took in her surroundings. Cold air seeped into the room. Her breath came out in wet heavy clouds. The shards from broken light bulbs and shattered windows crunched beneath her heels. Mangled chairs and upturned desks were scattered around the room. The walls were cracked and black with soot. Before her lay an unconscious Ethan, naked in a twisted knot. Just a few feet away a cluster of roots held a lolling Astrid within their gnarled grasp. To her right an injured Hawk Eyes leaned up against the wall. Blood trickled from the back of her head. Awestruck, she turned to Patterson.

"Anna what happened here?" She asked.

Patterson's brushed off the soot from her plum sweater.

"I spoke with Selena and her friends as you had requested." Patterson primmed.

Benson perked a brow, her expression demanded a thorough answer.

"And?" She replied impatiently.

Patterson's brown eyes glittered with contempt.

"And they attacked me." Patterson replied stiffly.

Benson narrowed her eyes.

Carmen Garcia's lithe figure strolled into the room.

She let out a disgruntled tch as she rolled a piece of plaster between her fingertips.

"How disappointing, and to think, I once had thought an educational facility would have a stable infrastructure. Where in God's name do our taxes go, anyhow?"

Benson released an exhausted sigh.

"Carmen will you please tend to the injured while I take care of this?"

Disgusted, Garcia flicked the white dust off of her lacquered nails.

"Listen, selkie. If you think I am going to play clean up crew you got another thing coming." Garcia frowned before nudging Ethan's unconscious form with the tip of her stiletto toe. "Besides, these fools have gotten what was coming to them if you ask me. May they rot in their failure."

Benson pinched the bridge of her nose. She was making an attempt at displaying patience but was failing miserably.

"That's funny, because I don't recall asking you your opinion. Now come help me prevent these-" She gestured towards us all with a look of complete bewilderment. "These *things* from turning into dead bodies."

Garcia heaved an imperial sigh. "If I must."

Within seconds, her slender figure blurred across the room with a snap and reappeared beside my bleeding friend. She knelt down and casually began assessing each wound. *The least they could do was show some sort of urgency.* I thought irritably to myself while Benson watched from afar with cool contemplation. I prickled with contempt. *How could she remain so calm during a time like this? Better yet, why hadn't she attempted to protect us in the first place. Was our well being not her intent?* The very thought made my stomach curdle. Confusion bubbled into realization, which quickly turned into rage.

"How can you betray us like this, after all we have done for you?" I accused. "We trusted you and you've fed us to the wolves!" I choked back tears of hate. Boiling outrage smoldered any ability to reason. I tore at my collar, desperately trying to free myself from the massive icicle that pinned me in place. "How can you side with Patterson when she is working with Lemmings?!"

Benson's mouth twitched.

Darkness bled into Garcia's eyes.

"Benson is here to help, you babbling half-wit! She hired Patterson to use a tracking spell to find Frank. She is also here to help Selena improve her craft. Like always, you meddled where you weren't supposed to and people got hurt!" Tenderly, she scooped Selena in her arms. Blood caked the back of her head.

I faltered for a moment.

Her words pierced through my cloud of rage and shook me to the core. *Had this really been my fault? I had been the one who struck first. Could it really be that I had fucked things up?* An icy wave of guilt washed over me. My heart crumbled when I saw Selena's face. Her bronze complexion had turned to ash. My stomach twisted when Garcia cradled the back of Selena's blood soaked skull. Ashamed, I averted my gaze.

"What happened, where am I?" Selena mumbled numbly.

She looked up, bleary eyed. "Ms. Garcia is that you?"

Each word came out slurred.

Garcia bit down on her wrist and pressed the punctured flesh to Selena's lips.

"Shh. Come on baby girl. Drink." She cooed and stroked Selena's sweat soaked head.

Anger, frustration, hurt and shame flared through me as I hung helplessly from the shaft of ice. In a futile effort, I kicked my feet. My body swung to and fro like a pendulum.

"How was I supposed to know she was hired help? She never

mentioned any of you. She was however very keen on admitting that she knew who and what we were. We already have two teachers smuggling kids into labs. So what would you propose I do? Let us hope for the best and assume we wouldn't get captured?"

Garcia gingerly laid Selena back onto the classroom floor.

"Take a look around. You took a chance and you blew it. Now everyone around you has to suffer for it. All we ask is for you to own up for your actions, Alexis. Can't you see? Each choice you make effects those all around you."

The head of the local vampire clan took a moment to asses Astrid's wounds. In the meantime, Benson went over the details of what had happened with Mrs. Patterson. Once satisfied, Garcia gave Astrid a solid crack upside the head. Astrid's eyes snapped wide open.

Her eyes burned molten gold. "Ow! What the hell was that for?"

Garcia scoffed. "It's good to know you're awake."

Astrid glared daggers Carmen's way. "Why you..."

Garcia's scarlet lips curled into a mischievous sneer.

Benson's voice cut through the chaos.

"Enough! All of you! What is done is done. Lexi made a decision that she felt was necessary. Quite frankly, I may have done the same thing if I felt you were all in danger. Let's not focus on the past but more so on the present. For starters, Anna are you ok?"

Satisfied, I watched a disgruntled Garcia scowl from afar. I took great pleasure in her discomfort. It's not everyday you see a powerful vampire in the throes of irritation without getting hurt. She didn't appreciate being told what to do but she held her tongue anyway. Patterson merely shrugged and rubbed her bruised arms.

"As fine as I will ever be, I suppose." She admitted with a resigned sigh.

Benson offered her a polite smile.

"Right. Now that we have established your well-being would you mind releasing my pupil?" She indicated towards a scowling Astrid.

"What about me?" I spluttered.

Benson raised a brow. "You will do best to stay where you are."

"It would be a pleasure." Patterson obliged.

The gnarled roots slithered away with the wave of a hand. Plaster cracked and crumbled as they receded back into the wall. Astrid crashed to the floor in a crumpled heap. Grumbling, she untangled herself from the foliage. Benson sighed and crossed her arms as she surveyed the room.

"There is a lot of damage here..." Benson said with a troubled frown.

"That there is." Patterson admitted tactfully.

All the while, the expression on her face remained reserved.

"Is it possible to make it appear as if a quake occurred?" Benson asked.

"Yes, but think it would be wiser to fix the place up cosmetically than to create a quake. Michigan isn't known for having quakes. Such a story will send the media into a frenzy. If we do choose to do a quake then there may be an investigation."

Benson whipped out her phone, with a few clicks here and there she snapped it shut.

"Consider it done, I have hired help. They shall be here within the hour."

Benson said as she continued to scope out the room.

"We truly do apologize for what has happened. We didn't mean to inconvenience you." Benson inspected the remaining contents within the teapot. She took a sniff. Her face sourced slightly.

"Do you mind?" Benson inquired, obviously referring to the teapot.

"No, not at all." Patterson offered graciously.

The twitch in her lip had said otherwise.

Cold blossomed from Benson's fingertips and frost began to spread across the pot's surface leaving a spidery web of ice across the ceramic surface. The contents inside crackled from the change of temperature. She meandered over to Ethan, letting the contents cool.

"Good, now that is settled let us begin."

Without further ado she tossed the ice water onto an unconscious Ethan.

He gasped and shot up out of his stupor, sputtering water.

"Sweet Jesus that was cold!" His teeth chattered.

Garcia's scarlet lips curled with amusement.

Meanwhile, Benson plucked something off of her blazer and then inspected her nails.

"Ah Ethan, so nice of you to join us. Would you be so kind as to cover your package? We all know that you are-" She wrinkled her nose and paused for effect, trying to choose her words carefully "well-endowed but there is no need to be sporting it in public."

Astrid cackled with laughter.

Ethan flushed.

"If I could just get to my locker..."

He fumbled for words as he desperately tried to cover himself.

Garcia tossed him her black cardigan.

Graciously, he caught it.

A sleepy Hawk Eyes stirred from her slumber.

"What's going on?" She inquired groggily as she ran her hand along the back of her head. She grimaced painfully and took in a sharp breath. The vampire blood must have helped speed things. By now all she had was a decent goose egg on the back of her head. Thanks to Garcia, Selena's sickly pallor had quickly faded.

"Oh good. You're awake. Benson is going to bring us up to speed on what's going on. While Lexi here *hangs* around." Garcia chuckled merrily at her own joke.

I narrowed my eyes and stared daggers in her general direction

"Awww, how cute, the sardonic vampire has a sense of humor."

"Now let's carry on shall we? Astrid please have a seat. Carmen and Selena will you care to join us?" She paused and looked me up and down with a pinched expression. "If you think you can behave I'll let you down. Do you think you can manage?"

I scowled but didn't argue.

"So be it." She waved her hand.

Instantly, the large spear of ice melted at her command and I crashed to the floor.

Patterson pulled up a chair and sat down.

Meanwhile a sullen Garcia sat at the back of the table.

"Let's get one thing straight." Benson announced. "Anna is not here to capture anyone. Earlier Ethan had inquired about a witch's ability to use a tracking spell." Benson inclined her head in Patterson's direction.

"Anna here happens to know how to do this spell and was more than willing to assist Selena with her craft. However, after what has happened now I do not know if she is still up for the task."

Patterson seemed to be miffed by the most recent turn of events but regardless she tilted her head in resignation.

"Yes, it would be an honor to guide a daughter of the craft. Despite what has happened it is still my duty to give her guidance."

Benson let out a breathy sigh. "We are in your debt, Anna."

Benson's watery blue gaze shifted from Anna to Selena.

"She is to serve as your mentor. Understand?"

Selena nodded numbly. "Yes ma'am."

Garcia leaned back and flashed Selena a seductive smile.

"If you don't listen to her we will skin you alive."

Anna cleared her throat and tucked a wisp of gray hair behind her tiny ear.

"As previously discussed, I can locate Frank's whereabouts but I am assuming the place is going to be packed with security. There isn't a question of finding him. The question is getting him out without being killed or arrested."

Benson offered her a curt nod.

"I am already working on that. I have voiced my concerns to the officials and informed them of my suspicions. In response, they have agreed to place a spy within the lab's quarters. I just so happened to have a play in choosing the observer that they have placed on the scene. However due to homeland security she hasn't been able to give me the specific whereabouts of the laboratory's location."

There was a significant pause. A moment of disappointment had blossomed within the conversation. *Would this person be able to get access to the security in time? Would Frank be able to last that long?* There were already people dying from their experiments. Each passing minute made it harder to guarantee getting him out successfully. *What if the person couldn't find enough evidence to have the program overthrown? What would happen to Frank? What would happen to us?* The program had to be stopped. The illegal abduction of unwilling subjects had to cease.

Everyone had held their breath.

The silence intensified.

A perturbed Ethan stared off into the distance.

In the meantime, a worried Astrid bit at her nails

I chewed on my lip and let out a weary sigh.

"I'll do it." I mumbled reluctantly.

Everyone stopped and turned to me.

Confusion swam in Ethan's eyes. "Do what?"

Defeated, I ran a hand through my auburn hair. I screwed everything up so I miles as well fix it. I had thought sourly to myself. I originally didn't want Benson or Garcia to realize I could alter my appearance with magic. Eventually, they'd figure it out in the long run anyway. However, if that were the case I'd rather that information came from me than from another source.

"I'll find a way to breach the security system."

Benson watched me with great interest.

Astrid's expression remained unreadable.

Selena had drifted back into a listless sleep.

Worry swam in Ethan's eyes. Silently, he begged me not to continue. He knew how paranoid I was about spilling my secrets.

Garcia leaned back and crossed her arms.

"And how exactly do you plan on doing that?"

I offered her a casual shrug and kept my tone as nonchalant as possible.

"Simple. I am able to twist time and use magic to create illusion of invisibility. I will sneak into Lemming's office tonight and use my abilities to get as much information on the lab as I can. He should have at least some sort of blue print on the place. He'd be a fool if he doesn't. The man is a conniving mastermind. That's how we got their notes on their supernatural serum they are working on."

Ethan's head dropped in resignation. Silently, he rubbed at his jaw while Astrid chewed her lip. A faint smile toyed at the corner of Benson's mouth. A hint of pride shimmered behind Garcia's expression while Anna tapped thoughtfully at her chin.

"Miss Adams. I think you are onto something." She rose and dusted off her hands. "Well now that has been settled, let's get this place cleaned up shall we?"

Benson's smile widened. "Yes. Let's."

CHAPTER 28

THE CROSS BAR on the door clanged. I jolted awake. Blinding light poured into the hallway. A dazed Bianca sat on the floor. She hugged her knees tight to her chest while a satiated Bright Eyes snored in the background. Her skin had paled significantly since the last time I saw her. Well damn, the little cockroach must have had his fill. I thought dryly to myself.

The metal door swung open and in stepped Marie Rousseau. Black heels clicked briskly against the stone floor. A ring of keys jingled against her hip. Theodore followed close behind. An exhausted Bianca rose from the ground like a newborn giraffe. Instantly, she leaned into the bars for support.

"Well it's good to see you got some use out of her." Rousseau murmured thoughtfully as she handed the woman a cookie and a bottle of orange juice. A sleepy eyed Bianca accepted the offering with a murmur of thanks. Theodore's shadow engulfed the two of them in darkness. I shifted nervously as Marie took in my malnourished form. She eyed me speculatively, paused, then glanced back at Bright Eyes and then back at me.

A flicker of disappointment flashed across her face.

I sucked in a breath.

Fierce gray eyes met mine. It was then that I realized she knew what had happened. I had disregarded her request and refused to follow her directions. She had intended on giving me an opportunity to heal but I had given that opportunity to the cockroach instead. The skin around her eyes tightened. It looked like she hadn't slept in days.

"Are you ready Frank?" She inquired with a bit of steel in her voice.

I sighed in defeat. "Ready as I'll ever be."

She only grunted in approval.

Theodore watched me warily. Golden light reflected off his chocolate skin. For a moment my eyes lingered on the pulse in his neck. The sweet scent of fear rippled off him in waves. His apprehension woke the predator within me. My stomach gurgled involuntarily and I forced myself to look away. *I couldn't lose control. Not now.* My will pressed against the burning hunger that seared through my veins. Then it occurred to me. *What would Theodore do if I were to try to drain him dry?* The very prospect excited me. Purple veins prickled at the corner of my eyes. A amused Bright Eyes watched us afar from his cot.

"Watch it *vampire*." Theodore rumbled. "You're a danger to yourself and everyone around you." The jangle keys and a metallic clicking sound tore me back into the present. Theodore exhaled slowly. "Step out real slow if you know what's good for you." I stared down the end of a steel barrel. Theodore flexed his sweaty hand but his index finger hovered protectively over the trigger. "You're going to walk real slow. If you try something I will shoot you. Understand?"

I nodded once.

Marie took the lead, I followed and Theodore fell in from behind. His rifle remained locked on the back of my skull. We walked into the bright yellow light. The steel door slammed behind us as two scientists scurried down the corridor. They wore white lab coats and were armed to the brim with pens and clipboards. I looked around. A pair of excited gentlemen on the far end of the hallway loudly discussed their discoveries with one another.

Pulsating necks were all around me. Their hearts thrummed like little drums. The beast within me whispered tauntingly inside my head. *Drink Frank, it's just one sip.. aren't you hungry?* Little droplets of sweat blossomed along my forehead. The predator in me growled, desperate to feed. I closed my eyes and tried to quell the beast within. I dug my nails into my palms. Beads of blood blossomed along the pad of my hand. I tried to focus on the pain more so than our current surroundings. We passed various rooms.

One with a shifting werewolf and ring of eager scientists with scribbling pens. Another room held a vampire, a doctor and a sickly little girl. In the background stood a guard at ease. It appeared as if the group were participating in a congenial conversation. He couldn't be there to feed. The girl was pale and feeble. No pleasurable meal would come from her. In fact, he himself was hooked up to her IV. There were no chains, weapons up in arms. In fact, it seemed as if he were there of his own free will. *But why?...* The very idea baffled me.

Why wasn't he trying to escape? Could it be he was a willing participant? The balding patient watched us approach from afar with hauntingly gaunt eyes. Marie Rousseau was the first to break the silence.

"Ze lab may participated in some activities that you and I don't approve of. However, they also have programs that are meant to improve mankind." She tilted her head towards the vampire behind the glass. "For instance, Seth here is participating in ze lab's quest to cure cancer. He is one out of ze many supernatural creatures that have agreed to support our cause. You and I can both agree that some practices here may be unconventional and some may be in need of refinement, however, deep down ze lab does have some good intentions that are worth fighting for."

I turned back to look. I couldn't hear what was being said. He must have said something funny because they were all laughing. Envy slithered around inside my chest. *Did they not see him as a threat?* The guard's posture wasn't rigid like Theodore's. Nor did he aim his firearm at the back of Seth's head. The hairs on my skin prickled with irritation.

Then again, in Theodore's defense, only five minutes had passed since I had contemplated on eating him. I suppose I too would have been a bit tense. As we left, Seth had glanced my way. For a brief moment our eyes met. Concern clouded his honey-eyed gaze. Within seconds, the conversation between him and the group had faltered. Then the girl had said something and he was immediately back on task.

Baffled, I turned to Marie. "But why? After all the tests he had to undergo why isn't he rebelling? Why are they treating me so differently than him?"

Marie clucked her tongue reprovingly as she removed her glasses and wiped them on her lab coat. "Now, now, cherie. Don't get testy. Seth had to undergo ze same preliminary tests as you. Unlike you, he follows all ze directions. He feeds when he is told and has proven zat he is a willing participant." She strongly emphasized the word feed and willing. She slipped on her glasses and gave me a pointed glare before moving on.

"Ze patient has been diagnosed with stage four cancer. Seth has willingly offered his blood to see if his vampiric DNA will cure her. You need to understand that ze lab rewards those who are eager to help. You may just feel that you are treated differently because you are in a different program. Seth belongs to ze medical program. You belong to ze military program. People view Seth as a medical remedy. You are viewed as a powerful weapon. That is why compliance is of the utmost importance. It's not a matter of different treatments more so than different perspectives. It's simple, follow ze directions and you will be rewarded with more freedom."

I eyed her dubiously when she mentioned the word freedom.

"What do you mean by more freedom?"

Theodore tensed Marie chortled and took a right turn. "Like going outside, getting time to roam. Receiving an allotted hunting time or an extended curfew. Things like zat."

Theodore frowned and looked me over with a sense of uncertainty. He hoisted his gun higher onto his shoulder. "Miss Rousseau shouldn't you be careful about disclosing too much information to the subject?"

He paused as if searching for the appropriate wording. "He is a *vampire* after all."

My eyes narrowed into little slits.

Theodore's grip tightened around his artillery weapon.

We approached two steel doors.

Marie let out a cynical snort. "Well, Theodore, the subject has a name and it is Frank. Nor do I see anything wrong with telling him how ze system works. In fact, maybe our subjects would be more compliant if ze lab were more honest about their practices."

She threw the steel doors open. We entered a white room with no windows and only padding. I blinked my eyes against the bright fluorescent lighting.

"What is this place?" I murmured in awe as my eyes adjusted to the light.

"Honestly I have no clue. I imagine it is for observation. They didn't tell me what your appointment was about. Regardless, I'll come back to fetch you in about an hour."

I frowned, mildly surprised. "He didn't tell you?"

She shook her head. "No, I am afraid not cherie but I will see you soon."

She stepped back and closed the doors behind her. I had a bad feeling about this. Marie usually knows what is going on and what I am being tested for. It wasn't like her to not be informed. Then again, I suppose there's not much she can do if they don't give her any details.

Uneasily, I stepped forward and looked up to see an intercom embedded in the vaulted ceiling. The windowless room had a screen mounted on the back wall and a long mirror embedded on the right hand side. The place reminded me of an interrogation room that you'd likely see in the movies, only it was much larger with no furniture. A small part of me wondered if they could see me on the other side of the mirror.

Curious, I stepped forward to sneak a peek. My famished reflection stared back at me with sunken gray eyes. So that's why Seth looked so concerned. I looked like a walking skeleton with paper thin skin. Due to malnourishment, my olive skin had faded to the color of yellowed parchment. I ran a skeletal hand through my brittle black hair.

The steel doors on the other end of the room rumbled. I whirled around to see a barefoot Jacob accompanied from behind by two guards. He only wore spandex shorts.

My eyebrows shot up in surprise. "Aren't you a bit underdressed?"

Jacob averted his gaze. His expression was sullen.

The guards that were accompanying him turned and left without a word.

A man's voice crackled over the intercom.

"He is not underdressed for the task at hand, my dear boy."

The TV screen flickered to life to reveal a bushy browed Lemmings smiling smugly back at me. "How nice of you to join us Frank."

I shifted my weight uneasily. "Not like I had much of a choice, now did I?"

Lemmings chortled and leaned back in his chair. A frown tugged at my lips. Uneasiness prickled along the hairs on the back of my neck. Something was fishy about this whole thing.

"Jacob, what's going on here?" I asked.

Jacob glanced at me then looked away.

Shame and disappointment clouded his visage.

The muscles along his jaw were tight.

Lemmings steepled his fingers and leaned forward. "You see, Jacob and you are going to fight. We need to see the differences between your species when it comes to battle." He paused and rested his chin on his fingertips. "Might I add that I am slightly disappointed in your condition? Didn't you feed, Francis?"

I bristled and narrowed my eyes into little slits. "First of all, my name is Frank and second of all I refuse to feed off the neck of a live person. I believe I have already made that clear." My voice didn't quaver. Each word cracked like a whip. *Whatever the case may be, I refused to gravel at the feet of a bully.*

A puzzled Lemmings frowned and stroked at his mustache. Distaste tightened his features. "This will affect the study." He mused aloud. He sighed with a wave of his hand. He dismissed the issue with a wave of his hand. "No matter, you will battle each other regardless. We can still gather some sort of information out of this predicament."

I cut him off. "I refuse."

All of his light hearted humor dissipated instantly. "*Excuse me?*"

"I refuse to fight Jacob just like I refuse to feed off the live vein."

Jacob averted his gaze and chewed on the inside of his cheek. A chilly smile curled at the corner of Lemming's lips. In his hand he held a letter opener. He tilted the object from side to side, admiring the shiny finish. "I have a proposition for you then."

My resolve hardened.

"You can shove your proposition up your ass."

His bushy brows perked in surprise. "Oh is that so?"

He twirled a silver letter opener thoughtfully in his hand. He sighed and he rose from his position in the chair. "I was hoping you would give me a reason to try out this new experiment but I wasn't expecting it to be so soon. In all honesty, I wish I had more time to prepare but I suppose I'll manage."

Someone whimpered in the background

Jacob stiffened.

The camera zoomed out to reveal a struggling Olivia hanging from the ceiling in chains. Sweaty blonde curls clung to her face. Her lips twisted with pain. Two rigid soldiers stood in the shadows. Darkness covered their visage. Lemmings tapped thoughtfully at his lips with the silver letter opener.

"Let's see. What should I do?" He paused for dramatic effect and snapped his finger. "Oh I know! Each time you refuse to do what I ask I'll stab Olivia with this letter opener." His smile widened. His icy blue eyes were devoid of emotion. "I have always wondered how a werewolf's insides reacts to silver."

Slowly, he ran the letter opener along Olivia's bare skin.

Her skin sizzled and crackled against the pure metal's touch.

Jacob's thundering heart rate quickened.

My stomach twisted with disgust.

"Fascinating, isn't it? How something so mundane can cause so much harm." Olivia shivered with revulsion and bit her lip as he made a smoking trail along the front of her abdomen.

The guard's hold on her gun tightened ever so slightly.

Jacob took an involuntary step forward.

"Please just do what he asks." Jacob whispered urgently.

Desperation welled up in his blue eyes.

I faltered for a moment. It had to be a scare tactic. Lemmings was a teacher, or at least he had been. There would be no way that he would stab a student. After all his educational training and his lifetime commitment to teaching one would assume that he was passionate about kids. Then again, he may have been the reason as to why we were all here in the first place. I decided to hope for the best and went with my first instinct.

"You're bluffing" I growled.

Lemmings raised a brow. "Oh really? Let's start with the stomach then, shall we?"

Without further ado, Lemmings drove the silver letter opener through Olivia's stomach. She let out a blood curdling scream as the blade pierced through her abdomen. Her flesh smoked and hissed against the purified metal. "Does this look like I am bluffing Frank?"

He twisted the blade to emphasize his point.

Olivia cried out again.

A strangled sound escaped Jacob's throat.

Pools of horror and despair flooded into his blue eyes.

"Don't do it Frank! Don't give this bastard what he wants!" Olivia screeched in between pants. A red stream of blood trickled down her side. Her body writhed in pain. My mouth dropped.

"He didn't.." I began, purely speechless by the outcome of events. The corner of my eye twitched. I grasped for words, struggling to speak. Wisps of fear scuttled across the back of my neck like little spider legs.

Lemmings rubbed his chin with a large hand.

'Fascinating isn't it?" Lemming mused out loud. "It appears that silver has an ill effect on werewolves as it does vampires." He twisted the blade, tearing more flesh. Olivia weeped. She panted, trying to ease the searing pain. Her skin bubbled. Blood trickled from her sputtering wound, leaving another wet trail of blood down her flat stomach. "A pity, really. I had hoped for a lesser effect." Lemmings exhaled in disappointment before giving the letter opener a good yank. A spray of blood hit the camera lens.

The corners of my eyes tightened. Purple veins prickled at the corner of my eyes. Hunger bubbled inside my stomach. I sucked in a breath of air and forced myself to look away only to stare into the sea of emptiness within Jacob's watery gaze.

"Please just do whatever he asks, for Olivia's sake." Jacob pleaded, his voice was barely a whisper.

Lemmings smiled with amusement. "Yes Frank, please do because next time I am going to see what this can do when it's in her neck and I don't intend on taking it out so soon." Lemming's laughter cackled over the intercom.

CHAPTER 29

MY CONTROL WAVERED as Olivia's blood trickled down the screen. Cold waves of panic shivered down my spine. The predator in me woke from its slumber. Hot desire trickled through my veins, unfurling my need to feed. *No, no this can't be happening.* My breath quickened. *Not now, I was doing so well. I can't lose control.*

I fell to my knees. Jacob's strong heartbeat thudded nervously in his chest. My hands trembled. *I had to get out of here. I had to go, anywhere but here.* Buds of sweat blossomed from my temples. The beast within me struggled for control. *Feed Frank, feed.* The predator within me cooed. No, I can't. I argued. *You must.* It coaxed, its voice silken with temptation. *Come now child, one sip won't hurt.* The animal within me purred. The thirst in me raged. I was seeing red. *Please, no, Jacob is my friend. If I start I won't stop.*

Jacob stepped closer. He reeked with the smoky scent of rage and sickly sweet fear. The deafening beat of his heart thrummed anxiously inside my head, sending me over the edge and into a red haze. I cradled my head in my hands. Inky pools of darkness flooded into the whites of my eyes. They narrowed into little slits.

"*Get away from me Jacob.*" I snarled, in a voice that was not my own.

I bared my teeth, revealing a pair of yellowed fangs.

His hands flexed. Fingernails lengthened into sharp claws.

"You know that is something I can't do." He rumbled.

The ice blue eyes of his wolf bore into me.

"Not if it brings harm to one of my own. I am sure even you can understand that." He replied apologetically as his muscles rippled and grew. His shorts ripped from the pressure. White fur sprouted along his back. His face elongated into that of a wolf. He stood up tall like a hulked out version of Anubis on steroids. White fur covered his body. Massive wolf paws supported the weight of his stocky five foot eight figure.

His bushy tail bristled and swished with agitation. Calculating blue eyes bore into me, watching, waiting, sensing.

His black nose wrinkled, taking in my scent. He stepped forward. The cement creaked beneath his weight. I crouched. My muscles coiled in anticipation. Tension made the air thick and heavy. His claws flexed. As did mine. Our gazes met. Our bodies tensed. We circled. Each step was measured slow and ready like two tigers circling each other in a ring.

"Please don't fight you guys." Olivia wheezed, breathlessly.

Lemmings rubbed at his jaw and watched with great anticipation.

"It's not worth it." She continued.

Lemmings held up his hand. She fell silent.

"You honestly believe that fighting me will end her suffering?" I snarled.

"Temporarily." Jacob growled back and pounced.

I charged.

We smacked into each other, spitting and snarling.

Explosive rage rolled off us in waves.

"You're a fool if you think he's going to let her off the hook that easily! He's going to do whatever it takes to get what he wants." I said as I snapped at his neck.

"It's better than doing nothing!" Jacob replied as he twisted away and swiped at my back. He took strings hardened flesh with him. I hissed and threw him across the room.

"You're only doing what he wants." I hollered back.

He yelped as he skidded along the concrete. He smacked into the mirror, cracking it on impact. "Please! Both of you stop!" Olivia pleaded in the background. The wounds within my flesh silently knitted themselves back together. My breath came out in heavy puffs. I reprimanded myself for falling back into my old human ways.

"Can't you see that? You are throwing away everything that Carmen and I have worked towards. Carmen and I befriended you, despite your werewolf heritage. Even after what your kind has done to my family. How can you just throw that away?" My voice cracked with rage.

Bruised and mangled he struggled to rise.

His bones cracked and popped into place.

"I am truly sorry about what has happened to your family. I am sorry about what happened between your kind and mine. However, Olivia is all I have left. You have to understand that."

Rage welled up inside me.

The predator in me screamed in frustration.

"Why can't you understand that he'll hurt her anyway?! Nothing is ever good enough for them. Her being the reason we are fighting like this is tearing her apart. She is a werewolf. She can heal physically in a matter of minutes but not emotionally. Why can't you see that?"

He swiped at me.

I ducked and rolled off to the side.

"I can't just stand here and do nothing!" Jacob growled.

"Oh, so you'd kill one of your friends instead? *Spare me the drama*."

I tackled him, moving at sonic speed. We tumbled to the ground.

He snarled, I hissed.

Spittle dripped from his elongated muzzle. Blood stained his white coat. We grappled, traded blows, punched, clawed and snapped at each other like a pair of wild animals. Blood trickled from my nose and from the cut above Jacob's right eye. The coppery scent of blood and acrid smell of sweat tainted the air. Hunger burned through my veins like molten lava. The predator within me flared in anticipation and took control. I licked my lips and dove for Jacob's neck.

"No!" Olivia screamed.

My fangs plunged into him, puncturing through the white fur and tough sinew. He thrashed against my weight. I pressed into him, holding him down. Hot blood gushed into my mouth. I took long pulls, ignoring the sour tang. Everything around me dulled. The pounding of his heart boomed in my ears. Someone screamed off in the distance. Nothing mattered. The only thing that mattered was the need to feed. I've never had werewolf blood before. Jake's blood didn't taste the greatest, in fact it was awful. However, at this rate I'd drink even piss water if I had to. It had been weeks since the last time I had fed. My body had already begun deteriorating. If I didn't feed soon I'd shrivel up like a raisin.

Meanwhile, Jake's life force gushed into me. My wounds began to heal. Muscles and flesh knitted themselves together. Broken bones cracked and popped into place. Bruises faded. Fiery bliss coursed through my veins. My senses heightened, overwhelming me with different emotions.

The bitter scent of sweat overpowered me. Bright lights burned my eyes. My hands trembled. My skin itched with agitation. Uneasiness blossomed within my core. *This wasn't supposed to happen. Feeding was supposed to heal me and nourish me, not make existence unbearable. Why was everything so overwhelming?* I itched with the need to rip, tear and kill. *Something was wrong. Is this why Carmen and the others refused to drink from the blood of a wolf?* The expectation for peace transformed into unbearable irritation. Bliss transformed into wild aggression. The flow of blood began to clot. I shook my head back and forth, growling, willing it to continue.

Jacob continued to thrash beneath my weight. *Why wasn't my venom working? Why was the blood clotting?* The fresh blood within me began to sour. The warm flowing liquid curdled in my gut. Healing turned into sickness. The room began to spin. Jacob wrenched me off of his neck and threw me across the room. I rolled across the ground. My stomach twisted and turned. My sides cramped. Cold sweat swept across my body. A wetness formed at the back of my mouth and I began to wretch. Olivia's sobs could be heard over the background. A satisfied smirk curled at the corner of Lemming's lips. The edges of my vision blurred. The room tilted.

"Didn't you know werewolf blood has an ill effect on vampires?" Jacob grunted as he struggled to get back up. The cracked screen on the left hand side of the wall flickered. Everything faded in and out. The image of Jacob faded, in a matter of seconds I was out.

Moments later there were a few bangs here and there and then Marie rushed into the room. Theodore trailed in behind her. Her jaw dropped at the carnage. Blood was sprayed across the walls. A long crack sprawled across the mirror on the right hand side of the room. The TV hung precariously from its mount. She paused and shot a bewildered glance at an unconscious Frank.

"What on earth has happened-"

She looked up to see a naked Jacob, who feebly attempted to hide his manhood behind his hands. Scuffs, bruises and scratches littered his skin.

"Mr. Parks!" She gasped and shielded her eyes.

The remainder of his clothes hung from him in tatters. The rest of the pieces were scattered amongst the floor. Theodore raised a brow. He barely managed to keep a straight face. Regardless, humor glittered in his eyes.

"Where on Earth are your clothes!" Marie demanded furiously.

Lemmings chuckled softly.

"It looks like he will have to make a few adjustments on the military jumpsuit and take in account the shift in mass." Lemmings said with a chortle.

Jacob flushed and averted his eyes.

Marie whirled on Lemmings.

"I demand to know what in ze world is going on here and I expect answers now Paul!"

An image of a frowning Lemmings flickered on the cracked television screen. Lemmings cleared his throat.

"Now, now Ms. Rousseau no need to fret, we were just observing the physical abilities between vampires and werewolves."

"Not much to observe, now is there?" Theodore said with a snort.

Marie shot him a scathing glare while still shielding her eyes from Jacob's naked presence..

"I'll be back with some-" Theodore began with a grimace.

He paused, fumbling for words. "With some appropriate attire."

A blazing red Jacob set his jaw and looked away.

"Yes, please do." Marie replied sternly.

She now flashed Lemmings with a menacing glare.

"You approved this observation when you already knew Frank was not up to par?"

Paul Lemmings sighed and rubbed the space between his fuzzy eyebrows with his two stubby fingers. "We've already discussed this Ms. Rousseau. The authorities gave me a deadline. If we don't meet that expectation then the funding for the serum will be suspended." He offered Marie a polite smile, leaned back and folded his hands. "I am sure you understand. Don't you?"

Marie gawked at him in complete bewilderment.

"You don't seriously intend to send them this *garbage*, do you?"

Lemmings inclined his head. "You can't be serious!" She sputtered. "These tests won't provide accurate information for your serum. They are biased, Paul. Both you and I know Frank is not up to his full potential. Whatever results you have gathered will be skewed in Jacob's favor. These don't display either candidates' true potential and even you know that." Paul's smile tightened.

Jacob shifted his weight.

"Then maybe you should have fed him" Paul suggested icily while Frank convulsed on the floor. Theodore entered the room and threw Jacob a pair of shorts. Jacob quickly threw them on and rushed to Frank's aid.

She threw her hands up in the air.

"I have tried! He wouldn't take a single drop from his blood nurse. We wouldn't be having this problem if you'll just *allow* him blood bags or an animal-" Lemmings cut her off before she could finish. "Why do you insist on treating him like a human? He is a vampire, Marie, a vampire for christ's sake. They may look human but let me assure you they are not. They are nothing more than a means to an end."

Her delicate features twisted with fury. "Theodore, call for medical assistance."

Theodore gave her a curt nod and then rushed out the door.

"This is ridiculous." Marie huffed. "Despite your philosophy he's a creature capable of reasoning, feelings and thought. Maybe if you practiced some sort of kindness then you wouldn't have to use so much force."

Lemmings' cheeks colored with ire. He rose to his full height. The camera automatically adjusted to his movements, revealing Olivia's limp form as it dangled in the background, her body stained with blood.

Marie gasped and brought a hand to her mouth.

"Paul," she stammered. "What have you done?"

Paul flicked his hand at the soldiers.

They approached and began taking Olivia down.

Jacob swallowed and looked away.

"Let's just say Frank and Jacob needed a little motivation to get started. Unlike you, I do whatever it takes to get the job done. I don't care if you have to use all of our blood nurses. You will confine Francis Marino and force him to feed. *Do I make myself clear?*" Each word came out like ice.

"I wouldn't do that if I were you." Jacob said with a sigh.

Paul's face soured.

He fixed Jacob with a lethal glare. "And why is that?"

His voice came out in a low growl, his patience was wearing thin.

Jacob ran a nervous hand through his tousled hair. Brown curls fell into his eyes. "Because, Frank turns feral when he feeds off the vein of a living human being. His inner predator kicks in and he loses control. He loses his ability to reason and goes on a killing spree, leaving trails of death in his wake. When he feeds he can't stop. The struggle for control may be due to the overwhelming sensations of human emotions. Who knows, all I know is that you don't want him to go down that road if you can help it. It was hard enough getting him back and you don't have Garcia here to assist you."

Marie nibbled on her thumbnail, listening carefully as Frank twitched on the floor. "Is he going to be okay? Is there a way to train him to master those urges?"

Jacob shrugged his shoulders helplessly as he kept Frank's head elevated.

"Honestly I have no clue but you're going to want to get him a blood transfusion and you'll want to be quick about it too, that is if you want him to live of course. If not he'll die from drinking my blood. He drank too much of it. Werewolf blood counteracts with vampire venom. It's a defense mechanism. If vampire blood mixes with a werewolf's it becomes tainted and makes the vampire extremely ill. That's why vampires don't drink from wolves."

CHAPTER 30

A FAINT BEEPING SOUND SLOWLY EASED me back to consciousness. Footsteps echoed in the hallway and a pair of hushed voices conversed quietly amongst one another just outside the door of my room. "It shouldn't be taking them this long. We should have had an update by now." A man groused. His pacing feet scuffed and squeaked against the linoleum.

"Maybe ze blood transfusions take longer with vampires. He was in pretty bad shape when they wheeled him in there." A woman replied, her voice was accented with French. The man grunted and then grumbled something sour beneath his breath. Jacob's blood must have muddled my senses because I could only understand bits and pieces of the conversation.

Everything came out as an incoherent mess. Then again, the last thing I remembered after feeding off of Jacob was blacking out from a sensory overload. *Damn werewolf blood. Regardless, I knew I was in a room but the question was where?* I sucked in a breath of latex laden air, taking in different smells as they ran across my palette. I caught a mixture of bitter bleach, crisp linen, sour sweat, fresh paint, stale blood and plastic all rolled into one. My eyes fluttered open at the sound of my name. A woman had said it, her voice was silky smooth and thick with a heavy accent. *Had it been the woman from the previous conversation?*

My vision tilted and blurred. The room was dark and I couldn't make out much of the details. Normally, I have exemplar night vision. *Hells bells, I hadn't felt this vulnerable in the dark since I was just a babe.* Nevertheless, the darkness made it easier for my eyes to adjust. Slowly, shapes and shadows came together in a jumbled mess. I was in a sparsely decorated hospital room with whitewashed walls and linoleum tiling. The place lacked a TV and only had plastic folding chairs for seating. Fresh white linens were draped over my body. My bedside curtain was partially drawn. The door to my room was ajar but was guarded by two heavily armed men. Between them a blinding shaft of yellow light leaked into the room. The dusty beam of light made my eyes water upon impact. The intensity of the light made me groan. Sharp jabs of pain throbbed behind my eyes.

The woman gasped at something the man had said.

"But you can't! Not unless you're prepared for ze consequences."

The man snorted. He stood in the doorway. His body blocked the invasive light and provided me temporary relief. "I am not, that is why you're going to do it."

The woman sucked in a breath and held it for a few seconds. She let it all out at once. "And if I refuse?" She inquired, her tone defiant.

The man in the doorway didn't move as he contemplated his answer.

"Then you can find another place of employment."

The woman had stiffened but I still couldn't make out her face. She chose her next words very carefully. "And how do you propose to do that?"

Her previous bravado had diminished significantly. My concentration wavered and exhaustion tugged at the corner of my eyes. I blinked, willing myself to stay awake. *Christ, it had been only five minutes since I had awoken surely I could stay up for a few more.*

"Let's just say I have connections" He replied coolly. "You have till morning to decide your next course of action." He paused and gave her thorough look over. "Choose well Miss Rousseau. The laboratory does not take kindly to insubordination."

He left, leaving the blurred figure to stand there in complete silence. His footsteps faded off into the distance. So did my concentration. Seconds later, her slim figure disappeared behind my fluttering eyes. I drifted into the land of dreams only to awake to what seemed like hours later.

Drip, drip, drip. Drops of hot liquid splashed against my withered lips. The coppery scent of blood drifted to my nose. The beast within me rumbled with pleasure. Insatiable hunger blossomed within my core once more. *Damn it all, can't a vampire mummify himself in peace around here?* I tried to squirm away.

The beast within me snarled in protest as it tried to lap hungrily at the blood. Hunger clawed through my veins. *Must feed.* It screamed. No way, if I began now there was no turning back. The shadow of a woman loomed over me. Her silky smooth skin reeked of peppermint. I couldn't fend her off. The werewolf venom had drained what little strength I had left. I ripped my head away only to have the bleeding flesh pressed harder against my cracking lips. Her heartbeat thrummed like the wings of a frantic hummingbird. Some of the hot sticky substance trickled into my mouth and tickled my tongue. It sent electrical shivers through my veins.

"Please Frank drink. If not for yourself then for your friends." She pleaded.

Her words were like honey to my ears.

My eyes rolled. *God I was so hungry it burned.*

The beast in me yowled with excitement.

"Please." She leaned in.

A silken tress of hair brushed against my sallow cheek. "Don't you realize if you don't drink you'll die? I know you won't hurt me. Drink, Frank. I forbid you to die."

My nostrils flared. I was drowning in her peppermint lotion and cucumber melon shampoo. I gagged, trying not to swallow the sweet nectar of life. *Didn't she know that if I didn't drink I'd only mummify?* That did not necessarily mean I'd die. I'd just be out of commission until I got a refill on blood. My determination faltered. The beast within me roared and rallied itself against my weakened defenses. *One sip.* It hissed. *One sip can't hurt.* It begged, coaxing me with silken words. One sip is all it takes I reasoned. The woman's voice cracked with desperation.

"The transfusion isn't working Frank. It took away ze venom but you're still not healing. Your body remains broken, bones and all. You've developed a few patches of new skin but that isn't enough. The organs within your body are failing."

A blood transfusion? It then dawned on me. So that was what the IV was for and that was why I had been slowly recovering from drinking Jacob's blood. Earlier I hadn't been able to maintain consciousness. Now it just felt like a really bad hangover. They had set up a blood transfusion to flush the venom out.

It was brilliant. Still, it would take me hours to fill up on this. Even so, the life force within blood bags wouldn't be enough. I needed fresh blood before any supernatural healing would take place. Surely she had to of known that. Hadn't she? She was a scientist studying the supernatural after all. I could fill up on these bags but I'd need to feed off the live vein to be brought back to my full potential. Vampires are known to get their nutrition when they draw the life force from a living breathing being. Sure blood bags had some of that but once the blood leaves the living body it begins to lose its potency. In fact, the amount of life force within one bag begins to degrade in a matter of days.

A singular drop of water splashed onto my skin. It was hot, wet and salty. Then another. Both drew my attention back to the present. I opened my eyes to see a woman hovering over me. To my surprise it wasn't a dream, it was Marie. Her skin soaked in the silver moonlight. Black loose curls cascaded around her face. I squinted. The edges of her figure were hazed.

I shoved her away.

"That's it? You're just going to give up?"

Her accusation bit into me like a knife.

My blood boiled with rage.

"You of all people *knew* how adamant I was about not feeding off the live vein and here you are trying to force me to drink. *Some friend you are.*" I snarled viciously.

Worry wrinkled her brow.

"Besides, It's not your place to tell me what I can and cannot do.'" I continued venomously. "What's it to you anyway? Are you obsessed with the fact that I am a freak? Do you want me to lose control and drain you dry? Why can't you people just leave me be?"

Marie pulled back as if she had been slapped.

Her silver eyes brimmed with tears.

Instant regret washed over me.

All the words had spilled out before I could reign them in

"Marie.." I began.

She shook her head. Tears spilled down her cheeks.

My heart nearly broke. "Marie, I am sorry,.. please don't cry."

Needles of anguish stabbed at my chest. I had made the one person whom I could confide in cry. Marie was my friend. Never once did I consider how my actions would affect her. Then again, I wasn't aware she had actually cared. Still, it wasn't her fault that I couldn't risk feeding off the live vein. *Why didn't I tell her?*

It was because I was afraid. I was afraid I couldn't turn back. I was even more so afraid of what our friendship would become. *If she were to see the other side of me..would she continue to respect me despite my thirst for spilled blood?* Regardless, she had already risked so much. Despite my lack of communication, she snuck in blood bags and fought on my behalf all on the assumption that my requests were based on pure personal preference. My throat constricted with guilt. *How could I be such an unforgivable ass?*

"Please don't cry." I whispered once again.

My voice came out cracked and hoarse. I reached out to bring her hand to my dry lips. I've never seen her lose control. She had always been poised around me. To see her cry was unnerving.

"How can I not? I'm going to lose my friend and my job all rolled into one and there is nothing I can do about it." She hiccuped

I let out a weary sigh.

Already my resolve to stay awake had begun to fade. *Maybe I did need to feed.*

"There, there." I mumbled as I showered her bloodied fingertips with kisses. "I don't want to see you cry. Let's get you cleaned up."

I pushed down my desire to feed and held the beast within me at bay. The cut on her wrist had been pretty deep and was bleeding profusely. With much practiced control I ran my tongue along the wound. I trembled with the desire but managed to maintain control. Vampire saliva promoted blood clotting and healing. That is how we feed without making messes and why the puncture wounds heal instantly when the fangs are removed.

Maybe, just maybe I could help heal the wound close with my saliva. I shivered. My fangs clicked down into place. The beast within me purred. Her blood was sweet and sticky like honey. Our eyes met and I caught a glimpse of my reflection. The skeletal gaze of a man in his early twenties stared back at me with sunken gray eyes supported by protruding cheekbones.

Unkempt hair fell into his face in a wild disarray. He had a five o'clock shadow, cracked lips and skin as thin as yellowed parchment. Translucent skin clung to his protruding ribs. Purple veins prickled from the corners of his eyes. I shuddered. Hesitant, I pulled away. My feeble struggle was transforming into a tantalizing interest. *Was it possible? Could I consume just enough and pull away?* An intrigued Marie watched me, her eyes burned with an intense curiosity.

"Frank?" She inquired. "What is wrong? Is everything ok?"

I paused and bit my lip. "I'm afraid.."

Her forehead wrinkled with concern. "Of?.."

"Of hurting you." She offered me a reassuring smile.

"It's okay. You won't hurt me Frank."

I bit my lip, a wave of anguish washed over me.

"What if I can't stop?"

She hushed me and brushed a stray hair out of my eyes.

"You can and you will because you are my friend." She crooned as she eased me back down onto the hospital bed. "Lay down and rest."

Tentatively, she leaned in and brought her wrist to my lips. Hesitantly, my skeletal fingers clamped down around the base of her forearm. Marie gasped as I plunged my fangs into her flesh. Her eyes fluttered when I pulled her life force into me. She trembled beneath the pressure. Her heart skipped a beat. I released my venom, in an attempt to ease the pain. Bits and pieces of her most recent memories trickled into me. They played across my mind like spools of film. One moment she was with Lemmings. He was demanding something from her. His words were as cold as steel. Hot anger coursed through her veins.

"You will make him feed." Lemmings demanded,

"I can't and I won't." She said.

"You will." He replied.

"You can't *force* someone to feed if they don't *want* to feed." She argued.

"You will do whatever it takes." He pressed.

"And if I don't?" She replied with a hint of flint.

"Then you can find yourself another means of employment."

Next she was outside a hospital room, arguing with Theodore about the ethics of medical treatment. Her posture was stiff, her expression tense.

" How many times must I tell you? He's not a parasite. He's a living creature and I am tired of hearing you bad mouthing our patients."

"He is a *vampire*, Marie." Theodore replied with an exasperated sigh.

"And you are a thug, Theodore. I will not tolerate you belittling our patients. *Do I make myself clear?*"

My lip quirked with amusement. A flame of pride kindled within my gut. *Who would have known?* Marie had been sticking up for me, a vampire of all things. A few seconds later she stood beneath the moonlight on the rooftop of a building. She had a flip phone pressed to her ear. She kept her hair wrapped up tight in a severe bun. Her face was etched in concentration.

"Are you sure?" The person on the other end inquired.

"I am." Marie replied without hesitation.

"Were you able to collect any evidence?" The sing song voice replied.

"I am in the process of collecting data" Marie said as she fiddled with her button. "I need to make sure our claim is solid before we make our move."

There was a significant pause in the conversation.

"And you're sure that this gentleman you speak of is the one I've requested for you to keep an eye on?"

"Yes, I am sure of it." Marie replied with a nod. "His name is Frank and he matches the description. However, he is refusing to feed. I am not sure how much time he has left."

There was a brief waver in her voice.

Everything blurred and I was back in the present.

My broken bones had mended. Grafts of fresh skin stretched across each muscle. Ripped sinew had begun to sew itself together. Marie's thundering heartbeat had slowed to a slurred thump. She let out a raspy gasp.

"Stop Frank, You're taking too much." Her voice came out in little rasps. She tried to pull away and I tried to break free but the beast in me snarled in protest. "Please." She whispered, her voice so faint it sounded like she was miles away.

The animal in me clamped down harder.

I cursed. *Why couldn't I break free from the beast's spell?*

A sweltering thirst for her blood continued to course through my veins.

"*We must feed. We need more, can't stop.*" The words came out in a garbled hiss.

It was the creature within me. She must have heard it too because her silver eyes widened. "Marie, I can't stop" I whimpered, hating myself for being so weak.

Her expression softened.

"You can Frank. I know you're still in there."

Her voice was a soft murmur.

The sea salt in her hair had intensified. Bits and pieces of her memories played behind my mind like a reel of film. The sounds of the ocean, laughter, water splashing and children swimming filled my brain.

"You have control. You just have to take it." She whispered.

"But I can't!" I snarled, we snarled, the beast and I snarled together.

I mentally kicked myself.

Was I not even going to try?

Was I going to allow this thing to tell me what to do? To control me?

"But you must." She breathed with a misty eyed gaze.

The light in them faded like the sun behind a rolling cloud.

My chest tightened with knots of regret.

"Please Frank. I can't see. Everything is so dark. Frank I am scared."

Her pulse slowed. Each beat came out slow and labored. The flow of her life force flickered like a dying flame. My stomach twisted with revulsion. *Damn you Frank, you cowardly sod. If you care for her in any way you'll stop now.*

Her heart beat sputtered beneath my lips. I strained beneath the beasts will. The beast that I had created, the manifestation of my fear, the fear to kill, smiled smugly in the corner of my mind. He had grown larger, feeding off my fear, the very thing I used to create it, paralyzing me from the ability to act.

Centuries ago, when I had been freshly turned I had killed my baby sister in a fit of hunger. It was a mistake but for some reason I couldn't accept that. She happened to be in the wrong place at the wrong time. She was only nine. She screamed, begged me to stop but I couldn't. I drained her dry. Back then I had no control. I was a newborn vampire blinded by the thirst for blood. I was so hungry. That very night I left a trail of death in my wake. I killed a string of town folk and dismembered anyone who got in my way. Only Carmen was able to to keep me at bay but by the time she did it was already too late.

The memories of her screams sent chills down my spine. I could never forgive myself. Each day I blamed myself for her death. My sorrow turned into hatred which transformed into fear. Since that day I vowed never to feed off the live vein again. A century later I ended up killing a human in the throes of passion.

The mistake pushed me past the edge. My fear of my own nature and the strength of my self-loathing had manifested into a beast. It turned into the beast that now loomed over me and haunted me ever which way I turned. No matter how hard I tried, I kept making the same mistake. Back then it was my sister, then it was Veronica, now it was my friend Marie. I could feel the pleasure blossoming in the beast's core. A seething anger kindled inside me.

My muscles tensed as I recalled all the times Marie had fought valiantly for me. Couldn't I do this one thing for her? I remembered the curl of her lips when she smiled. Her annoyingly sharp wit and the clever glint within her silver eyes. Her words echoed in my head. *You have control, you just have to take it*. They bounced around within my barren soul, knocking down the cobwebs of self-loathing and doubt.

They filled me with hope and inspiration. I wasn't going to kill her. The last time this had happened I had no control but this time I do. The word control ignited a mass of emotions within me. I am tired of being submissive to the overwhelming power of sorrow, regret and fear.

Her words had reassured me. I was a newborn back then but now I am not. Things are different now and I don't have to live in fear. Sure I have made mistakes but I have control now, all I have to do is take control of the situation. A flame of hate awakened within me. It pushed me to a snapping point, severing the bonds of regret that had held me down. The beast that I had created, howled with rage as I ripped myself away from its control.

I shook with effort. Slowly, but surely, I managed to release my jaws from her wrist. I have control, I reminded myself. I shoved Marie, almost too hard. It had been so long since I have fed. I must have forgotten my own strength. Her limp body slammed against the wall. Her arm hit the table lamp and it clattered to the floor. The ceramic base shattered. Pieces of glass scuttled across the linoleum. I cursed. *So much for showing control*, I thought bitterly to myself. *Was it really necessary to bounce her off the wall like a living basketball?* Probably not, but that wasn't my problem right now. Right now guards were running up to the door, demanding to know what was going on inside my room.

I zoomed over to Marie, scooped up her limp body and zipped back to the hospital bed. Gently, I laid her down and brushed the black curly locks off of her frosty forehead. She was pale as a ghost. Her rosy lips were now tainted blue.

"Come on baby girl. Wake up. Don't die on me now."

Someone was slamming their shoulder into the door with all their might.

"We know you're in there." A voice shouted.

I bared my teeth. Sharp fangs clicked down and I plunged them into my wrist. Hot blood trickled down my arm. I brought my bleeding wrist to her lips.

"Drink Marie."

The door began to crack beneath the soldier's weight.

She wasn't drinking.

The hinges creaked.

Cold dread took a hold of me.

The muscles in her throat weren't moving. Waves of terror washed over me. *What was I going to do?* My brain scramble for some sort of solution but my mind was coming up blank. Think, Frank, think! Then I thought of Marie. What would she do in a situation like this? Then it clicked. Immediately, I began massaging the muscles in her throat, willing them to swallow. That was how the human body worked right? The muscles in the throat moved to push down each morsel of food, didn't it? It wasn't like the food could move on its own.

Scientifically speaking this should work but I had no idea if Marie would be delighted or furious with me for forcing her to drink my blood. Quite frankly, I didn't care. As of right now desperate times called for desperate measures. She could be mad, as long as she was alive at the same time. The door splintered. The beat of her heart fluttered weakly in her chest. Her breath came out thin and reedy puffs. *Had I done it in time?* All I knew was that door was going to give in soon. The soldiers would be coming any moment now.

The door made a snapping sound.

I grimaced. Those hinges could only handle so much force within a given time. When they did come in I had to make a choice. Kill or be captured. The door came crashing down. A burly figure in a camouflage fatigues burst into the room. He was promptly backed up by a group of shouting men. His cobalt eyes locked on me. He pointed his firearm directly at my chest.

I could probably take him, but the other five? Probably not. Knowing from experience they were probably packing silver. These men weren't dumb. They knew that lead bullets couldn't and wouldn't take me down. Then there was that damn tranquilizer. I absolutely hated the silver nitrate tranquilizer. I'd rather be shot in the ass than be shot by the tranquilizer. *I had three options: Attack and get me and Marie shot for sure, run and possibly get Marie shot in the process or surrender.*

The soldier shouted at me, demanding me to stand down. The

other five echoed the same request. All of them were red in the face. I glanced at Marie. She was still in pretty bad shape. Could she handle a bullet wound right now? Besides, if I ran they surely would hunt me down. The laboratory was packed with security personnel and not to mention other objectives. Then I recalled Bright Eyes telling me about the black holes in the walls. His voice reverberated inside my mind. *Those things spray out silver nitrate and will knock you on your ass in no time, mate.*

My eyes flicked to the soldiers who created a half circle around me. Their bodies blocked the path to a speedy exit. I ground my jaw. Kill, flee or surrender. Those were my options. I decided on the latter. I owed it to Marie. I had drained her to the point of death. The least I could do is prevent her from getting shot.

"Put your hands up." Cobalt's voice rang with authority.

The vein in his temple throbbed..

"Easy now." I said, my voice steady and calm.

His grip on the firearm tightened.

"Don't you easy now me, *vampire*" He snarled.

I sucked in a breath of air.

"Put your hands behind your head and get down now!"

I exhaled slowly through my nose but the tightness in my chest did not recede. Slowly, I opened my palms in a submissive gesture. The corner of his eye twitched. He stiffened at my movement but his voice came out slow and controlled.

"I said get down!"

I prickled with disgust.

"Is that really necessary? Do you realize how dirty hospital floors are?"

Steel eyes tensed and the muscle in his jaw popped with rage.

"I said get down, *vampire!*"

I looked around. Multiple firearms were trained on me. Nervous fingers hovered over the triggers. He was right. If I didn't comply I'd end up looking like Swiss cheese. If I did listen however, I just may be able to break out of this God forsaken joint and see the light of day.

"Okay, but I'll only do it under one condition."

Steel Eyes quirked a brow.

His expression went cold but I rushed on before he could speak. "I want you to pass the word onto Lemmings. I'll feed but only with Marie, no one else." If she was gathering information on the lab then I wanted in. If I fed off her I might be able to slip her some of my blood to help enhance her hearing, eyesight, speed and clarity.

The soldier ground his jaw.

With a grunt he pulled the trigger. Barely a millisecond later something went poof and a silver nitrate dart stabbed itself into my neck. I sucked in a sharp breath. "Was that really necessary?" I ground out each word through gritted teeth. Then everything went black.

CHAPTER 31

BEFORE ME STOOD the door to the principal's office. *Just breathe Lex, the task at hand couldn't be all too hard, now could it? I mean, all I had to do was break in and snoop around for a few blueprints. I've done it before so why can't I do it again?* Despite my attempts, I remained frozen in place.

A few breaths later Astrid's voice crackled over the headset. "Everything okay in there Commander?" I let out an irritable sigh. *No, not everything was okay. Last time I had a team and now I'm flying solo. Now I am standing in front of a door not knowing what to expect. Regardless, time was ticking and I had to make a move. My invisibility could only last so long.* I bent down and fumbled for my lock picks.

"Yep, I'm just peachy."

I sucked in another calming breath and closed my eyes. *Pull yourself together, Lexi. What could you possibly be afraid of? Booby traps? For christ's sake he was the principal of a preparatory high school, not some criminal mastermind.* Little droplets of perspiration peppered the back of my hands.

The lock clicked beneath the power of my trembling fingertips.

"We're in..." I whispered breathlessly into the headset.

I could only imagine Ethan sitting on the edge of his seat with the headset pressed tight to his ears. Benson and Astrid agreed to let him listen but they refused to include a mouth piece. They argued that too many voices on the line would cause confusion besides his input really wasn't needed.

"Take a deep breath Commander, you got this." Astrid replied, reassuringly.

I let out a cynical snort.

Easy for her to say. She didn't have to worry about what was on the other side. The door creaked open, beckoning me into the shadowy abyss. I nearly jumped out of my skin as the door behind me clicked closed. The hairs on the back of my neck prickled with fear. My intestines twisted into a dreadful knot. *What if the mechanism in the door had locked? What if I couldn't get out?* Silently, I reprimanded myself for my skittish behavior.

C'mon Lex, get it together, most of the doors here were fire safe which means they are meant to close on their own. Besides, there's no way the mechanism should have locked from the inside after you've picked the chamber.

I exhaled and clicked on the flashlight. The room hadn't changed since my last visit to the principal's office. He still had the mahogany desk only now it was occupied with neat stacks of books and paperwork. The large bookcase stretched along the back wall and a potted tree still sat in the left hand corner.

If I were a big bad principal up to no good where would I hide important information? My eyes skimmed about my surroundings as I thumbed through various books and paperwork. *Would I place it somewhere inconspicuous, like out in the open? Or would I tuck it somewhere safe and out of sight?*

I tugged on a few drawers for good measure. Some of the contents rattled about inside their cage. Then the door to the main office made a clicking sound. I froze in mid stride. Astrid's voice crackled over my head set.

"Code red commander, we got a problem. The perimeter has been breached. Two subjects are approaching the main office and they're heading your way. You got to find a place to hide and I mean fast."

I scoffed. "A bit late don't you think?"

"What else do you want me to do? The feedback on these things take awhile to view."

Astrid retorted defensively. I scrambled for some place to hide in this god forsaken place. Beads of sweat blossomed along my neck. The energy I had reserved to conjure the illusion of invisibility was almost spent. The possibility of using my magic at its fullest potential was out of the question. *So where to next?* The footfalls grew closer. My heart hammered away inside my chest. I had to think of something and fast. Muffled voices spoke out into the quiet of the night.

"Why can't you keep track of your things? Is it so hard to use your pockets once in awhile Roger?"

Roger let out an exasperated sigh.

"Would you lighten up a little bit? *Jesus*, it's only going to take a minute."

The door handle jostled but the door didn't move.

I slumped with a sigh of relief.

So the mechanism did lock after all.

"But the Boss told us not to leave our post."

Someone inserted a key.

I stiffened and held my breath.

How on earth did this guy have a key?

"What the Boss doesn't know won't hurt him Ernie."

My legs had turned to stone. I knew I had to hide but I couldn't get myself to move. Waves of panic overwhelmed me.

"*But Roger...*" Ernie whined.

The door handle jostled. I couldn't breathe. How can I breathe in a time like this anyway? I twisted the molecules around me and warped time to my advantage. Time slowed. I managed to thrust myself beneath the desk. The door swung open to reveal two pairs of shoes. Their feet roamed the room while beams of light searched in earnest. One of them paused.

"I swear. I must have dropped it in here somewhere.."

The speaker stood stone still.

Roger's nose crinkled with disgust as he stepped towards me.

"Hey... do you smell that?" Was the musk from my fox going to give me away? I hugged myself tight. *No, no, no... please just go away.* I took a deep breath and tried to mask the scent of my fox. How the scent had leaked through my magical barriers was beyond me. My temples glistened with sweat.

His body twisted around. "What the hell? Is that musk?"

He inched closer to where I sat. I swear I was going to die of heart palpitations. If I got caught it was game over. There would be no help for Frank and no help for me. The very idea of being captured and caged terrified me. I bit my lip. Every molecule within me threatened to burst.

"What's this?" Ernie asked as he approached the desk. A pair of gray trousers stepped in front of me. Shiny black shoes were only inches away from my own. I closed my eyes. A droplet of sweat trickled down my cheek.

"Is this it Roger?" He bent down and reached for an item on the ground. I could smell the onions on his breath.

"Yes! That's it!"

I took a peek. In his hand he held a pipe.

"Good, now let's' get the hell outta here before the boss knows we've left."

The door clicked closed. Black pitch engulfed the room in shadow. I took a deep breath. A moment of silence seemed to stretch into what had felt like centuries. Astrid's voice shattered the quiet.

"Are they gone?" She asked.

"I don't know, you tell me." I replied.

"Easy now, the feed hasn't loaded yet. I am assuming you're safe. You going to be ok?"

I scrambled out of my hiding spot.

"Yep." I replied with an acidic snort.

"I am just dandy. I'll be even better once I'm outta this joint." I said as I dragged myself out from under the desk. For fucks sake, why won't my hands stop shaking? Then I saw it on the ground. It was a miniature safe. My heart nearly leapt into my throat. "I think I'm onto something here..."

I army crawled to get a better look.

"What is it?" Astrid inquired with.

"It's a safe..." I replied, cautiously.

Her breath hitched with excitement.

"Is there a keypad?" Astried asked.

"Yes." I wasn't entirely sure as to how I would describe the device. All I knew was that it bore a resemblance to some lock box that I had seen on the TV. That was how I knew it was a safe.

Astrid took a deep breath.

"Okay,... use your electricity to over power the lock's mechanics. Then apply the magnetic ring. If everything goes as planned the magnets should move the solenoid for you."

I exhaled.

"Here goes nothing.."

Electrical currents sprouted from my fingers and snaked along the curved edges of the keypad. Buttons crackled. Sparks flew. Tendrils of smoke drifted from the safe's keypad. I coughed and waved away the stench of burnt copper and melted plastic.

"Everything okay?" Astrid asked.

I covered my mouth with my shirt and sucked in a breath of filtered air.

"Yep. Don't mind me, it just stinks."

"Good thing I turned off the smoke alarm, huh?"

I grunted in approval before applying the magnetic ring as Astrid instructed.

The sooner I grabbed the blue prints the sooner I could head home. I held my breath and then gave the magnet a good twist to the left. The lock clicked beneath my trembling hands. There was a long pause. Something didn't feel quite right.

"Well? Did it work?" Astrid inquired impatiently.

"It worked alright, but something is wrong."

I leaned in and pressed my ear against the crack.

Sure enough, I heard a faint chirping noise. "There's a noise coming from the safe."

"Proceed with caution Commander.."

I offered her a nod and opened the door further.

The safe continued to chirp.

"There are papers." I murmured.

"Let's take a look." Astrid said, her voice wavered with trepidation.

I reached for the papers but the beeping increased in volume and speed. Waves of panic washed over me. A cold sweat broke across my skin.

"Astrid! It's going crazy. What should I do? It won't stop!"

What if Ernie and Roger had heard all the commotion?

Would they come sprinting back to the principal's office?

"Quick grab the papers and then shut the safe." Everything went silent. I quickly reached in. Wet smoke billowed from the safe. Needles of pain assaulted my eyes as the cool substance sprayed me in the face. Footsteps hurried down the hallway. I let out a horrified scream.

"Commander? Commander?!" Astrid shouted into the headset.

"What is wrong?" Astrid repeated, her voice cracked with panic.

I cradled my head in my hands as I rolled around on the ground, writhing in pain. The air was so thick. I couldn't breathe. The cool mist had set my lungs a blaze. I sucked in another breath but there was no reprieve.

"The safe was rigged." I rasped as I struggled to my feet. Waves of exhaustion overwhelmed me. I wobbled towards the door. My muscles trembled like jelly with each step.

"You need to get out of there now." Astrid began.

I gurgled with frustrated laugher. The door was so close but yet so far away. The floor tilted beneath my feet. Someone said something. I didn't know what. They were so far away. All I wanted to do was sleep. Every muscle within me ached. A blanket of darkness laid heavily upon my lids.

"Alexis! I mean it! Get out of there now!"

Voices rose and fell on the other side of the door. I stumbled towards the window with my arms out reached but two masked figures burst through the room before I could escape. Something pricked me in the chest. Everything went black and I crumpled to my feet.

"God damn it!" Ethan snarled as he chucked his headset across the room.

Astrid grimaced at the outburst.

An agitated Garcia drummed her lacquered nails against folded arms while a silent Zander remained slumped in his chair. "*Well?*" Garcia inquired irritably.

A defeated Benson silently slipped the headset off of her head.

"I was afraid it'd come to this..."

In the back Andrew ceased plucking at the dirt beneath his nails.

"What's wrong?" Drew asked, mildly distracted.

Ethan flexed his fingers and took a deep breath.

"They got Lexi." He growled.

"*And it's all your fault*." Ethan began.

Benson stepped forward.

"Ethan.." Benson warned.

Andrew's eyebrows shot up in surprise. "It's all my fault, because?"

Ethan jabbed a finger at Andrew's chest.

"If you hadn't encouraged her to do this then she wouldn't be in this mess!"

The eyes of Ethan's wolf peeked through his angry gaze.

Andrew lifted his palms in an acquiescent gesture.

"Hey now, I didn't put ideas into anyone's head. I may have supported and even encouraged her decision but in my defense she knew exactly what she was getting herself into."

Ethan's nostrils flared.

"And you think that's still ok?!"

His wolf came forebodingly close to the surface. Sharp talons sprouted from Ethan's fingertips. The beast within him returned Andrew's gaze with a menacing green-eyed glare. Andrew's jaw tightened.

"Look, Lexi has every right to do whatever it takes to help her friends."

Andrew replied evenly through gritted teeth.

His own wolf began to show through.

Astrid bit her lip. Garcia watched the whole ordeal with cool contemplation.

Ethan started forward. "Don't you start–" within seconds the vampire inserted herself between the two men.

"Enough is enough already! Ethan stand down, Lily's got a plan."

Ethan ground his jaw menacingly.

"Well it better be good."

CHAPTER 32

AN ICY DELUGE of water slapped me in the face. Gasping, I woke up in a sputtering haze only to find myself dangling from the ceiling in a set of chains. Delirious, I looked around. The room was dark, musky and dank. Harsh lamplight blinded me as it shined in my face. The familiar scent of mildew and oiled steel tickled my nose. Across from me sat a diabolical shape.

My stomach caved. *Well, if it wasn't Paul Lemmings himself.* I thought bitterly to myself. *For many reasons, I had hoped he had left. However, for some reason he decided to grace me with his continued presence.* Droplets sweat trickled down between my shoulder blades.

"Let's try this again. What are you and who do you work for?"

Funny, I thought sardonically more so to myself than anything else. *He had already beat me senseless. How he came up with the same insistent question was beyond me. Did he think my story was going to change? If so he had another thing coming.* He leaned in.

"Well?" He inquired impatiently.

I held back the urge to gag.

His breath reeked of old cigarettes.

I gestured for him to come closer with the tilt of my head.

He quickly obliged.

Eagerly, I spat in his face.

Growling, he punched me so hard my body swayed.

"I don't have time for your games!" He snarled.

I trembled with laughter and licked the blood off of my busted lip. "You got another thing comin' if you think I am going to tell you what I am and who I work for."

I said with a sneer. *He'd have to do more than beat me if he wanted me to spill the beans on the supernatural community.*

His flinty brown eyes narrowed as he mopped the spittle off of his face.

"Have it your way." He snarled and signaled to the guards with an incline of his head. One of the guards tightened the chains. I gasped in pain as another approached from behind and stabbed me in the neck with a syringe. Trails of cool liquid traveled through the network of my veins and left waves of euphoria in their wake.

"Listen here you little imp, you will be telling me what you are and why you are here or I'll be forced to take drastic measures." Lemmings began.

Glossy eyed, I stared at my captor through a drunken haze.

My vision blurred.

"What's a girl gotta do to get a break around here, anyway?" I murmured half heartedly. I was in a complete daze. The need to laugh and the desire to cry and sing all at the same time seeped into my veins. A drunken euphoria rippled through my body. Memories of home came back to haunt me.

Flickering firelight danced across my vision. Scents of pine and fresh dirt filled my nose. *Was I back home?* No, I couldn't be. My home was gone. Suddenly, I had this unrestrained urge to shift, to strip myself of all my worries and run naked through the forest. I couldn't comprehend this queer sensation running through my veins.

Was I intoxicated?

If so, what in hell's name was in that syringe? Maybe if I played along I'd have just enough time to recover? I delighted at the very idea of yanking Lemming's chain. I held my breath and tried for restraint. The urge to giggle was excruciating. All I had to do was play along right? Then he'd let me go?

I could only hope. I took a moment to pause and lick my lips.

"Please don't hurt me Mr.. Lemmings. I promise I'll listen."

I even stammered for effect.

It took everything within me to maintain my composure. I had to or it wouldn't work. Sure I was scared, jittery in fact. I could listen to what he had to say but that didn't mean I had to cooperate. A Kitsune can't lie but she or he can trick someone if the spirit is willing. It took every fiber of my being to restrain myself. The key here was to look the part, to be believable. Then again, all it took was one glance at his self-satisfied smile and I couldn't help but burst into a fit of drunken giggles. The poor sod thought I was taking him seriously. The very thought of it sent me into hysterics. The fool didn't even see it coming!

"Thought you had me there for a second, didn't you?" Tears leaked from my eyes. Lemmings on the other hand, was not amused. His mouth clamped shut and his face purpled with rage.

"So be it then." He growled and gestured to one of the guards with a wave of his hand. One of the armed assistants approached reluctantly and placed a silver blade in Paul's open fist.

He heaved a sigh and rolled up his sleeves. "You leave me no choice Alexis. If the truth serum won't work on you then I'll just have to cut it out of you."

I chortled with drunken laughter and tried wiping my tear stained face on my arm.

"Oh that's just rich. *I am so scared.* You have me *shivering* in me little boots. You really have me going here. You know that right?"

Even my own confidence surprised me.

The corner of his eye twitched.

I gasped. "Oh no! Did I strike a nerve?"

With each passing moment my intoxication swelled.

"Serves you right you filthy piece of shit."

The room began to tilt precariously in one direction.

His grip around the blade tightened.

"Oh no is the big bad teacher going to cut me up? All because poor wittle Lemmings didn't get his way? *Please*, you didn't dedicate yer whole life to teaching just to throw it all away in one night. Did you?"

Each word came out in a slurry mess.

His lips pressed into a thin line.

I cackled drunkenly as I swayed to and fro from my chains.

Then it hit me. Cold metal sliced through my corporal shell like a hot knife through butter. Searing pain ripped me out of my drunken stupor. Rivulets of blood dripped down my arm. Shocked, I gaped at him.

He cut me! The bastard actually cut me!

The very act of it was quite sobering.

An unnerved Lemmings pressed the wet blade further into my skin.

My jaw clamped shut.

The golden eyes of my fox glared back into his placid gaze.

"There she is.." He said in a satisfied whisper. "I knew you couldn't be human."

A smug smile curled at the corner of his lips.

An awkward silence passed between us as I eyed him ominously.

"Expecting bubbling of the skin, eh? I hate to disappoint you but I'm not a werewolf or a vamp." I snarled venomously through my gritted teeth.

"Ah, yes I can see that." He mused aloud as he probed at my tender skin.

I let out an audible grunt.

I had no idea how much more I could muster as I hung helplessly from the chains.

"No matter, iron it is then." Lemmings said with a pleasant smile.

Beads of sweat blossomed along my forehead.

"Do you know why I am here Alexis?" Lemmings inquired cordially.

I gasped as he twisted an iron bar experimentally inside my open wound. I flashed him a menacing glare and bit down on the corner of my lip. I'd rather die then giving him the pleasure of hearing me scream.

"Oh I don't know, maybe because you're a *creep*?"

He shook his head and leaned in."When I was younger I survived a werewolf mauling and lost both my friend and my leg." He pulled up his pant leg to reveal a mechanical leg. Well that explains why he smells like oiled steel. "Now I am here trying to take back the power that they took from me."

I rolled my eyes and let out a derisive snort.

"Spare me the drama. Boo hoo, so you lost your leg. Let me enlighten you on something." I paused for dramatic effect. "*No one cares*. Sorry to break it to you *pal* but nothing gives you the right to smuggle kids from the school and use them for your own experimental gain."

Lemming's brown eyes flared with rage.

"Why you little..." Seething, he reeled his hand back. I grimaced and steeled myself for the blow but there was a knock at the door. He paused mid strike. A muffled voice spoke on the other end of the door.

"Professor?" His grip on the blade tightened.

"What?!" He snapped.

"May I please come in?" Replied a meek voice on the other end.

"This better be good." He growled.

"There has been a breach within the security, sir."

A fuming Lemmings threw his blade across the room. The knife clattered against the wall. He whirled around and jabbed a finger at my chest. I involuntarily flinched beneath his menacing glare. "I'll deal with you later." He snarled before stalking out of the room. The room rang with an uncomfortable silence. After a while the intoxication had eased. A wave of sobriety washed over me as I went over the recent series of events.

Then I recalled all of the things I had said. A sense of realization overwhelmed me. Cold sweat blossomed across my forehead. Snakes of dread writhed within the pit of my stomach. *He was going to kill me. I had to get out of here or I'd be a goner for sure*. It was then that I realized the guards had left the room. I sucked in a breath of air and offered Inari a silent prayer. Desperately, I wiggled about as I tried to free myself from the jangling chains. Shards of pain prickled down my swollen wrists. Jolts of agony shot through my shoulder blades. My heart thundered inside my head. Moments later, I hung there panting from my fruitless efforts.

My shoulders slouched in despair. Any hopes of escaping had gone up in flames. It was useless, there was no turning back now. I was stuck here. Any chance of my friends finding me were next to none. *Who was I kidding?* I hadn't the resources or powers to go up against a batch of mad scientists all by myself.

Sure, I had a few tricks up my sleeve but my magic could only go so far. I could possibly siphon the lab's electricity but what if the electricity was the only thing that pumped fresh air into this room? For all I knew we could be underground and the generators may be providing the only source oxygen in this room. If I did anything to risk hurting this corporeal form I would be signing my own death sentence. Earth wasn't set up like home. There weren't many shrines here where my soul could take refuge for regeneration. A wave of sorrow washed over me. It was no use. The chains wouldn't budge. I let out a defeated sigh. I was doomed.

I'd be lucky if I got out alive.

A pair of footsteps pattered down the hallway. I bit my lip and held my breath. *He couldn't be coming back already, could he?* The footsteps paused and then came closer. I held my breath. I didn't know how much more I could take. Sure my wounds would heal, but my mind was about to break. I closed my eyes and waited for the outcome. Droplets of perspiration dripped down my brow. Whoever it was paused outside the door.

I closed my eyes and feigned sleep. The door creaked. Rubber soles scuffed quietly against the concrete. The door clicked close. My heart thundered inside my chest. My skin tingled in anticipation. I wanted to run but the chains withheld me in their iron grip. The feet paused in front of me and I held my breath.

"You poor thing..." A woman breathed.

Seconds later, a bucket of ice water was thrown over my head.

I bit my cheek so hard I began to bleed.

"What's with these people and their barbaric ways?" The woman continued to mutter foul things beneath her breath. Bits of blood, dirt and sweat swirled down the drain. I flinched beneath her touch.

Who was this woman and why was she dressing my wounds?

A whirlwind of questions swirled around inside my mind.

The woman continued to grumble venomously beneath her breath.

"I can't believe he did this to you."

I peeked through one eye to see a petite woman with a round face and a button nose. She wore her jet black hair in a tight bun. Rueful gray eyes roamed over my wound through square spectacles. She smelled like a mixture of sea salt, mint and earth. The scent of old earth reminded me of Frank.

"This will have to do... we don't have much time.."

Astonished, I watched her as she wrapped my wounds in gauze.

"Who are you and why do you smell like Frank?" I asked.

She shook her head as her tiny hands fumbled with the bandages.

"Zat is not important." She murmured quietly.

Her hand shook as she fumbled with the bandages.

I stared at her in complete bewilderment. She wore a black vest and a headset. Silky black tresses were pulled back in a tight bun. A set of white acronyms were splayed across her back. Her black combat boots scuffed with each step.

"Well, I beg to differ." I replied emphatically.

"This will have to do for now." She replied.

"Who are you?" I inquired once again, completely baffled by the recent change of events. She began fiddling with my restraints. Soon after, I tumbled to the floor in a crumpled heap. I recalled Benson saying she had someone on the inside, but never really took what she had said seriously. Could this be the very person Benson was talking about? Her supple lips tightened into a thin line.

"If you are who I think you are then you will help Frank, yes?"

I tried to speak but could only manage a simple nod.

"Good." Her mouth set itself in a grim line. It was only then did she begin to unshackle my wrists. The manacles clattered to the ground. "Now Frank is in ze thirteenth corridor. You need to grab him and get out of here."

I stood there dumbstruck as I rubbed at the broken skin. I still wasn't sure if I should say thanks. Everything was coming at me in a blur. She frowned and gave me a good crack upside the head. I cried out and rubbed at my head.

"Ow! What the hell was that for?!"

"*Do you understand?*" She asked crisply.

"Yes, yes I understand, *damn*, no need to get violent now."

Her jaw tightened. She slapped the red button on the side of the wall. A piercing siren began to wail down the hall. Red lights swirled around the room.

"Good. Now go!"

I gave her a brisk nod and ran out the door.

CHAPTER 33

THE THIRTEENTH CORRIDOR... the thirteenth corridor. I cursed vehemently beneath my breath. *How the hell would I find the thirteenth corridor anyhow? Possibly. Between the twelfth and the fourteenth?* I scoured the hallway, frantically searching for some sort of sign.

The swiveling red lights obscured the text on the wall. The siren kept wailing overhead, making it hard for me to think. An arrow pointed to the left indicating hallway eleven, twelve and thirteen while the other pointed to the right indicating hallways nine, eight and seven. *To the left it was then.*

I sucked in a deep breath and sprinted off to the left. The pads of my feet pounded into the cool concrete. I passed several unoccupied observation rooms on my way. Strange medical equipment cast skeletal shadows across each room. My footsteps echoed along the walls of the abandoned walkway. The hallway itself was hauntingly empty. They must have managed to to successfully evacuate this portion of the lab before I had escaped.

Moments later, I stumbled upon an open enclave. Further off, several corridors branched off along the curve of the enclave, like spokes on a wheel. Each one was labeled with a number.

Could this be the place?

My insides twisted into a dreadful knot. Crumpled bits of steel and debris were everywhere. A few bodies littered the ground and streaks of scarlet blood were splattered across the walls. No one else was anywhere to be seen. The hairs on the back of my neck prickled with unease. Astonished, I paused and did a three sixty. *Who could have done all of this?*

Rubble and metal rubbish were scattered among the floor. Clouds of smoke twisted lazily from a burnt out circuit in the wall. The door to corridor twelve hung loosely from its hinges. The door to the second corridor was completely blown away. Above the open entry was the number thirteen. My heart nearly leapt into my throat. It had seemed like ages since I saw Frank.

What would I say if we actually met? I highly doubt we'd be able to talk about the weather after him being stuck so long in such a dismal place. I started forward then paused mid step. *What if Frank was angry with me? What if he couldn't' bear to see my face?* We had taken a while to find him...or better yet, what if he enjoyed it here? Would he even want to come back? A whirlwind of doubt swirled inside my chest

I bit my lip and inched along the enclave towards corridor thirteen. The faint scent of mildew and wet concrete increased in strength. Hints of sweat, wolf and old earth also leaked into the wreckage.

The luminescence from the swiveling red lights revealed an open corridor with cells on the left and to the right of the hallway. Awestruck, I brushed my fingers along the brick walls. Frowning, I pulled away.

Wet dirt and mildew crumpled from my fingertips. *Is this where they kept them all this time? In a cold dank dungeon with nothing but a cot and an open privy?* Tentatively, I ran a trembling hand over the tangled sheets. Olivia's weak scent had brushed along my fingertips. I took a fistful of cloth and sucked in a deep breath of air. My muscles tensed and my stomach flipped.

They were here... I could smell them.

The scent of old earth and wet dog still lingered but there was something more.. something different... but I couldn't quite place my finger on it. Someone was with them but I couldn't be sure who. *Could it have been Jake?* Regardless, Olivia must have left first because Frank's scent was still fresh in the air.

Faint footsteps shattered my train of thought. They echoed just a few meters down the hall. A bouncing beam of light danced around the hallway in earnest pursuit. *Great*, I thought bitterly to myself. Just what I needed, more reasons to delay my search for Frank. *When were they going to cut me a break?*

I pressed myself along the wall. My heart thundered inside my chest. The light paused for a moment in my general direction. The swiveling red lights cast the pursuer's shadow across the room like a spinning poltergeist. I prayed with all my might it wasn't a vamp. I held my breath and willed my body to relax. No point in ringing the dinner bell. If it was a vampire I was screwed. He could probably hear my heartbeat a mile away.

Easy Lex, just take a deep breath. Everything is going to be all right, once we find Frank we can get the hell out of this godforsaken place.

After what had felt like centuries, the pursuer had turned and gone the other way. I let out a defeated sigh and stepped over the debris and back into the enclave. So much for all the hard work. Now I had to start from scratch and had no lead.

Frank obviously wasn't in corridor thirteen. So where in the world could he be? I headed back to where I came. We had come so far only to find him gone. Garcia was going to be devastated, Ethan more so if I couldn't find a way out of this dreaded place. A piece of metal skittered across the hall.

I froze mid step.

Then a shadow flickered out of the corner of one eye. Then a black shape shifted from one shadow to the next. Ripples of uncertainty shivered down my spine. Could it be the guard just making another round? *Did he happen to see me?* My muscle refused to move. Panic had froze me in place. A feral pair of silver eyes watched me from the shadows. They glowed like tiny beacons in the night.

"Frank is that you?.."

My voice wavered with uncertainty.

Someone cursed beneath their breath. Moments later, a skeletal figure stepped out of the darkness and into the glare of the swiveling red light. The wild haired man stared at me with a look of complete bewilderment. I stared back into the startled gray eyes of Frank Marino himself. Time stilled for both of us.

"Lexi is that really you?"

His voice was much deeper than I had remembered.

"Of course it is me... *sweet mother of Inari*, you've lost so much weight. Are you okay?"

A humorless smile curled at the corner of his cracked lips.

"Well let's just say this place doesn't have a menu that takes well to special requests." For a brief moment the red light swiveled over Frank. There was blood all over his face. He was covered in blood from head to toe. I reached out to touch him but he stepped away.

"Don't..." He warned. My eyes flickered to the blood spatters on the wall and to the bodies on the floor then back to him. My blood turned to ice. *Could it be?..*

"Hey!" Someone shouted from behind, immediately shattering the awkward silence between us. Frank's eyes widened in shock. Maybe he had thought he had killed them all? The very idea of Frank murdering a whole crew of soldiers made me shudder. I couldn't bear to take another look at the flood of bodies on the ground.

"You aren't supposed to be here!"

It was one of the guards I had seen earlier. Maybe he was the one making rounds. Frank bared a set of blood stained fangs. I flashed the man a pleasant smile and prepped myself to charm my way out of this. Maybe he could see this as a possible misunderstanding? Not likely, but enough lives were lost. The guard grabbed me as soon as Frank stepped forward. Sickly sweet fear rolled off him in rancid waves. Within a mere of seconds the barrel of a gun was pressed up against the underside of my chin.

"Oh no you don't buddy! You try to take a bite out of me then I'll blow out her brains. I know what you're capable of and I am not taking any chances."

The pistol trembled in his hands. Frank's eyes dilated. A sense of calm filled the room as he stepped forward. His voice came out in a cajoling lull.

"You will let her go." He began.

The guard on the other hand stepped back. It seemed that he was resistant to Frank's persuasive ways. "Don't try that compulsive crap! No way in hell am I gonna let you turn me into a vamp. You hear me?!"

Frank said something foul beneath his breath.

"Sounds like you've had a taste for vampire blood."

I rolled my eyes and let out a derisive snort.

"Oh *please*, it's not like one bite will turn you into a vamp. Trust me, it doesn't work that way. Besides, the blood all over his face is probably more for show than anything, right Frank?"

Frank didn't answer. The maw of fear that threatened to turn my wits inside out began to widen. "Frank? You didn't... you couldn't have... did you?..."

The guard's hold on me tightened. He shook me so hard my teeth rattled. Frank stepped forward to assist then stopped. "Shut up! Or I'll blow your fucking head off!"

I grimaced at the guard's violent tendencies.

"Frank? A little help here?"

Why did he stop? Why was he just standing there? Why wasn't he helping me? Was he really going to let this loon blow my brains out? Someone from behind clucked his tongue in disapproval. A man spoke from behind. His British accent came out crisp and cool.

"Now, now that's no way to talk to a lady, mate. Someone's got to teach you some manners eh?" Blue sparks of lightning crackled out of the corner of my eye. My captor's grip tightened involuntarily as he convulsed against me. Seconds later, he crumpled to the ground with smoke billowing from his head. Relieved, I turned around to stare into a pair of mismatched eyes. My stomach dropped. Shock washed over me. One eye was ice blue while the other was seafoam green. Unruly black hair fell in front of his angular face.

"Noah?.."

A smug smile tugged at the corner of his lips.

"Well hello to you too."

I sputtered in shock. Why was Noah here? Better yet how did he get here? Wasn't he supposed to be in Gaia? Did he follow me through the rift or did he know how to get back home all along? If he was here then what was his father up to? My blood boiled at the thought of him and Kane scheming behind my back. Speaking of which, if Noah was here, then where was Kane? I highly doubted Noah would leave Mount Kyoto out of the goodness of his own heart just to find me.

"What in the world are you doing here?"

Noah's smug smile faltered.

"Rescuing you, of course." He replied, flatly.

My hands balled up into tiny fists.

"I don't need rescuing, Noah..." I began.

Noah frowned and let out a derisive snort.

"This is where you say thanks and we hitch a ride back home, yes?" The corner of my eye twitched. *He wanted thanks? How dare he demand any thanks after what his family had put me through.*

"I never needed your help in the first place!"

Noah scoffed and rolled his eyes. Frank's silver gaze had volleyed from me to him then back again with each exchange.

"Oh is that so, eh? What about a little help here Frank?" He managed to mimic my squeaky request from earlier to the exact decibel. I flashed Frank a scathing glare.

"Yeah, Frank. What about that?" I asked.

Frank arched an archaic brow. "I take it you two know each other?"

It was Noah's turn to arch a brow.

"Well yeah, she's my wife." Noah said.

I nearly fell over from Noah's simple statement.

Frank's eyebrows shot up in mild surprise. "Is that so?"

Exasperated I threw my hands up into the air.

"That's it. I'm done."

It was so like him to just claim me when the ceremony hadn't even taken place yet. The very idea of it made my blood boil.

If that chump thought I was going to marry him, he had another thing coming.

CHAPTER 34

WHAT DID I get myself into? First it was Jake, then Frank and now Lexi? What were we going to do? It wasn't everyday your friends get abducted by some underground lab agency. Right now I'd give anything, to be a normal teenager. Even if it meant being dragged to some wretched mall on a Friday night.

However, I'm not a normal teenager. I'm a witch, who happened to be born into a highly devout catholic family. Not only that but I am best friends with a succubus and kitsune.

Did I forget to mention that I also have a thing for a vampire and my childhood best friend is a werewolf? Last but not least, I barely know a lick of magic! Sure, Patterson has been training me well and I might have some good tricks up my sleeve.

Even so, I don't know how much help I'd be in a situation like this. Some help is better than none, right? Carmen thought so, that's why she insisted I be added to Ethan's team. So, instead of sitting on some tropical beach for spring break I am here helping Astrid, Lily and the local super nats take down some secret government laboratory. Who happens to be kidnapping them for their own political gain.

"Hey Selena, snap to it girl and take a left." Astrid announced over the head set. Meanwhile, Drew's wolf bounded in the opposite direction.

"Well Drew's wolf is insisting that we go right."

There was a long pause before Astrid spoke again.

"But corridor thirteen is towards your left." Astrid said.

I glanced at Ethan, searching for some sort of confirmation. Splitting up wasn't what I had in mind.

I faltered for a moment and chewed my lip.

Drew's tawny brown wolf skidded to a stop.

Golden eyes stared up at me, expectantly.

Ethan also had paused to deliberate.

Silently, I hoped he would choose to follow Drew's wolf instead.

"What if they aren't in corridor thirteen?" I asked with a hint of uncertainty.

Astrid let out an exasperated sigh.

"Why in the world would they move their greatest supernatural specimens during a security breach like this? Honestly, what is the point of being navigator if you guys aren't even going to listen to me?" Astrid asked, purely irritated by my lack of confidence.

"Well, what if they have already left?" I insisted.

"We don't have much time to argue.." Ethan began.

"Look, all I know is our guts are telling us to follow the scent. I mean, your technology is one thing but how can you counter against a wolf's instincts?"

Astrid grumbled something sour about wolves beneath her breath.

Ethan narrowed his eyes in response.

"I heard that." He said with a foreboding frown.

I licked my lips. If I could salvage the situation between them then now would be a good time. The last thing we needed was a lack of teamwork on our hands during a battle that could cost us our lives.

"Look Astrid, I don't mean to intrude but Ethan may have a point. The entire place is on lockdown and everyone is going nuts thanks to your magical touch. If that's the case the group may have already escaped amongst the chaos."

When in doubt I've learned to just flatter the succubus. It seems to distract the demon from her temperamental ways.

"Besides... Drew is tracking them by their strongest scent signature. If he's leading us away from the corridor then it probably means they're on the move."

There was another pause.

"Selena's got a point Astrid..." Ethan pressed.

His voice came out urgent and crisp.

Exasperated, Astrid let out a defeated sigh.

"Alright, have it your way but if you're wrong it's on you."

Ethan gave us a firm nod.

"Let's move out then."

Drew took a right. We followed in close pursuit only to run into a hallway full of empty cells. We paused as Drew snuffled around for the scent.

The place smelled like mildew and sweat. Empty cells with abandoned beds and privies lined up along the right side of the hallway. Drew made a point to steer clear from the bars. Ethan frowned as he gave the bars an experimental tap with his finger. He sucked in a sharp breath and yanked his hand back to his chest.

"What's wrong? Are you ok?"

I reached out to assist him.

Ethan only shook his head in disbelief.

"They must have coated the bars with silver."

Drew let out a high pitched whine. I bent down to scratch behind his ear but he pulled away and bounded down the hall. The swiveling red light danced across his tawny coat. He led us to a large opening in the hallway that revealed a room with a two layered cage.

The vertical layer of bars were silver while their horizontal counterparts were iron. Astrid let out a long whistle when my camera took in the scene. I was the only one wearing one. My werewolf counterparts only had earpieces.

Senator Benson didn't want to risk having one of the cameras get smashed if either of them had to shift. The cage itself was the size of a professional boxing ring, maybe two. I took a peek inside. It looked like Jackson Pollock painted the floor himself with spatters of red and brown paint.

"They don't have much creativity when it comes to paint now do they?" Astrid mused aloud as I took in the scene.

An uneasy feeling slithered its way into my gut. Something told me that wasn't paint. A wet sensation nagged at the back of my throat.

A pale Ethan shook his head slowly in disbelief.

"That's not paint." He whispered. "That's blood."

Illness writhed within the pit of my stomach like a raging ball of snakes. My stomach heaved all it's contents. There went my lunch all over the cold cement.

"Aw come on Selena! Pull it together." Astrid groaned in disgust.

I let out a miserable moan and offered a pitiful apology. *How could someone claim that this is all good in the name of science?* The very idea of it disgusted me. The concept itself was unfathomable.

"What in the world were they doing here anyway?" Astrid inquired.

Ethan frowned as he took in all the cages.

"An experiment of some sort. I get why they have silver but why iron?" He asked, purely aghast.

I shuddered and rubbed the specks of vomit from my mouth.

"They must have fae." I murmured from behind my sleeve.

Ethan arched a confused brow. "Fae?"

It was then that I heaved again.

There was a pause, so Astrid explained.

"Yes, fae, like fairy spirits." Astrid began.

"Iron is like their kryptonite." I said.

"Like silver is for wolves." Astrid added sympathetically.

"I see.." Ethan murmured thoughtfully.

Drew skirted around me and my mess with great care. Thankfully, I had nothing else to give. He let out another high pitched whine and padded towards a control panel along the wall.

Astrid was right, I had to keep it together if not for me then for my friends. I followed in silent pursuit. White static crackled across the empty screen. Someone had taken a crowbar to the console and smashed the keyboard to little bits. Drew's wolf scratched at the control panel and look back at Ethan, waiting expectantly.

"Well, what is it?" Astrid inquired.

Ethan's brow crinkled with concern.

"She was here.. I can smell her."

He closed his eyes and leaned in.

"But I can't sense Frank."

Drew gave him an affirmative wag of his tail and nuzzled one of the control knobs with his wet nose. My stomach twisted.

"Who was here?" Astrid demanded impatiently over the head set.

"Olivia." Ethan said.

"Figures, he was tracking Olivia all along. Did or did I not tell you to trust me?" Astrid replied with a disgusted snort.

I hugged myself as I watched him run his fingers along the smashed keyboard. I could only imagine all the things that may be running through his head right now. His hand rested on the lever that Drew had pointed out. The label read emergency release.

"And she wasn't alone. There was a man, another wolf."

My breath caught in my throat. "Could it be Jake?"

Ethan offered me a helpless shrug.

"Who knows? It looks like she came back here to release the others and smash in the console with a crowbar, but now she's gone. All I know is she didn't come with Frank."

The voice on the other end of the headset remained unnaturally quiet. Drew's shoulders slumped as he hopped down from the console. I wanted to reach out and comfort him but we didn't have time for that. We were so close to finding them and now we had to start from scratch. Besides, I doubted he would accept my condolences anyhow.

"Why in the world would she do something like that? Especially when it risks the likelihood of her getting out of here?"

Ethan shook his head in disbelief.

"I don't know. All I can assume is she didn't want the lives of other super nats ending up stuck in the care of horrible people. Then again, that doesn't sound like Liv. Or maybe this is her way of fighting back? Who knows."

Something clattered down the hallway. Drew's ears pricked forward. A tingling sensation tickled my cheeks. The hairs on the back of my neck prickled with unease.

"Something's coming." I stammered uneasily.

Drew lifted his head and sniffed.

There was another crash.

His ears went back.

"Something's coming, something big and something magical."

Chills rippled down my spine. The air hummed with power.

"Whatever that thing is out there is it's dangerous. I can feel the magnitude of its energy crackling in the air. We have to get out now if we want to get out at all."

Ethan frowned at me as I searched around the room for escape.

"How can you tell?"

Ethan's suspicious voice was laced with concern.

I could only offer him a helpless shrug.

"Just lucky, I guess?"

The truth was I could tell by the air. Whenever I felt a magical presence the air would tingle. The larger the presence the stronger the vibration. As of right now the air was starting to hum. Patterson called it the sight.

However, I doubted Ethan would buy such an explanation but we didn't have time to delve into the tiny details. Bars of iron whined and creaked off in the distance. There was another crash and then a bone chilling roar. Astrid's voice crackled over the headset.

"What's going on team wolf? I can't get a read on you. The feed is going crazy."

A menacing growl rumbled deep within Drew's throat.

"It must be due to the magic." I explained.

There was a nervous tremor in my voice.

"Electronics never do well around magical vibrations."

"If that is the case we gotta get out of here, fast."

Ethan had replied hastily with a worried frown.

"No shit! What have I been telling you this entire time?"

Ethan heaved himself against the steel door just beyond the demolished control panel but the door wouldn't move.

"It's no use! It won't budge." Ethan said with a frustrated growl.

The creature stepped closer.

Another vibration rippled through the room.

The hairs along Drew's scruff rose against his skin.

"What are we going to do? Should we go through the hall?"

I ground my teeth, with all the banging he was making we may as well be screaming here I am come and get me!

"Are you trying to get us killed?" I hissed "There's no way we can make a run for it. That *thing* is standing just outside our door. Let's just stand still and keep quiet. Maybe it'll lose interest and go away."

In a perfect world that'd be the case but seconds later the archway crumbled beneath the power of a large paw.

Sweet mother of God, I couldn't believe what I saw.

Out from the rubble stepped a creature with blazing red eyes. A shiver of dread rushed down my back like ice water on a hot summer day.

"Is that a fucking *chimera?*" I whispered in disbelief.

Ethan sucked in a deep breath. "I believe so.."

Sharp claws sprouted from his nubby fingertips.

The creature itself stood ten feet high with two heads and a snake for a tail. One head was that of a lion and the other was that of a goat's. A tense Drew stood his ground between us and the mythical creature. His black lips curled, revealing a sharp set of yellowed fangs. Tawny brown hackles rippled down his spine.

Why wouldn't he move?

Did he not understand what he was up against?

The lion replied with an earth shattering roar as it whipped its snake like tail back and forth. The swiveling red light passed over her, revealing the front end of a lion and the back end of a mountain goat.

Snarling, Drew leapt towards the chimera. The muscles along his back rippled with tension. The chimera impatiently flicked her snail like tail and readied itself to pounce.

"Drew don't!" I reached out after him.

Ethan snatched me up held me back against his chest.

"Let me go Ethan! I have to help him. He can't go in there alone."

I wiggled against him, desperately trying to free myself.

"Don't Selena. You'll only get in his way."

His words had stung. He was right, there wasn't much I could do but I still wanted to help. A sense of helplessness overwhelmed me. I cringed as the chimera's massive paw swung at Drew's head. Ivory claws glinted in the swiveling red light.

"*Get out of the way!*" I screamed.

Blood roared through my ears.

Anxiety frayed at my nerves.

Was he going to make it?

He had to, if he didn't that swing in itself could have broken his neck. Drew leapt over the paw and latched onto the beast's throat with a ferocious growl. The chimera let out an aggravated scream as she clawed at her attacker. Drew shook his head back and forth and held on tight, beyond the lion's reach.

The snake tail whipped around. Fire spewed from the lion's jaw. I clapped my hands together and murmured a spell. A shield of blue energy encased us in it's protective shell just before the flames hit. The shield shook beneath the pressure of the flame. Waves of fire billowed around us but my enchantment still held in place. A wide eyed Ethan watched with gaping jaws. His hold on me fell away as he stared up in awe.

I stepped forward and withdrew the bow from my back.

Cold energy vibrated from the ground. The concrete was icy cool to the touch. From it I produced arrows of ice and launched them at the beast. Ethan had asked me earlier why I had brought such a thing, now he knew why. I hadn't told him earlier because I didn't want to have to pummel him for laughing at me.

Who knew I could do a lick of anything with a bow and arrow? Papi's hunting lessons didn't seem to go to waste after all. Nor did Patterson's training. Thankfully, water was nearby. I would have to use the elements to my advantage. Eventually, I'd be able to form a bow using my own spirit but Patterson said I wasn't ready, until then this would have to do. Locked and loaded, I continued to launch the shafts of ice at our opponent.

The chimera released an enraged roar as the lance pierced into its side. The goat head let out a deranged bleat as it bit down on the scruff of Drew's neck. My heart skipped a beat. Drew yelped. He hadn't anticipated that the goat could reach him.

The goat shook him around like a rag doll in a child's hands. Drew flew into one of the stone pillars. His limp body slid down to the ground in a crumpled heap. Snarling, the chimera turned to face us, her six eyes glistened like glowing rubies. Her snake like tail flicked with agitation. The snake ripped the icy shaft from her flank with its jaws and threw it aside. The arrow clattered to the ground and shattered into a thousand pieces.

Sharp talons scratched along the cold concrete. I backed away as the beast inched closer Her putrid breath came out in heavy wet clouds. Lithe muscles rippled along her shoulder blades. The creature was made of pure muscle and was built like a tank. Ethan began to strip.

"You think you can provide cover for us while we attack from the front?"

"I can try, why? What are you thinking?" I replied with a frown.

"I'm thinking we better come up with some sort of plan or we're all dead." He yanked me back by the wrist and headed for the cage. The beast stalked forward, watching us with hungry eyes. The mad eyed goat licked her lips while her snake like counterpart let out a volatile hiss.

A dazed Drew laid unconscious on the ground. Ethan threw me haphazardly into the cage and twisted the bars shut. Smoke sizzled from his hands.

"What the hell are you doing?! Let me go!"

He shrugged off his shirt.

"Stay in there and shoot from the cage, got it?"

My eyes narrowed into little slits. "When I get out of here I am going to skin you alive. You know that right?"

He offered me a helpless shrug. "Yep. Gotta go."

With that he threw off his pants and off he went. The chimera took off in full pursuit. Fuming, I prepared myself for another attack. It was then that I saw him, running in the nude, doing whatever he could to keep the creature's attention.

"Watch out!" I hollered as the chimera took a swing at his back. "Any help would be greatly appreciated right about now!" Ethan shouted back as he leapt out of the way and into the form of his wolf. His black shadow weaved in and out of the cages on all fours. The chimera went for the chase, cracking and snapping iron in her wake.

I sucked in a deep breath took a look around. All I had was metal and wet stone. I had no experience with either and earth magic was never my specialty when it came to the offense, so water it was. I closed my eyes and got to work. Patterson always told me when in doubt use the elements around you to your advantage. The earth provides the material while your spirit does the casting.

In cases of extreme emergencies you can always use your own spirit as the main ingredient but you must take care for you only have so much to spare before you die. Once it's gone, you're gone. Plain and simple. The question was, how much spirit did each arrow take to make? How many could I make before I ran out?

Regardless, I pulled another arrow from the ground and took a shot at the beast's shoulder. The arrow of ice arched through the air. Silently, I cursed myself for having sweaty hands. The chimera pounced to the left. The shaft soared past her and shattered against the stone. My heart dropped. How could I possibly make a hit? The two of them were so quick.

The chimera lunged, Ethan ducked to the right. The cat like creature followed in step. Ethan bit into her then tore away. He came back for a second strike. The chimera snarled and swiped. Sparks of fire flew from her mouth. Her ruby red eyes glittered with rage. Every muscle within me froze.

Ethan was a moment too late. The blow to his chest sent him sprawling back. He slammed into the stone archway with a broken yip. She stalked forward and licked her lips. I choked back a startled scream. *No, no, no. Please, this isn't happening, Ethan you have to get up.*

The bow shook within my sweaty hand. I forced myself breathe. *Breathe, just breathe, Selena. Everything is going to be ok.* Time slowed. The chimera was only a few feet away. I inhaled and drew the string to my cheek. *Just breathe.* I offered up a silent prayer, took aim, exhaled and released.

Please, please make it this time. Just make a hit, any hit. The arrow did just that, just below the goat's nape. The chimera let out a bone chilling scream. All the hairs along my back prickled with unease. She spun around and charged. Her ruby red eyes gleamed with hate. The ground quaked beneath her feet.

Then it occured to me, what if the cage couldn't hold her weight?

Terror gripped me in its claws. Desperately, I let loose one shaft after another. Beads of sweat blossomed along my brow. The creature came closer. My body swayed. My spirit was growing weak. One arrow hit, while another skirted along her flank. Another hit her square in the chest.

Regardless, she barreled through, yowling like a wild cat. The chimera closed in and lunged. A torrent of flame spewed form her open maw. The serpent's tail hissed. I clapped my hands together to form a shield but only a flicker of magic came forth, so I dove out of the way. Beams of fire shot past my leg.

I was a rat stuck inside a cage. Blood rushed through my ears. I could feel the beat of my heart thundering in the back of my head. We were going to die here, alone, and no one would know. The last thing I would hear were my screams.

The chimera came down onto the cage, snarling and spitting with rage. The bars creaked beneath her weight. Ivory claws glinted as they swiped at the cage. Her rancid wet breath was hot against my cheek. I scrambled away, just out of reach. She lunged again. I prepared myself for the final blow.

Just then, a blur of brown whizzed by and slammed into her flank. She stumbled backward with a feral snarl. My heart nearly leapt into my throat. It was Drew! He was back. Shortly afterward, a black blur latched onto her back. She let out a frustrated shriek. Her goat head counterpart screamed as it whipped its head back and forth, trying to locate the oncoming attack. Both wolves broke away with chunks of flesh. Drew went to the left and Ethan to the right. Together they came back for another onslaught but the chimera was already back onto her feet.

The serpent tail thrashed to and fro, spraying molten flames every which way it went. I ducked as streams of fire shot above my head. *So much for being useful.* I thought bitterly to myself. Magically, I was spent and the potion that Patterson had rigged up for me along with Ethan's extra clothes was just beyond my reach, just outside of the cage. I cursed myself for my stupidity. I should have never dropped it. *What was I thinking?* If Drew hadn't intervened when he did I would probably be dead.

I bit my lip as I watched the two wolves circle the three headed beast. Their paws skittered against the cool concrete. I held my breath as Ethan feigned to the left while Drew dove to the right. It was as if they thought as one. The chimera skittered just beyond Ethan's reach and spun around to meet Drew head on with her paw. I let out a strangled scream as ivory claws tore through flesh. I could hear bone crack as the paw smashed into Drew's ribs. With a yip he flew backward and crashed into the mess of crumpled cages. The chimera stepped forward and shook Drew's limp form between her blood stained teeth.

Ethan lunged but her serpent tail smacked him away. I couldn't breathe. Every ounce of my sanity was melting away. Frustrated, I tried yanking at the bars of the cage. The metal wouldn't give way. A wave of helplessness washed over me as I watched the chimera bat at Ethan as he tried to back away. She was playing with him, like a cat with a mouse before the final blow and there was nothing I could do, I couldn't escape. How much harm could I really do anyway? The shafts of ice that had once stuck out of the chimera had melted away, leaving oozing puncture wounds in their wake.

The chimera stalked forward as Ethan tried to hobble away. He couldn't run far on a broken leg.

Despite his werewolf heritage it'd take some time for his magic to heal the wound completely. Time wasn't something we had. In a matter of moments, the chimera would go in for the kill. It was just a matter of when.

Silently, I willed Drew to appear but no one came. Ethan couldn't do this alone. He needed a decoy that would keep the beast distracted. Panic gnawed at my nerves. *If I could do just one more arrow. One more arrow was all it would take.* I quelled the terror within me and reached deep within. I nearly buckled from the effort. I had no more spirit to give.

God damn it Selena. How could you be so stupid? What if you had pulled too much? You think you can help your friends if you're dead? You had one simple task... keep the potion on hand and you couldn't do just that.

Despair turned into disappointment and my disappointment turned into hate. Frustrated, my small hands tightened into tiny fists.

Sure I was new to magic but that didn't make me the one who was always in the way, now did it?

The chimera closed in. A flame of anger sprouted within my stomach. The very idea of it made me boil with rage. I'd be damned before that'd become me. I may be many things but useless was not one of them. I worked too hard to get here and trained too much to get where I am.

So, fuck the chimera, fuck the lab and fuck the men and women who took my friends. If I was going to die here, I was going out with a bang.

I reached for the splintered stick of metal just outside the cage and banged with all the strength I could muster. I hit over and over, making as much racquet as I could. Someone had to serve as a distraction, without one Ethan didn't stand a chance. The chimera's ears went back. She sent an aggravated hiss my way and bared her yellow fangs.

"Oh yeah?' I snarled and banged louder. "Don't like that, now do you?' Now c'mon you flea bitten bag of shit! It's me you want!"

She yowled in reply.Her serpent tail thrashed back and forth in . She licked her blood stained lips and turned to Ethan but he wasn't there. She screamed in frustration.

Cages went flying in her wake. Enraged, she fixed her ruby red eyes on me. My heart froze beneath her feral glare. Ice water ran through my veins. She stalked towards me. I backed away. I hadn't expected my plan would work, nor had I anticipated what would happen next.

All I knew was it wasn't going to be good. Beads of sweat blossomed as I watched the chimera soar through the air. I stepped back. I gripped the splintered bar so tight my knuckles turned white. I dug in my heels and steeled myself for the hit. If this was my fate, then I was going to die fighting. I was prepared to smack any fury knuckles that came within my cage.

CHAPTER 35

TWO HOWLS PIERCED THE AIR. Then something white leapt in front of the chimera and me. It stood on two legs, had the body of a man, the white fur of a wolf and the elongated head of a jackal. He reminded me of Anubis, the Egyptian deity of death. His furry white body rippled with power as he wrestled the chimera to the ground. He took her by the head and locked her in place. The goat's head flailed around and bit at its attacker the best it could.

Moments later, a gray she-wolf shot past. She danced to and fro, keeping the snapping jaws of the serpent at bay. She dashed in and out as she tore scaly chunks from the serpent's neck. Fur and scales flew everywhere. The chimera screamed and writhed in its attacker's grasp. A black blur of fur came to her aide. Together they kept the goat and snake at bay.

Thick muscle and sinew rippled with effort as Anubis held the beast in place. The chimera shuddered with effort but could not shake herself from the wolf-man's grasp. I watched in awe, with muddled confusion. Soon after, there was a series of audible crunching cracks. The chimera had stilled and the thrum of magical power had died away. To my amazement, the white wolf had snapped her neck. Awestruck, the splintered bar fell from my hands and clattered to the ground. We did it. I thought in utter bewilderment. *We had actually survived.* I couldn't believe it. *We were alive.* Tears of relief pooled at the corner of my eyes.

The humanoid figure doubled over. The muscles along his back rippled and shrunk. White fur fell away. I sucked in a sharp breath. Before me stood a panting Jacob. My heart stilled within my chest. Sweaty curls of brown hair fell into his face. My knees threatened to cave. I leaned into the bars for more support. *Could it really be him? If so, what would I say? Where would I start?* The gray she wolf let out a high pierced whine and dashed away.

"Jacob? Is that really you?" I asked with great trepidation.

He cast me a sad lop sided smile. Droplets of sweat trickled down his cheek.

"The one and only." He murmured through broken breaths.

I brought a trembling hand to my lips.

"I thought you were dead.." I whispered in disbelief.

He offered me a half hearted shrug and stepped forward.

I shrank away, not sure what to say or how to react.

The group said he was a werewolf, but I never really believed it. *Was this still the Jake I knew as a my childhood best friend?*

Dismay flickered across his face. "Selena, it's me, Jake."

I bit my lip. Everything thing within me was shaking.

"How can I be sure? I'm not sure of what's real or not anymore..."

I had murmmered the words breathlessly.

He let out a defeated sigh and ran a hand through his frazzled hair. The gesture itself was quite familiar but I couldn't be certain. "You love black jelly beans. Your first crush was Tommy Lee Jones, from first grade. Why is *beyond* me. The guy is a total geek. You love summer and your favorite musical is *Singing in the Rain.*"

My heart swelled. I thought I was going to burst.

"Dear God, it really is you.. You're here..."

I paused and struggled for words. "Are you going to be okay?"

He grimaced and twisted at the bars. I bit my lip as the silver seared his skin.

"Better than I'll ever be, now let's get you the hell out of this god forsaken place. You're lucky we recognized your scent. We were on our way out after freeing all the captives. Then you came along."

Smoke twisted from his blistering flesh.

"So it's true, you really are a werewolf..." I mumbled in disbelief.

He let out a weary sigh as the bars untangled beneath his grip.

"Yep, that I am. Shocking, right?" He replied with a sardonic smile.

I grimaced. A thousand questions swirled around inside my brain. I found it hard to breathe. When I spoke the words came out brittle and dry. "But how?"

Jacob offered me a simple shrug. "Born into it."

I licked my lips. "Does it hurt?"

He lifted one shoulder. "Every now and then, but you get used to it."

A high pierced scream shattered the silence.

"Jacob come quick! It's Drew!" Jacob and I rushed around the cage to see a sobbing Olivia. Golden curls fell into her tear stained face. Beside her lay Drew on his side, taking in shallow breaths. His limp form lay sprawled amongst the rubble of crumpled cages. Slick blood oozed from a gaping wound inside his chest. Ethan was doing his best to staunch the blood with his pants. Meanwhile, his shirt was draped Drew's lap and hips. Olivia looked up at me. Tears dripped down her chin.

"Ethan said you had a medic kit in your bag, do you think you can help?"

I cast Jacob an uneasy glance, I wasn't aware of a werewolf's customs.

Did I need approval to approach Drew?

Jake's bushy brows furrowed and he inclined his head.

"I don't know.. but I can try." I replied with a nervous smile.

Olivia choked back a broken sob and stepped out of the way.

"Please, do something, *anything*." Olivia begged.

A cool sheen of wet sweat broke across the back of my neck. I took one step forward. The ground seemed to tilt beneath my feet. I closed my eyes and and sucked in a deep breath. *Come on Selena, keep it together, you can do this. Just treat the wound like you do at home.* But that was the problem. We weren't at home and this wasn't some cut from a kitchen knife. This was a puncture wound to the lung, or even worse a collapsed chamber in Drew's chest.

Sure I knew a thing or two about medicinal herbs but that didn't mean I was a fucking surgeon. I have never dealt with a situation as complicated as this but I suppose it wouldn't hurt to try? If I didn't then Drew would surely die. I made my choice and cleared the gravel within my throat.

"Ethan?.." I inquired with a voice as dry as desert sand. He looked up at me. His eyes were eager and bright. "Would you be so kind as to grab my pack for me?"

I did everything I could to keep my voice steady and calm. Ethan offered me a solemn nod and off he went. I bent down to assess Drew's wounds.

The chimera had tossed him into a pile of crumpled cages. One of the bars had pierced through his chest. A good half of it stuck out of his back. Thankfully, he was laying on his side. Such a position would make the removal of the bar much easier.

Something was wrong, though. *Why hadn't he healed?* Pools of blood were everywhere. The wounds on Jacob's palms had healed in a matter of minutes. So why hadn't Drew's chest? Needless to say, Drew's wound should have begun to scab over by now.

Frowning, I knelt down and ran a finger over his gaping chest. His skin was hot to the touch. A small tendril of smoke sizzled out from the base of the shaft. My heart twisted at the sight. It was as I had feared. Silver had pierced him and by the way he wasn't healing I could only assume it had hit his heart. Who knows? By the way he rasped maybe it had hit a lung too? Drew cast me a wry smile.

"So doc, how bad is it?" Drew asked.

A brittle smile curled at the corner of my lip.

"How typical, even after you're severely injured and you still manage to have some snark."

Drew grunted in reply and gave me a cynical snort.

"You know me. I've got a reputation to uphold, but honestly, how bad is it?"

Olivia glanced at me warily as she took a hold of his hand.

I swallowed hard and offered him one of my best smiles.

"Not bad, we're going to try to patch you up, okay?"

Drew's expression turned to flint.

"Don't lie to me Selena. I just saved your life, so give it to me straight."

I swallowed hard, he had panted between each word.

It was an effort for him to even speak.

"It's silver, isn't it?"

I grimaced.

"Yes..and it looks like the bar may have pierced the edge of your heart too."

"Damn.." He replied with a pained grunt."That's why it burns.... God it burns so much...I tried to shift but I can't..it's the silver isn't it?"

I nodded while Olivia rubbed his arm reassuringly.

"We can try to take it out but..." My voice began to crack. He gave me another pitiful grunt. I struggled to continue. I doubted I could keep myself composed for very much longer. He was dying and I wasn't sure there was anything I could do. I felt like this was all my fault. Thankfully, Olivia finished for me. "But there's a chance it pierced one of your chambers. If that's the case your heart may collapse once the bar has been removed."

The possibilities were slim to none. By now Drew should have been healing but his magic flickered like a dying flame. We all looked at a concerned Jake, as if searching for some sort of advice. He offered us a helpless shrug.

"If we leave it in he will bleed out. The silver won't let him heal." Jake explained. His expression remained solemn but concerned. There were so much behind those eyes, so many stories that were afraid to be told. He had to hold himself together, not for himself but for his pack. The air thickened with tension. It was a choice between the possibility of life or death. In the meantime, Drew sucked in a shallow breath.

"Just do it." He said with a disgruntled sigh.

"But Drew you might die!" Olivia protested.

"You think I don't know that?!" Drew snapped.

Olivia flinched. It was as if she had been slapped across the face.

"Drew it's not her fault." Jake said with a grimace.

"You're right, I'm sorry." Drew replied with a sigh.

"I didn't mean to snap. I'm just in a lot of pain so bare with me okay?"

Ethan and Jake exchanged somber expressions.

"So what's it going to be? Let me bleed out or take a chance?"

Jake bent down and looked his Beta straight in the eyes.

"Are you sure you want to do this?" He asked.

Drew grimaced and offered Jake a stiff nod.

"Yes, now just get it over with."

Jake offered him a grim nod.

"Any requests before we begin?"

Drew flashed him a broken smile.

"If anything should happen to me, take care of Liv for me, will you?"

Olivia let out a choked sob. Jake leaned in and rested a reassuring hand on her shoulder. "I will protect her with my life." He inclined his head to Ethan. "Shall we begin?"

Ethan nodded and took his place. Olivia's lips quivered as Ethan took ahold of Drew's shoulders and Jake grabbed a hold of his legs. Together they held him in place so he couldn't flinch. Any movement could increase the tear in his chest. That was a risk we couldn't take. Sweat peppered my forehead. I looked back at Jake, searching for some sort of guidance. He offered me a reassuring nod.

"We owe it to him Selena. Do the best you can and make it quick."

Olivia's nails dug into Drew's arm. I dropped to one knee and licked my lips. My stomach had twisted with dread. Drew may have been an ass but that didn't mean I wanted him to die. I took a deep breath and steeled myself for the inevitable. If anyone should provide him relief it should be me. The others sure couldn't, unless they wanted to be burned. I was at a loss. The world all around me was closing in. *What if he died right here by my hand?* Either way, he had saved my life. All I could do was try. He was in this predicament after all because of me. Time slowed as I wrapped a trembling hand around the base of the shaft.

I became acutely aware of the cold metal as it touched my skin. I hesitated. *What if this didn't work? Would he be dead because of me? Why did everything have to depend on me? Why couldn't we just go back to the way things used to be?* Drew brought a trembling hand to my wrist. His mouth moved but nothing came out. I lost myself within those hard brown eyes.

"Come again?.." I asked, all I could hear was the blood roaring through my head.

"It's not your fault..." He paused and then the corner of his mouth curled into a half hearted smile. A trickle of blood dripped from his wet lips. "For what it's worth you did pretty good out there... for Sabrina the teenage witch."

I choked out a broken laugh.

"You're such an ass, you know that right?"

He offered me a tiny shrug.

"Someone's got to be." His eyes settled on me. All humor flickered away.

"Do it." He said with a dip of his chin.

I tensed my jaw and gave the rod a solid yank. Out slipped the rod, pools of blood gurgled in its wake. Drew stiffened and let out a pained gasp. His eyes went wide with shock. A bubble of blood escaped his lips.

"Drew!" Olivia gasped.

I stepped away as she scooped him up into her arms.

"Protect her." He rasped.

Jacob's jaw thinned into a grim line. "With all my heart, I promise."

Olivia let out a strangled sob.

My heart broke into a thousand pieces.

A dumbstruck Ethan stared at the scene in disbelief.

"What is happening to him Selena?" Ethan asked.

My heart constricted inside my chest. I couldn't find the words to speak. It was as I had feared. The bar was the only thing keeping his heart and lungs from collapsing. He was beyond repair, even pack magic couldn't mend that many ruptures within a short period of time.

"Please don't go Drew." Olivia begged.

"Shh..." Drew gurgled and cupped Olivia's cheek with a soothing hand. "It's going to be ok. You're safe now and that's all that matters."

He grunted and sucked in a shallow breath. "Promise me you're going to be okay."

Olivia sniffled "I can't."

Drew grimaced and rubbed a comforting thumb along her lips.

"You can. You have Ethan and Jake now." He said with a reassuring smile.

Olivia gulped and shook her head.

"Please don't go." Olivia begged.

Drew offered her a brittle smile and then went limp.

Wails of sorrow echoed down the corridor.

CHAPTER 36

FRANK, Noah and I skittered to a stop. Together, Noah and I peered around the corner. My stomach twisted with dread. The main corridor was packed to the brim like a package of sardines. How we were going to get past that was beyond me. A few moments later Frank yanked us back by the scruffs of our necks.

"Have you gone and bumped your heads?!"

He hissed through gritted teeth.

"If they see us we are surely done for!"

I grimaced and rubbed at the back of my neck.

"Easy Frank, that hurt."

Noah's eyes glittered like incandescent jewels.

"Now, now batman, there's no need to get your britches all in a knot." Noah replied sullenly.

Frank bared his fangs in reply.

Noah simply rolled his mismatched eyes.

I clucked my tongue in a disapproving manner and shook my head.

"Now, now boys easy does it. At this rate we won't need to worry about getting out alive because the two of you will have already torn each other in two."

The brief mania between the two bubbled down into a fit of tense silence. Together they exchanged menacing glares. Frank bit back a nasty retort while Noah shifted all his attention back to me.

"So what's the verdict, love?" Noah asked with a conciliatory smile.

I bit back some smart ass reply. *How many times did I have to tell this creep I wasn't his love?* Instead, I focused on the matters at hand. "Not good. The place is packed to the brim with security personnel. There's not much we can do without being seen."

Frank let out a weary sigh and rubbed at the back of his own neck.

"Well we haven't ran into Olivia or Jake." Frank began.

"So, what do you propose we should do next?"

Frustrated, I pinched at my brow.

We were in deep shit and time wasn't necessarily on our side.

"Well we can't just sit here." Noah grumbled bitterly beneath his breath.

"No shit, Sherlock!" I snarled back. "Honestly, even a person with a low I.Q would have figured that one out."

Frank bit his lip and glanced back at the main corridor, searching for some sort of escape. "The lines to the elevators are getting longer as we speak. We have to come up with a plan, and quick."

I chewed on my nail and began to pace.

"The longer we wait the likely we'll be caught. Line or no line."

Frank grunted in agreement but Noah simply shook his head.

"You won't want to take the elevators, not those ones anyhow."

I gave Noah a sidelong glance. "Oh, and why is that?"

Noah shrugged. "Because we'd be dead before we even got to the doors. It's like you said if we stay in one spot they'll find us. We're practically sitting ducks out there. Our best bet is to blend in with the crowd and use the chaos to our advantage. Besides those elevators open up to the main lobby and that place is crawling with security." He waved us over and pointed out the second hallway to the right. Frank and I exchanged looks of skepticism before looking over Noah's shoulder.

"We just need to make it to that second hallway. It will lead to an elevator that can get us to the top floor."

I eyed him suspiciously from the corner of my eye. "You know this, because?"

Noah offered me an illusive smile.

His calico eyes sparkled with mischief. "Because I've been there, pet."

I tensed and flushed all at the same time. Damn him and his sexy British accent. What gave him the right to call me pet anyway? Something told me he was full of shit. I glanced at Frank for confirmation.

Frank simply shrugged his shoulders. "It's true, I mean he's escaped the compound on three separate occasions. So why wouldn't he know where most things are?"

There was a long pause.

Noah watched me expectantly and waggled his brows.

"So what do you say, love? Willing to give this a shot?"

By now my blood was boiling. Just hearing him say the word love made my skin want to crawl. He of all people had no right to classify me by that nickname. If our survival hadn't been dependent on him I'd have half the mind to wring his skinny little neck. Fuming, I jabbed a finger at his chest.

"Let's get one thing straight. My name is Lexi, and I am *not your love*. I am a member of the Celestial Clan, the clan that you and your father pillage and raped. There are no mutual feelings coming your way. I am only betrothed to you by force, nothing more."

Noah's mouth tightened. His voice came out hauntingly low.

"For the record, I may have pillaged but I never did rape."

I stumbled for a moment. Was there a flicker of pain in those calico eyes? If so it was there for a hot second and then gone the next. Then again, I hadn't personally witnessed Noah participating in any acts of rape but I had seen his kin and that would reason enough for me. The air around us crackled with emotion. The tension itself made it hard to breathe.

Frank cleared his throat. "Alrighty then, shall we carry on?"

Flustered, I threw my hands up into the air.

"Oh for fucks sake, why not? We're all going to die anyway right?"

Frank offered me a sympathetic shrug. "The possibility is quite likely."

A boyish grin flashed across Noah's face. All the anger within me began to ebb. "Where's the fun if there's no sense of adventure, eh?" Noah said as he nudged Frank in the side.

Frank shot him a sideways glance but did not return the gesture.

I let out an exasperated sigh. "Alright Houdini, what do you got?"

Noah flashed me a triumphant smile. "Well it all depends. The best option is for you to alter your appearance and keep Frank and I cloaked. Do you think you can manage?"

I simply shook my head.

"No can do, I'm good but not that good. Besides, you of all people are pro when it comes to master manipulation. So why can't you do it?" I inquired sharply.

Frank grimaced. I bit my tongue. *What was wrong with me?* Noah offered me a tight lipped smile but remained polite. I faltered for a moment. Was my grudge against him unrealistic? *Sure, he happened to be the son of my father's arch enemy but he hadn't asked to be born that way. If that were the case, then what I had just said, was it uncalled for?* Something inside me told me yes.

"To be quite honest, I am knackered. Frankie here, and I spent a lot of energy earlier fighting off a fair few scientists in corridor thirteen. I am practically running on E." Frank narrowed his eyes at Noah's flippant reference to his name.

"The bloody sods haven't let me feed in nearly three days. I can alter my own appearance but I can't do both. Besides, I figured it'd be wise to save some juice just in case we run into anymore trouble."

Frank rubbed a thoughtful hand along his jaw.

"Hmm, well if that's the case then why don't the two of you pose as lab specialists while I will play the part of the unwilling specimen that tried to get away?"

Noah grinned and slapped Frank on the back.

"I had hoped you were worth some time saving. Now I know I was right, eh?"

Frank offered his old cellmate a peeved smile.

"Jeez, thanks *a lot*. Just for the record, I didn't need your help after all. I had everything under control until you came walking in. How many times do I need to tell you that?"

I arched a brow. Did I, for a moment, sense some sort of camaraderie between the two of them? I rolled my eyes and shook my head.

"Alright, alright. Let's get on with it, shall we?"

Together, after much deliberation, we took our forms and headed straight to the crowded corridor. A cloud of anxiety loomed over me. With each passing step the mass of conversation increased in volume, so did the pace of my thundering heart. Waves of worry riddled my spine with beads of sweat. We didn't know if this plan would work. If we put even one toe out of line we could end up dead. Sure, Noah and I were practically spirits but that didn't make us invincible.

Our vulnerabilities were aligned with whatever form we took. As of right now that form was in the shape of a human being. In short, our human shells could only handle so much damage. Regardless, illusion was a kitsune's specialty. I took on the appearance of a woman that we had found earlier in the hallway. Noah took on the image of her male peer that we had discovered a mere three feet away from her body. Noah assured us that no one should notice their absence in the middle of all this commotion. Despite his assurances, I still did not feel right impersonating the dead. Then again, I suppose it's necessary to deter from one's moral compass when your own survival was in question. Regardless, that was a personal battle I'd have to deal with later. Breathless, I dug my nails into Frank's flesh and pushed through the crowd.

Off in the distance stood a lithe figure with high cheekbones and silver hair. At her feet sat two lupine creatures made of pure muscle, and bone. Leathery gray skin, riddled with rot, clung to their skeletal forms. A chill ran down my spine. The very sight of them reminded me of the living dead. Noah dipped his chin towards the woman and her hounds.

"Careful with that one, love." He murmured out of the corner of his mouth.

Frank mumbled something but I couldn't hear him over the noise.

"Excuse me?" I inquired.

"I said *loosen* your grip. I can't feel my arm."

The hound watched me with it's milky white eyes.

Noah nudged me in the side. "Not so loud." He hissed.

The hound's lip curled, revealing a pair of blood stained fangs. *Could he smell the fox beneath my skin?* The hairs along my back bristled with fear. We kitsune could fool humans, possibly even vampires but dogs usually saw past the our wily ways. Silver lifted her hand, on command the hound's growling subsided.

"Easy!" I quipped back.

His voice dropped an octave or two.

"She's a vampire you half wit. If she catches wind of us then she will tear us to bits. You get me?"

I stiffened with irritation.

"Why didn't you just say so in the first place?" I replied tartly.

He let out a cynical snort.

"As if you'd listen in the first place, pet." He replied venomously through gritted teeth.

As if summoned the woman's strikingly green eyes roamed the room and landed on me. She was sex in a bottle. She had long silky strands of moonlight in her hair, lips made of periwinkle petals, and porcelain skin as smooth as a maiden's breast.

My nails bit into Frank's skin. *Did she happen to see us?*

Sweet Inari, I hoped she hadn't. I tugged Frank towards the second corridor on the right. He grumbled something about shape shifters and their barbaric ways. *Maybe, just maybe, if we moved quick no one would notice us.*

Noah dug in his heels. "Stay calm, love."

I began to retort. *How many times did I have to tell him? I wasn't his god damned love.* He pulled me close. I froze. His breath was hot against my ear.

"The goal is to be discreet."

I shivered, was it with pleasure or fear? The very idea of finding him pleasurable irritated me. I couldn't afford to be attracted to the son of the man who is at war with my family. That would be a form of betrayal, wouldn't it? Flustered, I pulled away. Damn him and his damnable confidence. How could I be discreet when every muscle in my body screamed run away? Regardless, Noah was probably right. If we were to run now we would only become prey. Still, him being right didn't make it any easier. I still wanted to run like hell. In fact, I wanted to shove the word discreet down his throat and beat him over the head, but someone had yelled "Hey!"

I froze. Little droplets of sweat blossomed along my neck. *Please, just let us go. I prayed. We are just three simple super nats that just want to go home. Is that all too much to ask?* We turned to see two heavily armed guards coming our way.

Noah muttered something foul beneath his breath.

Frank stiffened.

It took me a moment to find my voice. "Is there a problem, sir?"

The guard frowned. "Yes, as a matter of fact there is. Where do you think you are going? We are in the middle of preparing ourselves for an evacuation."

Silver watched us coolly from afar. Her emerald eyes glittered with interest.

Frank kept his head hung low.

Noah sneered and picked up an Bostonian accent.

"What does it look like we're doin'?" He grabbed Frank by the back of his neck and gave him a good shake. His head hung low in defeat but his shoulders tightened beneath Noah's grip. "We're taking this delinquent to the lab so he can't escape."

A shadow or two moved out of the corner of my eye. Two men had changed positions. While others stayed put in line. Silver brought a hand to her temple and the movement stilled. Something told me we were being watched. One moment the men were there then the next moment they blended back into the crowd. The distance between us and them had shrunk.

Did Noah even happen to notice?

The guard frowned.

"On whose orders?" One of the guards demanded.

"On Mr. Lemming's orders, of course. Surely you don't want to have to answer to him, do you?" I replied, almost instantaneously.

The guard pursed his lips while the other frowned.

Frank blinked for a moment He hadn't expected me to join in.

So, I took my chance and blundered on.

"I mean, I hear he has a horrible temper.."

I let the opportunity hang there, everyone knew Lemmings had a thing for authority but would the guards even dare to comment? In the meantime, Noah took what I had to offer and ran with it.

"Yeah, I heard he let the last person loose for not following protocol." He gave them a meaningful glance. "You don't want to lose your job over some simple orders, now do you?" Noah paused while the guards shifted their weight and exchanged uncertain glances. He scratched his chin for dramatic effect. "Gee. All that pay down the drain? *Just wasted*. Sad, really. God, what was her name again?"

Frank muttered something beneath his breath.

Noah grabbed a fistful of hair and leaned in.

"What did you say you *little* worm?"

Frank tensed.

I grimaced and held my breath.

"Her name was Marie Rousseau." Frank snarled. "And now she's in the infirmary now, you little pig."

Noah's eye twitched. "Why you..."

Both of the guards blanched. "Alright, alright. We got it. Don't mess with the bigwigs. Go finish your orders but make it quick. We depart in fifteen. Got it?"

We nodded and off they went. Silver frowned and dipped her chin. The men moved in. The hound from hell rose.

Noah dropped his Bostonian accent and tilted his head towards the corridor.

"You heard the man, now let's make it quick." Noah said.

The silence between us was deafening. I waited until we were well out of earshot.

"Enjoy acting much?" I said with an arched brow.

Frank let out a derisive snort while Noah dragged him along.

"It was a bit overstated if I do say so myself." Frank commented wryly.

Noah offered him a playful smirk. "Better to be overstated then under, eh?"

We made it to the corridor. Silver and the men were nowhere to be seen. We must have lost them. Noah looked around before releasing Frank's arm. "You alright mate? I had to pull on your hair for effect. If I hadn't roughened you up a bit then the bloody sods may have never let us through."

I arched a brow in mock disbelief.

"*Really?* You just had to roughen him up a bit?"

Noah gave me a disapproving glare.

"Jesus woman! Will you at least give me the honor of acting like a civilized gentleman?" Frank considered him from the corner of his eye.

Noah grimaced and offered Frank his hand.

"No hard feelings, eh?"

Frank grunted dryly and massaged his swollen wrist.

Regardless, he did not accept Noah's offer.

"You did what you had to do." Frank replied sullenly.

Moments later, one of the hellhounds burst through the crowd and veered straight towards us. His companion joined him. Silver and her men were not far behind. Noah hadn't noticed.

"Uh I don't mean to spoil the moment, but we got trouble at three o' clock. So let's get a move on, shall we?" I announced with a shaky smile. I was referring to the hounds that were closing in.

An open mouthed Frank backed away.

Noah blanched and grabbed me by the arm. "Run!"

A wave of fear rippled down my spine. We broke into a sprint. If something made Noah want to run then it couldn't be good. He was part of the shadow clan for Christ sake. Darkness was his middle name. Frank glanced back at the demon dogs with half eaten flesh.

"What the hell are those things?" Frank asked.

Noah grimaced as he pushed harder down the hallway.

"Hellhounds." He rasped. "Bloody buggers are fast and they have a nasty bite. If you're wise you'll do well to avoid them."

Silver was gaining on us and to make matters worse she had five other men with her. Whether they were human or not, I did not know. My instincts told me no. No human should be able to move at such speeds but in a place like this anything was possible.

Silver herself moved like lightning. One moment she was behind me, the next she was only a few feet up ahead. How was I supposed to compete with something like that? I nearly crashed into her. Thankfully, I skidded to a stop. Somewhere during all the mania, my webs of illusion had melted away.

A ghost of a smile curled along her luscious lips. The very gesture chilled me to the bone. She had the eyes of a green eyed panther and the face of a Roman empress. Silver strands of hair as smooth as spun-silk fell across her porcelain face. A wave of nausea tugged at the center of my core. *How could someone so beautiful be a part of a corporation that was so corrupt?* The very idea sickened me. Her voice came out in a soft Russian purr.

"I knew you couldn't be Darla." She said with a sultry grin.

I flashed her a jittery smile.

"Now what gave me away?"

The huntress stepped forward. I backed away. Oval fingernails sharpened into deadly points. She patronized me with the cluck of her tongue. "Oh, my sweet. Darla would never refer to the head of the military program as Mr. Lemmings."

I cleared my throat, squared my shoulders then offered her my best winning smiles. "Is that so? Well I'll be sure to take that into consideration."

Her eyes lit up with excitement. Seconds later, she swiped. I managed to throw myself out of the way. *Sweet mother of Inari, she was quick as a snake!*

Behind me Noah struggled with the hound's open jaw.

"This isn't the time for tea, love! Finish her already and go straight for her heart!"

I grimaced. Out of all the times he could have referred me by a pet name, why now?

Frank grunted in agreement as he sidestepped a punch towards the head. "Yes, please do make it quick."

Frank flipped one of the men on his back while another went for his neck. They moved with vampiric speed. *Could they be Silver's newborns?*

Five normal humans wouldn't have been a problem for Frank but five newborn vampires were a whole different ball game. Unlike their masters, newborns have no restraint. They were purebred killing machines pumped to the max with another ancient vampire's blood with only one thing in mind: the need to feed. Frank stepped to the side then just barely managed to duck to the right of another oncoming fist. If these were newborns and Silver had happened to sire them, then we were in some deep shit. We had our balls to the wall and we needed to do something fast. Meanwhile, the huntress cackled with glee. "Love? What are you, darling? His little boy toy?"

I flushed with embarrassment.

She dismissed Noah with the wave of her hand.

"Never mind him, my little vixen."

Her emerald eyes flared with desire.

"You're all mine." She said with a sultry grin.

Hot anger rushed through my veins. My lip began to curl and my hands tightened into balled fists. If she thought I was her's then she had another thing coming.

"Sorry to break it to you, *sweetheart*." I said through clenched teeth. "But, I belong to no one."

Silver rushed me. I twisted out of the way and threw her a kick. Together we clashed. She kicked, I rolled and popped back up to the left. We exchanged blows. Her fist bounced along my cheek. Fire exploded in my jaw while my knee met her flank. Her green eyes glinted with pain. Together we rolled around on the ground, slashing and clawing at each other like two wild animals in a fit of rage. Blood, spit and hair flew everywhere.

Meanwhile, Noah kicked the beast off his chest. Frank ripped a piece of piping away from the railing then tossed the bar to his cellmate. Noah caught it in mid air.

He let out a volatile hiss and bared his fangs. His five fox tails twisted and thrashed as he spun out of the first hound's way and stabbed the lunging beast right right between the shoulder blades. The hound let out a high pitched yip.

Noah's eyes flared as he drank in the hound's terror. Tendrils of black spirit swirled to his lips. His eyes glowed like jewels in the night. He was fully charged, he was a void Nogitsune after all and to them chaos was a delicacy. There was plenty of that to go around. The second beast went for Noah's back but he twisted out of the way.

A black crackling mass of energy shot out of his hand and blew the second hound away. I on the other hand am a thunder Kitsune and there wasn't enough electricity to go around. The creature bounced across the ground in a dazed stupor. An anguished Silver veered towards him. Desperately, I drew energy from the flickering lights.

"Oh no you don't!"

I hissed and threw a ball of energy in her face.

"Your fight is with me!"

Snarling, she charged. Melted flesh hung from her face.

"I will kill you, I swear. I will suck every droplet of life from your body and then feed you to my dogs!"

I flashed her one of my famous sneers.

"I wouldn't be so sure about that."

Little did she know I had very little energy to give. Together, we collided into spitting and snarling mess. Fists flying, hair pulling, claws scraping. Seconds later, three of the newborns latched onto Frank. One of the guards slashed him with a silver blade. Frank roared with rage and snapped the guard's neck. Black pitch filled his gaze. He threw one of the snarling newborns across the hall and zipped from one man to the next, ravaging necks with bloody fangs.

One of the men had a rifle. A series of poofs hissed through the air, moments later Frank's body was riddled with feathered darts. The metallic smell of silver leaked into his bloodstream. I let out a bone chilling scream as he crumpled to the ground.

Noah rushed in and grappled the man to the ground. He snatched up the firearm and cracked the guard upside the head. The man fell to the ground like a ton of bricks. My heart clenched with fear. I tried to assist him but Silver rushed me.

I tried to block but she kneed me in the side. I gasped with pain as I slammed her head against the wall. Together we wrestled each other to the ground. I could feel myself losing control as we rolled around on the ground, slashing and clawing at each other like two feral cats.

The vixen within me was taking over. My fingernails lengthened into sharp claws. Blunt human teeth turned into gnashing fangs. I saw the yellow eyes of my fox within the reflection of Silver's black eyed gaze. My two fox tails thrashed to and fro with agitation. Bit by bit,, pieces of my humanity fell away.

I kicked at her stomach but my claws couldn't connect. Silver sneered. Meanwhile, Frank was bleeding out while Noah kept the newborns at bay. Eagerly, they lapped up Frank's blood. We needed to act fast or Frank might not be able to see another day.

Violent rage boiled through my veins. Damn these humans and their god damn boots. If I could just get my hand in the right spot then I could blow her away. She was stronger then she looked. Based on the length of her fangs she may have been about three or four centuries old. Beating her was going to prove struggle some.

"It's over little vixen" Silver sneered as she leaned in.

"You're all mine!" She whispered in my ear.

I squirmed beneath her grip, desperately trying to get free.

"I am going to drink you dry." Her eyes glittered with glee.

"When I'm done with you there'll be nothing left."

I tried to bide for some more time.

"Oh come now, you wouldn't want to eat a stringy old thing like me." I replied with a jittery laugh.

This vampire had a few hundred years on me. I didn't know how much more I could take. I was in desperate need for some sort of distraction. For the love of Inari, someone please provide me with something. Anything would do, I could have built one of my own but I didn't have enough juice in me.

A howl split through the darkened hallway.

Silver stiffened at the sound and turned.

I took my chance and called forth the last of my magic. Flames from my own spiritual essence licked along my fingers as I plunged them into Silver's chest. She grunted in surprise. Triumph transformed into dread as sinew and bone collapsed beneath my burning fingertips. In a matter of seconds, I held her heart in my flaming hand. She let out an agonizing scream.

"*Who's dinner now, bitch?*" I hissed.

"*But how?*" She rasped.

I held my grip. An explosion of light boomed through the dark corridor, briefly blinding everyone in its wake. The remainder of the goons scattered away from Frank's fallen body. Shock muddled Silver's green aura with sickly gray.

Without hesitation, I ripped out her heart. Burning energy coursed through me. I drank in each droplet of fear and every ounce of terror until her body was a lifeless husk.

Bits of her lifeforce spilled into me. Moments later, I realized Silver's bleeding heart was still in my hand. Disgusted, I dropped the organ as if it were a diseased rat. Did I just ingest the terror that was within?

No, that couldn't be.

I was not, could not, would not be a Nogitsune.

Time froze. I found it hard to breathe.

Before me lay the husk of Silver's crumpled body. Shocked, I stood there, staring at my blood stained hands. A sense of realization washed over me. *I had just made my first kill.* A wave of remorse writhed inside me like a twisted ball of slithering snakes. *Sweet Inari, what have I done?* It all happened so fast. *Did I just kill someone for my own gain? This wasn't supposed to happen. I was a member of the celestial clan. I was meant to protect, not kill.*

Meanwhile three shadows shot past me and lunged for the remaining newborn vampires. The silhouette of a woman rushed towards me. She shouted something but I couldn't hear. Blood rushed through my head. *What had I done?* Her mouth moved but no sound came. She shook me. The words came out a bit clearer this time.

"Alexis?"

No response.

"Alexis?!"

She slapped me. Her hand met my cheek with a sickening crack.

"Alexis!" Selena snarled.

"Snap out of it and pull yourself together!"

Her face came into focus. Hawk like brown eyes pierced into me. Strands of black hair fell in her face. Her square jaw was set with determination. She was covered in blood, but whose it was I had no idea.

"Hawk Eyes, is that you?" I murmured in disbelief.

Her face twisted with frustration.

"Yes it's me you half wit! Who else would I be? What in the world are you doing here anyway?" Meanwhile, in the background, the werewolves snapped and snarled at their prey. I frowned and rubbed at the handprint that was upon my face.

"Escaping, or trying to anyway. What about you?"

Noah hopped back , just out of the range of a vampire's swipe.

"I don't mean to dampen your little reunion, but a little help over here would be nice." His eyes glittered like glowing jewels. Frank let out a feeble grunt as he struggled to get up, only to fall into a fit of frothing convulsions.

"Frank!" Hawk Eyes tried to rush to his aid but Noah beat her to the chase. His expression was grim.

"Poor sod.." He mumbled beneath his breath. Without another word he snapped Frank's neck. Together we gasped and took a step back. Everything went silent as an unconscious Frank crumpled to the ground. Ethan's wolf whined as his gray comrade licked her lips. Meanwhile, the arm of a ravaged newborn twitched.

CHAPTER 37

HAWK EYES STARED at him with a horrified expression.

"What the hell is wrong with you?" She asked, purely aghast.

"What?" Noah inquired. "It's either that or the poor bugger's in pain. He's asleep now, you see?" He gave Frank's limp form a solid nudge with his big toe.

Hawk Eyes' mouth dropped open in complete horror.

The wolves exchanged wary glances.

"Sleeping like a newborn babe." Noah exclaimed with a proud smile.

Exasperated, I pinched at the bridge of my nose and shook my head. "Noah, this isn't Gaia. You just don't go around snapping people's necks."

His mouth tightened in retort.

"Bloody hell, woman. Would you rather me let him die from blood poisoning? At least now the silver is not circulating through his veins."

I threw up my hands in frustration

"Okay then, Noah, then what the in Inari's name do you suggest we do?"

Noah flashed me a deadly glare as he threw Frank's limp body over his shoulder. "We don't have time for this horse shit. We need to find a place where we can drain him, somewhere safe."

Noah said as he adjusted Frank's weight.

Hawk Eyes' complexion went white.

"Drain him? You mean bleed him out like a stuffed pig?"

Noah narrowed his eyes. "Yeah, something like that."

Her jaw dropped in horror.

"What are you, some kind of monster? He needs blood to survive. You can't just take it from him." She sputtered in disbelief.

Noah's jaw set in firm determination.

"Think of it as a blood transfusion. Now let's move out." Without another word he shouldered his way towards the double doors.

Hawk Eyes called out after him.

"Who the hell do you think you are!? You can't just take him!"

Noah didn't respond as he tiptoed over one body after the next.

She whirled on me. Her eyes burned bright with rage.

"You are just going to let that creature take Frank?"

I grimaced and gave her a helpless shrug.

Her blazing brown eyes bore into mine.

What was I going to say? Oh, by the way that creature is my fiancé? I just managed to mend my relationship with her. I couldn't have all that hard work crumble in one day. Besides, Noah knew what he was doing, Frank had to be drained or all of that silver would stop his heart. Hawk Eyes grumbled something foul beneath her breath as she yanked her bow over her head.

"If you won't stop him, then I will."

My heart nearly leapt into my throat. *Was she seriously going to shoot Noah in the back? What if she hit Frank?* The white wolf's ears went back. She knocked an arrow. Every muscle within me froze. I knew I had to move but couldn't.

"You can't.." I began.

Her eyes narrowed into tiny slits.

"Watch me.." She proclaimed with a new sense of determination.

The white wolf's lip curled. She aimed. A low growl rumbled deep within his throat. Soon his gray counterpart joined in. Ethan's wolf watched with indifference. He never really cared for Noah anyway. A thousand thoughts zoomed through my brain. Before I knew it I was shouting stop and had managed to push myself in the way.

"*What the hell is wrong with you?*" Hawk Eyes snarled as she whipped her bow away.

"If you stop him then the silver will put Frank's heart through cardiac arrest." I protested, breathlessly, as I paused between each breath "Besides, he's the only one that knows the way-"

Noah turned. His calico eyes roamed over a fuming Hawk Eyes.

"Look ladies, if we don't get moving we're all going to die and if we don't make it fast Frankie boy here won't make it another day."

His expression remained aloof. "Get the picture, pet?"

Hawk Eyes stiffened but before she could respond he had turned away.

"Oh and by the way. That'd be my fiancee you're talking dirty to, so you best watch what you say."

With a flick of a tail he was gone. The wolves followed close behind and left her standing there, fuming. I took a step back. It would only be a matter of seconds before she turned on me.

It had looked as if she had been slapped in the face.

Should I run? Or should I stay?

Hawk Eyes stared murderously in my direction. The corner of her eye twitched. I grimaced. I knew I should have ran away when I had the chance. I steeled myself for what was coming next.

"*Fiancée?*" She inquired through gritted teeth.

"He is *thee* fiancée?' She continued in disbelief.

I flashed her a sheepish smile and rubbed at the back of my neck.

"Yeah, about that... that's a story for another time, eh?"

Seething, she snatched up her pack and stomped off in Noah's direction. Smoke practically billowed out of her round little ears. If I listened quietly I could hear the grinding of her teeth.

My stomach twisted with disappointment.

Well there went that moment of brief restoration between us. I thought bitterly to myself. Ethan butted me in the leg with his head and I too followed in her wake.

The atmosphere shifted as soon as we stepped through the doors. A wave of dread washed over me as we took in the room.

CHAPTER 38

SENTRIES OF LIFE sized incubators stretched towards the vaulted ceiling in organized rows. Noah's grip on Frank's body tightened. Awestruck, I stared as we passed a series of specimens. They were curled up in various fetal positions. Silently, they laid there, suspended in green fluorescent liquid. A silent chill rippled down Ethan's spine. Hawk Eyes sucked in a sharp breath. Olivia's wolf let out a high pitched whine. It took me a moment for me to find the right words.

"What is this place?" I managed to ask.

My voice came out raw and hoarse.

I looked to Noah for some sort of reply.

His brows knitted with revulsion.

"It's their library of creation." He replied quietly as he reached for something on a nearby countertop. Each word was laced with venom.

Hawk Eyes frowned as she ran her fingers along the glass.

"Better yet, what are they?" She asked.

Noah's calico eyes narrowed into tiny slits.

"Hybrids." He spat.

The white wolf looked up and licked his snout.

"They're the lab's hybrid creations."

Noah's knuckles whitened around what looked like a hammer.

"They mean to use them as military weapons. That is something I can't allow."

Without another word he swung the hammer at the incubator. Shards of glass exploded. Green water gushed forth through the cracks. Out spilled a twisted creature.

Breathless, he turned to us. His bright eyes were laced with apprehension. I looked to Hawk Eyes and she looked to me. Together we had a silent exchange that only two close friends could possibly experience. I turned to Noah.

He looked good standing there in blood soaked jeans and his hair all matted up with sweat. It never occurred to me that he would care about destroying weapons of mass destruction. A ghost of a smile curled at the corner of my lips.

"Need some help?" I asked.

His expression softened and Hawk Eyes pulled out her bow. Ethan and the other wolves let out affirmative barks while the three of us got to work, smashing each test tube we passed on the way to the elevators. Not too long after we stood in the elevator, silently waiting for the first floor to arrive. In the meantime, green goo dripped off of our bodies.

The silence between us was tense and the air was thick. What we had just done and everything we had seen was a lot to take in. I could still see the images of twisted figures spilling out onto the floor. The memory itself will be forever burned into my brain. Despite our reasons, I still felt dirty. Sure, the deaths of many innocent lives would have been astronomical if we had let the majority of those hybrid creatures develop to full term. Regardless, the outcome hadn't made me feel any better. For some reason I still felt the stain of blood all over my hands.

I couldn't help but wonder, was I changing? Had I traded my desire for balance for chaos and pain? Was it possible I was becoming less of a Mobutu and more like a Nogitsune? And earlier I had... the thought of soaking in Silver's terror sent shivers down my spine. Each step I had taken today made it seem that way. First the taking advantage of the dead, engulfing Silver's darkness and now this?

What would Pa say? Would he even recognize me anymore?

Hawk Eyes interrupted my self reflection when she cleared her throat.

The tension within the elevator had escalated to great proportions.

"Well.." She murmured reflectively. "That went well."

Olivia's mouth tightened into a thin line.

When she spoke her words came out like sickles of ice.

"That may be the case. Just remember, we did what we had to do."

Jacob didn't comment Earlier, Olivia and Jacob had shifted into their human forms while Ethan remained a wolf. The spandex gear they wore was able to morph with each shift, a new found ability designed by the lab. While Ethan's was not.

Hawk Eyes sighed. "Whatever you say, Liv."

She paused and frowned. "Where are we going anyway?"

We all glanced at a tense Noah, who happened to be staring straight ahead. His demeanor had been different ever since we smashed a handful of the hybrids back at the lab. We couldn't eliminate all of them but we did the best we could with the time frame we had.

"Well?' Jacob pressed. "What's the next step?"

"First step is to get the hell out of Dodge." Noah replied.

The western phrase sounded funny coming from his British accented lips.

It was now Hawk Eyes' turn to interrogate. "And then what?"

Noah's jaw tightened and he looked straight ahead.

"And then we'll drain Frank."

Olivia shifted her weight.

"Umm, there's only one problem with that plan."

Noah arched an archaic brow. "And what is that?"

She bit her lip and tucked a wet strand of hair behind her ear.

"How do you plan on replenishing his blood supply once he has been drained?"

Noah offered a polite smile. His eyes however, danced with irritation. Jacob's spine straightened at the gesture. Ethan let out a low growl. I didn't like where things were heading. "He will have to feed, of course."

Olivia displayed a hint of uncertainty. She glanced back at Jake then back at Noah. Jacob reached out and rested a reassuring hand on her shoulder. She hesitated and then continued. "Surely he will be under the fit of blood lust when he awakens, right?"

"Yes, that tends to happen now doesn't it?' Noah replied evenly.

His words came out short and clipped.

She fidgeted with a strand of hair.

"Well, how do you tend on restraining him?"

We all stared at him, waiting expectantly for some sort of logical explanation.

Noah offered her a nonchalant shrug and looked ahead. "I don't."

Olivia's eyes bulged and Hawk Eyes stiffened.

The elevator doors opened and off he went.

It took me a moment to register what he had just said.

Then it dawned on me and I caught my breath.

"You don't mean to let him have a feeding frenzy on innocent bystanders, do you?"

Noah didn't reply. We stepped out into the hall. I chased after him.

"Do you have any idea how many repercussions that type of thing would have?" Hawk Eyes sputtered with indignation.

"Not to mention what it would do to a vegetarian vampire's psyche."

I had muttered the words dryly beneath my breath.

Noah whirled around. His calico eyes were ablaze.

"Look, if you want to go all the way back there and get blood bags then be my guest. Preventing the death of a few extra guards is not high on my priority list!"

"You have got to be fucking kidding me." I replied with a cynical snort.

"After all you two have been through, you're just going to let Frank run a muck ripping out people's necks? Do you have any idea what that type of behavior may do to him once he's out of his trance?"

Noah jabbed an accusing finger at my chest. "You told me to do whatever it takes to get us out of here. This is what I have chosen to do."

I arched a brow. Exasperated, he threw his hands up into the air.

"What else do you want me to do? Grow wings and grant you your every wish? By the Gods woman, I'm not your bleeding fairy godmother!"

Hawk Eyes rolled her eyes. "Oh that's rich."

Something down the hall made a noise while the two of them exchanged heated words. Hackles of fur rippled along Ethan's spine. His black lips curled back in warning. Olivia nudged me with her elbow and tilted her head towards the black wolf.

"Something's coming." She whispered.

Jacob inserted himself between Olivia and the noise.

"Do something," He hissed.

"Like what?" I quipped back.

Meanwhile, my other two comrades continued to argue amongst themselves.

"I don't know, *anything*!" Jacob insisted, his expression was tense.

I flashed him a deadly glare. "Why don't you do it yourself?"

"I can't, it's not my place. Besides, he's *your* mate of all things and *your* responsibility. So be a leader now and step up to the plate."

Olivia's eyes went wide with panic.

"Will you two knock it off? Something's coming and it's quick!"

Fuming, I spun on my heel.

"*Your* mate, *your* responsibility" I grumbled mockingly beneath my breath. *Fucking werewolves, damn them and their damn rules. You can't rely on them for anything. If you want something done you have to do it yourself.* Without another word I stormed up to a blathering Hawk Eyes and delivered a blow straight to the soft spot just above her chin. She went down like a pile of bricks.

Thankfully, she hadn't seen anything coming. The possibility of blaming her injury on the laboratory's fragile state was quite likely due to all the magical attacks and crumbling foundation. Infact, maybe I wouldn't have to deal with the repercussions after all. I could always say something like *Oh jee, darn, a brick just randomly fell on your head.* Whatever the situation may be, I planned on exploiting it.

Olivia and Jacob exhaled in relief.

A stunned Noah gaped at me as I scooped up Hawk Eyes' limp body.

"What? She wouldn't shut up and something's coming this way. Now let's move out."

Instantly, Noah's mouth snapped shut.

"Come along now and be quick." Noah replied with an exasperated sigh.

He jutted his jaw towards the left doorway down the hall.

"There should be an exit down the hallway or some sort of entrance to a warehouse."

Jacob shooed Olivia in that direction.

I stood there and arched a brow as they passed.

"Should be? I thought you knew the way." I asked, purely irritated by the current change of events. Ethan's wolf chuffed in agreement. Noah turned to say something but a flash light flickered down the hallway. Jacob ushered Liv towards the door. Ethan's black lips curled back in warning. Instantly, he inserted himself between us and the men down the hall. I cursed beneath my breath.

"Let's go!" Noah urged. "We haven't got all bloody day."

My hands tightened into little fists. Reluctantly, I followed Noah's lead. However, if we ended up lost or even possibly captured I swear I'd clobber him over the head myself. The shadowy shapes down the hallway were humanoid. Only time would tell if they were human, I myself had preferred not to find out. When in doubt, it was always easier to distance myself from the unknown. Beams of light cut through the darkness like deadly lasers in the night. I picked up the pace.

"Hey!" Someone shouted after me in hot pursuit.

A cold clamminess seeped through my bones. All the while an unconscious Hawk Eyes bounced limply over my shoulder. Her head banged and bounced along the the stone wall as we went. *Did I care?* No. I couldn't really say that I did. A little goose egg here and there never hurt anybody. In fact, running was the best option that we had. I could however foresee a hot scolding in my near future, that is if she were to recollect her memories. Who's to say she would?

Shadows danced along the walls of the corridor. Most of the lights had gone out and all that was left was the flickering hum from the dying emergency lamps. Voices called after us. Our pursuers had picked up their pace. Cold sweat trickled down my spine.

"To the left, to the left!" Noah shouted.

Beams of light penetrated through the shadows and into my soul. My throat tightened in anguish. I refused to be caged. The very fear of isolation dominated my very being and thrusted me forward towards my goal. The high pitch whine of the dying generator rattled through my ears. The pounding footsteps came closer. Jacob rounded the corner and grabbed the nearest door. He ushered Olivia in and then hustled us in. Shouts of outrage echoed behind us but Jacob slammed the door just in time.

"Oh hells bells!" Noah snarled in disgust.

"I never even saw them coming. The blasted plan has gone to the bloody shitter." Frustrated he tossed Frank's limp body towards the ground in a gesture of frustration.

Olivia quickly stepped in and caught him mid air.

"What do we do now?" She asked as she eased Frank gently to the ground.

His body was slick with sweat.

White foam dribbled from his parted lips.

Noah ran a flustered hand through his wild hair.

"We need to drain him soon or he might not make it through the night."

A growling Ethan stood between us and the door. Black hackles rippled down his spine. I too had let Hawk Eyes fall haphazardly to the ground. She let out a feeble grunt. I am sure she would take time to thank me later, more so in blows than anything else.

"Liv, let's give Noah some time to recollect his thoughts. Come help me find some movable furniture. We're going to barricade the door, in the meantime Jake can guard the entrance." I announced with a reconciliatory smile.

Liv fussed at her lip. "But what about Frank?"

Someone banged on the door.

Ethan and I stiffened. Jacob's brows knitted together.

"Do as she says Liv. If we don't stave them off Frank will be good as dead."

The door shook behind Jacob's back.

"We know you're in there! Come out now with your hands up!"

Noah got to work with Frank. A series of bangs and a bout of angry voices could be heard beyond the warehouse door. My hands trembled with fear. *Was this it? We're we going to die here all alone?* Olivia and I had found a heavy shelving unit. Together we pushed. The possibility of not making it back home kept running through my mind. The very idea of it terrified me. The shelving unit wouldn't budge.

Would I never be able to take back what I said? The last conversation between Pa and I had been pretty intense. There were definitely some things that I shouldn't have said. Breathless, I tugged once again. A wave of anguish washed over me. Groaning, we strained. My eyes flashed golden. Auburn fur sprouted along my arms. Two fox tails flicked back and forth in agitation. Together we moved.

Our muscles ached but our resolve gave us strength. As one, we tore the bolts up out of the ground. The sound of metal creaking and bolts snapping was like sweet music to my ears. I exhaled in relief. Liv's eyes glittered with the visage of her wolf. Together, as a team, we stood there panting for air.

In the meantime, Noah had managed to bind Frank down to a few shelving units. Jacob on the other hand struggled to maintain the doors. We slid the unit in front of the entry. The door shook and cracked. We stepped away. A familiar female voice with musical undertones and a European accent shouted out on the other side of the doorway. "That's quite enough! Now move aside!"

There was an earth shattering boom then the door blew us back along with all the contents that were on the shelving unit. Splinters of wood went everywhere. Metal shrapnel, shards of glass, shredded bits of paper and book exploded into the air in a mass cloud of fury. Jacob just managed to scramble out of the way.

I found the very idea of being blown away by our own contraption quite peculiar. *Note to self: remove all contents from shelving unit before using it to barricade yourself in an abandoned warehouse.* A snarling Ethan inserted himself between us and the door. Jacob scrambled to his feet. Breathless, he joined Noah with his claws extracted. Together they hovered over an unconscious Frank. Their eyes watched the door with such an intensity it made my chest hurt. They stood there poised, ready to attack. Black swirls of energy licked up and down Noah's arm while drops of green venom dripped from Jacob's nails.

Together Liv and I crouched in the shadows, ready to pounce. Our hearts thundered inside our chests. Waves of smoke flooded from the demolished entrance. Ethan snapped his jaws. *Was this it? Was this how we were going to die?* If so we'd go out with a bang. Footsteps scuttled across the floor. I bit my lip. Time stood still. My breath froze. Olivia's muscles coiled like tightly wound springs, ready to burst.

Would I have to kill yet again?

Wearily, I focused on the task at hand. A shadowy set of figures emerged from the billowing fog. Ethan bared his fangs. Venomous saliva dripped from his open maw. Noah's muscles rippled as he took position, ready to lunge. Electrical energy tingled along my fingertips. I held my breath and braced myself for what came next. Out stepped the woman that helped me escape. Her mouth was pressed in a thin line. Raven black hair was pulled back into a messy bun. She wore black Kevlar vest around her chest. Senator Benson trailed behind.

My heart skipped a beat.

What in the world was she doing here?

Benson arched a brow and inclined her head.

"Mr. Parks. I see that you are well."

He silently returned the greeting with a stiff nod of his head.

The air crackled with tension.

I didn't know if we should attack or stay put. To make matters worse, out slinked a lithe Garcia. She was dressed from head to toe in military garb but she was still easy on the eyes. Damn vampires and their sexy ways. Couldn't they find one thing that didn't look good on them? Who has time to look smokin' hot during a battle anyway? I thought bitterly to myself.

"Vampire..." Olivia hissed and readied herself to lunge.

I yanked her back by the crook of her arm.

"Are you nuts?" I hissed. "Do you have any idea who that is?"

A sly smile curled at the corner of Garcia's luscious lips. "Alexis Adams, you can come out now, no need to be shy. We know exactly where you are, little fox."

A disgusted Olivia snatched her arm away.

A chill ran down my spine.

This was it. We were all going to die, me especially. Garcia was going to gut me alive. Just as I thought we were making progress too. Then again she never really did accept failure and getting caught by Lemmings wasn't part of the plan. I took a deep breath and stepped out of the shadows with my hands raised.

CHAPTER 39

SENATOR BENSON GREETED me with an arched brow.

"I see you got caught." She said wryly.

I grunted and rubbed at the back of my neck. "Yeah, about that.."

Garcia let out an impatient sigh and cut straight to the chase. It was never like her to wait anyhow. "Well, did you happen to get any blueprints on the serum, let alone the lab's security layout?"

I grimaced.

Leave it to Garcia to skip over the mild pleasantries.

The air between us crackled with tension.

"Well, no, not necessarily." I began.

There was an uncomfortable pause.

Meanwhile, a woman was barking orders in the background. The corner of Garcia's eye twitched. A grim Benson waited patiently for more clarification.

I blew out a big breath of air.

"No, I didn't get any prints on the serum. Nor did I manage to get any blueprints on the lab's security lay out." Disappointment shadowed Bensons visage, while Garcia threw her hands up in the air in a gesture of frustration. I bit my lip.

"Does that mean we're in trouble?" I asked.

Benson ran a hand through her blonde hair. The gesture for her was unnatural and it unnerved me. Benson never let on that she was frazzled. For her to be showing signs of concern was not a good omen.

"Perhaps." Benson said with a breathy sigh.

The pit of my stomach twisted.

Why can't I do anything right? I should have foreseen Lemmings was up to something before I stepped foot into his office. How could I have been so stupid?

A confused Garcia pursed her lips in disbelief. "I don't understand. The goal was simple. You were to go in, get the blueprints and get out. What happened?"

I sucked in a breath and rubbed a the back of my neck. What was I going to tell them? Lemmings put me to bed with a sleeping gas? The excuse itself was pitiful. I should have seen it coming.

"Well you see…"

Benson held up a gloved hand.

"We will discuss this matter at a later time." My shoulders sagged with relief. She inclined her head towards the French woman bustling around and barking orders.

"As of right now, Rousseau is leading the attack and we're taking over the lab."

I did a double take, something about the woman caught my eye. Then it hit me, she was the one who released me from the dungeon against Lemming's orders.

"You mean small fry over there?" I had asked in disbelief.

Benson nodded.

"What do you mean, taking over the lab and how?"

Garcia pinched the bridge of her nose and let out a patient sigh.

"Look here little fox, we don't have time to explain. So I am going to make it brief and to the point. Rousseau is Benson's confidant. They've known each other for years, centuries in fact. Benson used Rousseau's skills to infiltrate the system. She has done that now and we are taking over from here. Kapeesh?"

I chewed on my lip as I took all that in.

"So… does that mean we are out of the red zone?" I asked with a hopeful smile.

Together the two women cast me a meaningful glance.

Benson was about to reply when someone shouted.

"Get his vitals!"

It was Rousseau and she was frazzled. Together our heads swiveled in her direction.

Garcia stiffened when she saw her brother convulsing on the floor just a few yards away. My heart constricted at the sight of his twitching body. Rousseau jabbed a finger at the group of wolves. "All of you, hold him down. Now!"

Ethan was already to his feet, in the nude. He must have seen it coming and morphed just in time. Jacob and Liv scurried to Frank's side.

Rousseau whirled on one of the guards.

"Grab a box and stuff as many blood bags in it that you can manage. Pray that the box is big enough for all of our sakes."

The stunned guard stared at Frank's convulsing body.

"What are you dense?! That's an order, soldier!"

Quickly, he jumped to and out the door he went. Who could blame him? Her voice cut through the air like burning steel through ice. Meanwhile, the wolves were doing everything they could to keep Frank down while Rousseau hovered over Frank's wrists. She sliced them open with a Swiss Army knife. Garcia let out an anguish cry. "What are you doing?!" She exclaimed. Her face twisted in horror.

Black blood spilled from Frank's radial arteries. Garcia stepped forward to assist her brother but Benson pulled her back by the crook of her arm.

"Stay back, Carmen." Benson said in a hushed whisper.

"But Frank..." Garcia replied, her voice was laced with trepidation.

"You must." Benson insisted relentlessly. "His blood is tainted with silver. If you try to assist you will be burned. He needs to be bled. Rousseau knows exactly what she is doing. Let her do her job."

Frank let out an agonizing scream as he bared his fangs and went for Rousseau's neck. Ruthlessly, Jacob shoved his head back just in time.

Snarling, he arched his back.

"*Need to feed.*" He hissed. His eyes were black as pitch on a starless night.

Noah tightened his grip on the chains.

Garcia brought a hand to her mouth.

Her forehead crinkled with worry.

My heart thundered inside my chest.

Noah rolled his eyes with practiced patience.

"Bleeding hell, there he goes again. Come now Frank, come back, get to it!"

"The man has completely lost his marbles." Ethan whispered in awe.

"Bloody Christ woman, put your back into it. He's going to get away" Noah hissed.

"Do as he says, Liv." Jacob said.

"My God, it's the Beast." Garcia exclaimed in a hushed whisper. "And he's back.."

"The Beast? What's that?" I had asked.

"His alter ego, ever since he's changed Frank has two states of mind. One crazed with the incessant need to kill and feed while the other is well, just Frank."

"It would seem he never outgrew the thirst." Rousseau announced dubiously

"Tch. Give it time, it will pass." Noah said, unimpressed.

"Do you even realize how precarious the situation is at this current moment in time?" Garcia asked him, purely aghast with his lack of understanding.

Off in the distance Frank made little growling, snapping, snarling, grunting sounds.

"Oh bugger off. Have a bit of faith eh? These fits come and go. Give him some time, he'll come through. You'll see."

Rousseau did her best to make sure the wounds wouldn't seal.

"God damn it, when is that fool coming back?" A frustrated Rousseau snarled as she reopened the wounds on Frank's wrists. "I can't save Frank and go after Lemmings all at the same time. I need someone to go in my stead. I need someone who is quick and knows the way. Lemmings is nearly at the top of the tower. If we don't move fast he will get away with the serum."

There was a pause and a long breath of silence.

Frank's seizing had eased.

A troubled Noah looked all around.

"Well?" Rousseau demanded. "Who knows the way to the landing zone and is willing to go with Garcia to intercept Lemmings on his way there?"

He swallowed and then looked at me.

My heart skipped a beat.

Was he really going to volunteer?

Noah sucked in a deep breath.

" I will..." Noah said as looked back at me.

His calico eyes were hard to read. "Lex, will you come with?'

I stared at him, thoroughly taken aback.

Big bad Noah, the heir of the Shadow Clan was asking me for help?

I flashed him a reassuring smile. "Absolutely."

"I want stay to with Frank.." Garcia replied.

Rousseau's face darkened. "No, we need you to go with."

Garcia's forehead wrinkled with worry.

"But my brother.." She began.

"Your brother will be fine as long as I am here to aide him."

Garcia's face twisted with pain.

Benson placed a reassuring hand on Garcia's shoulder. "Do as she says, Carmen. We are at war. Let her do her job. She is doing everything she can and knows what she is doing. Besides, you are the only one quick enough that can assist the Kitsune. They may need your blood to help give them strength."

The furrow between Garcia's brow thickened. "And if my brother gets loose? What then? Who will be available to heal those that get bitten?"

Some of the soldiers exchanged uncertain glances.

"We have three werewolves that can keep him at bay. If injuries do occur, we have two newborn vampires that can step up to the plate. Now go before it's too late."

A flicker of irritation danced across Garcia's heated gaze.

"If you fail Rousseau, I will personally snap your neck."

An unperturbed Rousseau continued working on a trembling Frank.

"I am well aware, Carmen. Now please go."

Noah's eyebrows disappeared into his shaggy hairline. "Is she for real?"

Senator Benson offered him an apologetic smile. "I am afraid she is."

I nearly choked on my own spit. "Well alrighty then, now that we have put all pleasantries aside, are we ready to get this band wagon on the road?"

Noah and Benson exchanged looks of bewilderment.

"Bandwagon?" Benson inquired with a sense of uncertainty.

Benson was after all a mythical creature from Norwegian legend. Maybe they weren't up to par when it came to modern slang? And Noah, well, was Noah. Then again, I myself had only learned it at school just this past week.

Garcia's eyes narrowed into tiny slits. "Can it, Lex."

I grimaced. "Right then, you got it." The last thing I needed was for Garcia to rip out my tongue. I prized the art of talking. In fact, I viewed it as one of my specialties. Noah's surprise melted into pure pleasure.

"Well I'll be damned, I think I am liking her already."

Garcia arched a brow in Noah's general direction.

"Well, I myself am not very fond of you."

Noah scoffed in mild amusement. "A bit saucy aren't you?"

I let out a low whistle and rubbed at the back of my neck."You have *no idea*. Carmen this is Noah, Noah this is Carmen Garcia." Garcia simply inclined her head in greeting. Meanwhile Senator Benson gave him a good pat on the shoulder.

"There is more to be had Noah, now shall you do the honors?"

Noah offered her a nod. "With pleasure."

Then off we went.

CHAPTER 40

JUST AROUND THE corner we stumbled upon a dead scientist in a white lab coat. It appeared he had died from blunt trauma to the head. There were a few smudges of dirt here and there on his face. Other than that the corpse appeared to be in pristine condition.

"Well isn't' that a beauty?" Noah inquired as he skidded to a stop. Without pause he began to strip the coat from the dead. A confused Garcia watched the whole process with a look of disgust. I flashed her an apologetic smile.

"I am so sorry, he has a tendency to pillage the dead." I whirled around and flashed Noah a menacing glare. "What in Gehenna's name do you think you're doing?"

Garcia glanced at Noah then looked at me in complete bewilderment.

"Is he a bit touched in the head?"

"No, I am not a bit *touched* the head." Noah snarked. "This coat is in pristine condition. We can use it to our advantage. Thank you very much."

Garcia's face puckered with disdain.

"That's just barbaric. You expect us to wear a piece of clothing you've just pilfered off of the dead?"

I cleared my throat and began to speak.

"She has a point you know, besides..."

"Tch." Noah spat with a hint of disgust.

"You should talk. You're the one who sucks blood out of people's necks."

Garcia's chocolate eyes narrowed into tiny slits. "Look, *buddy*."

Noah didn't skip a beat. He kept on talking.

"Besides, I am not asking *you* to wear anything. You're bloody perfect the way you are." He gestured at Garcia's military outfit with an open hand. "Just look at yourself. You look like a bleeding soldier for Christ's sake! No, I'm not asking you to wear anything." He turned and shoved the dead man's coat in my general direction.

Garcia blinked.

"Who me?" I squeaked in surprise.

Noah's eyes narrowed with irritation.

"No, the goddamn Queen of England. *Yes, you.* You bleeding prat. Put on the bloody lab coat. It will make disguising you easier. No arguments now, *sweetheart*. Both you and I know I can only use so much magic and you are as dry as a bone. *So get to it.*"

Begrudgingly, I snatched the coat from his hands and did exactly what he said.

He was right. If I didn't cover more of my body with something people already associated with a member of the lab then it would be more of a hassle to getting me to fit in. Illusive magic took energy and Noah could only had a certain amount to go around. It just wouldn't be right if all the magic were focused on just me. The man had to fight after all. The less of my body showing the better.

Thanks to Noah's ingenious idea, we were able to pass a few guards without altercations on our way up to the top floor. I made a point to soak in morsels of electrical energy from the lights as we passed. Being dry as a bone wouldn't do in a situation such as this.

The place was practically a ghost town. Messes of abandoned paperwork were strewn along the floor. Red lights swiveled across the corridor, casting long shadows in their wake. I felt like we were hopping in and out of scenes from a Horror movie.

Thankfully, I hadn't drawn much attention. Noah was able to easily alter my appearance and maintain an illusive barrier all around me from there on out. Breathless, we stumbled upon the twentieth floor. The railing beside me had been ripped away. The lights above flickered hauntingly overhead.

"Too bad the elevators don't work, eh?" Noah said in between each breath.

"Yeah you can say that again." Garcia agreed.

"What the hell happened here anyway?" I had asked. I could comprehend the abandoned paperwork strewn across the floor, the overturned chairs and desks out of place. Everyone must have left in a hurry but I couldn't place my finger on the crumbling plaster and the numerous dead.

Garcia released a resigned sigh.

"Chaos made a home here once Astrid hacked into the lab's security system. Everything went a muck when the alarms went off. Doors opened that should have been locked. Monsters were let loose that should have remained contained. The scientists didn't know what to do so they attacked."

"And naturally the supernaturals fought back." Noah replied with a sardonic snort.

"How ironic?" I replied in complete bewilderment.

"The scientists were trying to use the supernatural to make the world a better place and it turned out to be something like this." I gestured to the destruction all around. "It is completely baffling, who would have known the fae could have been so violent? I mean look at the place. It's a bloody massacre."

"Needless to say, I am not surprised." Noah said.

"I assure you that wasn't our intention." Garcia protested. "The original plan was to override corridor thirteen and corridor thirteen alone. The residents in that hallway would have provided enough of a distraction on their own but we couldn't get past the security's firewall. Before we knew it, it was too late. The security codes were rigged. In a matter of minutes we had a mass massacre on our hands."

"Sounds like she tried overriding the security as a whole instead." Noah mused aloud.

"Precisely." Garcia replied.

"Well that's where she went wrong. Each corridor has it's own access code. If you don't have the key to that particular hallway you'll have to override the system as a whole. In result, a bloody massacre is what you get. Let's be honest with ourselves, if you release the key to the ones being caged against their will then something is *bound* to happen."

I sucked in a deep breath. So there was it. Astrid had made the same mistake she had with the governmental intelligence agency. She had underestimated the system and now everyone outside of the virtual world would have to pay for it.

"So that explains the carnage." I murmured aloud. "What will happen if all of this is let loose on earth?"

"Then we're fucked." Noah replied.

Noah would know. He had to live through the experiments. He knew what the scientists were capable of. The twisted figures within the test tubes had assured me that the outcome wouldn't be good. Who in the world would end up having to clean up a mess like that? I looked towards Garcia for some reassurance but she had none to give. I prayed with all my heart none of those creatures would be let loosed upon the earth. Just then, something clattered just above. Footsteps scuffled along the ceiling. There was movement on the floor above.

We all exchanged uncertain glances. My stomach dropped.

Could it be one of them? Were they getting away?

The very idea made me shiver. Noah jutted his chin towards the ceiling and tilted his head towards the door to the next floor. "The next floor leads to the roof. By the sounds of it someone is preparing to launch."

Garcia's jaw tightened with determination.

"We better get going then, that could be them."

"You're probably right." I agreed. "Let's head out before it's too late."

Together we headed towards the door to the top floor. Off in the distance I could hear a soft whirring sound. The whirring increased in volume as we approached the roof. We pushed our way through the double doors only to be greeted by the sun. I held a hand to my face to shield myself from the blinding light. Cold wind rushed through my hair. We weren't on a rooftop. In fact, we had made it to the ground level. Who would have known, all of the lab was positioned beneath the ground. The ground was paved with black asphalt. Here and there were trees but the place was surrounded by various military vehicles and aircrafts. I could hear the whirring of blades. Before us, just a few hundred meters off stood a black cobra helicopter on a launching pad. Everything was placed well away from the craft. The pilot to be was the one and only Paul Lemmings. Off in the distance there was a cliff.

"Well I'll be damned." Noah said.

"Sweet mother of Inari, he's going to get away!"

"Not if I can help it." Garcia snarled through gritted teeth.

CHAPTER 41

THE HELICOPTER up front was roaring with life. Swiveling blades sent gusts of wind our way.

Lemmings scrambled towards roaring helicopter as a handful of his goons headed our way. Many of them were dressed in military attire. Gusts of wind blew back from the blades.

"Oh no you don't!" Garcia screamed as she ripped the hood off of a nearby Hummer. "You aren't going anywhere without a fight!" With one more grunt she twisted the hood around and smashed a few of Lemming's goons in the face. Seconds later, she flicked the metal towards the hovering aircraft. With a whoosh the hood spun through the air like a giant Frisbee but only managed to clip the craft just below the blade. The cobra helicopter bobbed from the force. I took a few soldiers down by electrocuting them in the neck with the little power I had snuck from the generator on our way up here.

"Nice!" Noah exclaimed before dodging a blow to the chest. His calico eyes glowed with excitement as he twisted away from another blow only to return the favor by blasting a black hole through the man's chest.

Garcia let out a disappointed "Tch" noise between her teeth.

"Why can't you fight more like him?" She inquired with a tilt of her chin.

I scowled in her general direction.

"I am doing the best I can here. Can't you give a girl a break?"

Noah's eyes glittered with delight as he past me a ways up to take out a few more men. He offered me a playful wink on his way out.

"Can't imitate perfection, sorry babe."

Paul Lemming's face twisted with rage.

"Kill them you fools! Shoot them all!" He screamed.

Spittle flew from his lips as he tugged at the craft's door.

Garcia's hit must have bent the frame.

Many of the goons fumbled with their artillery weapons and took aim.

"Noah!" I screamed. "Get out of the way!"

He couldn't hear me. He was too busy taking down a guard a few ways off.

Smoke and fire spat from the barrel of the guns. My blood turned to ice. There was no way to make it in time. My muscles felt like lead. I twisted the elements of time. Everything around me slowed. I ran towards Noah and the oncoming onslaught of lead.

Plumes of smoke slowly drifted from the barrels. I didn't have much magic left but one could only hope that I would get there in the nick of time. I willed everything within me to move... *but why?* Could it be that I had cared? It had been so long since Noah and I had met. I wasn't ready for him to leave, at least not yet.

Something peculiar began to happen as the bullets began to stream out in slow motion from the rifle's lips. The air grew crisp. Panes of frost sprouted from the ground, slowly but surely developing them into sheets of ice. My grasp on time had slipped.

Everything blasted into full motion. Gunfire boomed. Black gun powder spat. Thick sheets of ice materialized instantaneously in front of us, absorbing most of the impact from the onslaught of lead before shattering into thousands of shards of frozen glass. We all paused and turned around, soldiers and friends. Behind us Benson panted. Droplets of sweat peppered her brow.

"Don't stop, you fools! Keep moving lest he gets away!"

Everything exploded back into action. She must have gotten to us just in time. By the way she was panting she must have sprinted up the flight of stairs. Two guards approached Benson from behind. Benson twisted, her fingertips. A sheet of ice grew from the ground. Behind her a handful of guards slipped and fell.

Noah whistled.

"Damn, who knew the selkie could fight?"

"Can it, Kitsune and get back to work." Benson replied through gritted teeth.

"Yes ma'am."

"If you think you can steal the serum from me you have another thing coming." Lemming's voice shouted over the Cobra's intercom. Somehow he managed to overpower the door and clamber into the cockpit amidst all the chaos. "I've sacrificed too much and have worked too hard to get to where I am at now."

"All over a leg, really Lemmings?" I shouted over the wind, my question was purely rhetorical. *Just keep him talking Lex*, I thought to myself. Maybe, just maybe I could buy us more time. There was bound to be another group heading our way, right?

"It's not just a leg, Adams. They took my *entire* identity."

"Identity huh? What about the identities of my classmates? Is the life of another person worth so little to you? What do you even have to gain from all of this anyway?"

"Adams, stand down.." Benson warned as she struggled with another soldier.

"The lives that were lost were not in vain, Adams. Can't you see this is one step close to bettering mankind? I mean, imagine a world where no one gets sick. Can you even possibly comprehend a situation such as that?"

Garcia took on another soldier from behind and snapped his neck.

Noah rolled his eyes and dismissed Lemmings with a wave of the hand.

"Mankind this, mankind that. That speech was blinding mate, really."

He twisted out of the way of another soldier and continued to shout above the wind.

"Honestly, If you ask me you're all off your bloody rockers. None of you scientists give a rat's ass about the earth or about bettering the human race as a whole. So shove off and hand over the serum, eh?"

An unconscious soldier crumpled to the ground. Lemmings simply shook his head. "Sorry kid, no cigar. The wolves took everything from me and now it's time to make things right. End of discussion."

"Why you..." Garcia began to step forward with her talons outstretched.

He made a series of movements in the cockpit and then the guns on the copter began to click.

"Look out!" I gasped as a stream of bullets spewed out from the aircraft's artillery unit. Benson ducked behind a wall while Noah took refuge behind a pile of dead. Immediately, I shoved Garcia behind a nearby Hummer. She let out a pained gasp and brought her hand to her hip. Dust and debris kicked up into the evening air as bullets whizzed by my face. They riddled everyone in their wake. Several of Lemming's men crumpled to the ground like broken marionettes. My heart ached. *They didn't have to die.* I thought miserably to myself. *All of this could have been prevented if Lemmings would just stand down.* Rivulets of smoke drifted from the barrel's holes.

"Did I or did I not tell you this man is insane?" I said as I took a peek around the corner. "I mean the man has completely lost his marbles!"

A disgruntled Garcia only grunted in reply.

"Yeah that's great and all."

Her voice was barely audible.

"And to think, he's taken down his own men." I continued, completely oblivious to Garcia's current condition. In the meantime, Noah curled behind a nearby truck.

"Better them than us, eh?" Noah replied with a wild eyed grin. He took one more blast at the copter before ducking out of the way. Smoke drifted from the tail of the aircraft. Garcia only groaned in response.

I frowned and did a double take. "Hey are you okay?"

She grimaced as she held her hand firmly to a spot just above her hip. Streams of scarlet liquid trickled through her fingertips. I brought a hand to my lips. It had appeared I hadn't grabbed her in time. In fact, she had been hit.

"Um, you guys, we have a problem."

"It's not coming out." She said.

"No shit, Sherlock!" Noah replied.

Then came round two. The force of the Cobra's blows made the hummer shake. Tires popped, metal ticked, glass shattered and alarms went off. I pulled a strand of magic from the source within my core. A shield of interwoven bolts of electrical energy wove itself around us in its protective embrace, shielding Garcia and me from any oncoming stacks. Benson gritted her teeth.

"Stand your ground!" Benson said as she launched lances of ice between each blast.

"You bet your ass I will!" Noah replied as he let loose on the helicopter's smoking guns. Black balls of fury slammed into the firing mechanisms. The craft lurched and recovered to the right. I looked around in search for some sort of solution. Dead bodies were everywhere. The air stank of death, sweat and blood. Bursts of wind blasted through the air from the copter's blades.

Garcia's mouth moved but I couldn't hear the words. Then I realized he was moving the craft around. I sought out a distraction, a solution of some sort that could possibly buy us more time. Then my eyes came across a tree just a ways behind the copter's swooping blades. He was facing us. Gears clicked and clanked. A few pointed weapons came to head. *Sweet mother of Inari, he was going to blow us to smithereens!* We had to do something and do it quick, but what? Benson screamed for us to move, *but where?* Where would we go that the missile wouldn't hit?

I looked back at the tree. Cold surges of wind moved through the leaves and then it clicked. If I timed it just right it might work. I sucked in a deep breath. Tingles of electricity rippled through my veins. The clouds around us darkened as Lemmings took aim. The sky rumbled and I drew forth all of my energy. A bolt of lightning came forth from the sky and struck the tree at it's trunk.

The tree came crashing down. I held my breath in anticipation. *Will the tree hit?* My pulse quickened. A shot of adrenaline buzzed through my veins as a few branches clipped the Cobra's front end. The cabin shook. Lemmings grimaced as a long crack crawled across the top of the glass. Splinters of wood and leaf spewed everywhere. My heart skipped a beat as the Corba's nose dipped.

Within seconds the copter swerved out of the way before heading out towards the cliff. Ice water ran through my veins. If he made it over the cliff's edge we wouldn't be able to pursue him.

"Hurry!" I shouted, breathless from the last attack. "He's trying to get away."

Garcia muttered something foul beneath her breath.

A pool of blood huddled at the base of her hip.

"Garcia, you aren't healing."

Garcia grunted and spat out a wad of blood.

"It's only a flesh wound,.. focus.. on the task at hand.."

She couldn't heal. I bit my lip. The bullets must have been silver and several of them must have been lodged deep within the issue of her flesh.

"Make it quick." She panted.

An exhausted Noah leaned his back against the wall of the truck.

"I don't know about you, but I'm all out..." He said.

Benson's face twisted in concentration as she called forth her magic. A blue haze of energy swirled around her fingers. The sky above us rumbled forebodingly. Noah squinted and looked up at the sky. Awestruck, I watched as the gray clouds whirled into a cohesive blob. Droplets of sweat trickled down Benson's neck as she called forth a deadly torrent of water from the sky. The very idea of it struck me as odd. *How could a body so small produce so much power?*

Dumbfounded, I watched as the torrent lurched and wobbled in Lemming's direction. Benson had did her best but the mass of water was too heavy to bear for smooth maneuverability. My stomach clenched as the water collided and spun against the craft's side.

The Cobra moaned and creaked against the pressure as it leaned away. By now they had past the cliff's edge. I held my breath. My heart thundered inside my chest. Benson was our last hope. She had to take him down or Lemmings would end up getting away. Benson grunted with effort. Her body was drenched in sweat. The torrent followed in hot pursuit. She guided the blast of water, slow but steady. However, Lemming's craft spun around and sprayed the twister with a healthy dose bullets. Water seeped everywhere, making the formation very difficult to maintain. Benson gasped.

Only moments later, the torrent erupted into an explosion of water. Splashes of water flew everywhere. Icy deluge fell from the sky as she doubled over in pain. She fell to her knees, gasping for breath.

"That's it." She panted.

Had she pushed herself too far?

"That's all I have." She said in between breaths.

I stared at her in complete bewilderment.

"That's it?" I had asked.

Benson shook her head and wiped the sweat off of her brow with the back of her hand.

"I can't regenerate energy like you do, Lexi. I am sorry. I'm simply spent."

I stared at her with my mouth ajar. *She was spent? How could she be spent in a time like this? We practically had him! How in the world could it possibly come to this?* A pit of despair opened up in my chest. I tried to speak but my tongue was as dry as desert sand.

I looked to Noah, desperate for some sort of chance, but he too had used up everything he had left. There was no more chaos left for him to consume. Whatever emotions were left were now dead along with the humans that had once held them.

There went our ticket home. I thought bitterly, more so to myself than anyone else. Then I glanced at Garcia. Blood seeped from the wound just above her hip. My stomach dropped. She was at the brink of death. So I closed my eyes and tried to clear my head.

Instead, I was haunted by the screams of dying men, recalled the twisted bodies of all the creatures in the lab, remembered the pain on Selena's face, and recollected the bite of iron against my skin. The memories themselves played back in my mind like spools of film.

How many more will die now? Now that he had gotten away? How many more would have to live with that type of pain? I swear I could hear his laughter beyond the cliff. My panic had turned to despair and my despair turned into hate. My hands shook, I seethed with rage. I could hear his engine puttering off in the distance. *He was not getting away. Not this time. Not if I could help it.*

I took a deep breath and opened my eyes. Bodies of men and women were everywhere. They were once brothers, sisters, father and mothers. All of them were dead now because of him. I let that idea sink in and allowed it to fill me with hate. I took in their terror, drank in their pain and reached deep within the center of the lab. I let it all soak in, the chaos, the electricity and the energy.

A gust of wind rustled through the leaves. Energy poured into me. Electricity crackled along my fingertips. Benson opened her mouth but no sound came. I couldn't register what she was trying to say. Noah had something, his voice was urgent and crisp. "Bring her down Benson, or she's going to break."

Benson reached for me.

My vision went white.

Blasts of wind came forth from my body. The sky rumbled overhead.

"He's not going to get away." I replied in a voice that was not my own. Lightning danced off in the distance. Thunder clapped. Fur sprouted along my body, Bits and pieces of my humanity fell away. Human teeth turned into gnashing fangs. My two fox tails whipped around within the wind. The remaining lights exploded overhead. Shards of glass rained down like drops of ice. Electricity crackled along the downed power lines. I consumed the world around me.

Trees dropped, power lines buzzed, glass shattered. Noah pushed through the wind but I blew him back. If I had to engulf the whole earth to make him pay I would do it in a heartbeat. Pure ecstasy ran through my veins. *Was this what it was like? To not have control? To have limitless power? To control the moon, the sun and the sky? Was that why Kane thirsted so much for our land?* By now I had a deeper understanding. Now I knew why Kane did what he did. He wanted power. I couldn't necessarily blame him. The desire to engulf everything around me was overwhelming. Currents of electrical power unfurled and flicked along my fingertips like wild snakes. Garcia's head lolled off to the side.

"She's gone completely mad!" Benson hollered over the wind.

A bolt of lightning skittered across the ground.

She tried to step forward but the maelstrom around me threw her back.

Noah shouted over the wind.

"She's using the electricity all around her, consuming it and making it hers. If we don't stop her she's going to blow the bloody building and all of us in it to bleeding smithereens!"

I closed my eyes and let it all in, consuming the energy all around me.

When I spoke my voice came out an octave or two lower.

"He will wallow in his own blood and experience a death consumed in terror and pain."

The eyes of my fox glowed white. All illusions fell away. My canines sharpened. The tails of my fox twisted within the gale. Gusts of wind roared around me. Lemming's craft was just a pin prick above the horizon. Clouds of darkness rolled ominously in and swooped the craft up in it's windy grasp. A haze of rain fell from the sky. The copter faltered beneath the pressure of the pounding rain. Thunder cracked. Lashes of white lightening skittered across the sky like clawed hands.

"Alexandria,..." Noah warned. "You need to stop."

He reached for me. "You're taking too much."

I opened my eyes. They were white as snow and cold as a winter's wind. I focused on the objective at hand, the need to kill. *He couldn't get away. Not now, not ever.* I peered through the squall. Wind and rain spattered my face. *One more shot..* I reached further. *Just one more was all it would take.* I concentrated and took aim. Then something hit me in the face. I tumbled to the ground. Stars exploded across my vision. Off in the distance the lightning struck. The helicopter swirled to the ground in a fit of smoke and flame. When I hit the ground everything went black.

My spirit form had drifted from my body.

Just above my unconscious form stood a panting Noah.

He was visibly upset

Rumbling thunder clouds began to dissipate along the horizon and the icy deluge slowed to a misty haze. My stomach dropped once I took in the scene. Death and destruction were everywhere. Trees were uprooted from the ground. Downed power wires crackled with live electricity. Hummers were overturned. Asphalt was cracked. It was then that I realized I had given into the taint and understood the importance of training.

Most of this destruction was caused by me. I had given into the tainted desire to consume and the training that I had not taken seriously was meant to keep that desire contained. All kitsune are born with the tainted desire to consume an overwhelming amount of energy. Consuming just enough to live is well and good. However, giving into the desire to consume more than what is needed is a matter of ease.

Naturally, it takes skill to keep our desires for power reigned. If we give in with no restriction to the desire to feed then we consume everything all around us, including our home and friends. Thankfully, Noah cracked me hard enough over the head to prevent that from happening.

"That was a bit much, don't you think?" Benson inquired.

Noah only grunted and shook his bruised fist.

The two of them were soaked.

"I don't know, you tell me." He said with a half hearted smile.

Benson eyed him skeptically as he bent down to check my pulse.

"I don't mean to get cheeky here Senator, but you're lucky she didn't blow this place to smithereens." He took a moment to analyze my face. "Young vixens can be a challenge if they don't know how to channel their energy. You know, control and all that jazz." He sighed and leaned over to pick me up. "Come now love, show's up. Time to hit the sack, if you know what I mean."

Senator Benson bit her lip.

"Will she be alright?" She inquired with a sense of uncertainty.

Noah offered her a simple shrug as he went to scoop up my body.

"At this point we can only hope,"

He dipped a chin in Garcia's direction.

"I'd be more concerned for her sake."

An awestruck Benson brought a hand to her mouth once she witnessed Garcia's broken body. "Dear God, you're absolutely right."

As if on cue a panting Selena Rodriguez rounded the corner.

She too must have sprinted her way up the stairwell.

"Thank God I've found you!" She panted. "Are you all okay? Did he get away? I came up here as soon as I heard the crash." She stopped mid sentence and gasped when she saw Garcia's state. "Sweet mother of Mary, *what happened?*"

"Looks like she got shot with some silver bullets and they got lodged within her wounds. If we don't get them out then she'll probably die at this rate..." Benson explained.

"Hey Selena, do you have a knife?" Noah asked absentmindedly.

"I'm already on it." Selena replied as she rummaged through her pack.

Distracted, Noah turned. His calico eyes watched the trail of smoke drifting just above the horizon. His expression remained grim.

"Do you suppose he got away?"

Benson managed to frown and shook her head. In the background Selena got to work on Garcia's broken body.

"Not likely..."

Hey Friend!

Thanks for joining me on this spectacular journey! It was honor and I hope that you enjoyed the read. Please don't forget to leave me a solid review on Amazon. I truly appreciate your assistance in spreading the good news! In the meantime, don't forget to connect with me via my mailing list where you can get snippets of the journey into the next book.

Sincerely,
Carly Seyferth

Newsletter: http://eepurl.com/dlYiDz

facebook.com/CarlySeyferth

goodreads.com/17764755.Carly_Seyferth

Made in the USA
Lexington, KY
12 July 2018